# LET ME IN

# LET ME IN

WITHDRAWN

## DONNA KAUFFMAN

BRAVA

KENSINGTON PUBLISHING CORP.
http://www.kensingtonbooks.com

BRAVA BOOKS are published by

Kensington Publishing Corp.
850 Third Avenue
New York, NY 10022

All Kensington titles, imprints, and distributed lines are available at special quantity discounts for bulk purchases for sales promotion, premiums, fund-raising, educational, or institutional use.

Special book excerpts or customized printings can also be created to fit specific needs. For details, write or phone the office of the Kensington Special Sales Manager: Kensington Publishing Corp., 850 Third Avenue, New York, NY 10022. Attn. Special Sales Department. Phone: 1-800-221-2647.

ISBN-13: 978-0-7582-3129-1
ISBN-10: 0-7582-3129-6

First Kensington Trade Paperback Printing: March 2009
10  9  8  7  6  5  4  3  2  1

Printed in the United States of America

*For Angela . . .*
*Thank you for the support, the laughter,*
*and the sisterhood*

# Chapter 1

He was the last person she ever wanted to see again. She'd done her time, she was out now. For good. Free. Free to be whatever she wanted to be, and what she wanted to be was alone.

It had been three years since they'd parted ways, and not under the best of circumstances. Derek Cole had been her boss then; the man who decided where she went, what she did, and how long she stayed. To say he hadn't been happy with her decision to resign would be putting it mildly. *Too damn bad,* had been her feeling at the time. The intervening years had done nothing to change that sentiment.

Tate Winslow didn't just like her newfound solitude, she reveled in it. Home used to be wherever she laid her hat. And her gun. Now home was the stunning vistas and peaceful beauty of the Hebron Valley, framed by the gently rolling Blue Ridge Mountains in Madison County, Virginia. She'd been Agent Winslow in her previous life. She went by Tara Wingate now. Not a stunning change, she'd tried to keep some sense of herself, but change enough to start fresh, leaving no tracks. Hers was a privately designed protection program created by someone who knew firsthand how to make a person disappear. Her former boss hadn't been pleased with her choice, but he'd respected it and her request for help in creating a new life for herself. She'd made certain no one here knew of her past . . . and he'd made certain no one from her past knew she was here. There had been no contact since and there would be no contact. Ever.

She'd come here battered in both body and soul, desperately in need of healing. She'd expected it to take time, and was willing to give herself whatever it was she needed to feel whole again. She'd given enough to others. It was time to take a little back for herself. Not that she'd really had a choice. There hadn't been anything left to give.

Surprisingly, adjusting to the quiet life in the valley had come easily, and the healing had followed more swiftly than she'd imagined possible. She'd found her rhythm quite naturally here, the slower pace of life calling to her in more ways than she'd known were possible. She'd only wanted a break, an escape, a place to lick her wounds and heal in private. She hadn't known the true depths of solace there was to be found in such a new way of life, but was profoundly grateful for every scrap of it. She hadn't realized how much faith and trust—two commodities she'd never had in large supply—that she'd put into it always being there for her. Until the instant it all changed.

The adrenaline pumping into her system right now was the exact opposite of everything she'd come here for, everything she'd become. It made her physically nauseous. Worse was the ease with which her training kicked right back in. That she'd ever need for it to, ever again, made her emotionally sick. And mad as hell.

It was a brutal revelation, discovering her peaceful existence could be so easily and swiftly shattered by something as simple as a rattling doorknob. Three years in the valley had healed wounds, soothed scars, and introduced her to a world where joy was found in morning blooms and evening bird calls. But apparently no amount of soul-soothing would ever erase the training ingrained into her from her previous life. A life where distinguishing between, and identifying, even the tiniest of sounds could mean the difference between life and death.

So when the rattling sound came, she knew it wasn't the

wind whistling over the shaker roof and vibrating the frame of her log cabin home. She had made casual friends of a few neighbors since moving here, but not a single one of them would have come calling after midnight without advance notice . . . even in an emergency. She had no family, no relatives. No one who would simply enter, or try to, without knocking first.

And yet, someone was at her door. A door no one from her previous life should know existed. Or certainly not where it existed. Derek hadn't been happy she'd left the team, but he'd promised he'd allow her the permanent exile she sought. And though he'd been a tough boss, he'd never expected anything from his team that he hadn't taken, or couldn't take, himself. He never shied away from making a blunt observation, and he never made promises because he knew reality didn't always come with the luxury of keeping them. So, when he gave his word, he backed it up. Without fail.

The return of that sickening, heart-pounding sensation, where every second was crystallized into a completely separate, fully realized moment in time, was something she'd never wanted to experience, ever again. But, in less than five seconds, she had palmed her gun from under the corner of her mattress—a security blanket, she'd told herself, smart for a woman living alone in the middle of nowhere—and had her back flat against the wall next to her bedroom door. She hated this, hated it with a deepening rage that was almost as bone-chilling as the sound that had launched her into it.

Drawing on every shred of training she'd had, fury mounted as she made her way out of her only bedroom, and crept down the short hall to the front room. She paused to peek around the corner, making a slow visual sweep of her small cabin, then moved in along the front wall. Staying low to the ground, she peered cautiously out of the panoramic front window, silently cursing the lack of night vision goggles, hating that she'd even thought of it. She'd bought the cabin mainly for that window, and the view of the valley and the endless rippling vistas of blue mountains that it showcased. The idea that someone was out there, using the very same window to stare in at her, made her even more livid.

She was crawling toward the door, already leaning toward shooting first and asking questions later, when a hushed, gravelly voice whispered, "Tate. It's me."

She went stock still, her heart lodged instantly in her throat. Hearing her old name . . knowing only one person could connect the woman living in this cabin to that name, only increased her fury. She knew that voice. Knew it belonged to a man who was quite capable of getting himself into any structure he wanted to. So why was he rattling her door knob? Unless . . .

She crept closer, and positioned herself on the hinged side of the door. Not smart, but Derek would expect her to do as she'd been trained. Especially considering he'd been the one to do the training. It was the smallest of edges, but with him she'd need every one she had. She didn't respond.

"Tate. Let me in." There was a long pause, then a choked, "Please."

*Please?* The almighty Derek Cole *asking* instead of telling?

He had to be in trouble. The most serious kind. And of all the places in the world he could go and drag that trouble with him, he'd chosen her doorstep.

"How dare you," she hissed, not intending to speak at all, but her rage at his gall robbed her of her better judgment.

"Had no choice."

"There are always choices."

"Open the door. I haven't—I can't—"

There was a thump against the door, as if his body weight had collapsed against it. Or the body weight of someone else. Holy Mother of—if he'd brought some wounded team member to her door, thinking she would play doctor—

"I will shoot you both if you so much as set foot inside this house. Find somewhere else to bleed to death. Anywhere else." To anyone else, the comment would seem callous at best, heartless at worst, but they had all been trained to do what they could to right very difficult wrongs in exceedingly impossible situations. Every single time they went to work, they put their lives on the line, knowing every mission could be their last. The risks sucked, and nobody wanted to die, but that was part of the job. And the other part of the job was to accept those risks . . . and never put innocent bystanders in danger in order to save yourself. You'd inserted yourself willingly into a potentially deadly situation. They hadn't.

There was a grunt. Then another thump. "Just me, Tate." Another thump, then a scraping sound. "Just me."

She leaned against the wall of the cabin, willing her racing heart and even more swiftly racing mind to slow down long enough so she could think and act clearly. "It's Tara. I don't work for you any longer, and I sure as hell don't owe you anything. Get off my property, Derek."

"Can't."

"Won't." And that was just it. Short of calling the authorities or putting him out of his misery right there on her front porch, there was going to be no way to get rid of him. She looked at the small table on the other side of the door, and the drawer where she kept a charged cell phone. She'd only gotten it for emergency purposes. Otherwise she didn't need one. There was no one to call, and no one who would call her. But if anything constituted an emergency it was this. Only without knowing the parameters of the mission that had driven him to her doorstep, even calling the locals to haul an apparent unknown trespasser off her property could unwittingly put others in danger. Which meant she couldn't make that call, and she hated him even more because he damn well knew it.

"You need to be anywhere else but here," she informed him.

"It's about CJ."

Tate's heart stopped all together. A split second later, she was yanking the door open, and dragging a half-hunched, half-crumpled Derek into her living room. He grunted when she left him to lie where she'd dragged him, stepping over his prone body to close the door, unable to tell, in the pitch darkness, whether he'd left any telltale signs of his presence on her porch. Like a backpack. Or a pool of blood.

She rolled him to his side, not particularly caring what injuries he'd sustained—and it was clear he wasn't healthy at the moment—or how much worse she might be making them by her rough handling. She gripped the collar of his black, Kevlar-lined jacket and yanked up so his face turned up toward hers. "CJ is dead. I saw her."

"You were wrong," he choked out.

"*Wrong?*" She shook him, stunned, beyond even fury now, unable to process the whole of what was happening. Her training might never wane, but she wasn't as mentally sharp as she used to be. In any other instance, she'd be happy—proud, even—to know that about herself. It wasn't healthy to have your brain wired to register, analyze, and process life-or-death information in an instant, and do so as if it were as natural as breathing. "Wrong how? I saw her. I know I'm not wrong. She's dead, Derek. Has been since three days before they pulled me out of that godforsaken village."

"No," was all he managed.

"How could that be? Is this some kind of sick hoax? How dare you come here and—" She made herself stop, and swallowed hard, jaw so tight it ached. "Tell me, all of it, right now, or so help me, God—"

"They still had her. After you . . . she was still there. Is still."

Tate's grip loosened. "No," she said, the whisper sounding like it had been tortured out of her. "That's impossible. Not after what we—oh God." Her fingers went completely slack. His head thumping against the floor barely registered as wave upon wave of unwanted memories flooded her mind. "It's been three years," she said, her voice toneless now, hollow, as she fought against the swiftly resurfacing past and the wave of nausea that accompanied it. The fury that had built up inside her fled so quickly it left her feeling lightheaded.

*Think about CJ. Not . . . not what had happened back then. Back there.*

CJ. Alive. She simply couldn't put that together. Not in any rational way.

She looked at Derek, who hadn't moved. Her eyes had adjusted to the low light, but it was still too dark to make out much. He was in significant pain, that much was certain. *Tough shit,* she thought, resisting with all her might the avalanche of nightmares that were piled up behind a mental door she'd very carefully, and very thoroughly, closed the day she'd left Washington. "How?" she choked out. "How do you know this?"

"Not now," Derek ground out. "Not yet. I'm—I've been . . ." He grunted as he struggled to lift his head on his own, scan his surroundings.

"I'm not bugged," she retorted sharply, thankful for the sudden resurgence of fury. "No one has been here."

"I have."

Her throat closed over as the new reality she was trying to stave off battered its way through her carefully constructed walls.

He'd been here. In her space.

Her world here, her life, was truly compromised, then. She wanted to shake him, hard, wanted to scream and shout and inflict pain, the likes of which he was inflicting on her. "How dare you!" she half-sobbed, half-growled.

"Better me," he managed, his voice, what there was of it, wavering badly as he let his head loll back to the floor. She could barely make out his features, but it looked like he had his eyes squeezed shut.

Interrogation and detainment rule number one: never shut your eyes. Never.

"Derek—"

"Than them," he finished, then his head rolled to the side and his jaw went slack.

"Derek?" She leaned over him again. Despite her earlier threats, her heart tripped. "Don't you go dying right in my foyer, dammit. You've already brought enough trouble to my door. You're not about to leave me to figure out what to do about it by myself." She pressed her palm to his cheek, turning his face to hers, trying to catch what little moonlight there was so she could better assess his condition. She didn't dare turn on so much as a flashlight until she learned more about what she was up against. The muscles in his face had gone slack, but his eyes were closed, and she could feel the warmth of his breath. He was still alive. "Good," she breathed, relaxing a little. She turned his face a bit more toward the spare wash of moonlight coming in through the front window. "Don't think that means I won't personally strangle you, though," she warned, leaning closer to get a better look.

He'd either taken a hell of a fall, or a hell of a beating. She was betting on the latter. There was a gash over his left eyebrow. A black and blue contusion swelling over his right cheekbone. The corner of his mouth was dried with caked blood, and his chin was all scraped to hell. And that's just what she could make out in next-to-no-lighting. It was also a bitch of a time to notice how thick and dark his eyelashes were.

She lowered his head back to the floor and rocked back on her heels to look over the rest of him. He was five years her senior, which put him at thirty-eight now. And while her past and what she'd gone through had left an indelible stamp on her, aging her in body, mind, and soul, whatever he'd been through in the past three-plus years—or hell, even in the past three days—hadn't diminished one iota of his natural, God-given beauty. Of which he'd always had an abundance. Didn't change the fact that he was a hard-ass, son-of-a-bitch who'd just compromised her whole world. And, quite probably, her life.

"Derek," she repeated, sharply this time. "Don't fade on me now. I need to know why you're here, all of it, and what the hell happened to you." She leaned over him again, and debated on doing a quick once-over with her hands to see if he was bleeding. He was lying in an awkward position, and she wished she had more light so she could get a better idea if he was suffering from any obvious fractures or dislocations. She refused to feel bad for her rough treatment of him earlier, but though she was still furious with him, it wasn't in her to totally disregard his condition. Besides, she needed him to be alert so she could get information out of him. He'd sounded pretty out of it, which made her worry that he'd suffered something more than just a good ass-kicking.

She tried not to think about how he'd let himself even get in that position. He was better than that. But then, she'd been better than that, too. Sometimes, even the best weren't good enough.

She started to slowly move his arm, hoping she could ease him over to his back, when she realized that the reason he was lying so awkwardly was because his wrists were bound behind his back. *Shit.*

She scooted around behind him, staying low to the floor, well below the line of view through the window. The cords wrapping his wrists together had been tied off neatly and thoroughly. A professional job. Her gut squeezed as a dozen new questions formed. He'd managed to loosen the bonds slightly, but from what she could feel of the skin around the cords, he'd paid a price for that, too.

She shifted her gaze to the rest of him, but had to run her hands down his hips and legs to get a true read on the rest. Her hands didn't come away sticky, so no bullet holes, but his ankles had been bound as well. Which meant he'd made it to her house and up onto her porch in his current condition. That explained the weight of his body thudding against the door, and why he'd rattled the knob rather than simply entering the cabin using the skills they all possessed.

It also made her wonder where the hell the beating had occurred. It couldn't have been that far away. She fought the sick dread that realization brought. Had he escaped? Or been left for dead? And just how imminent was the threat to her?

There was no way he could have been remotely stealthy getting from wherever he'd come from, to her door, in his current condition. Which meant anyone could easily follow his trail, literally to her door.

She glared at him, wanting to beat the ever-loving shit out of him, all over again.

"*I have.*" His confession ran through her mind. He'd been here, either in the area observing her, or physically in her home. Why? They didn't work on home soil. Obviously it had something to do with CJ, if a semi-lucid statement made by someone in his condition could be believed. Maybe he wasn't in his right mind. From the beating, or who the hell knew why. But, for whatever reason, he was on American soil, in the middle of nowhere, bound, beaten . . . and presently unconscious on her living room floor. So she'd better figure it the hell out, and fast.

How long had he been watching her? Could he have really been here, inside her cabin? He was a highly trained agent, but so was she. She'd like to think that she'd have noticed, either way. Hell, she should have felt it. She had truly gone completely soft. She'd wanted to distance herself from that hyper-aware, excruciatingly cognizant world she'd been a part of for far, far too long. And, apparently, she'd been even more successful at it than she'd known. At the moment, she didn't feel all that victorious.

He let out a soft groan just then, and moved his head slightly. She shifted back around to the front of him. "What happened to you?" She leaned closer, close enough to see his eyelashes flutter and his throat work. "Derek. I need to know what was done to you. Who beat you? Why? Come on, you got yourself here, so you can't be too bad off."

She, of all people, knew that for the colossal lie that it was. Adrenaline and the will to survive could give a person near superhuman abilities, but even those wore off at some point. "You're not safe yet," she told him, trying to keep desperation from entering into her tone. If she let so much as a speck of panic filter through the anger right now, the past would barrel right through all of the mental barriers she'd worked so hard to build and refurbish. She simply couldn't let that happen. Her life—her soul—depended on it. "And, thanks to you dragging your body onto my front porch, leaving God knows what kind of trail, neither am I."

He worked his jaw, making a guttural noise, then followed with what sounded like a hoarse whisper. She was forced to lean closer still, and push her hair back so she could put her ear right next to his lips. She was furious and sick to her stomach with fear, and far and away yet from coping with even the first shred of what all this was going to do to her. So it was a damned inconvenient time to look at those lips and remember the thoughts she'd once had about them. Private thoughts—intensely private—that she'd shared with no one, ever. Not even CJ, who'd routinely made up fantasy scenarios about what they could do with and to their gorgeous, tough-as-nails boss as a way to pass the time during the more stultifying moments of whatever case they were on. And there were always plenty of those moments. She'd blamed her partner for her own vivid, highly erotic daydreams. But, truth be told, she'd done quite well with those long before CJ had started her frivolous game.

Thoughts of her former partner definitely weren't helping her maintain, so she blanked out the fantasy scenarios, CJ, her own past life, and what had led her to leave it—as well as the man who had run it, and her—then did her damndest to look at that same man, now lying half-comatose on her cabin floor, as if he were nothing more than another problem to be solved, another mission to deal with.

And the only way she had a hope in hell of doing that was to revert to who she'd been before, or who she'd been trained to be, and completely disassociate her newfound inner self from the proceedings. It was the only way she could focus, so she could think, so she could analyze, so she could solve. It had been second nature to her once. It was the only thing that had kept her alive three years ago.

And it was how she'd stay alive now.

She willed the calm to come over her, a chilling calm that did little to soothe her raw nerves, or ease the acid eating her gut, but she knew that was merely a matter of time. They would smooth eventually. She couldn't stay angry, couldn't feel betrayed. Emotions of any kind clouded critical thinking. Critical thinking was paramount if she wanted to solve this problem, and live long enough to solve another.

When he didn't speak again, she turned her own lips to his ear. "Only for CJ," she whispered, curling her fingers into two tight fists. For a brief moment, she let the deep-seated anger, the hatred, the bitter fury and resentment flood through her. She'd never once allowed herself to feel anything so powerful as that toward anyone. Not even her captors. Especially her captors.

It should have rattled her more than it did. It exposed an alarming weakness. Hatred was a toxic poison that always did more damage to the one experiencing it than to the one it was directed at. In her line of work, that damage was often lethal. But, in that one instant, it felt good, so damn good, to channel all the horror, the fear, and the terror, into one black, twisting funnel of venomous fury and aim it directly at him.

Captivity had taught her the true nature of the precious gift of life. Her life. She, better than anyone, understood just how mighty a gift that was. One that she had a right to enjoy for herself. So, how dare he? How dare he take from her the one and only thing she'd ever asked for, or wanted, strictly for herself?

She shouldn't have given in to the temptation, even for that one, blinding moment, knowing it could consume her whole if she let it. But, for the length of that instant, she didn't regret it.

She rocked back on her heels and slowly uncurled her fists, feeling each finger as it relaxed and steadied.

"I'm in this now," she said, her voice low, toneless, dead, as she cleansed herself of the last of the dark rush. "You've left me no choice." She ran her gaze over him and mentally prepared herself to do a systematic, thorough check of his clothing, then every inch of his body. Just as she would with any person she encountered in his condition during a mission. She needed answers and she needed them fast. He might not be able to speak, but there were other ways to gather information.

First, however, she found herself leaning over him once more. She turned his face toward hers, then lowered her own until her lips were a breath away from his. "But understand one thing, Derek Cole. This time, you will answer to *me*."

# Chapter 2

Derek fought the haze. He was in a fairly significant amount of pain, but that was secondary. That he could compartmentalize. It was just basic mechanics. What worked, what didn't, and how long it would take to repair. The haze . . . that was different. He couldn't divorce himself from it, he couldn't ignore it, he couldn't bend it to his will. Which was why drugs were often so much more effective than physical torture.

Controlling his thoughts was still a slippery endeavor. Staying focused could last several minutes, or mere seconds, before his mind would wander off down some path that could be fact, could be hallucination, or some devilish combination of the two. In the past twelve hours, he'd gotten better at distinguishing which was which, but he still couldn't control the slide in and out. He didn't know what they'd pumped into him, or how long the effects would last.

Worse, he had no idea what he'd told them. Had his years-long, intense training, which included subliminal subterfuge, even under duress and drug induced confessionals, held up? Or did they know everything he knew? Which was admittedly damn little, but more than anyone else knew at the moment.

He didn't even know who the hell "they" were.

"Derek?"

Her voice. Tate's voice. He felt his thoughts begin to slip away from him again and fought like hell to keep them in check, under his control. He'd missed that voice. Always so crisp, so businesslike, so succinct. He'd fantasized about that voice, about making it break, making it tremble. No . . . no, that was the drug talking. He'd never allowed himself to think of his best agent as anything more than just that. Only she wasn't his anymore. In any capacity. Never would be. More's the pity. But what other choice did he have? What other choice would someone like him ever have?

"Derek! Do you hear me?"

*Yes.* And he wanted it to stop. It was torture, that voice. So close, and yet so far. He'd watched her. For days now. So close, and yet farther away than ever. Torture, indeed.

"Don't slip out on me," she commanded. "You need to hold on. Wake up. Tell me what you've done."

Done. What had he done? Bits of the past two days floated in and out of the pain-fogged haze that was his brain. He'd failed, that's what he'd done.

He grimaced, trying to separate the pain from the haze. Focus past the haze, latch on to something, anything, that was real and solid, then build on that. But all he heard was Tate's voice. All he saw was her cabin. With her safely in it. And him, forever on the outside, looking in. Keep her safe. But how? How to do his job, and keep her safe? He had to. He'd given his word. He never made promises. Yet, he'd made one to her.

And then darkness. And pain. And . . . limbo. No boundaries, infuriatingly elastic limbo. If this was purgatory, he'd rather just go to hell.

"Derek."

"Right." His voice . . . had that croak been his voice? Had he spoken, or just wished he had?

"Stay with me," Tate's voice implored.

"Want to," he managed. Hadn't that been the fantasy he'd never allowed himself to indulge in? Striding up to her door, announcing he was out, and would she please, for the love of God, take him in? Fantasy. Hallucination. He would never do that. Never ask that. He had a job to do. Always a job. Always . . . something.

"You can't just come in here and die on my cabin floor without telling me what the hell you've dragged me into."

Cabin floor. Tate's voice. The drug, he was hallucinating again. He'd come inside. She'd let him in. Sanctuary. Hers. Now his.

Someone gripped his chin, shook his head a little. It had the effect of tossing his thoughts like mental salad with a side of pain, and it took him another moment to sort through the jumble. "Don't," he grunted. It was hard enough, fighting this battle.

"What did they do? Is it just physical? Mental? Internal? I don't want to call anyone in, but if you need extreme medical care—"

"No." It was an automatic response, one that was as much an intrinsic response due to his training, as it was an actual accurate assessment of his current situation.

"I can't help you if I don't know what I'm up against."

Derek gritted his teeth, and worked hard to open his eyes, to swallow against the gritty sandpaper that was his throat, to find some way to surface long enough to figure out where he was. Who was prodding him. Separate fact from drug-induced fantasy. He'd already gotten himself in this much trouble, no need to extend the streak any further.

He thought he'd managed to blink his eyes open briefly, but it was just as dark as before. Blind? No. No, he'd seen her face. Felt her touch. Not a dream. Not a hallucination. Which meant . . . "Tate?"

"Right here," she said, matter-of-factly. "What did they do to you?"

She was here. He wasn't going to make contact unless absolutely necessary. He groaned as she began working on the cords binding his wrists. Pain shot up through his elbows, then screamed when his shoulder moved.

The pain had a clarifying effect that was costly, but one he hung on to. He was with Tate. She was here. Talking to him. So, he'd made contact. He'd . . . *fuck.*

"I'm going to cut the cords on your wrists, but I don't want you to move until we figure out if anything is broken."

"Not," he managed. Dislocated, but not broken. "Fine."

She laughed. It was a short, harsh sound. And it made him want to smile. Which was proof right there how fucked up he really was.

"Hardly. But maybe you won't die. Maybe you'll live long enough so I can have the pleasure of killing you myself."

He closed his eyes and stopped trying to roll his head so he could see her. "Please . . . do." Then he could blessedly stop worrying. He hated worrying. It was a completely foreign concept to him. Worry was a luxury he simply did not allow himself. Focused, emotionless clarity. That was how he functioned. It was the only way someone in their profession could function and be successful. And survive.

No worries. Only the job. And how to get it done. Sometimes you won. Sometimes you lost. Sometimes people died either way. Cost of doing business. It wasn't something you could lose sleep over.

But tell that to the sap of a conscience he'd suddenly developed. At least where Tate Winslow was concerned. Or Tara Wingate. Shit.

He'd apparently blown that all to hell anyway, considering his current location.

He'd never been good at that sort of thing anyway, having a conscience. It's what made him good at what he did. Now he had to pray that Tate was still good at what she did. It was the only hope either of them had. For him, to get the job done. For her . . . to stay alive.

A long groan escaped him without his consent when the bonds slid free and gravity pulled at his arms as his hands relaxed against the floor. He wanted to move, to blessedly find a different position, one that would allow him at least a shred of control. But he wasn't truly capable of assessing his injuries and, for Tate's sake, if not for his own, he needed to at least relay to her what it was he'd dragged her into. Why he'd come.

"Don't move."

"Don't worry."

He felt her hands at his ankles, and then the pressure there eased as the cords slid away from them, too. He wanted, so badly, to just flex his legs, get the blood flowing back to the muscles, feel what the damage was. Pain was an incredible clarifier. It was excruciating, but this was the longest he'd held any real thought pattern in what felt like an eternity.

"Let me do a check."

"Check," he repeated, moving just enough to jolt himself alert, as the haze began to seep in around the fringes again.

"Don't," she warned, holding his legs still.

"Have to."

"You have to do what I tell you to do. And only what I tell you to do."

He smiled, then grimaced as the action pulled at abused, blood encrusted skin on his face and mouth. "Bossy."

"I'm about to be your worst nightmare if you don't lie still."

"Can't." He'd already spent the past two days doing that.

"Will," she said. "Since you can't string more than two words together, let me do triage and try to catalogue the numerous sources of the pain you're presently in."

The haze was battling valiantly for a return, but while he was reasonably sure of his situation, he managed to tell her one critical detail. "Drugged."

Her hands paused on their journey up his thigh. A journey that actually made him glad he was in the diminished physical capacity that he was at the moment. Because the drugs in his system wanted to have a field day with the hallucinatory scenarios her mere touch brought to mind. At least, he was going to blame it on the drugs. Easier than admitting he was human.

"How long ago?"

"Days. Think . . . two."

"Two days?" She moved back up near his head, then gently prodded his eyes open.

She was nothing more than a vague, wavery image to him, zooming in and out of focus as she tried to see his pupils. It made him nauseous.

"Too dark, I can't see. What did they use?"

She'd shifted back and he mercifully closed his eyes again. "Don't know," he croaked, fighting to stay above the pain, above the fog.

She leaned closer again, putting her hand on his cheek. It felt almost . . . comforting. He focused on that. "What do they know?" she demanded. "What did you tell them? And who the hell are they?"

So much for comforting.

He would have smiled if he had it left in him. He was sliding away, and he knew there was nothing he could do to stop the void, or the vivid hallucinations that were sure to follow. For how long, he didn't know. Frustration made him instinctively curl his fingers into fists. The renewed blood flow to his fingers now that his hands were unbound caused needle-pricking pain to shoot straight through to the pads of each finger. Even his fingernails felt like they were on fire. Several of his fingers weren't right at all. It wasn't enough to jerk him back.

The void claimed him again.

The next lucid, or semi-lucid, thought he had was about the light. It was piercing, blinding, painful, and he was pretty sure his eyes were still closed. Had he finally ascended from purgatory? Was this the white light that signified the end of the road? Surely he wasn't destined for that finale. But at this point he was simply thankful to get out of limbo.

He tried to move toward the light, tried to open his eyes.

"Derek?"

The voice of angels?

"Derek. Open your eyes."

The voice of Tate Winslow. Which, as it happened, was the preferable option. It meant he was still alive.

"Try—" His voice stuck on one syllable. His throat was dry to the bone and swallowing didn't help much.

He felt the plastic tip of a straw press against his bottom lip, and he instinctively sucked on it.

"Whoa, not too much. Sip," Angel Tate instructed.

He choked a little, coughed, which reunited him with the pain that had been his constant companion now for what felt like an eternity. He tried to be thankful for the jolt of awareness that always accompanied the shock of pain, but he had things he had to accomplish, and these brief moments of pain-induced lucidity weren't going to get the job done.

"Must . . . talk," he finally managed, though the words came out more like a hoarse croak.

"I'm in full agreement on that," Tate replied. "But you taking off to la-la land every five minutes isn't making that an easy proposition. I have to know that what you're telling me is what's actually going on, and not some drug-induced hallucination."

"Not . . . hallucinating now."

"Right. And five minutes ago when you grunted something about snakes, you weren't hallucinating then, either?"

Snakes? He'd always hated snakes, ever since he was a kid. Every nightmare he'd had until the age of ten had generally featured the slithery devils. He'd stopped being afraid of them a long time ago, but he still hated them. So it shouldn't be any surprise they'd popped up again, given his current state. Especially given the nature of the situation. Snakes abounded, only they were in human form.

"I thought you were trying to tell me you'd been bitten by one, and that was why you were delirious out of your mind, but someone has delivered quite a beating, and that was no snake. Well, not the reptile version, anyway."

He wanted to smile at their parallel thoughts, but the simple act used way too many parts of his face that had no interest in cooperating without making him pay, so he just tried to corral his thoughts and focus his awareness—such as it was—on assessing himself, his situation, his current specific location. He was no longer on the floor. He was on something soft. He didn't bother trying to determine how she'd moved him from where he'd collapsed to wherever the hell he was now. Tate had been one of the most resourceful agents he'd ever had.

Then another thought occurred to him. "Where?" he said. "Hosp—?" He didn't think she'd have made that kind of mistake, but then from what bits and pieces he could recall of their initial conversation, she hadn't been too happy to see him. Of course, if she had dumped him in the authorities' laps, he doubted she'd have stuck around to see how he fared.

In response to his attempt to speak, she pressed the straw to his lips again. He sipped slowly this time, and was grateful when she left the straw positioned there for a bit longer, giving him the chance to take several life-giving sips. It could have been the finest champagne, and it couldn't have tasted any better. "Thank you," he managed.

To which she replied, her tone as dry as his throat, "Well, well, a please and a thank-you, all in the span of four hours. You must really be in trouble."

"Trouble," he repeated. "Yes." Trouble he'd brought right to her door, and in possibly the worst way he could have. "Sorry."

"The miracles continue."

"Tate—"

She pressed the straw to his lips again, effectively shutting him up if he didn't want to choke. "Right now, the only miracle I need, barring all of this being a really bad nightmare from which I would love to wake up any time now, is for you to get better as fast as possible so you can tell me what the hell you've done, and why the hell you've dragged me into it."

"CJ."

She didn't say anything immediately, so he tried to open his eyes again. He realized that the blinding light was actually the sun coming in through the window. He squinted against the brilliance of it, and just the act of squinting pulled at enough tight spots on his face to tell him that she hadn't been kidding about the beating he'd taken. He'd only had to squint his right eye, as it seemed his left was somewhat permanently squinted at the moment, being as it was swollen half shut.

He started to lift his hand to do a cursory touch test, but Tate put a quick stop to that.

"No moving. I haven't inventoried all of your injuries yet, but I think we can safely say you suffered a dislocation of your left shoulder and a few of your fingers weren't looking too hot, either."

He carefully tried to curl fingers in both hands, wanting to gauge her assessment personally.

"Honestly, what part of *no moving* didn't you understand?" She trapped his wrists with the palms of her hands, her touch gentle, but restraining nonetheless. "You're in my cabin. You're on my bed. I haven't alerted anyone to your presence here. All three of those things will change if you don't do as I say."

He closed his eyes again, mercifully escaping the piercing light. "Bossy."

"I learned from the bossiest."

A chuckle rumbled in his chest without his permission. "True," he managed, even as he winced through the renewed daggers of pain.

She pressed the straw against his lips. "Drink."

He sipped, but this time the taste was bitter. He immediately clamped his lips and tried to pull back.

"I'm not poisoning you," she told him, sounding more weary than pissed. "Trust me, if I was going to do something to you, it would be direct and unadulterated. I'm trying to give you something to ease the pain. You can't swallow pills, so I crushed up some pain reliever. Just sip as much as you can. I'd give you something stronger, but I don't know what they pumped into your system."

"Don't . . . want that."

"You can handle some ibuprofen. That's all this is. I won't give you anything stronger."

He relaxed again. "Okay." He sipped. A little pain reliever probably wouldn't begin to touch the problems he was currently dealing with, but it sure as hell couldn't hurt.

"I'm going to make some soup. We'll see if you can get a little of that down."

He nodded once, but he was starting to slip away again, and that was all he could manage. As sleep claimed him, he was faintly aware that this time it was just that, sleep. The room didn't feel like it was spinning. And he still had control of his thoughts. Maybe the fog was finally starting to lift.

"I'll check back in on you. Don't do anything stupid."

He didn't smile at that. He'd already done something so monumentally stupid, he couldn't possibly do anything worse.

He'd told her he was sorry, but that didn't begin to cover the depth of his remorse. She still had no idea how badly he'd fucked things up.

But she was going to.

He just had to hurry the hell up and heal enough so he'd be the one to tell her what lay in store. And not the guys with the tranquilizer guns and the happy juice.

# Chapter 3

Tate leaned on the doorjamb and watched him sleep. At least it seemed as if he was sleeping now. He was resting more peacefully, at any rate. Far better than the fitful, twitchy, complete-with-delirious-rambling unconsciousness that had passed for sleep the last time he'd checked out on her.

She tried not to think about some of those ramblings. In his drug-induced delirium, her name had been on his lips more than once. And not in a professional, teamwork kind of way.

She shifted her weight, crossed her arms more tightly, as the echo of those feverish, highly sexually-oriented ramblings made her body twitch in ways it hadn't in a very, very long time. And had absolutely no business twitching now.

All the rest of her parts, however, ached with fatigue. And yet, she knew another cup of coffee was going to be necessary, as sleep was a commodity she wasn't going to be able to indulge in quite yet. She could smell the fresh pot she'd put on as it began to percolate. The rich scent alone was enough to both perk up her brain synapses and make her feel a bit queasy, all at the same time. She'd really rather just close her eyes for a few hours. "Dream on," she murmured, still standing in the doorway, watching him.

She found her gaze once again roaming over his body. He'd always been well-muscled, but not big or bulky. He moved quickly, economically, always in control, and light on his feet.

More panther than lion. He generally slipped into whatever space he chose to occupy, rather than stride his way into it. He was stealthy with his dominance, rather than overt or kingly, despite his leadership position.

So it surprised her how overly large he seemed to her now, in the way he dominated the space in her bed. It was a big bed. A sea of bed, actually. She didn't like small spaces, didn't like to feel limited in her range of motion, even if she didn't use it or need it. She needed to know it was there, the room, the space.

She knew quite well that need was tied directly to her time spent in captivity and didn't really give a flat damn what that said about how well and thoroughly she'd healed. She'd healed more than she'd ever expected possible. So if she wanted to sleep spread-eagled on a mattress the size of Kansas, she wasn't going to apologize to anyone about it.

She covered her mouth with her fist as a yawn overtook her, which made her feel every tense fiber in her neck and shoulders. She was exhausted from the lack of sleep, but hauling his half-dead weight into her bedroom—and away from that giant picture window in her living room—before the sun came up hadn't exactly helped matters. He'd been back in her world less than twenty-four hours, and she needed him to wake the hell up so he could help her come to terms with exactly what his intrusion was going to do to her.

Her innate training had kicked in whether she wanted it to or not, and she realized she'd been subconsciously making damage-control lists almost from the time he'd collapsed on her floor. First order of business was to make sure he was stabilized and secure. He was still fighting off the effects of his injuries and whatever drugs had been pumped into him, but he was no longer bound, he'd been given sips of water, and he was as comfortable as he could be. She still needed to strip him and clean up whatever wounds he might have, do a more thorough investigation of his injuries, but getting him into bed had been an epic struggle, done in fits and spurts whenever he was lucid enough to help her maneuver his weight. At the moment, that was going to have to be enough.

Moving him off the floor had been a risk, as she couldn't be a hundred percent certain there weren't life-threatening internal injuries, but given his continued improvement, and the fact that she couldn't haul him into the nearest emergency room no matter what shape he was truly in, she'd done what she thought was most important.

Which was to make him comfortable and get him out of any possible public view. There were windows along the back wall of her bedroom, but as the rear of her cabin jutted out over a steep hill, someone would have to either be sitting on the deck which circled the back of her home, or have shimmied very high up into some skinny pine trees, to get into binocular—or scope—range. Not that there weren't agents who could pull that off, but it was unlikely. She'd done a thorough visual scan of the rear area anyway. Because unlikely didn't mean impossible.

As soon as she could be relatively certain he wouldn't do anything to further harm himself—or her—she needed to get outside and repair the obvious signs he had to have left in his drugged and disoriented trek to her front door. They might not be obvious to a neighbor or casual passerby, not that she had any of those way out here, but anyone who was actually looking for him would find a trail as easily as if he'd left bread crumbs.

If they hadn't already.

"What in the hell did you think you were doing?" she murmured, tucking suddenly cold hands deeper under her arms. It was little comfort. It was frustrating, the lack of progress she'd made so far in information gathering. She knew he'd been watching her, that he might have even been in the cabin at some point. What she didn't know was why. She did know that someone had found out, or found him, and beaten and drugged him. And that it might have something to do with CJ being alive. It made her heart clutch and her mind flinch every time she allowed her thoughts to go there. So she did her damndest not to. She'd get to all that eventually, process it, deal with it, but to do that she had to get to him first.

And he was still mostly out of it.

Her coffee-maker beeped from the kitchen. She still didn't lever her weight off the door frame right away, despite needing caffeine like a bleeding person needed a transfusion. If she had any hope of figuring things out enough to get them both through the next couple of days without unwanted visitors and the very unwanted consequences that would follow, she needed to be as alert as possible at all times.

And yet she continued to watch him for a few more moments, turning things over, sorting, analyzing. Hating. She still had some work to do on the detached and unemotional thing. Had he been telling the truth about CJ? Or was that just a hallucinatory effect of the drug? Except where in the hell would that have come from? And if this wasn't about CJ, what else on earth could bring him, literally, to her doorstep, or anywhere even remotely close?

He'd seemed somewhat certain when he'd told her that much, but then he'd also commented on things like how incredible she would taste, and how long he'd wanted to do just that. "Come on," she demanded angrily, tightening her arms even further as she finally shoved away from the door, hating how her body continued to respond so readily to even the mere thought of his garbled ramblings. "Wake up, dammit. Tell me the things I need to know so I can keep us both breathing. Because when it's all over, I really want the satisfaction of kicking your ass myself."

She turned toward the kitchen and the freshly brewed transfusion that awaited.

"I wouldn't blame you."

She turned back around to find him blinking his eyes open, but making no effort to move. Which was a good thing, since a lot of his movable parts really shouldn't be for the time being. "For?"

It took him a moment, during which he blinked a few more times, apparently trying to clear the mental haze, then turned his head fractionally, almost experimentally, in her direction. "Kicking my ass," he said, sounding more groggy than alert. "Least I deserve."

She stepped into the room, but didn't go near the side of the bed. This was the most alert he'd sounded since he'd conked out after dropping the CJ bomb on her. She had no idea how long he might have been awake, or what was going through his mind. Or, for that matter, what state his mind was in. Which was why she maintained a safe distance.

In the past, they'd always been on the same side, with the trust that naturally comes from playing on the same team. Now it was different. Completely different. Something had gone terribly wrong somewhere. For him to be out here, attacked, drugged, and presently in the bed of a former agent who'd buried her previous life in favor of a brand-spanking completely anonymous new one—one which only he'd known about . . . yes, something must have gone horribly wrong. Better damn well have.

"I'll agree with that," she replied at length. She drew close enough to see his eyes, which looked clear, or clearer, anyway. Still, she stayed on his weaker side, where he'd sustained most of his injuries. If he'd made it to her door, from God knew where, in the condition he was in, there was no telling what he was still capable of. Or what, in his delirium, he might think he needed to do.

*You would taste so damn incredible, do you know that? Do you know how badly I've wanted to know that?*

She blinked away the memory. Of his face turning toward her, pressing into her breast, as she hauled his semi-lucid self onto her bed. She hadn't been intentionally burying his face in her chest, it had been happenstance, as she'd tried to minimize any further damage to his very damaged self.

His eyes had been glassy, overly bright, and his smile far too sexy, as he'd sprawled on his back in her bed, keeping her pinned on top of him with a fist of her shirt in his hand. He'd used it as leverage, but hadn't released it—or her—even when he didn't need leverage any longer. She'd been an inch from his face, had clearly seen the unfocused look in his eyes . . . and yet her skin had gone all tingly, her nipples hard as rocks, and the muscles between her thighs tight to the point of aching.

She'd levered herself off of him immediately, or as immediately as she could, while simultaneously disengaging his fisted hold on her shirt and trying not to hurt him any further. It was ridiculous, letting herself get jumpy over a guy who was clearly half out of his mind and saying things he'd never remember, much less ever mean.

He wasn't glassy-eyed now, despite still sounding a bit groggy. He seemed to know where he was, and who she was. Which would hopefully preclude his ever discussing any fantasy that involved taste tests of any kind. If he did remember. Which she hoped he didn't.

"How long have I been out?"

Her gaze darted from his mouth back to his eyes. "You arrived in a heap on my foyer floor approximately thirteen hours ago. That was around three in the morning, which makes it almost four o'clock now." She stepped closer. "Your turn. How long have you been watching my cabin?" *Watching me.*

He squeezed his eyes shut for a moment, then opened them, blinked twice, then slowly shifted his head until his gaze found hers. "What day is it?"

"Tuesday. Twentieth of May."

She saw his jaw tighten, and his throat work. "Ten days, then."

He was angry, upset, she assumed with himself. *Get in line,* she wanted to tell him. "And how many of those did you spend drugged, unconscious, and trussed up like a Thanksgiving turkey?" She'd asked him before, but, as a gauge, she wanted to see how accurate his assessment had been when he'd been mostly out of it.

His gaze narrowed on hers then, but he didn't otherwise

react. "I was tranq-darted approximately sixty hours ago." He cleared his throat again, trying to get the rest of the gravel out.

She could have offered him more water, and she would, but now that he was more awake and alert, she wasn't approaching him that closely. Yet. She was close enough to see the frustration in his eyes as clearly as she could hear it in his voice. A man like Derek Cole was rarely, if ever, caught with his guard down. It made her wonder how they'd found him. And who the hell "they" were. At least his assessment of the length of time that had passed while still fighting the effects of the drugs had been spot on, which was good. She hoped his other training had been working subconsciously as well. "Of that time, how long did whoever tranq'd you have you?"

"Can't be sure. But not very long. If they'd had time, they'd have kept me clearheaded and worked me that way. Tortured what they needed out of me, make sure it was the truth."

"Looks like they did a pretty good number on you anyway. Maybe you weren't all that responsive, even drugged."

"I think the method they used and the act itself was as much a message being delivered as whatever they got out of me, or really wanted to know."

"I'm guessing you didn't escape as, given your condition and being bound, you wouldn't have been that hard to retrieve. So, why do you think they left you alive, but trussed up?"

He didn't answer that. Instead, he asked, "Have you been outside? Tracked?"

She shook her head. "You haven't exactly been stable. It took me awhile to assess your injuries, get you out of sight. I'm still not sure I can really assess how bad off you are."

He turned his head very slowly, just enough to take in the room around him. "Yours?"

She wanted to ask him if he was being disingenuous. He'd mentioned being here. Perhaps he hadn't been inside the cabin itself, which made her feel slightly better, both from a security position—though that was clearly an illusion—and, pride forced her to admit, from a personal one of having had someone in her home and not detected it. "I only have one. Don't get used to it."

His gaze tracked back to hers, but again he remained enigmatically silent. Suddenly she wasn't so sure about anything.

"I found the dart mark on the back of your left shoulder. Pressure syringe marks on your neck."

"Plural?"

"Yes."

He just grunted at that. "Explains why it's taking so long."

She assumed he meant to get over the effects of the drugs. "Apparently you're just as hard-headed drugged as you are lucid."

He gingerly moved his legs, then immediately stopped. "Apparently," he ground out. "How bad off am I? What do you know? I assumed you did some kind of check before moving me."

"Given my lack of X-ray vision, I don't know what the internal situation is, but you're not running a fever and you seem to be recovering rather than getting worse, so my guess is whatever damage you sustained, you'll live."

"Until you kick my ass, anyway." The corner of his mouth kicked up the tiniest of fractions, which still made him wince.

"True."

He held her gaze for a moment longer, then let his head relax back into the pillow more deeply, and closed his eyes. "I feel like I've been hit by a truck. Possibly run over by one as well. And that's not counting the pharmaceutical fun I'm having."

"Well, I wouldn't rule out the run-over part, but there were no tread marks, so maybe they stopped just shy of that. I think you have some bruised ribs, a seriously wrenched shoulder at best—"

"Dislocated. It happens. They didn't dislocate it. I did, trying to loosen my bonds. I got it back in. Sort of like a trick knee."

"Yeah," she said, staring dubiously at him. "You're tricky

all right." She had to actively keep from rubbing her own shoulder, as she imagined the contortions he'd put himself in, trying to regain his freedom. "If they'd broken a rib, you could have punctured something, trying that stunt."

"Considering I'd been left for dead, I figured it was a risk worth taking." He opened his eyes again, turned his head so he could look at her directly. "I would have done whatever I had to. I knew I had to get here."

"You give me too much credit if you assumed I'd give you safe haven. You're only still here because I don't know why you were watching me in the first place."

"I told you. At least, I think I did."

She folded her arms, resisting the urge to rub at the goose-flesh that now covered them. But she waited for him to say it again.

"I told you, about CJ."

All she could do was nod.

"Tate, I wouldn't have compromised—"

She lifted her hand, effectively silencing him. "I don't want apologies. It's too late for that. I want answers. You've already been here too long, leaving me in the dark for too long. With someone out there who knows you're here."

"Not here—"

"Here," she reiterated. "Just how good could you have been in covering your tracks from where they left you, to my front door? A child could track you here. A blind child at that."

He let out a long breath and closed his eyes. For a moment, she thought he'd either passed out again, or fallen back asleep. Then he said, "Storm was coming."

"And you thought that would hide your trail?"

His eyes remained closed, and he was sounding groggy again. "Best shot I had. Had to warn you. Tell you."

"If you wanted to keep me safe, you could have dragged your beaten ass anywhere else in this valley, drawn them off me, away from here."

"Too late for that."

A cold chill raced down her spine. "Why? What do you think you told them?"

"Doesn't matter what they know. What matters is what I know."

She stalked over to the bed and it took all her willpower not to shake him. "What do you know, Derek? What the hell do you know that was worth putting my life in jeopardy? Haven't I done enough for you and the agency? Don't answer that. I know damn well I have."

He opened his eyes, found hers unerringly. "Your life was already in jeopardy before I got here."

"You're the only one who knew where I was."

"CJ is trying to make contact with you. If she couldn't do it through me, I'm assuming she'd have tried other means. I'm not entirely sure she hasn't, or that my visitors a few days ago aren't a result of her digging."

Tate froze. "What the hell is that supposed to mean? And why, if she's alive, would her knowing my location put me in any kind of danger? She was my partner. She wouldn't—" Tate choked down the sudden hot rush that stung the back of her eyes. "She died for me, Derek."

"That's just it, Tate." Derek's gaze burned brightly into her own. "She didn't die, did she?"

# Chapter 4

He just wanted to sleep. A year should do. He was weary down to his soul. What he didn't want to do was look into Tate's eyes and see the shattered pain she no longer tried to hide. He knew what she'd been through before she'd left the team. He had led the team debriefing her. He'd heard every last detail, from her own swollen, cracked, bleeding lips. He'd seen her when she'd been broken, beaten, and reduced to something that barely seemed human. And yet, through it all, she'd never once let it reach her eyes. The last time he'd seen her, spoken to her, they'd been dead, hollow, completely void of all emotion. It should be encouraging to see her now, like this, looking so intensely human.

Except the feelings she should be experiencing these days were peace, tranquility, and, if she was very lucky, joy.

Not more pain, more anguish. She was the last one to deserve that. And he hated it that he was the one bringing those things back into her world. But he also refused to believe that staying cold and emotionless would have served her better.

After all, look where that had gotten him.

"According to you, she didn't die," Tate stated, jaw hard as granite, eyes bright with unshed tears. "She took a bullet for me, Derek. Several, if my hearing served me correctly, and it did. I might have been beaten until I could barely see, but I wasn't deaf. Are you saying that didn't happen? That I just dreamed it when I had to listen while they tried to torture out of her what they couldn't torture out of me? While they threatened to shoot her? When they did shoot her? Was it a hallucination when they dragged her past the open door to the room I was being held in, with two holes in her chest and one in the center of her forehead?" She towered over him at the side of his bed, fury now replacing pain. "Are you telling me that those sightless gray eyes that will stare into mine for all eternity weren't real? Because, even in my diminished capacity, they looked pretty damn real to me."

"I don't know, Tate," he said, speaking the God's honest truth and wishing he had some other truth to offer her. "I don't know what happened in that room, or what you actually saw—"

"*Actually* saw? *Actually?* I know what the hell I actually saw because I *was* actually there!"

Derek let her rage rain down on him, knowing the source of it was as real as it got. "The only person who really knows what went on in that room is CJ. And whoever was in on it with her."

"In on *what?*" Tate all but shrieked that last word. "We had no leverage, no way out, nothing to barter with."

"Except the truth."

"Which would have gotten us just as dead the minute we got done giving it up."

"Apparently she found a way to barter with it."

"How?"

"I don't know. All I do know is that both of you are still alive."

Tate said nothing more, but the fight was still in her eyes.

"Did you ever ask yourself why, after they supposedly killed CJ, they didn't finish you off, as well?"

"Of course I did. If you recall, that was a big part of my debriefing. The torture didn't stop when they shot CJ. It went on for two more days—"

"But, despite watching your partner die at their hands, you gave them nothing."

She jerked her head, looked away briefly. "They thought

killing CJ would weaken my defenses. They guessed exactly wrong."

"So they just up and left."

Tate sighed. "The assumption was they received orders to move on to other targets."

"Why leave you alive?"

Tate looked directly at him. "I don't think they believe they did. I might have been breathing, barely, but I was hardly alive. I assume, if they thought of it at all, when they left me there they believed I'd starve to death, if my injuries didn't get me sooner. I wasn't exactly freed, I was abandoned, as useless to them as the house they were using to torture us in.

"As I stated in my debriefing, they didn't treat me as a human being, merely as a conduit of information. When that conduit wasn't forthcoming, they saved further expenditure of energy and moved on. The last day, they were talking with each other as they left the room I was held in as if I wasn't there. They didn't so much as look back when they walked out. Shortly after that, the house was abandoned. What was left of the village was already burned out and deserted. I was discovered a day later by an old villager looking to see if there was anything useful left in the rubble to loot. I was retrieved by the team two days after that. End of story. A story you know full well. So, what part of the story don't I know?"

"They never did find CJ's body."

"I'm aware of that. Doesn't prove her death was a hoax." And just like that, the fight went out of her. She took a moment, and he watched as she tried to gather herself, regroup, but it was apparently beyond her at the moment. "I saw it, Derek," she said, sounding emotionally raw, bruised. "I saw her."

"I know," he said quietly. "But I've communicated with her, Tate. She is alive."

"I don't understand." Tate turned then, and paced to the window, stopping abruptly and staring out of it. "Make me understand."

He closed his eyes and willed himself to focus. "I will," he said, knowing his battle against the dark void that was pulling at him once again, was going to be a losing one. At least this time it was pure exhaustion, not the fuzzy fugue of drugs, that was pulling him under. "Rest, Tate. We both need it."

"Derek—"

"You'll know everything I do," he said, promising her. He rarely made those. "I just . . . I'm fading. Let me rest. Then we'll talk."

She paced from the window to the bed, arms folded. "I need to get outside anyway. Damage control."

"The storm."

"The sky is black, heavy, but the ground is just as dry as when you dragged yourself here."

"Shit."

"And then some."

He opened his eyes into slits, enough to see her roll her shoulders and take a deep, silent breath. "Let me get you some water—"

"Just need some sleep. You should, too."

"I can take care of me."

That was a fact he knew better than most. "There's more," he said, his eyes closing again, this time without permission. "A lot more."

"Really," she said, her tone dry and harsh. He could hear her footsteps moving toward the bedroom door. "And here I thought it couldn't get any more exciting."

He listened to her walk away, thinking that was the closest she'd come to sounding like the old Tate.

If he didn't already know he was going to hell, he certainly would for that alone.

The next thing he remembered was being jolted awake by a booming crash. He instinctively tried to dive off the bed to the floor for cover until he determined the situation, then came screamingly awake when hot daggers of pain knifed through him, pretty much everywhere.

"What the hell do you think you're doing?"

That was Tate's voice, shouting, then she was there, pushing him back down onto the bed from his slumped-over position, half on–half off the mattress.

"Heard—a crash. Thought—"

"Never mind," she told him, her matter-of-fact tone telling him she'd likely figured out the chain of events. "Just lie back down, you're in no condition to—"

"Actually," he said, bracing his weight on one hand, on his good side, as she helped shift his legs back to the bed, "I don't think I'm as bad off as I thought."

"Why? Because you didn't actually explode an internal organ just now? We still don't know what's busted up in there, so—"

"I know what shape I'm in." Or he certainly did now. Now that the rainbow of consciousness-threatening pain was settling down into something that was merely excruciating, he was beginning to sort out the sources.

White light flashed through the room, creating a strobe-light effect, followed almost immediately thereafter by a wall-rattling crack of thunder. Neither of them flinched, but simply continued maneuvering him back into bed.

He put his hand on hers when she started to pull the covers around him. "I can manage."

She stilled. "Three hours ago you could barely move your head two inches to the right, so you'll have to forgive me if I make assumptions regarding your general health and well-being."

He wanted to tell her he was the very last person whose well-being she should ever care about, but they both knew the only reason she was nursing him back to any level of health was so she could find out just how much jeopardy he'd put hers into.

"I'm beaten, not broken," he told her, then immediately wanted to bite his tongue off at the look that flashed across her face. "Tate—" he began, only to have her cut him off with a quick tuck of the coverlet over him, making him grunt a bit in pain.

She continued on, straightening the corners with crisp efficiency, her gaze no longer anywhere in the vicinity of his. "Rest," she instructed. "I'm making soup."

His stomach growled at that announcement, but she merely arched a brow, still not looking at him as she stalked to the door. "Sounds like a 'yes, ma'am,' to me. I'll be back later."

And she was gone, down the hall, and from the sounds of it, out the front door, which he heard slam shut behind her a moment later.

Straight out into the storm. But then, he supposed she was in a storm regardless of whether there was a roof over her head or not.

*I can take care of myself.*

Her words echoed in his head. As did all the others he'd heard her speak. Both here, and during her debriefing.

He blocked those out. All of them. Because she was right. If she'd ever proven anything, and she certainly hadn't needed to at that point in her quite illustrious career, it was that she could take care of herself.

She hadn't needed him then. And she most definitely did not need him now.

The best thing he could do for her was to figure out the fastest way to get on his feet, so they could solve the problem at hand before the problem took them out of the equation.

Of course, it would be a hell of a lot easier if he knew exactly what the problem was. He didn't look forward to the moment when he had to explain that little detail to her. All he could hope was that she had, unwittingly or not, the information he needed to fill in the crucial parts of the equation that were still blank.

*So focus, dammit. Focus.*

And though his head pounded like it was being used as an anvil, and his body screamed like a little girl every time he moved any part of it, he spent the next twenty minutes doing as thorough and methodical an assessment of his physical situation as he could. Tate's assessment was that his physical situation wasn't all that great, and if anyone could be an observational judge of that, she could. But he was the best judge of all. And while realistically, Tate wasn't that far off, he knew that willpower and a high tolerance to pain would expedite him through a fair chunk of recovery time.

Mostly he was thankful that the past twelve hours seemed to have been the trick needed to get the last of the drugs out of his system, or at least diminished to the point where all he had left was a splitting hangover of a headache. He could live with that.

Thunder rattled the cabin walls again as Derek slowly worked his way into more of a sitting position. Well, his head was propped up higher than his chest now, anyway. It was a start. His stomach rumbled again, which he took as a good sign, despite the fact that the idea of food at the moment made him want to puke. By tomorrow, he estimated, he'd be closer to tackling that endeavor without turning green at the thought, but he'd try to get some of Tate's soup down later. The faster he could get some nutrients back into his system, the better. He glanced at the open door on the opposite side of the room, the one leading to the master bathroom. Another adventure to be tackled as soon as humanly possible.

He might have seen Tate at her worst, but she'd kept her recovery process an intensely personal one, dealing only with a few hand-selected medical personnel throughout, until she could leave the team for good and retire here to continue healing on her own. He understood the need for that kind of privacy, on many levels, when dealing with such catastrophic injuries, both physical and mental.

Given her intimate acquaintance with those kinds of privacy issues, he realized she'd be more than capable of helping him with his far more rudimentary needs. However, he was just as determined as she'd been to handle as much of his recovery privately as possible. And it had little to do with modesty or pride. They had a mission ahead, and as partners they would have to know, have to be able to trust, that they could rely on each other. He needed her to believe, without question, that he was capable of leading this mission, of getting them through this.

The front door to the cabin banged open and shut again, drawing his attention to the bedroom door. She didn't come immediately down the hall. He heard her in the kitchen first, making a clatter, then finally her footsteps coming closer. Thunder continued to rattle walls as heavy rain slashed at the windows. The gloom was so thick now, the lightning strikes barely penetrated it. He guessed it was early evening, which meant he'd slept another couple hours before the storm had woken him up.

"I should have turned on a light for you before I left," she said as she entered the room, a small tray balanced in her hands.

"That's okay. And you didn't have to go to all the trouble," he said, grunting as he tried to shift his weight a bit further upright.

"Derek—"

"It's enough I'm here, doing . . . this to you. You don't have to spoon-feed me on top of it."

"Your shoulder—"

"Hurts like hell, but will be fine. If you've got something I could fashion into a sling to take the weight off of it for a bit, that—"

"I've got a sling. Just stop what you're doing before you make things worse."

"To quote you earlier, I can take care of myself."

"If by that you mean you can drag yourself, half-dead, to the doorstep of someone who can keep your sorry ass from dying, then yes, you most certainly can. Now, if you're determined to abuse your already abused body, then fine, but at least suck up your pride long enough to let me help you sit up."

She set the tray down on the nightstand with something of a clatter, causing the soup to slop over the side of the bowl a bit. She turned to him, hands on her hips.

"I know I look like hell, but I'm not as bad off as it seems," he told her.

"Right."

He found himself smiling, and didn't even wince this time when it pulled at the broken skin at the corners of his mouth and eyebrow. His cursory once-over before she'd come in from the storm had revealed that she'd cleaned the dried blood from his face, hands, and wrists at some point during his unconsciousness and put ointment on the cuts. He tried not to think about those narrow, strong fingers touching him. Mostly because the thought of her ministering to him didn't bother him nearly as much as it should have. "I don't recall you ever taking such a tone before." He lifted a hand, and did wince a little when his shoulder protested. "Not that I don't deserve every sharp tone in the book. I'm just saying it's a different side of you."

"Get used to it. I might have to suffer whatever hell on earth you've brought back into my world, but I don't have to suffer arrogance or condescension along with it."

"Is that how you see me? Arrogant and condescending?"

"What, you think you're all sweetness and light?"

"Tough, but fair, would be a closer assessment."

"You were both, true. I respected the way you ran the program, and I respected your personal work ethic."

"But you didn't like me much."

She simply stared at him. "I knew I could count on you to do whatever had to be done to ensure a successful mission, and I knew I could trust you with my life and those of my fellow agents. Nothing else mattered."

He nodded. "Fair enough."

"But I don't work for you any longer. So, if I'm thinking something, or reacting to something, you'll be the first to know about it. Whether or not you approve of what I have to say, or the way in which I say it, means little to me."

"Understood."

She turned her back on him and walked over to a tall dresser situated to the side of the bed, opposite the wall of windows. He hadn't been in the position to pay much attention to how she'd furnished her home, but while she rooted through the drawers, he did now. He used the term "furnished" rather than "decorated," as there were the necessary items, all sturdy and durable looking, if not exactly stylish or even matching, but next to nothing extra added beyond that. A small matted and framed print of some kind hung next to the bathroom door, and a colored glass jar with a spray of dried flowers in it sat on the dresser. The nightstand held a generic-looking lamp and a clock. No books or clutter of any kind. Although she might have moved that kind of stuff out of reach or sight when she'd moved him in here.

It wasn't exactly barracks, as the log walls, beamed ceilings, and woven rugs on the plank wood floors, leant the room warmth, but it didn't look much like a home either. Made him curious about the rest of the house. He watched as she dug through first one, then another of the dresser drawers. Other than through a high-powered scope, it was his first opportunity to truly look at her up close. His head was still pounding with a blistering headache, but his eyesight was blessedly clear now.

He knew from watching her over the past week that she moved relatively smoothly, if not exactly gracefully, which, considering how broken she'd been, was somewhat surprising. Clearly, if she'd moved his bulk from the front room to this bed, she'd regained both her strength and range of motion, and the muscles to throw behind it. She was leaner now, he thought, recalling her once solid, sturdy frame. He wouldn't go so far as to call her skinny, though there didn't seem to be much to spare on her frame these days. More . . . rawboned.

He thought about her face, which he'd mostly only seen with a scowl since reentering her world. Not that he could blame her, but he'd thought her drawn features were more a result of that expression. Now he was thinking that it went with the rest of her. Not exactly bony or narrow, but definitely harder, and a bit weathered. He wondered whether it was the natural result of her rehabilitation—her face had been pretty banged up by her captors—or a result of living a rather elemental lifestyle out in the middle of nowhere.

Her hair, which she'd kept chin length during the time she worked for him, was the only luxuriant thing about her now. It was long, or longer than he'd ever seen it, brushing below her shoulders, all at one length. For all her physique was spare these days, her hair was anything but. During his observation of her, she'd always had it pulled back, or under a hat, so he hadn't noticed it so keenly. Now he couldn't seem to stop looking at it. It was thick, surprisingly wavy, and had a natural shine that drew the eye.

She slapped the last drawer shut and turned to face him, but he found himself still watching her hair move and swing around her shoulders. She dangled a sling in her hand, finally drawing his attention.

"I'll have to make some adjustments for your size, but I think it will work."

He stared at the sling a moment longer, and images of the last time he'd seen her, three years before, swam uninvited through his mind. She'd been leaving the hospital's long-term rehabilitation wing. Leaving the entire area, for that matter, for good. He'd come to see her with the idea of talking her into taking a sabbatical rather than terminating her job. He'd used logic, telling her she'd retain benefits that way, and seniority. He'd argued that she'd go crazy sitting out in the middle of nowhere, that she was too vital a person for that, with a need to be involved rather than sidelined. He thought he'd been giving her a long-term goal, something to focus on. A future.

She'd been sitting in a wheelchair when he'd walked in, but only because the nurse was more stubborn than she was. At least that was his take given the byplay between the two. One leg was still in a heavy brace, her head was still partially bandaged where they'd had to shave it. Her face was recognizable by then, but still pretty banged up. And her arm had been in a sling. The one presently in her hands, if he wasn't mistaken.

She'd quietly listened to all his arguments, then turned to the nurse and informed her that she was ready to leave. She didn't bother to look back after she'd been wheeled past him. Though she had probably felt somewhat humiliated by her physical limitations at the time, he recalled thinking it had been one of the more dignified exits he'd ever seen. And though he'd sincerely believed she was making a mistake by resigning the team, that dignity alone demanded he respect her decision. And he had.

Until he'd been given no choice.

"You didn't have to—"

"What?" she said, rather brusquely. "I have a sling, you need one. Don't get all maudlin on me."

"Maudlin? I'm hardly—"

"Here." She walked over to the side of the bed, already making the adjustments to the strap. "You'll need to shift your weight forward just a—"

"Got it," he said, for some reason annoyed rather than amused with her no-nonsense demeanor. She bent across him, all but burying his face in all that hair, and he didn't want to know how fresh it smelled, or how silky it felt. He didn't want to know that it would make his body respond in ways that, while heartening to know everything still functioned properly, was entirely inappropriate. Especially when it was very damn clear he didn't then, and certainly didn't now, hold any of the same distraction or appeal for her.

Using his good hand, he tugged the strap from hers. "I can do it."

She immediately let go and straightened. "I'm sure you can."

Hearing the thread of amusement in her tone had him looking up. There was little hint of it on her face, but he knew what he'd heard. "What?" he asked, knowing he sounded almost petulant, and not seemingly able to get himself under control. It shouldn't bug him in the slightest that she wasn't aware of him the way he was suddenly aware of her. He certainly wasn't at his best at the moment. And just because she'd never thought of him in that way, certainly shouldn't have been any kind of blow to his ego. They'd worked together, and that kind of distraction held all kinds of dangerous potential he continually instructed his team to avoid at all costs. Not that all of them did. Being put into highly dangerous, life-and-death situations, especially with someone you had to trust with your life, had a way of creating sexual tension, even between people who otherwise couldn't have imagined it.

He'd never been in that kind of close quarters situation with Tate, and never knew her to have gotten involved with anyone she'd worked with, but it certainly hadn't kept him from thinking that, had life been different for the two of them, he might have been interested in her that way. So it shouldn't have been a stretch to think that she might have felt something along the same lines.

Christ, he really needed to get some food in his belly and get some rest, because his entire train of thought was bordering on the ridiculous. He finished situating the sling, using motions that caused more pain than necessary, but if that's what it took to clear his head, so be it. "If you could prop the tray on my lap, I can take it from there," he said, not remotely interested in eating anything at the moment, but needing the distraction almost as much as he needed the nutrition.

She did as asked with a minimum of fuss. "I'll leave you to it. Let me know when you're done." She moved to the doorway, but paused by the frame and looked back. "Then I'll want a complete debriefing on everything you know so we can start getting me my life back."

# Chapter 5

Tate made it as far as the kitchen before giving in to the shaking in her knees. She sank down onto a kitchen chair and wrapped trembling hands around the mug of hot tea she'd made herself after coming in from the storm. She let the warmth seep through her skin, willing it to soothe the rest of her.

She shouldn't let him rattle her. The situation he'd put her in was rattling enough. Maybe that was it. Maybe it was the return of the tension and the adrenaline and the worry that was making her hyper-aware of him in ways she had absolutely no business being. Of course, he'd never been in her home before, much less in her bed, so she could probably be forgiven for having a few wayward thoughts. Which didn't explain why that awareness had begun when he'd still been lying half-conscious on the floor inside her front door.

It was the situation, that was all. She took a fortifying sip of tea, then swore silently when it burned the tip of her tongue. She had to get her wits about her if she was going to reclaim her life and get him and whatever he'd brought with him the hell out of it.

While she'd been outside, trying to beat the storm from hell and losing that battle handily, tracking and covering his movements all the way out into the hills, she'd made a promise to herself. She didn't care what was going on, or why he'd come to find her, she wasn't leaving here. This was her home now, these were her mountains, her retreat, her corner of the world. Her haven. And she'd be damned if she was going to let anyone take it away from her.

She blew across the surface of her tea, hating that her breath was still a bit uneven. She could blame it on the aftereffects of her long hike through the wind and rain, but she'd bundled up against the elements and had taken appropriate precautions, using her walking stick when she had to. Covering her tracks as well.

She popped a few over-the-counter pain relievers as she took another sip. These days, it was thankfully the only medicine she required, and only then when needed. She didn't hurt now, but she knew she'd pay the price tomorrow, so a little preemptive strike was in order. Plus, it was likely only the beginning of the strain she might have to put on her still relatively newly-healed body. She closed her eyes and tried to clear her mind, meditate, even briefly, reclaim the calm she'd worked so hard to find inside herself.

But every time she closed her eyes, it was like a myriad of images coming at her in high speed, making her head hurt, drawing her thoughts down paths they had no business traversing. Whether they be inappropriate thoughts of her former boss, or unnecessary flashbacks to a life that no longer mattered.

So she stared instead across the small kitchen, past the foyer, and out the large picture window beyond. Even though the heavy rains shrouded her view, she could clearly visualize the rippling chain of velvety mountains that hugged the valley. Her valley. Keeping her gaze there, she focused her thoughts on the immediate future. On what lay in store for her now that Derek was here. What threat had he brought with him that, right at this very moment, might be laying siege to her peaceful existence?

She'd been heartened by the fact that she hadn't found any other tracks between her house and the tangle of bush and brush she'd tracked him to, that he appeared to have literally crawled out from. Then the storm had come gunning, so she had opted not to track further, though she'd wanted to. She'd wanted to find out where he'd made camp, and perhaps even pick up the trail of who had gotten to him, as he hadn't been in any condition since their surprise ambush to do so himself. The more information she gathered on her own, saw firsthand with her own eyes, the better she'd feel. It wasn't a matter of not trusting Derek, but he operated in a world—once her world—where information was power, and often the line between life and death. He'd share what he knew accordingly, even if he thought his choices were governed by his concern for her best interests. She'd been fully in charge of her own best interests for some time now, and she had no intention of giving up any of that power unless absolutely necessary.

The storm and winds were fierce enough to make any tracking after the fact close to impossible, but she'd also been well aware of her physical limitations, and she knew just getting back to the cabin was going to exhaust what little energy she'd had left at that point. It was with regret that she'd turned around, but with the promise that she'd head back out after the storm to see if there was any salvageable track left to follow.

She absently massaged her left thigh, even though the steel rod that was in there now wasn't exactly going to respond to any amount of rubbing she could do. The muscle tissue wrapped around that rod needed constant coaxing and care to stay limber and flexible. Her muscles were strong now, and she was more resilient than she'd ever thought she'd be again. But there were limitations, and some of them would never be surmounted. It was a compromise she'd accepted.

But she wasn't the average person, living the average life. No matter how badly she'd like to think she was. Not before, and apparently not ever. The proof of which was currently taking up residence in her bed.

As if summoned by her thoughts, he called out not a second later. "Done."

She dragged her gaze from the picture window and her

thoughts inward along with it, gathering her strength, and her wits. She'd need both for what was about to come. "Okay," she called back, hearing the fatigue in her voice, knowing she was going to have to find some way to mask it. She pushed her chair back. The time had come to find out what was going on. And what it was going to take to re-secure her life here.

She topped off her herbal tea and poured Derek a cup of coffee. She breathed in the rich scent, sorely tempted to relax her self-imposed limits on her daily intake. The punch of caffeine would be welcome, but during recovery she'd learned that it would also leave her jittery and unable to relax, much less sleep. She'd initially thought to eliminate it all together, but eventually she'd found a balance. It was harder, possibly, to maintain, but as a constant test of discipline, which was vital if she was to maintain her hard-won rejuvenation, it wasn't such a bad thing, all in all.

She carried both mugs into the bedroom, then immediately put them on the dresser top so she could intercept his shaking attempts to put his food tray back on the night stand. "If you couldn't wait for me to take it, you could have just set it on the bed next to you."

He didn't apologize or look remotely repentant. It almost made her wish he was still in a drugged stupor. Derek with all his faculties in order was going to demand much more control on her part. Unfortunately, he needed all his faculties in order for her to get the information she needed.

"I didn't want to slosh it on the bedspread," he said by way of explanation.

"If you'd eaten all of it, there wouldn't be anything to slosh."

"I got more of it down than I thought I would."

She set the tray on the dresser and picked up the mugs. "Is that commentary on my cooking?"

"No, just commentary on the state of my body."

She started to hand him the coffee, but handed him the tea instead. "You might want to stick with this, then, at least for the time being."

He looked down in the weak brown contents. "Tea." He looked up at the mug in her hand. "I smell coffee."

She set the mug on the dresser, next to his uneaten soup. "When you can finish your food, then we'll talk about coffee. Your system needs the former more than the latter."

"Nurse Ratched," he grumbled, but she noted he sipped the tea. She tried not to think about the fact that it was her mug he was putting his lips on, because it was completely ridiculous to even go there, but go there her thoughts did.

She purposely kept her gaze off his mug of coffee. She needed more than a caffeine jolt at the moment. "Let's just say I know of where I speak, and leave it at that."

His gaze lifted to hers, but he didn't say anything. She fervently prayed it stayed that way. She had no plans to discuss anything about her life here, her recovery, any of it, with him. "Tell me, from the beginning, what happened that led you to come all the way out here to stalk me."

"I wasn't stalking you. I was observing you."

"Why not just contact me directly?"

"I needed to make certain you weren't part of . . ."

When he didn't continue, she walked around to his side of the bed. "Part of what?"

Derek sighed and briefly closed his eyes. For a moment she thought he was succumbing, once again, to either his injuries, the drugging, or both. But just as she moved forward, he opened his eyes. "Things have changed within the agency since you've left. Nothing is the same, and I don't know who to trust."

She had no idea what she'd expected him to say, something about CJ contacting him and him being concerned about what connection she might play in that startling discovery that her former partner was still alive. But this . . . was entirely unexpected. "What do changes in the agency have to do with CJ still being alive? I thought that was what drove you to come out here and drag me back into a world I very specifically left behind."

He stared into her eyes for a long moment, then closed his again. "It's a long story, Tate."

She folded her arms. "I find I have the time. And you're certainly not going anywhere."

He let out another long breath, then looked at her again. "Go and get a chair, or something. This might take awhile. And it will be easier on us both if you're at least comfortable while I tell you and not glowering over me."

"I've a right to glower. And you will tell me everything, Derek. And when you're done, you'll answer all my questions. You came to me, not the other way around, so—"

"I'll answer what I can."

"You'll answer what you know. Not what you choose. It's my life that's being put in jeopardy here, if the condition you arrived in is any indication, so any trust issues you might have, get over them." She walked over to the stuffed chair in the corner and dragged it over to the side of the bed. She sat, masking the relief that the comfort of getting off of her feet and sitting on something soft, gave to her. She shouldn't have had to worry about exposing her weaknesses or vulnerabilities, even to him, maybe especially to him, who'd seen her at her lowest, most vulnerable point, but she'd been too well trained to reveal anything she didn't need to. "If it eases your mind any, since the day I left the rehabilitation wing of the hospital, I have not been in any kind of contact, in any manner whatsoever, with anyone connected to, or pertaining to, my former life, in any way, shape, or form. And certainly not my heretofore dead partner." It sounded harsh, saying it like that, but the truth was, she still hadn't—couldn't—fully process, in any real way, that CJ was alive.

She had his full attention now, his gaze tightly focused on her own. It was a visceral thing, his full attention, even when he was injured and laid up in bed. She found herself shifting back in her seat, almost bracing herself.

"As far as you know, anyway," he said.

"What on earth does that mean?" she demanded, sitting forward again. "I'm very well aware of who I'm in contact with and who I am not. Unless you're intimating that the handful of neighbors I've befriended since moving here, all valley residents for decades prior to my arrival, are actually a network of undercover foreign operatives . . . then I believe I can state with fair certainty that I've been totally cut off from that world."

"That was the conclusion I'd drawn as well."

She clapped her hands several times. "Bravo, then. So, I ask again, why not simply approach me?"

"I was about to do that very thing when I took a dart to the shoulder."

She sat back again. "How long had you been out there?"

"Before the attack, a week."

"And watching me for a week is all it took to make certain I wasn't secretly in cahoots with someone?"

"You know better than that. I ran a thorough search before coming out here."

"Now, that sounds more like the Derek Cole I knew." She frowned then, as something else occurred to her. "Why you?"

"What do you mean? CJ contacted me, and only me."

"Okay, but surely you weren't going to keep that information to yourself? I mean, it's a fairly major event, an agent rising, literally, from the dead. You'd need help. Why not put someone else out there in the hills on watch for me? And who tranq'd you?"

"As I started to say earlier, things have changed tremendously in the agency since your departure."

"Retirement. You can't say it even now. Do you have such little respect for my decision, even after all this time?"

"Actually," he said, sounding suddenly weary, "I have far more respect for it now than ever before."

"What, you thinking about getting out of the game, too?" She'd said it, half-kidding, knowing that their agency was her former boss's entire life. He'd said so often enough, and said it with pride.

So it came as something of a shock when he responded, quite seriously, "I don't know. It's no longer the game I signed on to play."

Now it was her turn to be intently focused on him. "What are you saying?"

"I'm saying that our agency isn't what it once was. Our mission, under Mankowicz's direction, was to use intel that our regular channels of security couldn't sanction, to privately infiltrate known threats in order to bring an end to similar privately funded, non-military, covert operations against our country."

"And what's changed? Are you saying they replaced Mankowicz? But he was the best agent our country ever had. Our agency was his brainchild and he had the blessing—hell, the relief and gratitude—of everyone who knew of our existence. No way did he step down, so—" Her face fell. "Wait, you're not saying he's—"

"He's very much alive, but there was a shift in power, and our agency got caught in the crossfire. Mankowicz was, to all public eyes, promoted to ambassador, which is a polite way of saying he was given a choice of taking a prestigious position, or retiring."

"Who did they put in his place? And why keep the team at all, if they didn't think—"

"Oh, they thought we were doing a grand job."

"Because we were!"

"'Were' being the operative word there."

"What do you mean? We couldn't possibly—"

"It took me awhile to figure it out. Too long, actually. I was like you." A brief smile ghosted his bruised lips. "A little cocky and arrogant about our team."

"I prefer to think of it as pride," she said, meaning every word. "We earned that right."

"Well, whatever you want to call it, I never thought, even with Mankowicz out, that things would change all that much. Northam is a controlling, micromanaging asshole, but, push come to shove, he needed me to run the program, because I always have, and successfully so, and it was more important for him to be racking up wins than try and push his way into a situation and job he had little real understanding of, just because he has an ego the size of Asia."

"Wiley Northam? He—they gave it to him? Why in the hell would anybody give that windbag such a delicate job demanding diplomacy on a level that—" She broke off, rubbed her forehead as she let the information sink in. "Political assignment, clearly, I get it, but still there had to be somewhere else they could stick him and make him feel important without risking our agency."

"My sentiments exactly, but stick him with us, they did. I wasn't happy. In fact, I was downright pissed off, but, as I said, I knew if I kept the marks high in the win column, he'd stay out on the golf course with his blowhard cronies and leave running the team to me. I didn't care if he took all the credit, as long as he left me and the team the hell alone."

"I'm guessing that didn't happen."

"No." He paused, and shifted slightly, lifting his hand to stop her when she began to rise to help him. "At first, I just chalked it up to him being the asshole we all know he is. But over time . . . I don't know. Things weren't adding up, but I couldn't figure out why. Our intel was still good, but things weren't rolling as smoothly."

"Your intel was good because you developed your own extensive network of informants that only you had access to. Don't tell me he expected you to hand that information over to him? Even he has to know that the only way that kind of chain works is—"

"No, he didn't demand anything of me. In fact, that was what was so confusing. He stomped around the agency and tried to act as if he was the one making all the decisions, which I let him, because it was easier on all of us . . . but then, like I said, the missions started not going smoothly, at least in the areas where they should have, which made it all the more difficult to get anything accomplished in the more deeply embedded operations. With no foundations being built properly, we weren't getting people inserted at the levels they needed to embed themselves into. Our wins were becoming fewer, and the ones we did get weren't as impressive."

"Didn't the chain of command realize this coincided with Northam's assignment to the agency and can his windbag ass?"

"I honestly don't know what command thought, as my requests for face time with, well, anyone, continually got postponed, under the guise of a variety of plausible, yet exhausting excuses."

"So, what are you saying is going on? If the agency isn't performing, are they threatening to disband it altogether? Was Northam sent in for that reason? Maybe he was the sacrificial lamb, sent to slaughter a program that was no longer politically advantageous for someone higher up the foodchain than he was."

His lips quirked again. "We think alike."

"Is the agency in jeopardy then? Is your job on the line?" She was so caught up in his story, she'd momentarily lost sight of the fact that they hadn't even begun to discuss where CJ fell into this tangled web, much less why Tate had been brought back into it, or who was trying to stop Derek. More disturbing was the dawning realization that, somehow, all of it was tied together. Which made her heart begin to pound.

Because if it wasn't simply a mission gone bad, with the possibility of a rogue agent, thought to be dead, still alive and perhaps working against their interests . . . if this went higher than that—way higher, from the way Derek was talking—rotting from the inside out, then whatever it was he'd gotten her tangled up in was far, far more dangerous than even she'd dared to imagine. And, with her past experiences, she didn't have to work too hard to imagine the worst.

"I don't know where I stand with my job," he said. "Well, that's not entirely true. By the time I set out to do reconnaissance on you, I had figured out that something wasn't quite kosher with our agency's chain of command, and given our dwindling number of cases, and slowly disintegrating track record, I thought it was only a matter of time before I was replaced, but no one had actually broached the subject. Northam wasn't threatening me with it, anyway. Which was also a red flag. They should have been all over me for underperformance and the dip in our success ratio."

"So, what do you know now that you didn't know then?"

"When I left, I was running this mission, regarding CJ, completely covertly." He held her gaze. "Even from my own team. It's why I'm here, and no one else."

Her eyes widened, truly shocked now. "Are you saying you're here unsanctioned? *You're* rogue?"

"I wasn't certain what I had, what in the hell it involved. All I initially had was a coded message from someone claiming to be CJ."

"You didn't tell anyone? Why? Because the agency was looking bad, and telling them, 'ooops, we really didn't lose an agent three years ago and now maybe she's working for the other side,' would make you look bad? That doesn't sound like you."

"Because it isn't me. And no, that had nothing to do with it. My gut was—is—telling me something's off inside our agency, and I've done my own digging, trust me, but I can't figure it out. I trust my immediate team, but I don't trust command. Certainly not Northam. I don't know what's going on, but whatever the hell it is, it's not on the up-and-up. We're floundering, then out of the blue I get intel, intel that came to me outside of channels, containing information only a very, very limited number of people would know about. In fact, that number would be two. One, if you still counted the fact that CJ was no longer alive."

"Me," she said quietly, a chill creeping down her spine. "You thought I sent you false intel on CJ? That's crazy."

"A lot of things are crazy. And I didn't know what to think. Your story about seeing CJ die was pretty damn convincing and, after all this time, I saw no reason to believe otherwise. Except, there was this coded message."

"Purporting to be from her? Or, you thought possibly from me?"

"I believe now it was from her, but I had to know, find out, verify, whatever I could. Too many things aren't adding up to go into this bizarre, sudden revelation without my eyes fully open to every possible contingency."

Tate slumped back, rubbed her temples. "But you'd heard direct from me that I saw her dead with my own eyes."

"Exactly. And . . . add in the things that aren't adding up, I had no idea what to think. I didn't know if it was some kind of trap, designed to catch me in something that would discredit me. Because Northam is doing a fine job of that, all on his own, with his singular ability to destroy everything we've ever accomplished."

"So you came out here to check me out, see what was what, before telling anybody." She folded her arms. "You did plan on telling somebody, at some point."

"That, or determine it was some kind of hoax and set it aside completely. But I needed to know more before I decided who to trust with it, if anyone. I needed to validate the transmission."

Tate hugged herself and let the latest volley of information sink in. She hated what he'd done to her life, but, from his perspective, she began to see where he'd had little or no choice in the matter.

"If I came out here, and couldn't determine any active connection between you and your former partner, I'd have gone away and you'd never have known. Nor would my agency. I took a risk in coming in on this myself, for going solo, outside of channels without sanction."

"Are you saying it was an altruistic gesture? To protect me?"

"It served both purposes, but believe it or not, my intent was to protect your privacy at all costs, unless you gave me a reason to do otherwise." He held her gaze. "I gave you my word. And that still means something to me."

She nodded, taking it all in, but still having a hard time processing all the levels of it. Then her head shot up as she recalled something he'd said when she'd first dragged him inside her cabin. "Wait a minute. You said you communicated with CJ. You made it sound like you'd talked to her, or had some kind of direct give-and-take. Not just some coded, third-party message. Was that the drugs making you hallucinate?"

He shook his head. "No. I have communicated with her, in a manner of speaking."

"So, then . . . you believe it's her. She's truly alive."

"Yes, Tate. I do believe it now. Now that I've been here, I don't think it's all some elaborate hoax." Derek lifted his good hand toward her. "She's alive."

Tate merely looked at his outstretched offer of solace, then back at his face. "What did she say?"

"I only had five seconds with her direct, live time."

"In person?"

He shook his head. "I wouldn't be here if I'd actually had her in front of me. It was a satellite voice transmission, via my laptop."

"How long ago?"

"The day before I left to come out here to watch you. I believed it, believed her, but only to a point. I had to know for sure. Too many things still don't add up."

Tate's heart was drumming so fast now, she had to fight to keep from pressing her hand against her chest to keep it from pounding straight out. "What did she say?"

"She gave me the code word that I developed for you two on your last mission together. That was never debriefed, because it was—"

"A code you developed for us, outside channels, if we ever needed to reach you outside protocol."

"Right. Only you, me, and CJ knew that code."

She clutched at her arms, pressing them against her middle, as the chill began to radiate outward, threatening to freeze her heart over completely. "Then what?"

"She said she was still there. She'd found a way to infiltrate, to make them think she'd switched sides, become one of them, but her ultimate goal was to get back to us, provide us with the kind of intel we'd never been privy to before."

"With no contact? In three years?"

"When I say she was deeply embedded—"

Tate lifted her hand. "I change my mind. I don't want to know this. You're putting me directly in the line of fire by disclosing highly secure information and I don't—"

"You don't have a choice. You were right about that. And you need to know. Because she said she needed to be extracted. I asked her how, what exactly she needed." He rolled his head, pinned her with his dark gaze. "Which is the other reason I came out here, to watch you, to try and put all the puzzle pieces together."

"I don't follow."

He rolled his head again, pinning her with his gaze. She couldn't look away.

"When I asked her what she needed for extraction, she said to get you. That you'd know."

# Chapter 6

She stared at him for a long moment, then said, "I thought she was dead. I still can't believe otherwise, frankly. So how in the hell would I know what she needs, apparently alive, working deep undercover, three years later?"

Derek hated putting her through this, but he had no choice. *They* had no choice. "You were the only other one who was there. You know your captors—"

"How many pictures did I look through? Thousands. And I came up empty."

"Maybe she thinks they will show up now, if you look again. I don't know what she thinks, or thinks you know. Our transmission cut out then, and that was our last contact."

Tate was doing a damn fine job of using anger as a shield against whatever terrors might be lurking from her past, but he didn't miss the light shudder that went instinctively through her at his comment.

"I won't look through your database again."

"You have a computer?"

She arched a brow. "What? You're going to hack in? Because if you sign in from any location, you must know it would be like waving a huge red flag."

"I have alternate means."

She tilted her head, and he thought she'd ask him to explain, but she didn't. She'd only demanded he answer whatever questions she asked, and he planned to do just that. He also planned to honor her silent request to not provide information she could have requested, and didn't. When he could. If he felt she had to know something in order to get them both through this, he'd tell her whatever he had to. She already hated him. If it meant keeping them both alive, what did it matter if he pissed her off a little more?

"Is that what you think CJ wants me to do? Waste hours on end looking through what amounts to the who's who of terrorist mug shots?"

"It's a place to start. Do you have any other suggestions?"

"Yeah, that we start anywhere but there." She slumped back in her chair and rubbed a hand over her face.

"Tate—"

She held up a hand, stalling whatever comfort he might have tried to give her. Probably just as well. Nurturing didn't come naturally to him. Unless it involved how to raise a good agent.

"I can mentally go back over it," she said quietly. "Our time out there. Not just at the end, when we'd been found out and taken into custody, but before, when we were still undercover. I know CJ, or I did, better than anyone. I can try to figure out how she might have gotten back in with them, and how she might need to get out, but even with all the mental analysis I can apply, given my three-year-old intel, it would, at best, be a stab in the dark if you don't have any additional information on where she might be, specifically, and with whom." She looked at him expectantly.

"I don't have anything else. We only had those two communiqués. She hasn't been in contact since. And I wasn't able to verify anything through what proper channels I felt I could access. My only lead was you."

"Do you know, for certain, that the faction that held us is still in existence, in power? Are they still operating as they were? Three years, as their world turns, is an incredibly long time for them to remain intact."

"We've of course kept them in our sights since extricating you. But we haven't been assigned to anything on them since then. As you say, their world changes quickly, as does ours, and they ceased to be the dominant threat."

"Did you look to see if, perhaps, there has been any other activity with them? Other countries working anything having to do with them? Our allies? Or enemies? Or possibly some other faction within our own government?"

He slowly shook his head. "I did look, yes, but no, there have been no operations that I've been able to uncover dealing with them or those who surround them. Definitely not with us." And they both knew his clearance was the highest there was. What he didn't have personal access to, he usually had an alternate source to tap into. However, this time he'd been limited in who he could reach out to. "I had to be careful how deeply I searched, and who I asked."

"But you feel confident that you didn't miss anything."

"As confident as I can be."

"And yet your entire department missed the fact that CJ has been alive for the past three years and apparently working with the same group we were sent to infiltrate."

"You know as well as I do how easy it is to fall off the radar if that's your goal."

"Harder today than it used to be."

"True. But intel is only as good as the direction we're aimed in. We can't gather information on what we're not looking at."

She dipped her chin, but her attentions seemed turned inward. He didn't want to know what she was seeing in her mind's eye. "So, if they're no longer a threat, no longer the focus of any kind of real scrutiny, then are you saying they abandoned their plans to acquire plutonium? I know it's been a couple of years, but surely they haven't given up on their quest to gain global presence by becoming a nuclear power?"

"No, they haven't. But the world changes, partnerships change, channels of communication become harder to maintain in the face of continued opposition. Hell, the opposition itself changes."

"But they're still trying to do exactly what they were trying to do when CJ and I were sent to infiltrate them? So why aren't we looking at them? Why aren't they dead center on our radar?"

"The chain of command changed, theirs and ours, and so did our focus. Some of their alliances crumbled, new ones were established, it's not the same game now. From what I could learn, the division that held you shot and killed their leader in a double cross six months after you were extricated. It was chaos for a short time as a new power grid was established, but the man who finally prevailed and restored some order to the regime didn't trust anyone who was left from the original group, so he brought in his own guys. Same mission, same game, but new alliances, new mergers, new connections. The new internal faction was tight and impenetrable, so our focus shifted upward and outward."

Tate looked up. "So, if all the players changed, then who is CJ working for?"

"Specifically? She didn't, or couldn't, say, but she intimated she was working for the same group, so I can only assume she moved up the chain when the regime changed."

"Then how in the hell can I be of any help? I don't know any of those players. We infiltrated the lowest level, as supposed foreign operatives working with Italian counterspies they'd tapped a year before. It's the only reason they'd have anything to do with us as women. We'd just begun to make inroads when Buonfiglio was found out to be a triple threat, working for the Afghanis as well as his government and ours, and flipped on all of us to save his sorry, cowardly ass."

"Which he didn't, by the way. He was killed shortly after you retired."

Something flashed across her face, but she said nothing. Derek thought about letting it go, but decided to nudge, just a little. He needed to know where she stood. "What?"

"Nothing. I just—" She held his gaze, and hers was all steel now, reminding him of their days working together. She'd been rock solid then. She still was now, though she probably thought she wasn't. Some of that had been trained into her, but mostly it was who she was. You couldn't make an agent out of nothing, you could only hone and enhance the elements that were already there. And being unshakable was one of her sharpest natural components. It was why she was sitting across from him today, and not in a dusty grave in a desert halfway around the world. "I'm not sorry he's dead," she said, at length. "I don't know what that says about me. No one deserves to die, especially not like he probably did."

"He was directly responsible for the death or torture of a half dozen people, four of them his own countrymen and working directly on his team. He was a mercenary and, you're right, a coward. Neither of those qualities generally lends itself to a happy end."

She didn't say anything.

"What else?" he asked.

She looked up. "What else, what?"

"You had a look. And it wasn't simply satisfaction over Buon's death."

"You know what I miss the least about not being part of the team any longer?"

"*The* team, or *my* team?"

"Yes," was all she said.

His lips curved slightly. "What do you miss the least?"

"Having my every blink of the eye, flicker of emotion, twitch of the lips examined, analyzed, and probed."

"You know better than anyone that you can't just keep your opposition under a microscope. In the world we operated in, you had to keep close watch on your own as well. As Buonfiglio so rightly proved. If the Italians had been paying closer attention to their own, he'd never have gotten far enough to do what he did."

"We could say the same thing about CJ."

He nodded. "We're far from perfect. But that doesn't mean we don't try our damndest."

"I know. I didn't say I didn't understand it, the need for it, or even approve of the need for it. I said I don't miss it. Here in the world I'm in now, no one cares what I'm thinking about, or what my next move might be. I'm not on anyone's radar. Ever. Claiming that kind of absolute independence and freedom is a heady thing, Derek. Giving up even a shred of it grates. Deeply."

"Understandably."

"Then you'll forgive me if I don't allow you insight into my every thought."

"I'm not being nosy. I need to know my partner." His lips quirked again when she scowled. "Recalcitrant though she may be." He turned serious again. "It's been three years. I need to know you, what you're thinking, the conclusions you are drawing. It could be the difference between success or failure." He didn't have to add that that usually equaled life or death. With her, he didn't have to.

"You'll have to settle for knowing what I see fit to tell you. As I said before, I don't work for you any longer. You don't own me, or have rights to anything I don't care to give you access to."

"We're partners, not team leader and agent. You're stuck with me now, like it or not." He lifted a hand, briefly, off the bed. "No need to clarify which side of that you stand on."

"Derek—"

"I may not have any rights where you're concerned, but we're in this regardless of whether or not it's right, fair, or anything else. We both know that life is often none of those things. I can continue to apologize for dragging you into this, or we can accept that this is the lot we've been handed and get to work on solving it."

"I thought that's what we were doing."

"Okay. Then when I ask you a question, I need you to answer me. I'll do the same for you. Partners, Tate. You know better than anyone what it takes to make a successful partnership. You and CJ were the best team I ever had."

Now it was her turn to quirk her lips, only there was absolutely no humor in her eyes. "And yet, look where it's gotten me. The irony, eh?" She stood and shoved her chair back.

"We just started," he said. "We still have an enormous amount to cover and time is something we can't waste any more of than we already have."

"We?" she asked, arching a brow.

"Tate."

"You need to rest. And I need to . . . regroup."

"Tate—"

She picked up the food tray from the dresser. "Neither of us is going anywhere right this second, Derek. I'll be back later." She paused in the doorway. "As your partner, I'd advise you to get as much rehabilitative rest as possible. We have no idea what the next few days will bring, but I think it's a safe bet to assume that the stronger you are, the better chance we'll have of getting through them." She didn't wait for his reply.

But when she turned to leave, she caught the tray on the edge of the doorframe. She corrected the movement immediately, before anything could topple to the floor, but the sudden action revealed two things to Derek: her reflexes were still sharp as ever. But her body was not. It would have taken someone with his dedication to detail to notice, but there'd been a slight, yet definite hitch in her step when she'd readjusted her trajectory and that of the tray. She'd healed from her injuries in a far more superior way than even he'd have ever projected, even knowing her for the bulldog she was.

But while she might give the impression of being one hundred percent, or damn near it, she wasn't. He knew she'd undergone multiple surgeries to repair the damage done to her limbs, all four of them. You wouldn't know it to look at her today that she'd ever been as broken as she was. Until that brief, but telling moment.

She'd been out in the rain, hiking the hills. Then she'd come in here and sat in that chair for the past half hour. And now she was paying the price. A price she'd never want him to see.

Pride was a luxury people in his line of work often couldn't afford. She, on the other hand, had every right to it now.

Which was why he didn't ask, didn't probe. Now, anyway. He needed to know her limits, both mental and physical. But, for the moment, he'd content himself with whatever knowledge he could gain from keen observation, and past knowledge of his partner.

It was frustrating as hell, but then he doubted he had the corner on that emotion at the moment.

Surprisingly, he must have dozed off shortly after her exit, because the next thing he was aware of was opening his eyes, only to find it had grown fully dark outside. The storm continued to rage on. In fact, as thunder rattled the walls and roof once again, he realized that that was what had awoken him. At least he hadn't tried to dive off the bed this time.

His eyes adjusted relatively quickly to the darkness which was a relief on more than one level. He was still fatigued, but not groggy. The headache lingered, but was milder now. It felt like the last vestiges of the drugs had finally left his system.

He looked around the room, but even in the darkness, he could see he was alone. Nature was calling somewhat insistently now, and he knew he was going to have to tackle that little adventure shortly, but for the moment he lay still and listened. Once he sorted out the sounds being made by the rain pounding on the roof and slashing at the windows, he could focus on the sounds of the house itself. There were none. No music, no television, no voices. No sounds of domesticity coming from the kitchen.

The latter thought made him smile, imagining Tate's reaction to that notion. Which led to wondering where she was, and what she was doing. She'd closed his door at some point, but there was a yellow glow seeping through the cracks, so lights were on somewhere. His thoughts gave pause at the idea of her watching him while he slept. On the one hand, he didn't like the vulnerability implied in the very act, and yet there was something undeniable . . . comforting, about the idea that any-one absent of nefarious plans would want to watch over him.

He wasn't sure how late it was. She could be asleep on the couch. The idea of flipping the favor and watching over her in return was oddly far more arousing than it was soothing. Which brought him right back around to the necessary trip he had to make. As he mentally prepared himself to manage the pain he was about to endure in order to get himself upright, his thoughts strayed back to Tate. He should logically be con-cerning himself with locating her immediately, and making certain all was still well and secure. But his instincts weren't clamoring. And despite the manner in which he himself had been recently subdued, he doubted the same would happen within the walls of this cabin without rousing him from his sleep.

Which left him to decide between being smart and pinpointing the location of his partner, and updating himself on the time and whatever else might have happened while he slept—but that meant risking her immediate presence, and worse, her help, with his pending adventure—or he could take care of that chore first, then track her down. First, he decided to get himself up-right, or as upright as he could, so no matter what happened beyond that, she couldn't negate his trip altogether and sug-gest any other solution.

His shoulder screamed in protest as he worked at shifting his weight toward his good side—or better side, anyway—but he'd dealt with his shoulder dislocating before and knew how to manage that pain. It was the other combined radiant points of torture that had him catching his breath, then grunting as he levered himself carefully to a sitting position.

His ribs were seriously not happy with this venture, but careful probing before had already told him they weren't bro-ken. It wasn't the first time they'd been banged up, so he knew the difference, but this time the external damage had been to the front, side, and back of his torso, all of which were protest-ing. Loudly. He knew from his attempts at eating the soup that his left hand was a mess of purple and blue, but Tate had re-aligned and taped three of his fingers before, leaving him his forefinger and thumb for navigation when needed. At the moment, he had that hand tucked into the sling supporting his shoulder, so, though essentially out of commission and throbbing, it was at least stable and not much of a hindrance.

His face hurt, and his scalp felt like someone had snatched half his hair clean out of it, but he'd already probed it with his good hand and, other than a few lumps and some split skin here and there, everything seemed to still be there. His nose wasn't broken, but the rest of his face didn't feel so good. But the split on his cheek and along one eyebrow felt like they were healing, and his jaw, though sore as hell, didn't feel damaged beyond the bruising. One side of his mouth was still messed up, and he imagined he didn't look terribly lovely at the moment, but ultimately all of the damage felt minimal. A quick run of the tongue had told him his teeth were all intact. Always a bonus.

His wrists and ankles burned like hell, but with Tate's quick and thorough attention and ointment, they were healing quickly. That left his legs. It was too dark in the room to see them clearly, and he couldn't bend at the waist to reach down past his knees, but a gingerly flex of one ankle, then the other, then one knee, then the other, told him they were in pretty much the same condition as the rest of him. Beaten and bruised, but not broken. Still, he wasn't keen on immediately relying on them to hold him upright. Not without at least a little support. His head felt clearer despite the pounding, but the physical exhaustion he felt was still pretty keen. He knew he'd be wobbly from pain and fatigue, and falling right now would not be well received by any part of his anatomy.

He debated caving, and calling out for Tate, at least for help in getting him upright and to the bathroom. Why he resisted, he wasn't sure.

Well, that wasn't entirely true. As it happened, there seemed to be one part of his body that was functioning quite fine, thank you very much. He chalked it up to something like early morning hard-on syndrome, even though he knew damn well it hadn't started until he'd thought about watching Tate sleep. And just in case he thought about trying to lie to himself about that, the very act of thinking about it right now made him twitch.

Yeah. It was going to be humbling enough just getting himself to the bathroom. He didn't need to do it with her trying not to look at his raging hard-on, while he did it. He also needed that little problem to subside between here and there, and despite the potential shrinking factor her presence might have on his ego, something told him having Tate in the room, touching him in any way, was not going to help diminish anything else.

He eyed the chair she'd been sitting in earlier. It was too far away to even use his toes to drag it any closer. So that was out as a possible support while he stood for the first time. The bed had no footboard or headboard to use for bracing his weight against. Which left the nightstand. Which was located to his left now that he was sitting upright with his feet on the floor, and therefore out of play, as his left arm was in a sling. Wonderful.

He was debating on pushing himself to a stand and angling himself toward the chair as he launched himself upright, but it would also be on his left. "Fuck," he muttered under his breath, already feeling the effects from just sitting upright for this long. If he didn't find some way to get himself going, he wouldn't be going anywhere.

"Derek?"

The overhead light flipped on a moment later making him wince as the sudden glare brought a whole new level of throb back to his headache. "Don't," was all he said.

The room went instantly dark, but a moment later, the nightstand lamp on the opposite side of the bed clicked on, bathing the room in a much softer glow. "Better?"

"Mmm," was all he could manage.

"I'd ask what the hell you think you're doing, but I'm guessing there's no point in that."

Her voice was still coming from behind him, on the opposite side of the bed, and for that, at least, he was grateful. He wasn't a modest man, not in the least. His body was a tool for him, and, as such, he kept it in good shape. Beyond that, he didn't much care what anyone thought of his appearance. He simply did whatever was needed to get the job done. To that end, it didn't so much bother him that Tate was seeing him sitting there in nothing more than his skivvies, all battered and bruised. She'd already seen it all, as she'd been the one to take his muddied and torn clothes off in the first place.

But that was just the logical part of things. The part he controlled. What was suddenly out of his control, was his almost hyperawareness that he was sporting a whole lot of bare skin that would be available to her direct touch, if she were to so much as consider helping him get up and take even a single step. And his body's reaction to that notion was also, apparently, well beyond his control. It was crazy, and he could chalk up that heightened sensitivity to everything from the aftereffects of being so heavily drugged, to the damage to his body, to the very difficult situation he'd landed them both in.

But why start lying to himself now?

"I need something to help me balance myself," he told her, fighting to maintain a level voice. The frustration of his limitations was only compounded by his frustration with his lack of control over himself, but he didn't need her to know any of that. "You wouldn't happen to have kept your crutches along with your sling, would you? Just one would do."

"And you need to balance yourself upright because why?"

He opted for directness. He tried not to snap the words, despite his rapid loss of patience. It wasn't her he was impatient with. "Because I need to use your bathroom."

Rather than give him a hard time, or, thank God, suggest an alternate solution that involved a bed pan of any kind, there was a silent pause, then she simply said, "Okay. I'll be right back. Stay put."

"Not a problem," he muttered, but he could already hear her moving down the hall.

She returned a moment later. He felt her presence rather than saw it, as she paused in the bedroom doorway before entering. He tried to shift his weight to look over his shoulder, but that was asking a bit too much of his ribs at the moment. "What's wrong?" he asked instead.

"Nothing," she said, and came into the room and around his side of the bed. She was carrying a beautifully carved oak walking stick. The handle was a large, gnarled knot of wood, plenty big enough for his wide hand, and the stick itself was thick and sturdy.

He looked from the stick to her. She had no expression whatsoever on her face. Which told him far more than she likely thought it did.

"It's beautiful," he told her, quite sincerely. "More like a piece of art. You sure you want me handling it?"

"It's the walking stick, or me."

He reached out his good hand. "Thank you," he said simply.

"You're welcome," she said just as simply, handing him the cane, which clearly was hers, and from the burnished shine on the head of the stick, it had been palmed often by her own hand. "Do you need any help levering yourself up?"

She was handling this about as well as anyone who couldn't read his mind. Quite probably because she'd been faced with similar indignities in the past. And it was the quiet, simple dignity she was offering him that forced him to get past his own stupid issues with his renegade body parts and accept her offer. "I just need to get my weight over my knees, and I'll be fine."

"Okay." She moved immediately, without needing to ask what to do, and sat next to him on his right side. "I don't want to hurt your ribs, but I need to wedge my shoulder under your arm. You need to lean forward, as best you can, with your palm firmly wrapped around the cane. Use your thighs to push to a stand, staying bent at the waist as best as you can until you have your weight centered. Then slowly—slowly—straighten upright. I know it's going to be hard with your ribs, but—"

"I can handle it," he said, cutting off her string of instructions. Not because they were annoying or unnecessary. She was definitely the voice of authority here. No, he cut her off for quite the opposite reason. "Let's give it a shot."

"Wait," she said, and got up again. She moved the stuffed chair until it was angled right in front of him. "If you lose your balance, I won't be able to keep you upright." She sat next to him again. "If you can, drop back to the bed, but if you over-project, shift your weight and soft land in the chair."

He turned his head and looked at her. "Pretty good foresight."

She smiled a little then, and there was no sharpness to her wry tone this time. "It's possible I might know a little something about being stubborn and insisting on moving around and taking care of myself somewhat earlier than might have been strictly recommended."

"You don't say."

Her smile widened and reached her eyes for the first time. "I think I just did." Then she turned face front and leaned in to wedge her shoulder into his armpit. "On three."

# Chapter 7

Tate leaned outside the closed bathroom door, knowing full well she was hovering. But she also knew exactly what it was like to want privacy when she'd been shakier than she'd wanted to admit. All she needed was for Derek to lose his less-than-solid footing and crack his skull on the sink or the tub. "Everything okay?"

"Under control," came the dry response. "Do you happen to have any more of that soup?" He was trying to sound casual, but there was no mistaking the strain in his voice.

She folded her arms. "You don't think I'm falling for that one, do you?"

"I think we can both handle this without falling at all. And I'd like some soup."

*And some privacy.* She well understood that. "Okay. But don't even think about falling and breaking anything, or I'll crack your skull myself."

"Stop. You're embarrassing me with your touching concern."

She tried to stop the responding smile and couldn't. "What'll be embarrassing is me coming in there."

"If I need a helping hand, you'll be the first to know."

Images of exactly what she'd need to handle flashed through her mind and she quickly decided she wasn't up to verbally sparring with him. She was still trying to process everything he'd told her earlier. And if there was any doubt left, he ended it by adding, "And don't mistake my desire for privacy as a sign of modesty."

A little instinctive shiver went through her at all the unspoken ramifications of that. And the fact that he was inducing shivers of any kind was enough to alarm her into stepping back from the door. "Soup, coming right up."

She heard him chuckling as she left the bedroom, which didn't help her growing awareness of him. She couldn't decide which was more dangerous, his sexual advances while he was hallucinating about her, or his dry charm while completely lucid and aware.

Pulling the container with the leftover soup out of the fridge, she popped it on the counter with perhaps a wee bit more force than absolutely necessary and forced herself to steady and remove the lid without ripping it off and throwing it in the sink. But he was so completely frustrating. And she was far too entirely aware of him. Hard not to be, with him invading hearth and home as he had, and in such dramatic fashion, but considering all that, she should be far more frustrated by him than turned on by him. In fact, she had no business whatsoever being charmed or anything else. Especially after what he'd told her before his last trip to la-la land.

Right now she needed to focus all her mental faculties on what they were going to do about the situation with CJ, and whatever it was that had someone hunting Derek into the Hebron Valley. If it wasn't for the condition he'd arrived in, and the reasons behind it, she'd be sorely tempted to boot him out on his battered behind and tell him to take care of the CJ situation on his own. It was both horrifying and miraculous to know, to even consider, that her former partner was still alive. Miraculous, because even now, fully ensconced in her new world, the only thing Tate missed about what she'd left behind was CJ. To think her partner was still out there somewhere and they could once again spend time together, was an amazing, wondrous, unbelievable gift. And also horrifying to contemplate, given the very thought of what CJ had been doing for the past three years, what she might have had to further endure . . . or, even more unthinkable, the choices she might have had to make in order to survive.

But even with all of that to consider, to think about, to possibly even hope for . . . it wasn't her job or her responsibility to personally do anything about it. She had never been one to shirk her responsibility, or even that of any others where she could be of assistance. But this . . . in this, she thought she had the right to no longer be involved. The right to be left alone. To make the same hard choices in the name of survival that her partner might have had to make. CJ, of all people, would be the one to understand.

But she didn't have the luxury of throwing her former boss out on his very fine ass and reclaiming her peaceful existence. Whoever had tracked him down within spitting distance of her cabin, and drugged and beaten him, and more tellingly, left him alive afterward . . . they had taken that choice away from her.

She could be as mad as she wanted to be that he'd all but directed them to her doorstep, but that wasn't a productive use of her time or energy. Neither was wasting even a second of her thoughts on erotic visuals and unwise attractions. She'd managed to work with him for a long time without ever once being tempted to do anything about her little CJ-inspired fantasies about her boss. Of course, she'd usually been pretty preoccupied with getting the job done. And staying alive long enough to do so.

Here . . . here she didn't have those distractions. No stresses, no myriad of details demanding her full attention. Here, she could be at peace, left alone with her own thoughts, to manage her days, all of her time, to suit her own desires. Which, until yesterday, had been a welcome blessing. She'd led a very overstimulating life. A life that three years of solitude and serenity were only now beginning to balance. So, while she was alone, she was far from lonely.

She supposed it was only normal though, living a relatively

tranquil existence now, that his arrival in her personal space would send all those blessedly desensitized sensory receptors into a suddenly saturated state of hyperawareness. Maybe rather than trying to ignore her response to him, she should simply work through it, like she was now, in order to understand why she was reacting the way she was. Then she could come to terms with it and learn to channel those reactions effectively into a more professionally based, work-oriented mentality.

Anything would be a more productive use of her time and energy than wanting to jump his bones every other second.

"Which would all be a hell of a lot easier to manage if he could put some damn clothes back on."

There came a clearing of a throat from behind her.

Mercifully, her back was to him so he couldn't see the flush of mortification that was surely flooding her suddenly very warm cheeks. "What the hell do you think you're doing?" she demanded, perhaps a wee bit more sharply than entirely warranted.

"I don't know how they do things out here in the country," he said, by way of response, "but I think the soup heats up a lot faster in a pot on the stove. Or in the microwave. I'm not picky."

Her fingers curled inward on the countertop as she tried, and failed, to rein in her frazzled nerves and take control of herself. Instead, she whirled around and let fly with all the pent up emotions that had been building up inside her since his abrupt appearance in the middle of the night—and there was quite a range of those roiling around inside of her at the moment.

"How dare you," she said, and she could hear the seething in her tone, so she understood why his expression changed to one of surprise. She was a bit surprised herself.

"I've already apologized for—"

"There is no apology great enough for what you're doing to me by being here. But here is where you are, so I'll deal with what I can't change. But if you think that means I'm going to

like it, or be amused by your attempts to be charming or disarming, you are sadly mistaken. And I definitely don't appreciate you skulking around—"

"I sounded like a herd of buffalo coming down the hall.
Your neighbors, who live an easy two miles away, likely heard
me," he said, leaning quite heavily on her walking stick, and
resting his weight on the doorframe as well. "You were lost in
thought." He pushed away from the door and moved into the
kitchen, which suddenly shrunk down to a very tiny space. His
grin was slow, and knowing, as he came closer, and she wanted
to smack it off of him, but she was suddenly rooted to the
spot, immobile, as he stopped right in front of her. "Wishing I
had more clothes on."

She refused to look him over as his comment urged her to
do, though it took considerable willpower not to. He was wearing loose black boxers . . . and a sling. And she didn't have to
look to know the rest of him was exceptional. "Derek—"

His smile faded, his tone grew serious. "I'm not trying to
charm you, Tate. Trust me. I know it's the last thing you think
I am. I'm trying to make a bad situation as tolerable as possible. We have to work together, and it would be easier if we
could find some kind of rapport—"

"Rapport I can handle. I am—or was—a professional. Having you invade more of my personal space, however, I cannot
handle. And I won't. So I'd appreciate it if you'd step back."

"We worked together for years. Often in high tension, life-
and-death situations."

"Yes, we did," she said, frowning a little. "What has that got
to do with anything?"

"I always found you to be an attractive woman, Tate."

Alarm filled her. But it didn't come close to matching the
rush of . . . what? Anticipation? Surely she didn't want him to
acknowledge, much less act on, the other kind of tension that
was swirling around them.

"But, even in the most extreme situations, I never once considered doing what I can't seem to stop thinking about doing now."

She was the one hallucinating now, that was it. He was still in the bathroom and she'd come into the kitchen to get soup, and had somehow fallen down a rabbit hole or something, because surely he was not standing right in front of her, saying what she thought he was saying. It was wild enough that she was having any thoughts in his general direction, but at least she had the excuse of being retired and no longer the sharp professional.

He was still team leader, actively on the job. And the only person who'd been even more the consummate professional during their years working together than she'd been. All work, no wink. That was Derek Cole. Not ever. With her, or anyone else. At least not that anyone had ever known. CJ had made it her favorite topic of conversation on more than one occasion. So, if he ever had . . . flung, he'd been remarkably discreet about it, which was saying something around people whose job it was to know every damn thing. It was another aspect of his character that she'd admired. So, what the hell was this?

When she finally found her voice, it was damnably shaky. "You're injured, and recently injected with God knows what, so—"

"It's not the drugs talking, Tate."

"Well, it doesn't sound like you talking, either. At least not the you I worked for. We've got enough to deal with, without—"

"Oh, I know. Believe me. I came down the hall just now to see if I could sit in here and eat some soup. No ulterior motives. No skulking intended. Then I hear you commenting on my—"

"Must you repeat it?"

His lips quirked a little then. "See?"

"See what?"

"How is it I missed this?" he asked, sounding sincerely perplexed.

"Missed what?"

"You."

He was looking at her like he'd just discovered something amazing, and couldn't quite believe it.

"I'm the same me, I've—"

"No. You're not. I always admired your capable, no nonsense work ethic. You and CJ were the best agents I ever had. Which, considering the talent I had assembled, is a high, but deserved, compliment. I said before that I found you attractive. I did. And do. But I always viewed that through the filter of being your team leader, looking at that as simply another attribute you possessed, to be executed professionally where and when best deployed."

"Just because I don't work for you now—"

"It's not just that. You're . . . more you now. Still everything you were, but there's so much more. I'm seeing the rest of you, probably the you you've always been, but who I never had the pleasure of meeting. You're dry, sharp, outspoken, and surprisingly sarcastic."

"You're right, the professional filter is off, but maybe I'm not who I was before, either. I'm leading a very different life now. I'll pull it back together, focus, find my professional balance once again, but only because I have to. And believe me, no one is more motivated to get through this and make it go away as quickly as possible. To make you go away," she added truthfully. "To get back to the life I earned, the life I deserve. The life I *need*, Derek." If there was a quiet pleading in her tone, she wasn't going to apologize for it. Things were complicated enough without this sudden revelation from him. Especially considering she'd been thinking very similar things about him.

Which, if he hadn't known before, he did now, given her comment about his lack of clothing. Now he knew she was noticing him, too.

Which meant one of them had to get their act together, and get it together real quick. He moved closer and leaned his weight against the counter, along with the walking stick, so he could lift his free hand.

"Derek—" She broke off when he lightly brushed his fingertips across her cheek. His touch was gentler than she'd expected. She should be smacking his hand away, not wanting to lean into the unanticipated warmth she found there. She didn't need nurturing, or caretaking, but that's not what the look in his eyes was telegraphing, What she saw there was bold, unwavering, unapologetic want.

And what he wanted, was her.

She swallowed against a suddenly dry throat, but the words she needed to find, to end this before it went any further, didn't come.

"Maybe we should just get this out of the way," he said. "Do you want me to stop, Tate?" He lowered his mouth toward hers excruciatingly slowly. "Tell me if you do, because I'm pretty sure it's the only thing that's going to stop this."

"Derek," she said again, only this time it was more plea than rebuke. She just wasn't sure if it was a plea to stop . . . or a plea to hurry up.

His lips were warm on hers, but his kiss wasn't gentle. Probing, yes, and definite in purpose, but not tender. He slid his fingers into her hair and cupped the back of her head, tilting her mouth more fully into his. He parted her lips, and took her.

And, God help her, she let him.

His groan of appreciation as she took him into her mouth reverberated deep in some untouched part of her. Her hands grappled for the counter behind her, looking for purchase to support her suddenly wobbly knees. Then he rolled his weight to trap her between his body and the countertop, and she grabbed at his hips instead, instinctively keeping him steady on her. He groaned again, or maybe it was her this time. He was a damn good kisser. And she was quickly lost as they both gave themselves over to the moment. The way he kissed her, took her, with such absolute conviction, left her feeling . . . claimed.

Her body sang to life, the sensory demands so rich and vibrant, she felt both tingly and lightheaded at the same time. After the torture and all the painful rehabilitation afterward, she'd thoroughly cut herself off from feeling anything. She'd worked hard on just being blessedly, mercifully numb. So this . . . this onslaught of sensation, all of it so intensely pleasurable, was completely overwhelming.

And just as her innate self-protective instincts finally began to kick in, and panic began to ebb in around the saturation of pleasure, he lifted his head and rolled his weight off of her so he was leaning back against the counter beside her.

They were both breathing heavily.

"So," she said, at great length. "That was amazingly unprofessional of us."

"I'll agree with the amazing part," he said, sounding slightly stunned himself.

Which was the only thing that enabled her to reclaim even a shred of rational thought. Had he been remotely cocky or smug, she wasn't sure what she would have done. "We can't do that again."

"You're probably right," he said, and she had no business whatsoever feeling even the tiniest bit disappointed. Then he chuckled and turned his head to look at her. "Good luck with that, huh?"

She surprised herself by smiling back before she could catch herself. She quickly regrouped, but it was far too late. "Derek—"

"Tate."

"I'm not kidding. It's all I can do to wrap my head around all the other things you're telling me. I can't—we can't—"

"Oh, I know. Trust me, I had absolutely no intention of being distracted from my job, especially right now, when I'm not so certain I still have one. But—"

"Wait," Tate said, turning to face him. "I didn't think to ask you that. You've been out here, what, almost eleven days now. What do they think you're doing? Where does Northam, the team, think you are? Are you truly rogue?"

"I don't know how I'm being classified. I'm out here in the

wilds of central Virginia, not on assignment, getting myself drugged and half killed, while following a case that not only was I not assigned to, but that my superiors don't even know about."

"So you've still told no one, even after the second transmission," she said, as if verifying the fact. "Not a single soul knows but you?"

"I can't trust anyone right now. Given how the team has gone off kilter, and I still don't know what's behind that, I had no idea how the information would be received, much less acted on. CJ was one of mine, and when the time came, it was me she contacted. It's my responsibility to handle that in the best way possible."

"Even if it means jeopardizing your whole career?" She braced a hand on the counter as she turned more fully toward him, so busy trying to make sense out of this latest bomb drop that she wasn't aware she hadn't made any attempt to move out of his personal space. Her hip was inches from his. "You could lose everything, handling things like this."

"I have no idea what career I have anyway at this point. I do know I'm her best shot right now. And, flipping that around, I'm also protecting my team by making sure this is on the up-and-up before I drag anyone else in."

"Besides me, you mean."

"Tate—" He went to shift his weight to look at her and wobbled dangerously.

They both grabbed for the walking stick at the same time, her hand landing on top of his as they each gripped the handle. "I think you'd better get back to . . . lying down," she said. Her head was struggling to get back to business, but her body was still all on board with the extra curricular activities of a few moments ago. And touching him, even incidentally as she was now, was not helping.

"Just help me get to the kitchen chair. I need to work on getting mobile."

"You need to not pass out. Might I remind you that at this

time yesterday you were still half delirious." *And saying things you had no business saying to me.* Things that might not have been so drug induced after all, but merely uncensored while under the influence.

"It was the drugs more than the beating messing with me. I think they've pretty much cleared out. The rest I can handle. I know my limits."

"And if I said the same thing to you, exactly how much latitude would you be giving me?"

His lips quirked, but she could already see the strain tightening his jaw. "None."

"Exactly. Now, let me help you back down the hall. I'll bring the soup in when it's heated up." She didn't ask if he needed help, but simply put herself in position on his right side until he was away from the stability of the countertop and standing on his own.

He wasn't hulking big like a linebacker, but he sure seemed to tower over her all of a sudden, not to mention swallowing up all the air in her small kitchen. Or maybe just out of her. But she was feeling mighty breathless by the time she got him to the doorway. For someone who was busy trying to be professional.

He paused for a moment, and let the doorframe replace her for assistance with balance. "I should probably apologize. For . . . you know."

*Kissing me senseless?* "Yes, you should."

He turned his head and met her gaze. She worked to keep her expression direct and defiant. His, on the other hand, was openly searching and undeniably curious. "Except you went and kissed me back." He smiled slightly then, and made her wonder how a face that was so banged up could still be so beautiful. "And I find I'm not feeling all that sorry about that."

"Bed," she said, albeit a bit shakily now. She nodded her head toward the hallway, struggling to stay all business. It was damn hard when he wasn't playing by the rules and looking at her like he wanted to devour her. Especially now that she knew she'd enjoy being every last bite.

His eyebrows lifted at her unthinking command, and there was a very mischievous twinkle in his eye. In all the time they'd worked together, she had never once seen that devilish flicker. Or thought him remotely capable of being mischievous. Much less flirty. He'd always been strictly business, and not just with her. It made her wonder again about his personal life. Not that any of them had much of one. None of them had family to speak of, and their work had been pretty consuming. Some of them managed. CJ was forever involved with this guy or that. Tate simply hadn't been as good at compartmentalizing that way, but she'd had her moments. She wondered if Derek had had his . . .

"Ordering me to bed?" he said. "Now that's more—"

"Don't even go there. It's too easy and it's beneath you," she said, then rolled her eyes at herself when he laughed. "And I'm shutting up right now."

To his credit, he said nothing, but the twinkle was downright sparkling now. Talk about seeing a new side of someone.

"Move," she said, motioning him down the hall.

"Yes, Nurse Ratched," he responded, not making the smallest effort to move away from the doorframe.

She huffed and turned away, walking back to the stove and the container of soup, deliberately and quite willfully refusing to look at him or speak to him again until she'd gotten herself fully under control. He could stand there until his legs atrophied for all she cared. Staring at her, smiling at her, twinkling, and thinking whatever the hell he wanted to think.

Because it didn't matter what he thought. So her hormones had been dormant a bit too long, and he'd been drugged with some kind of happy juice, and they'd both allowed themselves to get a little distracted by that. Distraction over.

CJ had hunted Derek down. Derek had hunted her down. And now someone had hunted Derek down. Within a mile of her cabin. They had a whole hell of a lot more to concern themselves with than playing libido roulette.

She slapped a pot down on the burner and flipped the flame on, then dumped the entire contents of the container of homemade soup into the pan. It was late, but she'd need sustenance, too, if she had a prayer of getting through this without losing what was left of her precious sanity. What the hell had he been thinking? And what the hell had *she* been thinking to let him get away with it?

She stirred the soup a bit too vigorously, sloshing some onto the burner with a sizzle. She flipped the overhead fan on. "Seriously," she muttered, thinking back over what just happened, "and in my own kitchen." More stirring. She adjusted the flame. "If he thinks he's just going to come barging in here and drag me around by the hair all caveman style, he has another think coming."

The soup started to bubble and she clapped two bowls on the counter and poured the chunky vegetable broth into both. She rooted around in the cupboard for some crackers, grabbed two soup spoons and some napkins, then arranged everything on the tray. Turning toward the hallway, relieved to see it empty of half-naked man, she took a moment to steady herself, and take a deep breath. "I will not let him affect me," she murmured. "I will not get near him. He will not get near me. We are going to talk business. He is going to tell me the rest of what in the hell is going on. With CJ. With his job. All of it. No more kissing. No more flirting. No more twinkly eyes."

She continued her little motivational speech under her breath, all the way down the hall to her bedroom door. Then forgot everything she'd spent the past ten minutes coaching herself not to do when she found him on the floor next to the bed.

# Chapter 8

He'd felt like Superman back in that kitchen. Now he just felt like an idiot. "I'm okay," Derek assured her as Tate set the tray on the dresser with a clatter and rushed to his side.

She crouched beside him as he pushed himself into a sitting position with his good arm. An action his ribs painfully protested.

"What happened? I told you it was too soon to be up."

It took him a moment to get his breath back. "Let me guess," he said, grimacing as his ribs continued to wreak havoc on his pain tolerance. "You know this because your nurses used to say the same thing to you."

"Except I didn't end up in a heap on the floor."

"I notice there was no denial in there," he said, grunting a little as he continued to work himself closer to the chair next to the bed. "And I was hardly in a heap. More like a controlled collapse."

"You're lucky you didn't crack another rib. Come on, let me help you get up."

He wasn't sure he hadn't, or just worsened the strain on the ones already in trouble, but he wasn't going to tell her any of that. He was going to refuse her help, just to prove a point, but the stumble had taken whatever he had left out of him, and he was pretty sure the only point he'd prove would be hers. "God,

I hate this," he said as she helped him slowly move to his feet, then back onto the bed.

"I know," she said, sounding utterly sincere this time. "Just as I know you're going to push yourself to get better as fast as possible, but you can't push the limits too far, or you'll be going in reverse. I need you to be putting Humpty Dumpty back together as fast as possible here, you know? We're kind of on the clock."

He knew. And that reminder, coming from the person whose life he was presently endangering simply by being here, was all the nudge he needed to get his head out of his pants—and hers—and back to taking care of business. "About the kitchen—" he started, never more serious.

She was leaning over him, trying to arrange his pillows behind his head as he levered himself to his back, a grunt of pain escaping him no matter how much he tried to contain it. "Forget the kitchen, okay?" she said. "Subject dropped. You need to rest. I'll bring the soup back later. Or better yet, I'll fix you something in the morning. You should just sleep now. It's late anyway. Did you hurt anything when you fell?"

"I didn't fall, I stumbled. The stick hooked the foot of the bed. And no, other than my pride, I think I'm in the same busted-up shape I was in before."

He was grumbling, he heard it in his voice, and feeling sorry for himself was something he never indulged in. But then he'd never come on to someone on his team in her own kitchen, either. Maybe it was the drugs still in his system.

Then he looked up into her concerned face and his body twitched to life, and if there was any lingering thought that the chemistry going on here was pharmaceutically induced, those doubts were forever quashed. He knew he had to find a way back to how things used to be, back when she worked under him. He swallowed a groan and squeezed his eyes shut. The last thing he needed, with him in bed and her leaning over him, was even the slightest provocation to think about her beneath him in any fashion. "I'm good," he told her, sounding strained even to his own ears. Hopefully, she'd take that as the pain talking. And it was part of it. Just not all of it.

She finished getting the covers up and over him, then finally, mercifully, straightened and stepped back. Only then did he dare look at her again.

"Thanks," he said, meaning it. "I'll sleep this off, then we'll eat and talk through everything."

"In the morning. But I want some answers, Derek."

"You'll get whatever I have," he promised. *And I'll get myself under control if it kills me.* Which, watching her walk out of the room, then pause at the door to look back at him, seeing real concern clouding her face, was going to be harder to do than he might have imagined. And he'd imagined it being pretty damn impossible.

He closed his eyes and worked on relaxing his body, head to toe, mind over pain, willing himself to get into that mental head space he had to be in if he was going to be effective in solving this situation to everyone's satisfaction. But hearing her puttering around the kitchen distracted his efforts, and behind closed eyes the only scenes that were playing out had nothing to do with the job at hand. More an extension of what might have happened if neither one of them had stopped what they'd started in that kitchen. Which only served to compound his pain management issues with other body demands that weren't entirely comfortable either.

At some point, he'd dropped off to sleep again, but clearly his sleeping thoughts had mirrored his waking ones if the condition of his body upon awakening was any indication. At least he'd been trying to do something about it, as he came fully awake enough to realize where his good hand was at the moment. And what it was doing.

He opened his eyes just enough to slide his gaze around the still dimly lit room, toward the door. No sign of Tate. Good. Things were disconcerting enough between them at the moment.

Still more asleep than awake, he let his eyes drift shut, and continued what he was doing, opting to enjoy what little pleasure he could amidst the pain that was presently his constant companion. His mind very willingly helped him out with his endeavor, easily providing all the stimulation he needed to continue his quest for extended pleasure. As his body slowly shifted gears, growing a bit more demanding, he became more fully awake, and had to decide whether to continue on and finish, or stop before things got, well, out of hand.

If he thought it would have helped to take the edge off his desire for Tate, he'd have quite willingly risked it. But he doubted anything was going to take the edge off of that need, except Tate herself. He glanced toward the door, listening for any noise that might indicate where she was at the moment, but the cabin was quiet. Still, he regretfully let his hand slide away, despite knowing there was little likelihood of taking the edge off in any fashion in the near future, but not willing to risk making the situation any more awkward than it already was.

As it happened, Tate arrived at his door not two minutes later, and though things hadn't completely subsided, he was able to bend one knee enough to disguise the state he was in. "Hey," he said, figuring that was as safe a thing to say as anything, while buying himself as much time as possible to get himself under control.

"Hey," she responded, staying in the doorway. "You still hungry?"

*You have no idea.* "What time is it?"

"A little after midnight. But I can't sleep. I thought I heard you rustling around, wanted to make sure everything was okay."

If it had been possible for him to blush, he might have at that moment. Thank God he'd had the wherewithal to stop before she'd come to the door. Rustling, indeed.

"But seeing as you're up—"

How he managed to stifle a groan, he had no idea. "Some

soup would be good, if you don't mind. Or whatever you feel like fixing."

"Not a problem. Did you get any sleep?" She frowned a little as she asked the question.

Which prompted him to say, "A little, why?"

She took a small step into the room, but didn't come closer. "Nothing, you just look a little flushed. I hope you didn't do something earlier, push too hard, and get a fever started."

It took considerable control, but all he said was, "I'm fine. Getting more food in me wouldn't be a bad idea, though." *Anything to help me stop thinking about getting more of me into you.*

She seemed to pick up on something in his tone, because she immediately stepped back. "Right. I'll be back with that shortly." And she vanished down the hall.

He wasn't sure what lines she'd read between, but her response had been more a snapping to attention than anything else. Maybe she mistook his edge of impatience with himself for a desire to keep things professional.

"Right," he muttered, sliding his leg straight again, and staring at the only slightly smaller tent still visible where the covers draped across his hips. "Clearly, I'm all business here."

He debated the wisdom of trying to get himself to the bathroom again, more as a means of diverting his attention to another activity than because he needed to, but decided he'd had enough adventure for one twenty-four hour period.

Tate came back just then, bearing the same tray as before. "I brought bottled water with it. I didn't think you'd want coffee this late."

"Water is fine," he said, shifting carefully to a sitting position, or something approximating it, so she could put the tray on his lap. The stabs of pain weren't as unwelcome this time as they took care of what he had not earlier, and by the time she'd come out to his side of the bed, he was ready for the tray in more ways than one.

"Are you up to talking more? I can come back after you get the chance to eat some."

He nodded to the chair, already having spooned up some soup. "We can talk while I eat. I don't want to keep you up any later than I already have."

"I think I can miss a little sleep if it means not sleeping permanently." She sat in the chair, an oversized cup of what looked like hot tea in her hands, and got right down to business. "We need to talk about what's happening with CJ, and what you plan to do about it, but first I want to hear more about why you think your job is in jeopardy. What did you tell them? About being here? I know they don't know about CJ, but what do they think you're doing? Are you in contact?"

It was a relief to jump straight into it, and made him feel that much worse for doing this to her and her new life. It was that remorse that made him redouble his decision to keep his hands—and mouth—off of her. To that end, he looked at his soup as he ate and listened.

"So do you have any suspicions at all on who drugged you? Did they take any of your personal effects? I didn't find anything on you when I—uh . . ."

"No," he said, not wanting to direct the conversation in any direction that included his lack of clothing at the moment. "I wasn't carrying anything at the time."

"Do you think they knew where you were making camp?"

He did look up then. "I realize my current condition makes it hard to take exception to that question, but still—"

She lifted a hand to ward off the rest. "I wasn't being insulting. I don't know where you were relative to camp when they ambushed you, and given this wasn't an active assignment, you might have felt comfortable enough to create a less-than-hidden home base."

He shook his head. "I kept to standard protocol. Never slept in the same place, kept my gear stashed when I was awake and moving."

"They'd watched you enough to tranq you, so what makes you think they didn't observe where you stashed your gear?"

"I don't know that they watched me for any length of time. I think I'd have sensed that. My guess is, given the rather random nature of how it all went down, that they were hunting me, and when they finally got me in sight, they took me down."

"Are you certain, then, that everything is where you left it?"

"No," he admitted. "I have no idea what I might have revealed under the influence of the drugs they shot me up with. Afterward, I wasn't in any condition to go back and check."

"And if they tracked you back to your gear from where they tranq'd you?"

"They couldn't. I don't leave a trail."

She nodded, accepting that as fact. At least she still had that much faith in him. It shouldn't irk him that she questioned things, but considering his less than professional behavior, well, pretty much since arriving half dead on her doorstep, he could hardly fault her.

"If you tell me where to go, I'll retrieve your stuff. Depending on how long you were out after they were done with you, they've had plenty of time now to find it, if they were so inclined."

"Given the duration and severity of the storm, I doubt, even if they were still out there, that they'd have had much luck."

"Do you think the storm—"

"My gear is where I left it, which means it's safe. And dry."

"Your confidence is appreciated, but you said yourself you don't know—"

"I have to believe I held up."

"And if you didn't?"

"What I did have was as tamper resistant as it gets."

She nodded, but they both knew that depending on who found it and what technology they had on hand, anything could be tampered with, hacked into. "I listened to the weather while you were sleeping. It's supposed to let up by morning. I'll head up and bring back your gear then. Or not, as the case may be. Either way, we need to know, and get it gone if it's still there."

"You're right. That will also be some indication of how I held up under the interrogation." And any reassurance he could get on that score was quite welcome at the moment. Especially seeing as he wasn't exactly holding up that well under the onslaught of Tate.

"True. Whatever the case, until we figure out who the players are, the less there is to find, the better."

Now it was his turn to nod. He watched as she tucked one foot under her other leg and shifted back more comfortably into the thickly cushioned armchair. There had been a slight awkwardness to the movement that he'd only noted because he'd been trained to . . . and because he was looking for it purposefully now. Which meant he was staring at her, which wasn't part of the game plan. He returned his attention to his soup, but not before noticing how the soft cotton of the loose pajama pants she wore revealed the curve of her thigh when her new sitting position pulled the fabric tight.

It occurred to him that since he'd been observing her, and further, since he'd been here with her, she'd never worn what he'd consider flattering or even particularly feminine clothing. Not that it had diluted his attraction to her. Which had little to do with her body, anyway, and a whole lot to do with her as a person. Her expressive face, and maybe her hair, had his attention, but other than noting that she'd grown leaner and less sturdy-looking, he hadn't really been caught up in the physical aspects of who she was.

From their time working together he'd known her to have a compact, strong body. He knew she cleaned up well when necessary. But he realized now his attraction to her didn't stem from any of that. And the hitch he'd noticed when she'd moved didn't turn him off, either. He knew how broken she'd been. Only now, now that he'd tasted her, did that realization tug at him in an entirely new way.

He spooned more soup, and wondered what she'd think about that. Which was easier than figuring out what he thought about it. She'd probably see it as pity, or worse. Which it wasn't. He'd hated it before, when it had happened, hated the ones who'd done it to her, hated that their overzealous methods were going to cost him his best agent, after nearly costing her her life. He hadn't felt sorry for her then—she hadn't allowed anyone that luxury, making sure everyone knew that she was thankful for her life, given that her partner had been robbed of the same. The rest were the risks inherent in the job they performed. She'd signed on for that.

He still hated it. All of it. But now it somehow seemed a lot more . . . personal. Which was ridiculous. Partly because he still didn't know her, not in the way he'd just begun to know her. And partly because it didn't speak well of him that it only touched him now, because he'd stepped past his role as team leader and mentor. He'd wanted to believe he was more naturally empathetic than that. It was a harsh realization to discover that perhaps that wasn't entirely true. Or hadn't been.

Which begged the question of who the hell he really was, and how did that reality sit with him?

He realized they'd been sitting there for some time now, in silence, while he ate. Without looking up, between bites, he said, "Which thing do you want to discuss first? My job?" God knew he'd done enough thinking about it over the past eighteen months since Northam had stepped in to take over. This latest turn of events was only serving to add an even wider spectrum of consideration to his thoughts.

If she was aware of any of the maelstrom of emotions running through him at the moment, she certainly didn't let on. "You say you didn't trust your chain of command to properly handle the news of CJ's return from the dead. If you did tell them, what do you think they'd do?"

"That's just it, I have no idea what they would have done. There is a definite disconnect between Northam and the team."

"What is his standing with the higher-ups? Has that changed, too? Are we still assigned to the same division, working under Howell?"

"Oh, Northam and Howell are like peas in a pod. Might be why they put him there. The disconnect isn't with NSC, it's between Northam and us. Maybe indirectly with Howell. Our assignments have changed—"

"How?"

"We're not targeting the same resources and groups, and what assignments we do get are micromanaged to death by Northam."

"Why do you think that is? Is it just him being a micromanaging ass? We had an excellent track record, so surely it can't be because they think we need overseeing."

"I wouldn't think so either, but my reach with the team now is very limited and strictly controlled. Everything I do, every decision, has to be vetted through Northam."

Her eyes widened. "But how can that possibly work? There isn't any time for that kind of protocol in the field, which is why you—"

"I'm left wondering about a lot of things lately, Tate."

"But you don't think we're being phased out? I mean, I can't believe that could be true given the need for the specific kind of jobs we handle. The world certainly hasn't suddenly gotten safer, and even with the recent change in the Oval, there is no way we're getting complacent on international threats to our security."

"I don't believe so, either."

"So . . . what do you believe? How have you been handling it?"

Derek smiled, but knew there was no humor in it. "Probably not as well as I should be. I butt heads with Northam constantly and am a major pain in his ass, but it's the only way to keep the team running effectively."

"Which can't be helping your career—"

That caught him by surprise. "Do you think I base team decisions on personal career aspirations? Have I ever given that appearance?"

"No, but you've put in a lot of time, built this team to what it is today. Without you, they have to know—"

"We're all expendable, Tate."

She dipped her chin.

"I didn't mean it like that. But if you're going in that direction, yes, even losing you and CJ didn't put the team out of commission. Losing me wouldn't stop them from going forward, either. Especially now."

"Is that what they're trying to do, do you think? Push you out? With your record, they can hardly axe you. If they want you out of the division, I guess they could promote you, but—"

"Actually, I was made an offer."

She sat back. "Really? Not that it's surprising," she hurried to add when he arched a brow. "Why didn't you take it?"

"It was a lateral move, though admittedly to a more upwardly mobile track, but I wasn't interested. It was internal, essentially a political job that had more to do with mediating between security and the military than actually doing anything. That's not what I want to be doing."

"So, you do think they're trying to get you out, then. Make you quit, or do something outside of protocol so they can get you out? Because it's working, especially if you reconsider that the CJ thing might be a hoax created for that express purpose."

"At the time they made the offer, no, I didn't think that. Northam was just being installed at that point and a lot of changes were happening. They accepted my refusal gracefully and let me know they'd continue to look for ways to utilize my skills. I told them I was happy utilizing them the way I already was." He gave a half smile. "I'm not sure they know what to do with someone who isn't all about being career- and advancement-hungry, but I was hoping they'd just be thankful I was willing to continue running the team."

"Then Northam takes over, and things change, and . . . do you wish you'd taken the position?"

"Hell, no. What I want to know is what the hell is going on in the agency I'm already in."

She leaned forward then, propping the cup of tea on her knee. "Could it simply be something as simple as a shift in how the new team in the White House wants to run things? Trickle down and all that?"

"Could be."

"But it doesn't feel like that."

He shook his head. "No. No, it doesn't. It feels like something else is going on, and they'd really like for me to not get wind of it."

Now it was her turn to smile a little. "Maybe you've been in intelligence too long. Maybe you're paranoid."

"You're only paranoid when they're really not out to get you."

Her smile faded. "You're really serious, aren't you? You really think there is something else going on. But you don't think the CJ thing is a hoax?"

He nodded. "I have no proof, but my gut instinct tells me otherwise. And it's that gut instinct that has made our team the most successful division in international security history."

"So . . . what are you going to do about it? Or what have you been doing?"

"I dig where I can, where it won't be looked at or questioned. But it's a painstaking process. I can't just pump people for information. In the meantime, I've been doing my job, or trying to, and forcing Northam to deal with me, work through me instead of around me, which really pisses him off, but I thought maybe if I make him mad enough, he'll make a slip."

"So you think he's directly involved . . . in whatever it is you think is happening."

"Honestly, I don't know. He's got his nose so far up Howell's ass, I can't tell if they put him in the position so they could control it, whatever it is they are doing, through him—"

She laughed then, and he looked up from his soup. "What's funny?"

"Well, it makes sense. Putting Northam in to gain control of our division, our team." She met his gaze. "They certainly weren't going to get that kind of access through you."

"No," he said, feeling slightly better, realizing only then how much her earlier comments about putting career over duty bugged him. He wanted to know her, the real Tate Winslow, which was astonishing enough for a man who purposely kept the personal interaction with those in his professional life at a professional distance. Made the job much easier. But even more shocking was that he wanted her to know him. And respect and like what she came to know.

If he'd thought he was in dangerous territory before, he realized now he was in a whole new world of jeopardy. And he was putting her there right along with him.

"So, you're doing your job, butting heads, pissing people off, and then you get the call from CJ."

He nodded. "Coded message first. Then the satellite transmission."

"And you made the decision to handle it on your own. At least to start with, anyway. No one on the team knew."

He shook his head. "I never brought anyone in. Except you."

"Maybe they do know. I mean, could they know? The second transmission—"

"Came to me through private channels. I'm as certain as I can be, on my end anyway, or was, that no one knows about it."

She paused at that. "So, do you have an idea who tracked you here? You said it might be from CJ trying to find me. Would the faction she's with have that kind of wherewithal? To hunt me here on American soil? For what purpose? Does she even know I retired?" Her eyes widened. "Is it possible she contacted anyone else from the team?"

"I don't know. Given the code she used, and staying out of channel, I didn't think so. Other than I thought maybe she'd tried to contact you."

"She wouldn't have known how."

"Unless you'd already been in contact, which I know now isn't the case, but it had to be considered."

"I know. I hate it that you ever even suspected that, but I understand why." The wind had gone out of her sails on that point almost as quickly as it had blown in. It was one of the other things he'd always liked about her. She was quick to defend herself or anyone she felt was getting an unfair shake, but she was just as quick to consider a logical, reasoned response, and move forward.

"And, just so you know, I already said there has been no contact, but I also made very sure there were no threads connecting my new life to the old. You're the only one who could have made that connection for her."

He understood what she was asking. "She knows from me that your last mission together ended your time with the team, but that's all. It was a short transmission, there wasn't much time, and I didn't know how secure things were on her end. She doesn't know from me where you are, and there is no documentation of it, I made sure of that at the time."

"Do you think maybe someone from her end tracked you, hoping you'd lead them to me?"

"It's hard to say, but it made the most sense. Looking exclusively at the CJ situation thus far, and discounting my concerns about my home base, it would appear they're the only ones who'd have a vested interest in tracking me out here, or torturing me to get information. Ostensibly on your whereabouts."

He noted the slightest of shudders at that, and realized in that moment, maybe more than any other, even when he'd first seen her in the hospital, how forever changed she'd been by what had happened to her in that deserted village. It seemed an obvious conclusion to draw, but only another agent could appreciate how thoroughly trained and deeply committed they were to their jobs. In most cases it was all they had, all they knew, and nothing, not even life-threatening torture, would stop them from sticking with it.

She hadn't. And now he realized it might have been the best possible choice not only for her own sanity, but for the safety of the team. It had been only the tiniest of flinches, but if even the thought of being subjected to any kind of brute force could visibly shake her, that alone would put anyone around her at risk.

"Maybe CJ needed out because she was found out, and if that's true they could have intercepted her transmission to you and, therefore, are trailing her to me. Especially if she cut out and is on the run. If she was as deeply embedded as you think she was, then who the hell knows what intel she might have. That might make it worth their while to run an operation here, on American soil, to flush me out."

"Possible."

Tate tilted her head. "But you're not thinking that's it."

"I certainly can't rule out any possibility."

A frown creased her forehead and there was real concern in her eyes. "So . . . what other possibility could there be?"

Derek put his spoon back in the bowl and pushed it away, suddenly no longer hungry.

"The ambush, the beating, and leaving me alive afterward . . . doesn't feel like an outside job, and most certainly doesn't fit the pattern of the group you and CJ were infiltrating, despite the changes of command." He held her gaze then, tightly. "They've never once, to our knowledge, concerned themselves with things happening on American soil. They usually only get agitated when we're on their turf. I don't know what CJ thinks you might know, but given she knows you're out of the game and have been for the past three years, that means if they intercepted the transmission, they know that, too. I don't know what they'd think your involvement could possibly be. Hard to say—they could suspect you're still involved, or deep undercover in some way yourself, but . . . given what we know about them, the tranq dart, the subsequent questioning . . . none of it feels like it was their methodology."

"So, if you don't think the attack was coming from CJ's end, then that can only mean . . ." She drifted off and her cup tilted dangerously on her knee. "Derek, you don't honestly think it's—"

"Us?" He hated this. "Yeah," he said quietly. "Yeah, I think maybe I do."

# Chapter 9

Tate sat perfectly still, and let the shock of his quietly spoken words settle inside her brain, where hopefully they'd eventually make sense. "But . . . why?" she asked at length, grateful he'd simply given her the time to process, without continuing to talk. "What would be the reason to come after you like that?" She looked up. "Given they don't know about the case, how could they think you've gone rogue? After only seven days? Given your career history, wouldn't benefit of the doubt give you some cushion—"

"Initially, I wouldn't have been cosidered rogue, but certainly now I could be. Even though I'm on a leave I requested, I only requested a week, and I haven't checked in even though I'm currently running two active missions and made it clear I'd still be actively available for those."

"Who—"

"I say I'm running missions, but that would be misleading, because Northam has his hands, nose, and fingers in everything I do, passing it on to Howell."

"Okay, so going with this scenario, why would they assume rogue and not that something happened to you?"

"They wouldn't, unless my supposition is right and things are off to begin with. Then they're going to worry that I'm off doing my own thing, suddenly, out of the blue, and panic, thinking maybe I'm figuring things out and taking this time to do some hunting of my own. I certainly have been vocal enough about my displeasure on the turn the agency has taken with our team, and with my concern about our success ratio dwindling as, what I see, is a direct result of that."

"So, why not capture you and bring you in for questioning? That's protocol if you've refused to communicate and they feel it's intentional and classify you as rogue. Even drugged, if necessary. I mean, it's extreme, but if they're truly panicking, that would resolve the issue one way or the other. They can always apologize afterward if it was a giant misunderstanding."

"Good question," was all he said.

She swallowed hard and the various ramifications of what he was implying continued to sink in.

"By doing it this way," he said, "no apologies necessary because no one will ever know it happened. I won't know it was them, and now they have their answer on what I know, based on questioning me under the influence of drugs. I was left alive, perhaps, so as to keep them from having to deal with the mess of a suddenly dead agent on their hands, especially their team leader—"

"But won't they worry that you're going to be a hell of a lot more suspicious now that this has happened?"

"Maybe they think I'll take it as a warning and stop poking my nose in."

She sat back and didn't say anything for a few moments. "I hate to say it, but that sounds more plausible than anything else we've come up with. Except . . ."

"Except what?"

"Well, if they did think you were off on your own, ostensibly on a requested leave, but really so you could dig into things you might be suspicious about . . . but then they track you to the middle of the Hebron Valley . . . what in the hell could you possibly be looking for here? Our agency doesn't operate on American soil, and what could they be doing anywhere around here to be suspicious of? I mean, finding you here, I think, would play more into proving you were doing just as you said you were doing, taking a break."

"I don't know. And I wasn't thinking like that when I came down here, which is probably why they got to me in the first place. I wouldn't have seen it coming. Not like that."

"It would only panic them if they somehow found out about CJ, or think that you really are on some kind of secret mission—"

"I don't know what they think. I piss off Northam on a regular basis. I told him I was taking some personal time, which didn't go over well, but since I have never taken so much as an hour of personal leave, and have accrued more than I could ever use in a lifetime, they couldn't say no. He knows himself that he's running the show, so he couldn't very well tell me I'm not expendable for a few days."

"I don't know," she said. "There's a link missing somewhere, and it seems obvious it has something to do with CJ, but I don't see how that connects to them, either. I don't know . . ."

"I'm wondering if maybe they've been monitoring me for some time. If my taking off just gave them the chance to finally do something about their concerns about me. Maybe they've been concerned about me for longer than I think. It's the only thing I can imagine, and maybe I haven't been as subtle in my digging around as I thought, maybe I slipped up somewhere. For all I know, they've just been waiting for a moment like this and I handed it to them on a silver platter."

"These are very serious allegations we're supposing here."

He lifted his bad arm slightly and winced. "Yeah, well, it felt pretty serious from my end, too."

"I'm not minimizing that. I'm just saying, you need to really think long and hard about this angle because you still have a complete absence of proof of anything nefarious going on that would lead to this kind of paranoia and attack. You still aren't any closer to proving that."

"Unless I can prove it was them. It's a backwards way of

getting to the heart of it, but they tipped their hand by attacking me. It's a solid link and proof not all is right."

"If you can prove it was them. And even if you do, they could have some story in place about why they think it was necessary, and it would be Northam's, and maybe Howell's, word against yours. I don't know, Derek. On the one hand it seems more plausible an idea, if you're right about there being a cover-up, than it being anyone connected to CJ's overseas infiltration. But . . . what in the hell would they be covering up?"

"I don't know. Which may be the reason I'm still alive, because when they drugged me I had nothing to give them."

"You don't think you told them about CJ?"

"They wouldn't have known to ask, and . . . I have no idea. But I think they'd have already been on your doorstep by now if they knew."

"So you think they trotted back on home, convinced you really are just on vacation for a few days? What about now? You've been gone longer than you said you'd be—"

"Well, they know the condition they left me in. They can be all concerned and wondering and saying they're trying to track down my whereabouts, all along knowing I'm out there, recovering from their beating—or not. One way or the other, I'll surface eventually and they'll spin that however they need to."

"And you? How will they spin you? What do they think you're going to do? Won't they be keeping an eye on you? Know you're here?"

"I don't know, Tate. Anything is possible. But they don't know it's you here, and that will take time to uncover. If they are watching me further, to see what I do post-attack, they may think I just dragged myself to the nearest house and asked for assistance. It will take them some time to track down who lives here, since I buried that under a bunch of layers for your protection."

She looked at him. His expression was dead serious, but open. "I think I want to switch gears a little. To the situation with CJ. We still have that to discuss. She did contact you. Maybe there's some kind of connection. It's all too seemingly random for me. I can't help but think—"

He slid the tray to the bed. "Tate, it's pretty late, are you sure this is a subject not better left for morning? I know I've given you a lot to think about, and I know you won't be taking my theories on face value, which means you'll likely lie awake and go over them, analyze them, put your own mind to the matter at hand. Which, frankly, I'm counting on. I'm missing something, and I don't know what it is. I want you to tell me whatever is on your mind about this."

"Even if it's that I think you've gone around the bend?"

"Do you?"

He was so serious, it made her smile. "I don't know what I think. I haven't been there, though, to witness any of this. Northam is a new player for me, and I never had to deal with Howell. On those rare occasions he felt the need to bless us with his presence, you were the one called in." She sighed and stood, then walked to the other side of the bed and picked up the tray. "What I do know is that your instincts were rarely, if ever, wrong. It's possible you're putting too much on what could just be a new regime with a new focus, but then the attack on you doesn't really back that up."

"I have no proof it was them."

"And even less proof it was anyone else."

He sank back against his pillows with a weary sigh, and Tate suddenly busied herself moving the tray to the dresser top by the door. She knew what he tasted like now, and he looked too damn good in her bed, even with the sling and the bruises. The less visuals she had to toy with after he was gone, the better.

"Okay, so we'll tackle the rest in the morning," she said. "I'll fix breakfast, we'll get you up and see how you're feeling, moving, then go from there. I'll want to get up to retrieve your gear earlier rather than later. Then we can go over everything that has to do with CJ's contact with you, and try to see where that might fit into what is or isn't going on back at home base."

She looked back at him, then. He was clearly fatigued, and more than a little frustrated. But there were a lot of things out of his control at the moment, including his own stamina and health, and she well knew what that felt like. "Is there anything else I can get you before I turn in?"

"I'm fine." He turned his head and pinned her with that direct gaze of his. It packed even more of a punch now, given their earlier involvement. It was like a physical touch now, and she knew exactly what that felt like. "I am sorry I dragged you into all of this."

"I think you have the apology part covered."

"I know it's not fair of me to say, but as much as I hate that you have been pulled into this mess, I'd be lying if I said I wasn't glad to have you on board." *On my side*, was the silent, but clearly added sentiment.

She didn't know how she felt about that. It had been one thing when he'd invaded her home, mid-mission, bringing with him whatever danger and chaos was involved in the case. But now she realized that he had no backing, that he was truly alone, truly rogue. And, worse, that the very security offered by home base might, in fact, be the source of the danger and chaos in this situation. It was going to take awhile for all that to sink in. And for her to decide how she felt about Derek's role in this.

Right now, the only side she was on, was her own.

She lifted the tray from the dresser, as much to provide a shield from his penetrating gaze as anything else. "I can't say I'm happy to be on board, but you know I'm going to do whatever it takes to figure this out. I have a lot at stake here, too." That much was the truth.

He held her gaze for what felt like an eternity. "Yeah. I understand that, too."

It seemed there was a lot more being left unsaid, but she

wasn't brave enough to push for clarification. Not that it mattered what he thought, or felt, regarding her. It took two to make that a problem. She could control what happened between them. And she would. Just as soon as she got some distance, some rest, and some of her sanity back. "Do you want the light on or off? There is an automatic night light in the bathroom."

"Off, then."

She balanced the tray long enough to switch off the small lamp on top of the dresser that had provided the only light in the room. There would be no moonlight coming in tonight.

"'Night, then."

"'Night."

She balanced the tray once again and turned to go.

"Leave the door open, if you don't mind."

"Okay," she said. She had just stepped into the hall when he called her back.

"Tate?"

She angled back so she could look into the room. The glow of light from the hallway bathed him in an almost otherworldly glow. "Yes?"

"About earlier—"

Her heart kicked up a notch. She knew exactly what he was referring to. Despite the incredible and overwhelming situation they'd been discussing, it had never been far from the surface of her thoughts, her awareness . . . and apparently not from his, either. "It's—don't worry. Like I said before, it's past. We need to focus, and I plan on—"

"I want to promise you that it won't happen again. It shouldn't. Because you're right. We need all of our faculties sharp and our mental game clear of distractions."

"I know. No worries, Derek. I'm an adult, you're an adult, we've worked together for a lot of years, and—"

"And it's a promise I'm not sure I can make."

She went still. "What?"

"I'm well aware that I have many things to concern myself with at the moment, not the least of which is getting us both out of this in one piece. I've always been the consummate professional, and I don't plan on putting in anything less than my best. But that doesn't change the core fact that I am distracted. By you. And I have absolutely no experience with how to channel that, or compartmentalize that, because you seem to defy any of the rules I've always set for myself in the past. I don't seem to get to have any say, or control, over the timing, or the right or wrongness of it. It exists, and I need to be clear and up front about that."

"Derek—"

"I'm not saying I'm going to jump you, Tate, or do anything I'm not invited to do, I wouldn't—I won't. But I'm going to want to. I do right now, even with everything we just talked about, knowing full well the ramifications. It's not like me, but then I haven't been like me in some time. And . . . I don't see that changing. Thought it was only fair to let you know."

The tray shook a little in her hands and she realized his words had her trembling. She just couldn't exactly say why. Or she didn't want to. "I already know that there are many things in life that aren't fair," she said, damning the shakiness of her words. "You being here is proof enough of that."

"Tate—"

"It's okay, Derek." Which was a complete lie. Nothing about any of this was okay. Not the problem she had to solve if she wanted her life back. And definitely not her surprising attraction to the source of the problem. "I appreciate you telling me. I—I'll—see you in the morning."

This time when she left, he didn't call her back.

And morning came far, far too soon. He'd been right, she hadn't slept much at all. And even with the precautions of pain relievers and stretching before bed, she was paying the price today for her activities of the previous day and night. The dampness was as much the villain as the physical labor, but it didn't matter why she ached. What mattered was that she was going to have to find some way to get herself mobile enough to get back up in the hills again today. And in order to even attempt it, she needed two things. And both of them were presently residing in her bedroom.

She wasn't ready to face him yet, though. She needed a bit more time to walk the floor, get the tightness in her thigh, and the corresponding knot in her hip, to ease up a bit, or she'd risk him seeing her at less than her best. Mostly she was buying time because lying awake all night hadn't given her any additional insight into what to do with either of her problems. Now she was confused and fatigued. Not a reassuring combo at best, and definitely not preferred when gearing up to deal with Derek.

But the day wasn't getting any younger, and neither was she. She finished up her stretches and rolled up her mat. She usually did them on her front porch, when the mornings were warm enough. But the combination of the storm debris and potential human debris out there had kept her indoors. She stowed her mat behind the door, then tugged the sheets and blanket off the couch and folded them up, too. Her sofa pulled out into a bed, but she hadn't gone to the trouble. If she didn't feel any better by tonight, she would.

After one last procrastinating stop in the kitchen to put water on to boil for tea and a morning bowl of oatmeal, she finally went down the hall to her bedroom. The door was still open, but Derek wasn't in her bed. It was only then she heard the shower running. Which meant her walking stick was in the bathroom. With him.

It wasn't like she could have just headed out without talking to him first, as she needed the location of his gear, but she'd hoped to retrieve her stick while he slept and use it while she puttered around the house this morning, to give her hip and leg a bit of a break. At least she could get her clothes, get dressed. Thankfully the pajamas she was wearing now had been in the dryer yesterday, so she hadn't had to sneak in her own room last evening while he'd been sleeping to pilfer them. Not that he'd have minded, or even known, but after the kitchen situation she didn't trust herself not to stand there and ogle the man, and think things she had no business thinking. Her luck, he'd open his eyes and catch her staring, and—

"'Morning." Steam wafted into the room through the open bathroom door. The mixed scents of her own soap and shampoo mingled with the heavy mist.

She stilled for a moment, trying to ignore all the delicious little sensations just the sound of his voice had sent skittering along her skin. "'Morning," she managed, then resumed digging in her dresser drawer. "You took a risk there, with the shower—"

"It's big enough to drive a tank into. Between that and all the handrails, I figured I was safe."

She'd had her bathroom converted while she'd still been using her wheelchair, even though by the time she'd moved out here, her need for it had almost completely ceased. She'd bought the little four room cabin mostly for the rural location and the views, but the accessibility and open design of the one-floor structure had been a selling point, too. She'd known when she bought it she'd be back on her feet again, but she'd also known from the start that whatever plans she made, or activities she took on as her time in the Hebron Valley unfolded, she had no intention of ever leaving.

Living so far out, living alone—a situation she didn't see ever changing—it only made sense to make adjustments for the future. Her previous injuries would forever haunt her, and likely expedite the aging process, so she'd had the remodeling done right off and been done with it.

"Still, you should have let me know. If you'd fallen—"

"I'd have gotten back up. I'm fine."

"You're hardly fine." She dared a glance over her shoulder to look at him for the first time today, and immediately wished she hadn't. Because fine didn't even begin to describe him. She wanted to look away, look anywhere but at his freshly showered, still damp skin, tousled wet hair, towel-wrapped hips, clean-shaven jaw, piercing blue eyes . . . but made herself maintain eye contact. She was going to have to get a grip at some point, right?

"I feel a lot better this morning." He stepped closer and she found herself gripping the edge of the drawer. "How about you?"

If he touched her, she was going to melt right into a little puddle on the floor. That gravelly voice, the sincere concern in his eyes . . . that naked chest right there within touching distance. It was still such a sensory overload. She could hardly be blamed. Self-preservation won out over proving herself, though, and she turned her attention back to the drawer, belatedly realizing it was her underwear and bras she was digging through. "Fine. I'm fine. Just let me grab a few things and I'll cook breakfast."

As if on cue, his stomach grumbled quite loudly, and she smiled before thinking better of it. She glanced at him and he lifted his good shoulder in a slight shrug. Then, before she could react, he reached up and smoothed the skin across her cheekbone, continuing the motion and brushing her hair from her face. "You sure you're okay?"

Her knees did that wobbling thing they did whenever he touched her. "I might have slept better," she told him, opting for honesty, hoping it would steady herself . . . and him. "But I've certainly handled worse. A little fatigue isn't going to kill me."

"Rain stopped," he said, and she breathed a small sigh of relief when he dropped his hand away. A second longer, she might have leaned into the warmth. She'd never, not once, wished for nurturing during her entire healing process. Not from anyone. She'd wanted strength of mind and strength of body, and she'd most definitely wanted the absolute knowledge that she could regain and sustain both completely on her own.

So why was it he could rouse that desire in her so easily, that need? It was as disconcerting as it was unnerving. Which, when melded with the physical arousal aspect, just left her in

the kind of mental muddle she'd never really experienced before and found herself completely ill-equipped to handle. And
that, in turn, a new vulnerability was being shoved at her right
in the midst of everything else that was being dumped on her
plate, which was really starting to piss her off.

"I can go up and retrieve my gear," he started to say, but she
cut him off quickly. Her sharp tone was not entirely commen-
surate with his comment, idiotic as it was, but that was his
problem to deal with.

"You're not going anywhere," she flatly stated. "First, no
visible sightings of you until we determine a game plan. And
second, with your ribs and shoulder just barely on the mend,
not to mention the fact that your body is still recovering from
any lingering aftereffects of the drug, and the laundry list of
minor contusions and other injuries you sustained, the last
thing you need is—"

"As you've also said, I've certainly handled worse."

"Yes, well, hiking in boxers and a sling isn't recommended
even on a good day. The rest of what you crawled in here
wearing isn't suitable for rags at this point. Once I retrieve
your gear, which hopefully contains clothing, we can argue
about who's going to do what."

She caught his grin from the corner of her eye. "Really bossy."

She snatched whatever lingerie was at her fingertips and
closed the drawer with a snap before stepping back out of his
personal space and away from any chance of another distract-
ing touch. "Let me get dressed, then I'll start on breakfast. If
you want to be all macho and bullheaded, then see if you can
make it down the hall and turn the burner off under the tea
kettle. It's going to whistle any second now."

"I can make the tea."

"And oatmeal," she said. At his confused expression, she
added, "It's what I eat every morning. I figured it would be good
for you, too." She really should tell him to sit down, or lie
down, or something. But at the moment she was just relieved
at the prospect of getting him away from her for a few minutes

while she dressed and regrouped. Again. She was doing a whole lot of trying to get a grip and not a lot of actual gripping. Once he was dressed properly, she told herself, this would all be much easier. And all the other body parts that went wonky every time she laid eyes on him would calm down and do what she wanted them to do.

If anyone had mind over matter down to a science, it was her.

She was in the living room, pulling her shirt down over her body as she heard him thumping down the hall, still leaning pretty heavily on her walking stick if the reverberation on her wood floors was any indication. She turned as he passed by the open archway into the living area. He had a fresh towel wrapped around his hips and tucked in at the waist.

At her questioning look, he said, "I thought I'd wait for my other clothes."

She thought it might be more likely that he couldn't maneuver his boxers back on after his shower, which brought to mind how, exactly, he was going to get fresh clothes on. Without her help, anyway.

At this rate, she was never going to get a grip.

Standing in a beam of sunlight, the first bright light they'd had since his arrival, she saw the bruises and welts on his torso for the first time. She'd seen far worse, on her own body in fact, so it didn't freak her out, but it did concern her.

He noticed her focus. "It looks worse than it feels."

"I think I'm pretty much the last person you can pull that crap on, but it's good to know you have a high tolerance. You sure you're not experiencing any other difficulties? You sure they're not cracked?" she added, motioning toward his rib cage. "You're leaning pretty heavily on the walking stick."

"Most of the bruising is on the same side as my shoulder, so it just takes the weight off if I lean to the right. The stick helps. But no, they're not fractured or broken. I do know the difference."

She nodded, knowing he spoke the truth. "Would it help if we wrapped them, just for stability?"

He shook his head. "It'll be okay. In a few days, I'll have a good range of motion back. I can start rehabbing my shoulder today."

She folded her arms as a response.

"My shoulder does this. Trust me, I'd know if I'd torn anything or done damage. I have to start getting the motion back." He stopped trying to explain and just said, "I know what I'm doing." He shifted his weight a little, causing the towel to part over his thigh. There was a particularly nasty bruise there, too. He glanced down. "I'm thinking size ten." He looked up to see her frowning, and added, "Shoe. That stomped me."

She turned abruptly away and started straightening and stacking the linens and blanket she'd used the night before, despite the fact that they were already neatly stacked.

She heard him move into the room behind her. The floor vibrated beneath her feet.

"Tate, I didn't mean to—"

"It's been three years, Derek. And the last thing I was then, or now, is fragile. Please don't censor whatever you're thinking or feeling on my account." As soon as she said that, she wished she'd worded it differently. There were a few thoughts and feelings she'd prefer he did censor, such as his sudden desire for her. It would certainly make it a hell of lot easier for her to do the same.

"Well, it clearly bothered you, so—"

"Brutality bothers me. Having to witness it, or even think about it, bothers me. I'd like to think it would bother anyone, but I'm not trying to be all activist here." She turned to face him. "I may flinch, or wince, or turn away from something." She shrugged. "I cope how I cope. But just because I don't want to look at something doesn't mean I'm weak, or vulnerable. Right now, here? I have a choice in how I handle things and I'm not going to hide from that. When we're out there, however, I'll handle things in whatever way the situation dictates."

"I wasn't questioning your professionalism or your abilities—"

She laughed. "You should be. I would be." The kettle started to whistle in the kitchen. "I wouldn't lie and say I wouldn't rather be doing anything else, with anyone else, than facing even a tiny element of my past life again, with or without you. But I beat amazing odds to come back to what I have today. That took guts, focus, determination, and superior mental fortitude."

"You're made of pretty tough stuff. It's what makes—made—you a superior agent."

She took the compliment in stride. She had been good and it had nothing to do with being cocky, smug, or egotistical to know that, to own that. It was simply fact. "I'd have never gotten into the profession if I hadn't thought I could handle it. But you don't really know what you can truly handle until you're tested all the way. I thought I was strong. Now I know I am." The kettle's whistle grew more shrill and she stepped around him. "I'm going to make breakfast, then you're going to tell me the rest about CJ. I'll get your gear, then we'll decide what our first move is going to be."

She walked into the kitchen and didn't look behind her. That had been a pretty damn good little speech. So there was no point in ruining it by letting him see the stark terror lurking behind that mask of solid confidence.

# Chapter 10

Derek positioned himself on the far side of the living area, out of direct line of sight of the big picture window, but still where he could maintain a visual track of Tate's trek out to where his gear was stashed. He'd lose sight of her shortly, long before she reached her destination, but he kept his eye on her until then. Maybe a few long minutes after she'd disappeared into the underbrush and trees of the incline across the narrow strip of valley that lay between her cabin and the next low range of mountains.

He could see why she'd chosen the place. The view would be considered spectacular to anyone. But to someone trained as she'd been, it also provided protection, given the wide open visual of anyone approaching her cabin from the front. From the back, it would take enough planning and equipment to scale the several-stories-high pilings driven into the ground, supporting the deck and house that hung over the steep incline behind her cabin, that a surprise visit would be almost impossible.

He didn't remember much of his initial entry into her cabin. How she'd been when she'd dragged him inside, bloody and half-conscious. He doubted she'd simply thrown the door open.

He was quite sure she'd have preferred to keep it slammed and bolted shut, once she found out who it was lying half dead on her porch.

It had been two full days—now going on three—since he'd been left shoved under a bush, bound and drugged. Three days he couldn't afford to lose, but he'd had little choice. He kept in mind that he could easily have lost all of his days. He wished he could take off on his own, leave her out of it, but that wasn't going to be possible. She'd wanted to talk during breakfast, but the act of sitting upright at the small kitchen table had quickly begun to take a toll. Perhaps the shower had been pushing it, but he felt a hundred times better and his head felt much clearer. He'd given her directions and sent her off, with the promise to resume the discussion upon her return. After he'd gotten some more rest. Which he wasn't going to get standing here.

He shuffled back to the bedroom, moving slowly now that he didn't have the support of Tate's cane. Correction: walking stick.

He smiled a little, despite the little stabs of fire shooting through his ribs with every step he took. She hadn't liked it much when he'd insisted she take the stick with her on her hike. For someone who was quite blunt about her capabilities as well as her limitations, she didn't like it when he noticed the latter. Especially when they were physical in nature. Odd that she wasn't nearly as defensive when he noticed the mental or emotional scars.

The smile flickered to a grin, then quickly to a grimace when he inadvertently dinged the elbow of his bad arm on the bedroom doorframe. He'd called it a cane, not intentionally, but her correction had been automatic. She was unapologetic about the wheelchair-adapted shower and the fact that she still had a hospital-issue sling in the house, but let him call her walking stick a cane and she got bitchy. Of course it was, truly, a walking stick, devised and created as such, but that hadn't been the point, he didn't think. She hadn't felt compelled to further elaborate and he'd let it go. For the moment.

She was still the Tate Winslow who'd worked for him. And yet she was so much more now. Or perhaps she'd always been more and he'd carefully screened that out. As he did with most people, he'd realized. Or had come to realize over the past year or so, as he had numerous other introspective things. Introspection, never high on his list of indulgences. In fact, it wasn't on the list at all. But the last eighteen months had changed a number of things. Northam taking over had just started the ball rolling. So many things had changed since then that the list now didn't resemble at all the one he'd lived by his entire adult life. And he had no idea what to do about that.

Rules had changed. Others', and, therefore, his own. Boundaries changed, his deeply ingrained ideals . . . all new permutations he wasn't sure what to do with, much less how to feel about them. Feelings . . . his or others'. Caring and accounting for them. These things were new to him, too. All he could do was make decisions based on knowledge gained through careful study and hard work, thorough training. And a gut instinct he'd learned to trust above all else. That's what had guided him in life. Not always infallibly. But he was still here, with very few regrets. So he hadn't been interested in changing the status quo.

Until the status quo had changed on him and taken away that choice.

Tate had left a legal notepad on the bed, with a pen, as he'd asked. There was a mug of coffee on the nightstand, along with a bottle of spring water. The oatmeal had been just the right choice. The pain sucked, as did the easy onset of fatigue. But the vitamin-enriched hot breakfast was a step in the right direction, as would taking the ibuprofen she'd left by the water bottle. Since he was alone, he swore long and loud as he carefully lowered himself to sit on the edge of the bed long enough to swig down the pain relievers. He had intended to sit in the overstuffed chair that was still angled beside the bed. Prove to himself he was that one step closer to being upright and back on his feet.

"Idiot," he said, as he carefully levered first one leg, then the other, up onto the mattress. He tucked the towel back around his waist and did his best to shift the pillows so he could sit as upright as possible. In the end, he settled for a half-sitting position that took the pressure off his ribcage and his shoulder. And tried to swallow the supreme frustration that admitting further defeat had handed him.

He slid the pad of paper to his lap and positioned it so his bad hand, still resting in the sling, pinned it down, stabilizing it so he could take notes. Notes he'd have her burn later in the fireplace, but which would help him sort things out, formulate, extrapolate . . . and hopefully have more to offer Tate when she returned than the limited information he had at the moment. He tapped the pen on the paper, his thoughts drifting not to CJ, the communication they had had, the moments leading up to his drugging and interrogation, or anything having to do with the past year and a half, during which everything had changed at work, and therefore, in his whole life.

No, his thoughts drifted to Tate, and her present climb through the hills. It wasn't entirely foolish to worry. She wasn't a civilian out there, but she wasn't one hundred percent either. She'd already been up there once, at least as far as where he'd been jumped. As it turned out, it had been a fairly good distance from where he'd stashed his things, which was good news for them in general, but not so great for her today.

Now that he was paying attention, he'd immediately noticed the slight hitch in her step this morning, the way she favored her leg in the way she stood, the way she balanced her weight at all times. She hid it remarkably well, so well he doubted anyone else would notice. He had, and now he couldn't seem to stop himself from looking for any other telltale signs of her past. It was easy to say it was simply what one did with a partner, a full and constant assessment, just as she was naturally doing with him and his laundry list of injuries at the moment. But he knew better than that. What he didn't know, was why it mattered so much to him. If his interest wasn't tied to his concern that her past might make her less effective in handling the present situation, then what was it tied to? It didn't make her less appealing to him, or more, for that matter, if he was looking for vulnerability.

For the moment, he wondered just how much work it was taking for her to hide her vulnerability from him. And why she was bothering. And why the fact that she felt the need to, with him, was seriously pissing him off. It wasn't like he wasn't fully aware of what she'd been through. Of all the people on the planet, he was one of the very few she shouldn't feel the need to hide anything from.

He tapped his pen on the blank sheet of paper, and tried to force his thoughts back to the business at hand. She'd be back somewhere around an hour to ninety minutes from now. He had work to do, best he get to it. She'd gone out once before, he reminded himself, and hadn't brought anything back with her. Or anyone. If they were still out there, watching, then they already knew where he was and had chosen not to approach. They hadn't approached her when she'd trekked out in the storm. Didn't mean they wouldn't today. Or any other day. If they were still out there.

His gut said no. But then, what the hell did his gut know anymore?

He came instantly awake when the front door to the cabin swung soundlessly open. He couldn't have said how he'd known, deep in sleep, that she'd returned, but he had. He blinked his eyes open and stared, his vision still blurry with sleep, at the pad of paper on his lap. And the still blank page staring up at him. Fuck.

"Derek?"

He squeezed his eyes shut. And he'd been worried that she was going to be the weaker partner of the two. "Yeah," he said. "In here."

She was already at the bedroom door when he opened his eyes again, in time to see her all-business expression falter to one of concern. Which just pissed him off more. At himself.

"You find it?" he asked, cutting off any possible inquiries

about his current state, knowing he sounded gruff, but tough shit for the moment.

She lifted the small black gear bag and the two separate black plastic tubes that were now Velcro-strapped to either side. "I did."

"You can just put it on the bed."

She lifted an eyebrow at the continued short tone, but did as he asked. He watched her move into the room. She had the walking stick in her other hand, but wasn't using it. She propped it by the bed. If she was any worse for wear from her hike, she wasn't showing it. Which also pissed him off. Unreasonable though he knew that was. There was no way she wasn't in some kind of discomfort. She'd been all but limping before she left. What bugged him was that she thought she had to work to keep it from being obvious to him.

"I'll get some clothes on and meet you in the kitchen. I don't suppose—"

"I'm starving. I'll throw something together."

He thought she'd ask him if he needed help getting dressed, but she simply left the room. Her only concession to his condition was to leave the bedroom door open. Presumably so she could hear him if he fell or called out.

Of all things, her indifference should have been the thing to jerk his chain, but like all the rest of his irrational behavior it just made him smile. "Teach me to be snippy," he murmured under his breath, then pulled the gear bag close with his good hand.

He heard sounds of lunch being prepared, with cabinets opening and closing, a pot or pan being put on the stove, water running. Domestic sounds, never a part of his daily routine, and yet oddly comforting all the same. He turned his attention to getting some clothing on, which took quite a bit longer than he'd thought it would, draining what little patience he had left with himself.

"Lunch is ready," she called out.

He was standing now, boxers on, jeans on, zipped but unbuttoned, shirt on but hanging open, unbuttoned as well. The little pains in the asses just wouldn't go in the little slots. He hadn't even tried to get the T-shirt on. Giving up on the buttons, he left the shirt untucked from his pants so it covered his undone jeans, and pinned the shirt together under his suspended arm. He didn't bother with a mirror. It was what it was. She'd just have to deal with it.

He debated on not using the walking stick, but figured it was a stupid point to try to make to himself or her. Which was when he realized why she was, essentially, doing the same thing. Trying to hide her deficiencies from him, especially the physical ones.

So, at least they were both being a little ridiculous.

Feeling a little less moody, but a lot hungry, he maneuvered himself into the kitchen chair she'd thoughtfully already left angled just right for him. She was at the stove, stirring something, and didn't look up when he came in.

"Smells good."

"Campbells. Can't really go wrong with that. Hope you like chicken noodle."

His stomach responded. Loudly. And they both snorted a little.

There were already plates on the table at each place, and a larger one in the center covered with slices of cheese, some grapes, and a plastic sleeve of sesame crackers. He slid some of the crackers onto his plate.

At the sound of crinkling plastic, she said, "Not much, I know, but usually I go to market on Tuesdays. I made some ice tea. Is that okay for you? Or do you want another bottle of water?"

"Both, if that wouldn't be too much to ask."

She made the drinks, grabbed another water bottle, set those on the table, then carried over two bowls of soup. At no point had she looked directly at him. He didn't think it was because of his gruff tone.

"This is good," he told her. "Thanks."

She nodded and crushed some of the crackers into her soup.

They ate in silence for a few minutes, then he just decided to up and ask. "What's wrong?"

She glanced up then. "Nothing, why?"

He opted to take a different tack. "Why do you try to hide your bad leg from me? How much it bothers you, I mean."

She looked momentarily surprised by the question, further proven when she looked back at her soup again, rather than hold his gaze. "I don't want you to have doubts about my ability to function."

Which sounded like the flat truth to him.

She continued to eat.

"You don't have to hide things from me. In fact, I'd prefer you didn't. It's best we know exactly where the other stands. On all things."

She looked up then, and pinned him with a gaze so direct, it sat him back a little. Then her lips curved just the tiniest bit. "Okay."

Now it was his turn to be wary. "That was easy."

"I'm not so sure of that."

"Meaning?"

"Your mandate goes both ways, you know."

*Ah.*

Her smile grew. "Exactly, Mr. I-Can-Handle-It." She nodded toward his bowl. "Finish up. You're going to need your strength for this afternoon." She lifted her spoon and waggled it. "Don't even think about going there."

Now he smiled. "Too late." But he said nothing more, and they finished their meal in companionable silence. Something else he wasn't used to. At least with the women of his association. But then, Tate had never been in that category. And though his thoughts regarding her had strayed far from the professional, he knew he'd never presume to compare her to anyone else.

She stood—carefully, he noted—and cleared the table. When she caught his look, she paused and said, "What?"

He glanced down to her hip, then back to her.

"Sorry," she said. "Habit."

"Habit, how?" he asked, thinking she'd said it so off-handedly, it wasn't a habit she'd just formed in the two days since he'd arrived. "You make a habit of denying your—" He faltered then, unsure of the exact words to use.

"Disabilities? Limitations? It's okay, Derek, I'm well aware I'm not one hundred percent whole."

"You can fill in the blank then. But why pretend to yourself?"

"It's not a matter of pretending. Or any kind of denial. I know exactly what's going on with my body, and all the signals it can give me on how to take the best care of it. I guess it's more mind over matter. I control it—"

"So it doesn't control you," he finished.

"Something like that."

"How bad is it?" he asked, deciding to see just where the line in the sand was with her willingness to be blunt and truthful. Better to establish that now, even if it pissed her off a little. "Now, I mean. I know how bad it was then."

"I could make the obvious statement that nobody knows how bad it was but me, maybe CJ, but I know what you meant. I have a steel rod in my thigh, several metal plates in my hip, enough plastic in my knees to be co-opted by Legos. My left shoulder has been completely rebuilt, as has part of my jaw and one of my eye sockets. A few of the disks in my spine had to be fused together, which is part of why my hip aches more than it should, as it's thrown my skeleton a bit out of whack. My ankles will both set off metal detectors in any airport, and I'm down a half a toe. I have a place on the back of my head where my hair will never grow back, but since my newly longer hair covers only part of the lovely scar that starts at the nape of my neck and travels the length of my spine, it's not something I really worry about."

He'd known about most of the list. Had seen her, so the list was a visceral one, not just one recited to him by a doctor or fellow agent. But hearing her list them, so casually and yet so intimately, twisted something inside him. Not pity. Not even on the range of that. No, this was something much darker, more along the lines of seething. Of anger, of an almost malevolent desire to smash something. Maybe obliterate it. He didn't have to ask what kind of human being could do such inhumane things to another. He'd seen it. Countless times. He knew more about it than anyone should.

And he'd always felt a certain rage, a certain need to right the wrongs, to seek justice, maybe even vengeance. It had always been that way for him. Which was why he did what he did.

But this . . . this sensation was thicker, more insidious, and not truly his to control, or even understand . . . which made it more than a little terrifying.

Worse, he had to sit there, in his beaten, busted-up body, and take it in while being able to do exactly nothing about it. Forced to feel it roil around inside him, and accept that this was part of him, too, this darker, ugly thing, this . . . hate. That knowledge, along with the truths she'd just handed to him—upon his request, no less—was something that he couldn't escape from, even if he wanted to.

He gripped his good hand around the coffee mug she set in front of him, while curling the fingers of his bad hand into a fist inside his sling, uncaring, welcoming even, the blistering pain that accompanied the action. "Where does that leave you now?" he forced out, trying to sound like the civilized human being he now knew he was not. Because if the men who had done this to her were standing before him right now, it wasn't going to be something as clean and righteous as justice that he sought.

"Most days, it leaves me a little stiff, but not much more. I have exercises, a laundry list of them, stretches mostly, that I do every single day without fail, to keep the muscles as supple as possible, the joints as flexible as possible. I also know my limits and try to work within them." She caught his look. "I'm serious. Pushing myself—which, yes, I did that at first—only sets me farther back. I learned patience—don't even think about making a comment—and that pacing myself is what, in the end, will give me a fuller and longer life, free of any real limitation or restriction."

She sat across from him with her own big cup of tea and slid the plate with the grapes on it in front of her. "Dampness makes things a bit worse. And yes, you don't have to point out that hiking in the rain yesterday, and in the damp air today, both pushed my limits in terms of distance and durability. But it's nothing I won't recover from. It just makes me a bit gimpy for a day or two."

He still kept staring at his mug of coffee. Not seeing it. Trying like hell not to see anything.

Finally she sat back in her chair, her cup cradled in her hands. "You asked."

He could only nod.

He could feel her gaze on him, but not the intent of it, not without looking up. And he couldn't do that just yet. Most people wouldn't have identified the blackness, the dark roil, behind what he knew could be an emotionless mask if he wanted it to be. Tate wouldn't even have to look closely to see all of it.

So much for revealing their true sides to each other.

"Your turn," she said, when the silence started to spin out. "Ribs, shoulder, fingers, for starters. Head, in terms of grogginess. Back, legs, anything else cropping up now that the pain of the major busted parts is settling a bit? Anything worse than you thought? Better?"

She was being direct and to the point. Which was her way of being kind. Both to him, and to herself. Because she knew something wasn't right with him after her little recitation. And he was pretty certain she was no more interested in digging into his reaction than she was into discussing herself any longer, either.

For both of their sakes, or so he told himself, he pushed his thoughts hard onto the path she was directing them to. And away from the black swirl. Not that it made it go away. He knew now, now that he'd tapped into it, it was never going completely away.

Just who—or what—had he become? When had a life devoted to what he'd always seen as just, edged over the line into something . . . else? And how had he fooled himself into believing his own righteous crap for so long? You didn't swim in the muck as long as he had, and think you'd never get any of it on you.

So he opened his mouth to tell her exactly the state of his injuries as he knew them to be, without gloss or pretense. Only, what came out of his mouth was, "What about the rest?"

"The rest of what?" she asked, sounding sincerely confused.

He should stop, but he didn't seem to be in control of this path he'd started down, any more than he had when he'd kissed her right here in this kitchen yesterday. She'd gotten to him, to some part of him he didn't even know he had, much less what to do with. "What you've done to overcome the physical damage done to you is remarkable."

"Thank the top-notch surgeons you made sure I had for that."

"It's a lot more than surgical, and we both know that," he said, sounding testy again. He knew that because she paused for the briefest of seconds before lifting her cup the rest of the way to her mouth.

"Okay. They patched and rebuilt. I rehabbed from there."

He looked up, finally. And he knew he hadn't been remotely successful in diverting himself from the dark place, because of the way her eyes widened when his gaze met hers. "What did you do about the rest of it? The mental part of it? And I don't mean the part that got you through post-op, then rehab."

Her cup was frozen a few inches from her lips, her gaze locked—or maybe a better word was trapped—by his. "Meaning how have I mentally reconciled what was done to me?"

He could only nod.

Slowly, too slowly, she set the cup back on the table. There was a fine tremor in her hands, revealed by the way the ceramic clattered a little against the surface of the table. The hands quickly disappeared into her lap. Her gaze followed a moment later. "I don't know."

"Do you hate them? Do you dream of revenge? Do you—"

Her head shot up and there was steel in her eyes. But not hatred. "I survived. They did what they thought was just."

"You can't possibly—"

"Don't you dare presume to tell me anything. Not about how I feel or how I should feel. Not now, not ever. You have the right to feel, to think, whatever you want to about what that—that event evokes in you. But don't you dare tell me how it should resonate within me." She shoved back her chair so hard it banged into the refrigerator behind it. She rose too quickly and had to grip the table suddenly for support when one leg straightened more smoothly than the other. "I don't know what you think this path you've decided to take will get you, but I'm all done walking it with you. I've told you once, and I will again for the last and final time. I'm in this because I have to be, and I have more at stake than someone like you could possibly ever understand. So I will fight, with everything I have, to regain what should never have been threatened or breached in the first place. We, neither of us, are whole, but I suspect you will do the same. For whatever reason and motivation it is that drives you. I don't need to know it, nor do I need to understand it. And beyond what I've just told you, you don't need to know a thing more about me, either. If my personal fitness or ability changes in any significant way, mental or otherwise, you'll be the first to know. As it pertains to getting the job done. Otherwise, you can back the hell right off."

She moved to the hallway arch. "I haven't had the chance to shower since you got here, so I'm going to take one now. I don't much care what you do in the meantime as long as it doesn't involve me, or put my life in more jeopardy than you've already managed to put it in."

She swung around then, to look at him one last time, and he

didn't think he'd ever seen her like this. He knew he hadn't. Tate Winslow might get angry, but she never lost control. She was teetering right on that brink. How was it he felt both humbled and shamed by being the cause of it . . . as well as more aroused than he could recall ever being in his life?

Truly, what the hell had happened to him?

"When I get out, we will discuss everything. No more distractions, no more subterfuge or personal line of questioning. And, at the end of it, either you'll come up with a next step, or I will. Because I'm also all done being a sitting duck. Crippled or not, injured or not, I want us out of this cabin in less than twenty-four hours. I might be a target, but the life I built here doesn't have to be. I want to know this will still be standing here when I get done. Even if I have to crawl back, I need to know there is something to crawl back to. You might not get that—"

He stood now—why, he didn't know, other than he had to somehow level the playing field. "I get that," he said quietly.

She turned away.

"Tate—"

She didn't stop. The next sound he heard was the slamming of the bathroom door.

# Chapter 11

Tate found him in the living area, sitting in the overstuffed side chair, his feet propped up on the end of the coffee table. He was dozing. So she took advantage and stared her fill.

He was clothed, but it hardly made any difference. His shirt was unbuttoned, as, she noted, were his jeans, and that particular combination, with him sort of sprawled and relaxed, even with the sling hiding most of his chest, did little to quell the jump her pulse gave every time she laid eyes on him. Or worse, when he laid eyes on her.

Despite his reassurances about his general health and well-being, the fact that he was sleeping this often was more telling than any update he could give her. She wasted a second debating on doing her own reconnaissance mission to scope out his injuries, but he wasn't sleeping deeply enough to risk it. All she needed was for him to wake up and find her hands all over him . . .

She ended that visual with a glance out the front window. The way the furniture was positioned, they'd be out of long-range view while sitting. But they'd both been here for going on two full days now since he'd dragged himself to her door. If they were going to have company, they'd have had it already. What concerned her now was that they were being observed simply to determine when either of them left the cabin. She'd been on full alert during her entire trek today, weaving her path, using trees as cover, making it as impossible as she could for anyone to get a clear bead on her for anything more than a few seconds at a time.

She hadn't felt any particular presence. But then, neither had Derek.

It had been somewhat more reassuring when she'd gotten to his hidey hole, that his gear hadn't been at all disturbed, nor did it appear anyone had tracked through the surrounding area, although with the heavy rains that had been a bit harder to determine. Hiding her tracks today had been something of a challenge as well, but she'd done a fair job. Just because she didn't feel a presence out there now, didn't mean whoever it was who'd started this wouldn't send someone else in later. No trail was no trail, now or in the future.

To that end, she'd done a lot of thinking in the shower. She'd taken a long one, letting the hot water pound her tight muscles and the steam relax what the pounding water couldn't. She'd stood there until she was pruned and wrinkly and the water had started to run cool. It had taken that long to once again come to some sort of terms with her newly acquired housemate. She still couldn't exactly say what the hell had come over him during their last conversation. He'd always been passionate about his job, but she'd never seen that look in his eyes before. There had been something dark there, something a little vicious. Not directed at her, but that it had been directed anywhere gave her a little pause.

It really made her wonder if he wasn't still suffering from side effects of the drugging. After all, in the initial twenty-four hours, it had lowered his inhibitions and had him saying all kinds of inappropriate things to her. Maybe it had boomeranged the other way and he wasn't entirely aware that he was still being influenced.

She couldn't say for sure. She'd endured a great deal over the course of her career, but one thing that she'd never encountered was being drugged. Short of lab work, there was no real way to know what might still be going on in his bloodstream. Looking at him now, he still looked far from harmless, more like a coiled cat, who, even sleeping, was only a blink away from striking if provoked. But that coiled readiness, the inherent athleticism of his body, right down to the hard line of his jaw, only radiated the elements of a highly trained agent to her. That other element, that darkness . . . that she couldn't see now. She almost didn't want to wake him, didn't want to chance what she might still see in his eyes.

But she had no choice. She hadn't changed her mind on the need to leave the cabin. She hated that she had to do so, for more reasons than simply being pissed off that she was being forced from her home. There was security here that she'd come to rely on, emotionally and physically. Perhaps more than was wise, but she hadn't figured that was a measure she'd have to ever concern herself with again. Whatever she'd done in her career had been done on soil far, far away from the red rocky clay of Virginia. Any foes she might have gained along the way wouldn't come looking for her here. As long as she was no longer in the game, or infiltrating their turf, she was of no interest to anyone from her former life.

Or so she'd thought.

"Derek."

She said it quietly, a little test, perhaps, to see how deep under he'd gone. His eyes instantly blinked open and unerringly found hers. "Your hair looks good down."

Again, he'd managed to put her off balance. He really had to stop that. Determined to keep on track this time, she took a seat on the end of the couch closest to his chair and propped the still-blank legal pad on her knees. "I want to set up a timeline first. When did Northam take over the division?"

She glanced at him as she spoke. His shirt had fallen open when he'd shifted up in his seat, giving her a nice view of bare chest all the way to where the arrow of fine dark hair disappeared behind the zipper of his unbuttoned jeans. Not that it wasn't anything she hadn't seen before when he'd been wearing next to nothing, but something about the casually draped cotton fabric and negligent opening of denim . . .

She looked back to the pad of paper, pen poised, and made no apologies to herself for keeping her eyes down. Clearly he was going to affect her no matter how many pep talks she gave herself, or how many layers of clothing he put on. Best that she just understood that and looked for other ways to keep her head clear and her thoughts focused. "How long ago?"

"Eighteen months," he said.

His voice sounded like warm honey coating a layer of thin gravel. Seriously, did he do anything that wasn't inherently sexy as hell? How had she worked next to him for so many years and kept her fantasies about him completely separate from the job?

"Things didn't change at first," he said. "We were all deployed when he came on board, and those missions were completed as planned."

She started taking notes. All business. That was her. "When did that change?"

"With the very next set of mission orders. We were called in—I was called in—and briefed on the new command channels and the new protocol, which I was to pass down to my team."

"Did that come from Northam or Howell?"

"Northam led the meeting. Supposedly the mandate came from Howell."

She glanced up briefly. "Supposedly?"

"He's been running the division all along, so it seemed a little odd that he'd been the one to change things up."

"But Northam worked for him, and is known as a pleaser, not a leader. Mankowicz wasn't a pushover like that," she added, referring to their old chain of command. "Maybe Howell was just waiting for the time that he could install someone he could roll over."

"Possibly. But there has to be more than this. More than just Howell wanting to implement his own ideas. What's happening now isn't just a new way of doing things . . . and it's not just micromanaging. Our mission directive has changed."

"Specifically?"

"No. That's just it. According to Northam, which comes down from Howell—because, believe me, I've been rattling cages and demanding answers—our mission isn't any different now than it was before. They've used the new power in the White House to explain some of the protocol changes, but it's like they don't think we're going to notice the fact that we're not being deployed in the same manner, on the same kinds of cases, much less the number of cases, as we were in the past. And I know that isn't because we're not needed, or that someone in a position higher up the food chain thinks we should go about handling the situations that require these types of covert missions in a different way."

"Meaning what, then? If it's not the new staff, or our direct chain, or a new president in the Oval, and you don't think Howell has become some egotistical tyrant who suddenly wants complete control over his division down to the tiniest detail . . . then what is the cause of the abrupt shift?"

"That's just it, I don't know."

She tapped her pen on the paper and tried to think, knowing that Derek was already way past the frustration that was just now beginning for her. "You said you think maybe they're watching you. Why? And who, specifically, do you think 'they' are?"

"Howell, I guess, or whoever he's directed to watch me. Might go higher up the food chain, I'm not sure. And the why is because I'm not going along with the game plan. I'm not playing nice and just doing as I'm told and pretending I don't notice things aren't the same. I'm asking questions and rattling cages and I don't think they're liking that a whole lot."

"Are you getting any answers?"

"Bullshit, yes. Real answers, no. Which is what led to me doing some digging, I thought discreetly, but who knows. Maybe they got wind, and the result was what happened out there in the hills. If I could prove even that, I'd be on the way to getting at this thing, but who the hell I'd take even that information to, I don't know. Whatever the hell it is that's going on, it's bigger than Northam, and possibly—probably—Howell as well. Where that chain goes, I have no idea."

"And you think they are afraid you'll keep digging until you find something?"

"I think they surely suspect it. I haven't quit, I wouldn't take a promotion away from the division, and I'm sure they don't think I just suddenly decided to play quietly."

"Did you find anything at all in your digging? Could they know if you did?"

"No, I haven't. I haven't figured out why we're not being deployed as we once were. I can't figure out why they want to monitor our every move, when the entire point of our agency was to create a freely moving, single-lead, command task force whose sole purpose for being created was the very autonomy it gave the agents in the field. Had our success ratio dropped, or had anyone in the division done anything to subvert our cause, I could understand the sudden precautions, even disbanding us if the trust was shattered."

"But that didn't happen."

"No. We had to regroup after losing you and CJ. I won't lie and say that was an easy adjustment to make. I had to rethink and rework strategies we'd long since taken for granted when using the two of you. I don't have other female agents who could do what the two of you did, and given those strategies, it's not a plug-n-play situation where I can slot a male agent in your place. We took full advantage of our adversaries underestimating your abilities due to gender, especially in the areas we were deployed into, so it took a great deal of restructuring and rebuilding, entire new strategies. But it was done. And we continued onward, well before Northam took over. Differently, but not significantly less successfully. Not in any way that would warrant this."

"So, what else could it be? Could it be you're reading too

much into things? Why couldn't it simply be the new power in the White House? Maybe they really are rethinking our stance on terror and international diplomacy—"

"Then disband us. But don't cut our balls off, then stick us out there to get our heads blown off anyway."

She didn't flinch at the less-than-gentle language. It was only surprising in that he wasn't more colorful, given what she'd long been used to working with in a male-dominated field. "Have you lost other agents?"

He nodded. "No one you worked with," he added.

Like that made any difference, she thought, but understood, after CJ, why he'd added the caveat. "Were they lost in a manner directly related to the change in mission protocol?"

"I'd argue yes, but it's a subjective argument that I can't prove. And in a game of my word against Northam or Howell's—guess who wins?"

"Still, any significant losses—"

"They aren't. Not to say that the loss of any agent isn't significant, you know that, but it's not out of keeping with the dangers inherent in the job. It's just out of keeping with the way I've always run my team. Our stats were never in line with the ones their analysts came up with as an acceptable ratio of loss. Ours were always significantly better."

"Now they aren't?"

He shook his head. Once, curtly. She didn't push further.

"What are your theories?" She lifted her hand. "I don't care how farfetched. Most people would be shocked to find out there are teams out there operating as we did. So I'm not going to be prone to disbelief no matter what you throw at me."

"That's just it, Tate. I don't have any theories. None that play, anyway. I really don't know what the hell is going on." He gestured to his discolored, beaten face. "But something sure as hell is, because I'm pretty damn certain nothing from any mission I've ever run has come all the way over to our turf, to hunt me down in the middle of the Hebron Valley, just for the privilege of drugging me to find out what I know. And that includes anything having to do with CJ and whatever the hell she's gotten herself into. Despite the timing of it, nothing that we know about them supports their doing anything like this here. And given she'd just contacted me, it'd be pretty damn fast for them to put something like that into play." He shifted in his seat again, but didn't look any more comfortable. "No, this," he said, scowling, lifting his right arm slightly, "was courtesy of someone from my own damn side."

Tate's heart rate accelerated. Because she believed him. And because she tended to agree with him. It made no sense to ascribe his drugging, out here, to some overseas faction who'd suddenly decided to kick into operation Stateside. Not that some didn't exist here, but operations were usually deeply covert and largely passive in methodology. Passive not to be equated with being any less dangerous. Infiltration wasn't exclusive to American agents overseas. Overseas agents were doing the exact same thing here, but their information gathering generally didn't involve overtly capturing and torturing a believed United States operative on American soil.

Still, she had to ask. "What were you currently working on when you took leave?"

"Nothing. I had two teams deployed, but was waiting on further orders."

"And that's when CJ communicated with you."

He nodded.

"And you're certain it was her." She lifted a hand. "I'm just reiterating for the sake of putting this all in a time line."

"She used my code, the one I'd set up for the two of you only. And she reached me outside of command channels, both with the initial coded message, and the satellite transmission."

Which had been another out he'd given them, totally off the record and out of the chain's protocol. But Derek had always been more concerned with successfully completing missions and doing so in a manner that kept his agents in one piece to be deployed again, and playing by the rules didn't always guarantee that, and in many cases made it next to impossible.

So he'd created his own rules, his own protocol, but as long as they remained successful, no one bothered to scrutinize too closely how they'd done it. Until now.

"Do you think someone figured out that you sort of colored outside the lines in the way you handled us? Could that be the reason for the crackdown?"

"It would have been cutting off their nose to spite their face. All they were worried about, and should still be worried about, was winning the battles, and thereby winning the war. The fact that they assembled us in the first place made it loud and clear, to me anyway, that playing by the rules wasn't exactly in the forefront of their list of concerns. I could see if we had some spectacular or embarrassing failure and they needed a scapegoat, but that hasn't been the case."

She agreed with him there, too. In all the time she worked for him, they were never once called on the carpet for violating mission protocol. And neither were they ever asked to explain in any detail how it was they had such a high success ratio.

"So, back to CJ. She used the channel you set up for us. Could it be possible someone found out about that channel and was using it to set you up in some way? I mean, if you think they're gunning for you, for whatever the reason might be, maybe they want to discredit your job performance in some way."

"No way could anyone else have that code. It's not in any documentation anywhere. You, CJ, and me were the only ones who knew it."

At least he was no longer worried she'd compromised it in any way. Which brought another, very unsettling thought to mind. "Unless CJ—" She stopped, then finished the thought. "Could she be playing both sides? I mean, contacting you via your pre-established code only she knows, so you'd know it was her, but also working—"

"Working for my side, against me?" He was incredulous and more than a little angry at the notion, if his expression was any indication, but he didn't immediately negate it as possible.

Which Tate took as a good sign. She didn't think it was the right string to pull either, or she was praying it wasn't, but she was glad to see that he wasn't so focused on his own scenarios that he wasn't willing to look at this situation from any and all angles, even ones that would be very difficult to consider, on several levels.

"Given what was shared in our limited communication, no, I don't believe that," he said finally.

She let him continue to stew over it, though, as she pushed forward. "So, if that isn't the case and it's just extremely odd timing that she shows up now, in the midst of this abrupt change in your team's mission protocol, then what prompted her to come back from the dead after three long years?"

Tate was trying her damndest to keep a strictly professional focus with her questions and viewpoint, but even she could hear the thread of resentment in her tone. CJ. Alive. All this time. Only to surface now.

"By her own admission, she hasn't been captive all this time," Tate went on. "I know what intel we had when we were captured, as we both had access to the same information since we were working together on it. And she didn't know anything so important that it would keep her alive that long. And given the huge subterfuge of making me think she'd been shot, clearly that wasn't the goal anyway." She tapped her pen in rapid, agitated succession on the pad of paper. "So, she somehow insinuated herself into working for the other side—either deeply undercover, or worse, as a double agent—and now, three years later, it's time to make contact. And she chooses to do it in a way that exposes her specific connection to you, to our team, outside the bounds of protocol. Why?" She stopped the tapping and looked at Derek. "What, exactly, did she say to you? Why are you so certain it was her? Maybe she gave them the code under torture."

It was a stretch, as they wouldn't have known about it to interrogate her for it, but she was reaching anywhere she could.

"Even if they had, which I doubt, why use it now, three years later?"

"You tell me! Maybe we haven't been paying attention to what the hell they're doing over there and now they're coming in via you. I don't know. Maybe it has something to do with whatever the hell it is you think is going on with the team."

"She told me that she was alive, that she never stopped working, which I took to mean for our side, and that she wasn't done yet, but that she had no choice, that she needed out."

"And she wanted you to do that. Without any further intel. Despite the fact that the last we saw of her, she had a bullet hole in her forehead."

Derek gave her a quelling look. "There was no time for further explanation. Which was when she instructed me to work with you."

Tate flipped the pad onto the coffee table and flopped back against the couch. "Great. Just great."

"Which is why I don't think the code was used by anyone else. Why would an opposing force use a dated code to flush out an agent who has been inoperative for three years? It doesn't play."

"Maybe they're afraid I know something."

"Times change quickly, and, as I said, their chain of command is completely different now. I just don't see where you could come into play for them at this point."

"Okay, okay, so let's say CJ is alive, and she's gotten herself in trouble with the guys she's embedded herself with, and now she's making connections Stateside, talking to you, and throwing my name around. So maybe they are behind your ambush. Maybe they were tracking me down, or you—you said you felt you were being watched, and maybe you were, just not from our side. Maybe they found out I'm inactive and started to track me down, or tracked you tracking me. Seriously, in this chaotic disaster of a mess couldn't it be them?"

"I don't know—"

Tate shot off the couch. "I don't know, I don't know! Is that all you can say? What the hell *do* you know? You drag me into the middle of this cluster and all you can say is I don't know? For that matter, why are you so damn convinced it was CJ you were talking to?"

"She transmitted a photo—"

Tate's eyes popped wide. "*Now* you tell me this? Of course, anyone could have her photo. They held us long enough to take a yearbook worth of pictures."

"This one wasn't taken in the village, or anywhere near where you worked over there, not with them. It was taken in London, in front of a construction site along the Thames. I looked it up. It's current construction."

"It's also the age of digital photography, where anything can be Photoshop'd."

"We're better than that. We can examine pixelation to the—"

"And you had that done? Had the photo authenticated?" she demanded. "How? I thought you shared this intel with no one."

"I didn't tell anyone. I know it might come as a shock to you, but I actually have some personal background experience in several of the departments that backed up our missions. It's why I was called on to lead the team."

"So *you* authenticated it."

"To the best of my abilities, with what I had to work with, yes."

Tate sat back down in a slump. Her hips protested and her thigh tweaked, but she barely winced. She hadn't had this much adrenaline pumping through her since . . . well, since she'd found him beaten and bloody on her doorstep two days ago. It was a pattern she didn't care to continue. "I saw her, Derek," she said quietly, a few moments later. "I saw her. I wasn't even five yards away. I know what I saw. They didn't have time to plan an elaborate hoax. From the time of the gunshots to the time they dragged her past my door—"

"Unless it had been planned before then."

"I don't see how."

"Are you saying it's impossible? You'd been separated the entire time."

"But held in adjoining rooms. She heard what happened to me, I heard what was happening to her. That was intentional."

"Everything?"

"I know what I saw."

"Okay, let's say you're right," he said, making her look up from where she'd twisted her fingers together in her lap. "Let's play that out. Because frankly, I felt the same as you do now when she first made contact. What else could I think, right?"

"Right," Tate agreed, frowning. "So . . . ?"

"So, using the same rationale, why? If she died in that small hut three years ago, why would someone plan an elaborate hoax now, trying to prove otherwise, this many years after the fact? You're the only other one who was there, and you've been inactive since that mission. If you'd given us anything to work with on them, we'd have moved on it by now. Not only that, but nothing we are doing now involves that group, in their current incarnation, in any way, and hasn't for a long time."

"Maybe something is happening with them to cause them to be concerned about my still being alive." She was reaching, but maybe it would trigger some other line of thought.

Derek looked at her. "If that was the concern, they could resolve their fears more directly, without the hoax."

"Unless there is reason they can't get to me here, solidly planted on American soil, retired from the game. Maybe they create a CJ, returned from the dead, in order to draw me out of seclusion, very possibly overseas, where they would have all kinds of power over how to handle me that they might not enjoy here in the States."

Derek's expression made it clear this wasn't an original line of thought.

"Right," she said. "I forgot, you've been stalking me, trying to determine if maybe I've been secretly working for them, or working for someone, while supposedly retired."

"It wouldn't be the first time a retired agent lent his or her services to current parties of interest."

"Thanks for the vote of respect." She started to stand again, but he leaned forward, grunting in pain as he did so, stilling her with one look.

"I didn't mean to imply that the parties of interest here could only be nefarious in nature. Our own country recruits from its retired ranks all the time."

"And you think our own country is beyond being nefarious?"

"I didn't say that. You and I both know better. And given my suspicions of late, obviously I'm already well down that trail of thought."

"Well, I can settle part of this. I'm not working for anyone, on either side of the ocean, in any capacity. Nor have I maintained, in any manner whatsoever, any interest in keeping up with what's going on anywhere in the world beyond about a five-mile radius from my front door. Hard to believe given my dedication, maybe, but true. I don't even get a newspaper. I've been completely and totally self-absorbed for the past three years, and, to that end, have very specifically locked the rest of the world out of my own little one. If I ever chose to invite said world back in, I would, on my terms, and my terms only. But three years later, I still haven't. And didn't have any immediate plans to change that."

*Until you showed up.*

"You have every right to live however you see fit. I'm not faulting you, much less criticizing you."

"Good to know."

"Nor did I ever think you were working for anyone." He lifted his good hand. "Not that I knew, or had checked up on you."

She cocked a brow. "Have you? Checked up on me?"

"Honest answer?"

"I should hope for nothing less at this point."

"I wanted to. Many, many times. At first it was professional in nature, strictly wanting to know how someone I admired and respected was getting on in a world so different from the one she'd left behind. But after time went on and you didn't come back—"

"You honestly thought I would?"

"Stranger things have happened. Even with your medical issues, it's like a boxer who just can't leave the ring. I was secretly glad you never showed up on my doorstep."

"Really? Why?"

He smiled then, and a little of the tension ebbed. "You sound a bit miffed by that. Make up your mind."

She waved a hand. "You know what I mean."

"I do. And the reason I was glad you didn't wasn't because I wouldn't have given or done anything to get you back on my team, it was that, like that beaten-down boxer—"

"No one wants to pay to see him fight anymore," she finished. "You didn't want to have to turn me down."

"Or worse, offer you some desk job, something out of the field."

"Would you have?"

He nodded. "I won't lie. Your body might not hold up to a field job, but your mind is something we could have always used. So, yes, I'd have insulted you and hurt your feelings, but I'd have done whatever it took to get you signed back on."

She thought about that, then smiled a little. "I'll take that as a compliment."

"It would never be anything less."

"But . . . I didn't come back," she said, getting them back on topic. "So you eventually just let it go."

"Not entirely true, no. You continued to stick in my mind, long after you should have. I told myself it was the aggravation of having to rework my strategies around your absence that kept you in the forefront of my mind. Not sure that was true, either. Then I wanted to follow up, just to get you out of my mind, threads neatly snipped."

"But you didn't."

He shook his head. "Not until now, not until CJ. Northam took over the team and my thoughts were diverted. Temporarily, or so it appears now." He looked at her. "To think I thought offering you a desk job was the worst thing I could do to you."

It was clear that he hated everything about this. And his respect for her, even when she added in the recent personal slant, did mean something to her. So she smiled, and let him off the hook a little. "Well, we never played by the rules before. I don't know why you thought things would change." She stood then. She needed to walk a little, keep her legs from getting any tighter. "I'm going to fix something to eat."

"Would you like some help?"

She didn't bother asking him what help he thought he might be. He'd offered sincerely. "I'd like some time to think."

"Okay." He maneuvered himself to a stand.

"You rest, I'll call you when—"

"I need to move. I'm going to the bedroom, start a little rehab. See what's what."

She just nodded. He was going to do what he thought he needed to do, no matter what she said, so she saved her breath.

Just before stepping into the kitchen, she turned back. "Derek?"

He paused in the hallway, looked at her.

"I don't miss it. I thought I might. But I don't. It's like it was another chapter in my life, a very, very big one, but one that is now closed. I don't find myself wanting or needing to reopen it. I did all that I was supposed to do there. The future . . . it's another chapter. I'm eager to find out what will happen next."

"Tate—"

"I won't be coming back. Just so you know."

"I know," he said, quietly. "I won't—" He stopped, then just said, "I know." And moved on down the hall.

# Chapter 12

They had to get the hell out of the cabin. Tate was right about that much. Derek slowly walked the taped-up fingers on his left hand up the wall in front of him, gritting his teeth when they moved past shoulder height. He just wished, after their talk, he had a better idea where the hell they should go.

"There's food in the kitchen," came her voice from the doorway behind him.

He felt like he'd done nothing but eat today, and yet just the mention of it had his stomach grumbling. Probably not a bad sign, hunger. Except for where it pertained to his hostess. "Be done in a moment."

He didn't hear her walk away, but didn't invite further conversation. Instead he focused on walking his fingers slowly back down the wall. Both the fingers and the shoulder protested. His ribs weren't all that excited about the maneuver, either.

She waited until he'd lowered his hand fully to his side. "Do you still have it?"

He thought about that for a second, while he debated on another round of finger-walking exercises versus putting his sling back on and mercifully giving every part of his aching body a break. Sling won. He'd tackle round two after he had something to eat. "Have what?"

"The photo."

Light dawned. Hadn't occurred to him, with everything else they'd been discussing that, of course, she'd want to see proof of her former partner's miraculous return to the land of the living. But when he turned around and caught her expression, which was one of serious trepidation, he realized there was a whole lot more to the request than simply seeking proof. "Not printed out, no." There was a mixture of disappointment and relief in her eyes, which tugged at that newly discovered place in his heart. Very disconcerting, that tug.

"I have a computer," she said.

"Which is the last place I'm going to upload it."

"Right. Stupid."

There were too many ways to retrieve data these days, even after a permanent deletion. "Not stupid. Understandable, you wanting to see her."

"I just . . . need to. With my own eyes." She made a short, snorting sound. "For all that's apparently worth."

"If you got played, considering the condition you were in, and the fact that the possibility would have never occurred to you—or anyone—I think you can cut yourself some slack there."

"So you say," she said, not giving herself an inch.

He didn't push it. She'd had to confront and handle a great deal in the past three years, far beyond healing herself. The information he just dumped on her was proof that, in one respect, she hadn't changed. She was just as tough on herself now as she'd ever been. He supposed it was also a large part of why she was still standing here, so he could hardly be critical. "So I say," he repeated. "I have it heavily encrypted in my satlink."

"Your what?"

"New technology."

"Satellite links were around when I was there," she said.

"Not like these."

"Still, you think that makes it safer? My god, anyone with junk in the sky is probably watching you."

"Works both ways. I can scramble a signal for a distance up to two miles."

"Your own bubble of white noise."

"Something like that." He adjusted the sling and changed the strap position slightly, before moving over to the black gear bag he'd stowed on the dresser. "I'll bring it to the kitchen."

Her gaze had already strayed to the bag. She looked at it with an expression that was a cross between a kid staring at a present under the tree . . . and one looking at the door to the haunted house on Halloween. Then, without looking at him, she turned and walked back to the kitchen.

He dug out the necessary equipment and met her there.

She'd put plates with sandwiches on the table, and some iced tea. Another bottle of water for him. A bowl of grapes in the middle. "It's not much—"

"Please," was all he had to say.

They sat, but she didn't eat. So he booted up the link and went about retrieving the image he'd stored.

"You're sure it's her?"

The photo of CJ blinked onto the tiny screen. "You tell me." He handed her the link and noted her hands were shaking just slightly when she took it.

There was no gasp, no nothing, as she stared down at the image. In fact, her face was carefully blank. Carefully, he thought, because he knew there had to be a lot of feelings running through her at the moment. This time, her game face was bullet-proof.

"She's standing in front of the Harrison-Gambault tower. Does that mean anything to you?"

"Should it?" she countered, still staring, still saying nothing, revealing nothing.

"I don't know if there is any significance, other than by researching it I discovered it was still being constructed, and therefore proves the location is current."

"And you're certain it's not digitally altered?"

"If it is, then the digitalization is surgical to a point beyond what my very sensitive program can detect. There is absolutely no pixel distortion between her and her surroundings."

"Was it strictly a text communiqué? Did you hear her voice?"

"No, I didn't. We communicated live time, but no . . ."

"Troubling."

"Perhaps." He waited a few more minutes. "What do you think?"

She finally tore her gaze away from the image. He couldn't begin to imagine what she was thinking, feeling. "I'm not sure what to think. I'd like to think the timing is coincidental to what's happening to you inside the job."

"You think it's connected?"

"I don't see how it could be, other than to rattle your cage and see how you'd handle the matter. Even so, seems pretty elaborate for that, with too many variables to control, in terms of trying to shake you loose." She reluctantly handed the link back to him. "You did go rogue with this. So, if I'm wrong and someone did go to these lengths to set you up, then you've fallen right into their trap."

"Possible, I suppose, but not probable. And the drugging seems a bit extreme, if the intent was simply to discredit my job performance as a means to get me off the team."

"Agreed."

"So . . . ?"

She didn't respond right away, but didn't pick up her sandwich either. "So, I can't speak to what's going on with the job. Or how your unexplained extended leave time is going over back on the ranch. On the off chance nothing is really going on with the job and it's just being handled like too many of the other government-run operations now that Mankowicz is gone . . . do you think it might be wise to call in with some handy story to excuse your delayed return?"

"I thought about that."

"And?"

"Maybe when we're no longer at this location. Even with the link and scrambler, I'm not contacting them from here and potentially confirming my location. They have access to the same technology I do."

"Which brings me back to the whole CJ thing. You're feeling that certain the group she's with is not behind this in any way?"

He lifted his good shoulder. "I'm not certain about anything. But I can't make those puzzle pieces fit well enough together to feel good about it."

"So . . . then what?"

"Well, the way I see it, we have two things in play here. The tranq and subsequent interrogation, which I can't make fit with CJ or any other case I've worked on recently. Leaving my concerns about the ranch, as you put it, in play."

"And the other thing is CJ surfacing and requesting help."

"Right."

"Okay, so let me ask you this. If we're saying CJ isn't involved in the current concerns at work . . . how certain do you feel that they're behind the drugging?"

"Certain enough not to call in yet, if that's where you're headed with this."

"I agree that any contact should be made away from here . . . but at this point, maybe we should treat that situation as hostile. Meaning—"

"Meaning if I'm rogue, I'm rogue. They drugged me and worked me over, so why give them anything to go on, from any location."

"If you feel that strongly it came from our side, then yes."

"You think that's the direction we should be looking? Leave the CJ situation alone and focus on proving my suspicions?"

Her gaze drifted to the link in his hand, then back to his face. "Yes."

"But—"

She lifted a hand. "I know it goes against everything you stand for, to leave an agent in the field, in crisis, if there is something you can do about it. But, at the moment, you've got your own crisis to handle. And, if CJ thought finding me was going to help her case, then I'm sorry to say, she was wrong, which may force her options to change anyway. Assuming she knew, from her inside position, that I survived our little detainment, maybe she thought I'd know something—anything—because she assumes I've been on the job this whole time and making it my business to keep myself informed about anything and everything having to do with the people who damaged me and killed her. Makes sense, except it didn't go that way, and I know less than nothing about anything. Now you're cut off from any inside moves you can make, essentially in the same situation as CJ. Do you have any way to contact her?"

He shook his head. "If I did, I'd have done that by now."

"Then given your current position with regards to the agency, I don't see how you can do anything else for her. At least not until she communicates further. I'm sorry."

Her tone was sincere, but she'd carefully put herself in the role of agent now, not friend, not partner. Derek knew more than a little about compartmentalizing, and approved of the skill, but that didn't keep it from bothering him a little, anyway.

"If she contacts you again, gives you more to work with, maybe then you can find a way in to help, call in a favor, whatever, but only as it doesn't compromise you."

"I'm not putting my safety before hers, I'm—"

"I'm aware of that, I'm not saying that. I'm saying that if you compromise yourself further, trying to help her . . . you're the only one who suspects what you do about your team, Derek. If you're gone, no one takes up that battle, that mission."

"You know."

"Yes, now I do. But I have no standing, no way in. And all I know is your suspicions. I'd have nowhere to go with that. So you have to be careful in what you do, because you staying in the game has more far-reaching potential than you being out."

"I understand that, but that doesn't mean I can't also try and find a way to help CJ. I can't just walk away from that."

"At this point, what choice do you have? I'm not saying I like it, but until she communicates, you're stuck. And even then, once you tell her your situation, inform her you've contacted me and I can't help, either, then it all might go in a different direction anyway, leaving you to focus on this. Which isn't going to just lie around dormant like before when you were just discreetly digging. Now you are, for all intents and purposes, AWOL. So, someone is noticing, someone is going to care at some point and ask questions. And if the attack did come from within, then they're going to have to figure out how they want to play this."

"To their advantage, which, without me being there to refute it, won't be difficult. But, even if we remove the CJ situation from the table, I'm not ready to just stride back into the office and improvise. I may not have a base of equipment to work with out here, but I have far more autonomy than I would there, and here, I'm out of direct reach, anyway. But you're right, we do need to leave this location, at least make it a challenge to get their hands on me again. Although, they have everything they need to get rid of me legitimately now, so I don't see why they'd continue the hunt. They don't know about CJ, so they don't know that I'm working a case. They'll be planning any one of a hundred ways to can my ass if I show up, and if I don't, then they've got me for desertion. If I didn't give them anything while drugged, I'm of no further use to them, and already signed my walking papers with the stunt I'm pulling now."

"So you think they just packed up and went home?"

"I'm not sure what level of concern they're showing for my continued existence, and we won't take any chances there, but I don't think, as it stands right now, that I'm in imminent danger, at least not until I actually do something. Even if they connect me to this house, and eventually to you, you're inactive and no amount of digging will show any different, so I don't know what red flag that would raise, other than me hanging out, even hiding out, with a former team member."

She took all that in and was silent for a few moments. "Are you planning on leaving the country? Would you go overseas, to London, or wherever, and try and get to CJ? If you try to leave, they'd know." She looked at him. "And don't get any funny ideas about me going over there for you. I know they're not tracking me, but I couldn't go even if I wanted to."

He understood why he couldn't leave. His passport, and all alias passports, were still government special-issue; it would be like sending up a huge beacon if he went through customs anywhere, using any of them. If anyone was looking. "Why can't you?"

"I had to surrender my passport when I left the agency, and I've never applied for one as a regular citizen. I wasn't planning on leaving here in a very long time, if ever. I've seen enough of the world."

"I have ways to circumvent—"

"Given the current international climate, do you want to call in those kinds of favors at this point? Your problem seems domestic to me, not foreign. Leaving the country is only going to be necessary if you plan on following up with CJ and we've already discussed that." She broke off, narrowed her gaze on him. "You aren't still planning to do that, are you? That's crazy."

"If they're looking for me here, it would help if I wasn't here. At least until I figure out what the hell is going on and who, specifically, is behind all this. So, if while doing so, I can be tracking down CJ, it kills two birds."

She gave him a quelling look.

"Sorry, bad choice of words there, but a valid point. If I get you out of the country with me, even if it's to stash you somewhere safe while I do what I have to do, it might not be a bad idea. And if we figure out what it is CJ thinks you know, then you'd be there to give me whatever intel you could. I wouldn't involve you directly unless absolutely necessary."

Her quelling look darkened. "I'm not flying over there, Derek. Not even for CJ."

"I've unfortunately made you a target here, so sticking around until we figure out who's involved might not be an option—"

"Well, that is an option, just not one I'm foolish enough to choose, despite the very real desire to take that risk and cross the bridge of what happens next when it happens. I've seen too much of what can happen next, so sitting here like a duck in water, not a great plan. But if you think I'm hopping a plane to the Middle East—"

"How would you feel about working independently?"

She frowned. "Independently how?"

"Well, what if I can find a way to get myself overseas, risk using other connections, and pursue the situation with CJ? I won't have the agency behind me, but I do have a career's worth of contacts. I can maneuver well enough. Better than sitting here doing nothing anyway. And it puts me off the radar. Given that Northam is essentially handling my current assignments and given the fact that when I disappeared, it was into the wilds of Virginia, I'm not thinking they're going to be looking for me overseas."

"You still don't know for sure what you revealed to them while you were under the influence."

"No, but the fact that they haven't done anything since is a clue that they didn't get enough, if anything, from me to do anything to or with me. Killing me, especially here, an ocean away from where it could be covered up as a job-related casualty, would create more problems than just leaving me be and watching me."

"Which, if they still are—"

"Is why we need to get out of here, already agreed."

"And what do they think you're going to do about being drugged and beaten? Assume that it was just some kind of unfortunate mugging in the wilderness?"

"I have no idea what conclusions they think I'll draw, but I think the fact that I haven't checked back in, and they haven't tried to make any contact with me, is ample enough proof to show that we all know I'm not a happy little agent, playing by their new rulebook."

She let that process, then said, "So, you head overseas,

throw them off your trail, give you time to search for CJ . . . leaving me here as what? Bait?"

"No. We'll both disappear. If we know we have to, we can do it in a way to make sure no one can track us."

"So you leave and draw them away from me—"

"No, that would still leave you as bait. When I don't pop up for an extended time, whoever came after me could easily come knocking here and ask the same questions of you they asked of me, and they may or may not be as gentle about it as they were with me."

"I realize that. I was going to say, you leave, draw them away from me, then I disappear, too . . . won't that just make them redouble their efforts?"

"Possibly. Only this time they'll have to work to find either one of us, and they'll have to split up whatever resources they have, diluting both. So . . . good luck with that, on their part."

She sighed and shoveled a hand through her hair. "Okay, okay, so you go chasing after CJ, and I what? Hide? I'm not interested in that."

"Good. Because while I'm gone, you can track the mystery here. No one will be expecting that, no one will be looking at you to be looking right back at them—"

"They'll suspect something when I'm not here any longer, assuming if they tracked you this far, they'd be keeping an eye on me, too."

"We'll leave together, then split up. They won't know where either one of us is. I can't believe that, without knowing where I am, they'd ever suspect or even consider you're tracking them. How could they? They'll be too busy trying to figure out where we went together. Splitting up will throw them off. And even if they figure out I'm alone, they won't know where in the hell you are, and I doubt they'd assume that you are coming after them. You parted from the team with the highest of honors. They won't see you as a threat. You have no grudge with them."

"But, ostensibly you do. And if I'm with you . . . tarred by the same brush."

"I think I've unfortunately tarred you either way. I say we use what little element of surprise we might have."

She stared at her plate and slowly peeled the crust from the bread, her thoughts clearly quite far away from the meal on the table. "What am I supposed to do? I mean, I can hardly waltz into headquarters, wave hello, and pretend I'm on a friendly visit."

"You know, that might not be such a bad idea. They won't know what in the hell to make of that."

"If you're right, and they're behind your drugging, I'm going to assume they've figured out we've had contact of some kind. I show up now? Talk about red flags."

"Okay, but then so what? Let the red flags wave. What can they do to you?"

"Well, I'm looking at a pretty good example of what they can do to a person—"

"I mean right there, in headquarters. It's probably the safest place you can be."

"Except at some point I'd have to leave, and I imagine I wouldn't be leaving entirely alone."

"We could use that to our advantage as well. I can set up a communication channel with you that not even they can break. So if you stay in town, they can watch you all they want—"

"Do you really think sitting in a hotel is any safer than sitting out here?"

"Make your visit high profile enough and they won't have a choice but to keep their distance. They'll surveil you, but we can use that to our advantage."

"How?"

"You watch the watchers."

"We both know that requires a lot of accessories I don't have—"

"I do. Or I can get them."

She tilted her head slightly. "Just how far outside the lines have you been playing all these years?"

He grinned. "Far enough to get the job done, not far enough to end up on the outside permanently."

She leaned back in her chair and loosely folded her arms. "And to think I thought I knew you."

"To think. You're not the only one making some revelations here."

"Speaking of which—"

"If I'm on one continent, and you another, you won't have to worry about what revelations I'm making where you're concerned."

"True, but as silver linings go—"

He gave her a mock wounded look.

She rolled her eyes, but he could see she was fighting a smile.

"Eventually, I'd have gotten to you."

"Such confidence," she tossed back, assuming he was teasing, which wasn't entirely the case. Not that he was remotely confident about anything in regards to where he stood with her, only that if their close proximity continued, he'd have likely pushed to find out.

"It will take me a little time to set things up," he said.

"How little is little?"

"A day. Maybe two."

She nodded. "Do we stay here while you do that?"

"I think it's best we don't."

She didn't question his ideas on that, but instead asked, "How are you planning to make contact with CJ once you get over there?"

"I'm going to start in London, check out the building where the picture was taken. Call in some favors, get as much current intel as I can, on the group she's with, the specific players, fill in the gaps I wasn't able to fill in here before I headed out to find you. I won't have to be discreet once I'm over there, as no one here knows I'm looking there. I only have to worry about being discreet from her side, which is what I do for a living. So

I'll call in favors, do what I can, and pray like hell I can either get word to her that I'm there, or she finds a way to contact me again."

"A definite maybe of a plan."

"You have any better ideas?"

"Specifically? No. But maybe it wouldn't hurt to run your intel contacts by me. You probably have better connections than I do, having been gone as long as I have, but you never know, there might be someone I know who could help, if they're still in play."

He studied her face, but it seemed like a straightforward offer. Since she'd handed back the link, since she'd looked at CJ, it seemed she'd found her balance a bit more, had shifted more smoothly into agent mode than she had thus far. He wished he felt better about that. "I'd appreciate anything you can give me."

"Most of my contacts over there were CJ's as well, since we ran most of our missions in tandem. Who knows, maybe one of them would know something about her still being there."

"It's another thread to pull."

"What plan do you have in mind for me? Am I to concoct some kind of cover story for why I'm suddenly showing up? What's my angle?"

"Maybe you want to return. As I said, it's not at all unlikely for an agent to want back in. It would be plausible for anyone who's not connected to whatever is going on. Those who are can hardly do anything while you're sitting there, chatting everyone up and talking a good game. You'll just have to be on the ball when you're not in the building, keep a very high, very public profile. Find a way to be there as much as possible, see what you can put together."

"And if they do know about CJ's communiqué with you? Won't that seem odd, me showing up suddenly, her former partner?"

"If they know about CJ, or worse, then we're already in it over our heads."

"And I'm just walking in, handing myself to them."

"Sometimes being in plain sight is the safest place. With all eyes on you, they can hardly do anything without tipping their hand and risking revealing themselves. Although . . ." He trailed off.

"What?"

"I was just thinking, in terms of covering bases and contingencies, if we're way off base, and they are somehow tied into the CJ situation, for whatever reason or angle, and they don't immediately do something about your reappearance but watch and wait to see what you do, as another lead to me, or her . . . that would still give you just as much leeway to watch and wait to see what they do. It just ups the ante."

"That would follow whether CJ is part of this on their end or not, really," she said, thinking the operation through. "Meaning, if they're after you, then once again, me suddenly showing up right after you disappear might not be looked at as a coincidence, no matter how good a story I tell them."

"Possibly. But you can still counterspy, maybe find out exactly what they do know, why they're coming after me."

"If they went so far as to play drug roulette with you, this isn't some idle concern on their part. I will be walking into the middle of things . . . and as we don't know what's going on, we don't know how high the stakes are. We know they're high enough to encompass what was done to you, which is no small thing."

"I know, but the other option is to let me get you a passport to travel with me."

She immediately shook her head. "I'll stick with the devil I don't know in this case. I know the devils over there and I'm not willing to put myself anywhere near their grasp."

"Then, okay. Plan B it is."

"Yep," she said, sounding as unenthusiastic as a person could.

Had the stakes not been so inordinately high, he might have laughed. As it was, there was very little that was amusing in any of this. "Let's eat," he suggested. "We can talk lists and contacts when we're done."

"Yippee."

He did smile then. "You know, I didn't realize how much I was capable of missing someone until now." He picked up his sandwich. "I'm going to miss you, Tate." He watched her dig into her sandwich rather than respond and ducked his chin so she wouldn't see his smile fade.

# Chapter 13

What, exactly, Tate wondered, did one pack for an espionage trip back to your former workplace? She hadn't kept much of her wardrobe when she'd moved to the cabin. Her body was different than it had been then, as were the demands being made on it, not to mention her new life came with fewer clothing requirements. "Not a single suit. Not so much as a pair of slacks or a black skirt." She looked down at the closet floor. "Of course, those hiking boots would be just the thing to set off a nice jacket/slack ensemble. And the Birkenstocks would be killer with a little black dress."

"Do you answer yourself, too?"

She didn't look over her shoulder. The last thing she needed now was to see Derek fresh from the shower, regardless of his manner—or not—of dress. "No, that would be crazy talk, then."

He chuckled, which oddly made her both sad and angry. And she was about as tired of the mood swings as she was of the pep talks she had to give herself to get out of them. When had she become such an irritating whinypants? No, she didn't want to leave her home. Yes, she knew she had to. No, she didn't want to care about Derek as anything more than the conduit to her getting her life and, along with it, her blessed peace and quiet back. And solitude. Solitude would be great. Because she was great out here by herself.

And yes, the longer he hung around in the private little

sanctuary she'd built for herself, the harder it was going to be to convince herself of that after he was gone.

*I'm going to miss you, Tate.*

Probably a good thing she was going too, then. Maybe by the time she returned, she'd be so thankful to be home again, there wouldn't be any lingering ghosts-of-Derek-past. And she refused to even consider that she wouldn't be returning home. Triumphant. Whatever that was going to play out to be.

"Let me guess," he said, closer behind her now. "You don't have a thing to wear."

She tried not to be obviously stiff or overly still, but she couldn't seem to be relaxed. Not with him so close. Not with everything she had to deal with today looming ahead, still to be confronted. "Sadly, I am the reason the cliché exists." She gestured toward the interior of her closet. "Not exactly the wardrobe for an international woman of mystery."

"Just be sexy, baby. *Rowr.*"

Eyebrows climbing toward her hairline, she turned to face him, an incredulous look on her face. "Okay, now I'm the one hallucinating. Because you did not just do an impression of Austin Powers. An incredibly bad one, I might add."

He lifted his good shoulder and smiled so disarmingly, she had to remind herself his body was actually a trained lethal weapon, not just lethal to a woman's libido.

"International man of mystery, that's me," he said. "And I'm not certain, but I think 'bad impression of Austin Powers' is a double negative. Or redundant. Or simply impossible to gauge, really. What scale would you use?"

He was being . . . playful. And did so quite well. As if it came naturally to him. Or . . . or something. When she'd have sworn, if anyone had ever thought to ask, that her former boss didn't know the meaning of the word, much less how to execute it. She knew she was still staring, but it was beyond her to adapt her expression to something more socially acceptable. "How do you even know that movie?"

"How could I not?"

"I—don't know," she said, stuttering when a smile—a very amused smile—spread across his face. How was it she was suddenly the socially awkward one? "You don't strike me as a man who keeps up with pop culture, that's all."

His mock wounded look was downright adorable. Equally disarming was the way he put his pinky up to his mouth. "It's all part of my evil plan to someday rule the world."

Seriously, she really needed him to be somewhere else in this cabin. Now.

He dropped his hand, and, mercifully, the horrible Dr. Evil accent. "I fly a lot. They show movies. It seeps in. Name a Jim Carrey movie and I can probably quote—"

She lifted a hand, palm out. "Stop now."

Now he cocked a brow. "Tate Winslow, a movie snob?" He lowered her hand by covering it with his good one.

Great, they'd moved from banter to actual touching. And she wasn't a movie snob, far from it. She'd let him believe it, though, if it meant he'd stop being so damn cute and charming. He wasn't a cute and charming kind of guy, and she was already feeling . . . distracted by him. Add in cute and charming to—to whatever the hell it was he was making her feel, and she didn't really stand much of a chance on that whole no-ghosts-of-Derek-past thing.

She needed to pack, dammit. She needed to find something, anything, that would magically restore her to agent mode. This . . . this bantering and touching and being all nothing-like-she-expected, was not helping matters. At all. "I picked you for a news junkie, maybe some sports, probably something eclectic, like rugby or . . . or cricket. But sitcoms, comedies, mindless entertainment—"

"Are oftentimes the things that keep a guy sane when he has to run around the globe doing what I do—what we did—seeing what we saw, fixing what we knew would never really be fixed." He curled his fingers over hers and lowered their hands as he stepped a little closer. "Hasn't anyone ever told you? Laughter truly is the best medicine in the world."

Laughter. And Derek Cole. Mutually exclusive concepts that, even after personally witnessing him being momentarily charming and endearing, simply didn't compute in her brain. And that *he* was telling *her* how to lighten up? The world—her world—had officially jumped off its axis.

On top of that, he was so close now, her breathing was affected. Her brain wasn't moving fast enough this morning to handle what it had to handle, today of all days, leaving her cabin and all—much less this. "Agreed. About the laughter. I just never thought of you as—well, that. You know?" And she was officially babbling.

"As what? Having a sense of humor? Enjoying a good laugh?" He seemed so surprised, and it wasn't a put-on this time. She frowned, confused. He had to be more self-aware than that. "I can't be blamed for thinking something wasn't there when I never once saw it on display."

"That's because we worked together." He said it so matter-of-factly, like, of course he wouldn't dream of doing something like laugh while working. If he didn't look so positively consternated, she'd have smiled.

"I hate to be the one to break it to you, but co-workers enjoy a good laugh with one another all the time. Even while working. Helps deflect all those things you just listed. CJ and I spent many a long night on surveillance—"

"I was careful with how I ran my team, we had important business to conduct," he said, as if explaining it to himself as well as her. "I couldn't risk not—"

"Being seen as a complete and total badass, at all times?"

Now he looked a bit wounded again, but sincerely this time, despite the fact that she'd delivered the statement in fairly dry tones.

"Total badass, huh?"

"In a good way," she added, for which she received his trademark quelling look. "Like that," she said, maybe enjoying a little amused smile herself now when the quelling look deepened to something scowl-like. "And that."

He was really perplexed by this, she thought. And that, along with his earlier little routine, grounded him in a way that made her look at him in a whole new light. And that was despite already knowing what a patriotic, devoted humanitarian he truly was, despite the total badass exterior.

"We all had great respect for you, you know, mostly because you were the baddest badass of us all." She did smile more fully now. "We all wanted to be you when we grew up."

When he rolled his eyes and went to move away, surprisingly she was the one who closed her other hand over their still joined ones, keeping him there, keeping him close. "I was complimenting you."

"I didn't joke around."

"No, you didn't. But we didn't hold it against you. Mostly because it never occurred to us that you would. Hard to miss what you never had, you know?"

"I mean, I didn't joke around with anyone. You're right, about not knowing. How could you? It was never my intent to be anything other than professional. You had each other, I guess, your peers, to let your hair down with."

Understanding dawned. "Not you, though."

"I never really thought about it, never missed it. It didn't matter to me where I was when I laughed, or what I was watching, or that I was alone while doing it. That's simply how it was. I'd long since accepted that as part of the overall equation."

"So why does it bug you now?"

"I don't know," he said, sounding truly mystified. "It shouldn't, really, I guess. I mean, it's kind of silly."

"What, wanting to share a laugh with someone?"

"No. Not that I wouldn't enjoy that, but I don't regret how I've spent my time, lived my life."

"So . . . what is it?"

He looked at her. "I never thought about it, but it's kind of strange, realizing that there isn't a single other person who knows who you really are. Or all of who you are, I guess."

"You mean a guy who is a badass by day, and a closet Mike Myers impersonator by night?"

"Something like that. Although I believe you said baddest of the badasses." He smiled a little then, and it was the self-deprecating nature of it that had her heart tilting a bit.

Which was entirely more alarming than anything else that had happened up to that point. It was bad enough he'd infiltrated her home and her head, riled up some dormant hormones. But her heart was off limits.

"Which . . . is somewhat hypocritical, I guess," he said, "if I truly have no regrets for the solitary nature of the job."

"Which you don't."

He shook his head. "None."

She slipped her hands from his. "Well," she said, trying for matter-of-fact, probably missing by a mile. "Look at it this way, now someone knows at least some of your secret self. You can sleep more easily." She started to turn back to the closet, but he surprised her by tugging her back around and cupping his palm to her cheek. There was a tenderness to the gesture that made it far more intimate than simply the default intimacy implied by such a personal action.

"You might know a little more, but even you don't know me, Tate."

"No," she said, her voice suddenly gone all tight and, well, needy, maybe, a little bit. But she could hardly be faulted for that when he was looking at her like he was. All intense and complex and multifaceted. He was damn good at his job, which required him to be all of those things, in spades, only now he was utilizing them in an entirely different way, and focusing them entirely on her. And . . . he was just as damn good at it, as it turned out. Her wildly leaping pulse was testament to that. "But I know what I need to know."

There was a flicker then, in his eyes, which she might have missed had she not been standing so close, looking so deeply where she couldn't not look. Resignation? Hurt? She couldn't be sure. All she knew was that a moment later, there was nothing to see at all.

He dropped his hand away, his expression flat, all newly-revealed depths completely hidden from view. To look at him now, she'd be hard-pressed not to think she'd just hallucinated that entire interaction.

"True," he said, his tone the distant, impersonal one she'd so badly wanted for herself earlier. Which kind of pissed her off a little, the ease with which he could shift gears.

"Best we stick with that," he said. "Go with our strengths."

Thankfully, before she could do something even more foolish, like asking him to elaborate on what, precisely, he thought those were, and suggesting that perhaps she could add a few items to that list, given the past ten minutes, he grabbed the walking stick he'd left leaning against the dresser and moved away. "Let me know when you're ready," he said, and left the room.

She turned back to the closet, but didn't see a damn thing in it. "Where you're concerned, Derek Cole, I don't think I'm ever going to be ready."

Suddenly, leaving the cabin didn't sound quite as terrifying as it had before. Staying, with him here, was fraught with a whole set of different dangers she hadn't anticipated. And though she was beginning to wonder if she'd lost too much of her edge over the past three years to reenter that world on any level, even as a visitor, at least she'd had training. So, it stood to reason that the knowledge, the skills, were all there somewhere, waiting to be tapped again. What had just happened with Derek? She had no prep, no training, absolutely nothing to fall back on there. Her job, she understood. Sex, she'd figured out. Working friendships, she'd made. Social skills, she'd cultivated.

However, along with escaping death on more than one occasion, she'd also managed to avoid ever being in . . . well, love. Not that she loved Derek. But, along with love, she'd avoided being in all the stages leading up to falling into it.

Lust, she was okay with. Gentle affection wasn't a totally alien concept. But that's where it ended.

She missed CJ. Every day, in some way, she missed her former partner, and, yes, friend. CJ had been the one person in her life she'd truly grown close to, bonded with, shared her real self with, as Derek had so eloquently and compellingly characterized it. CJ had been sister, co-worker, and friend. The only real family she'd had. So Tate knew she was capable of that kind of connection, that kind of love, if you wanted to characterize it as that. Just as she understood, quite personally, the depths of grief that balanced it.

So . . . she didn't want to ever miss anyone else. Not like that.

She massaged the place over her heart, as if that would fix the weird discomfort she was feeling there now. When she realized what she was doing, she stopped immediately and just started yanking clothes out of her closet and throwing them in the chair behind her.

The faster she could get out of here, the faster she could get her head out of whatever the hell place it had gone to, and start focusing outwardly instead of inwardly. Apparently all the navel-gazing she'd been indulging herself in for the past three years had done more than make her soft. It had made her an idiot.

Because only an idiot would waste even a second of time wondering what it would be like, what life could be like, with someone else.

A shared life. On all levels. Willingly, and with anticipation. It wasn't a concept she'd actively avoided thinking about, she simply hadn't. Not for herself anyway. Given the path she'd chosen, it wasn't her destiny. Of course, until three years ago she'd thought she'd be active in her chosen field until they forced her to retire at some decrepit old age, where she'd . . . hell, she'd never even thought it out that far.

Not that it mattered now, as it hadn't worked out that way.

She'd spent the past three years just quietly thrilled to be alive, living any life.

Now . . . now she was being dragged back. And by the very man she'd—delusionally—contemplated being any part of her new life. Yeah. Idiot didn't begin to cover it.

She knelt down to drag her one and only suitcase out from under the bed. It was one she'd bought—or bribed one of her rehab trainers to buy—on impulse before leaving the center for good. It was flowery, with a lot of pink. Two things she was most definitely not. Or hadn't been, anyway. But when she'd left she'd had no idea who she was, or what she'd become, so it seemed only right to start the journey with a different viewpoint all together. Try something new on for size, see how it felt, operate from there.

She looked at the flowered bag and smiled, thinking she didn't want to know what it said about her, three years later, that she thought it suited her perfectly. But more because it was just so truly out there, than because she was any more pink and flowery now than she'd ever been before. She wondered what Derek would think of it. A far cry from the somber and oh-so-serious government-issue luggage and totes they lugged around the globe.

"Oh for Christ sake." With a disgusted snort, she hauled herself upright and flipped the bag onto the bed. *What would Derek think*, she silently mimicked, making faces at her complete ridiculousness.

Seriously. Maybe it would do her good to get a dose of the outside world, of reality, even harsh reality. Because, clearly, living in a cabin in the woods in the middle of nowhere had demented her.

For a long time after she'd come back to the States, then come here, she'd found herself wondering what CJ would think of this, or say about that. It was only natural, as they'd been each other's sounding board for everything. But to find herself instinctively wondering the same thing about Derek was just another piece of proof she didn't need telling her it was a good thing they'd be putting some distance between them, and soon.

"Tate. In the kitchen."

She startled at the sound of her boss's voice. Because that's exactly what that had just been. Complete with badass command. But before she could decide how, or even whether, to comply, he added the one thing sure to guarantee she'd do as ordered.

"Communiqué. Coming in."

*CJ.*

She found him seated at the kitchen table, satlink cradled in his hand. "Dammit!"

"What?" she asked, unsure if it was alright to look over his shoulder, then deciding she'd do whatever the hell she wanted to. After all, she didn't work for him any longer, and she sure as hell didn't owe him anything at the moment. She moved behind him, but the screen flashed off.

"We're out in the middle of goddamn nowhere, with nothing between here and the heavens above, and I can't maintain a decent satellite signal to get one goddamn transmission."

"It's probably the mountain ranges, they screw up satellite dish reception and—"

"Wait—" The screen flickered back to life.

"Here," she said. "Come in here, by the front window."

"Take it," he ordered. "I can't move fast enough. I'll catch up to you."

"I don't know the scrambling code."

"Sure you do, it's the same one I taught you, the both of you."

"Right, right." Her brain was scrambled, that was the problem. She took the link like it was a fragile newborn and trotted into the living area, up to the window. "I'd go outside, but—"

"Stay to the left, if you can," he said as he moved more slowly behind her. "I don't know what—"

But she'd already complied, keeping as close to the window as possible without being in direct sight. "It's flashing, the screen. What does that mean?"

"It means the signal is still weak. Who knows, it might not be this location that's the problem. It could be any number of things." He reached her side, and leaning heavily on the walking stick, looked over her shoulder rather than take the satlink back from her.

There was so much adrenaline pumping through her, it brought back so much, so many sensations, feelings, from her past life, when she'd existed more often than not in that constantly charged element. Mostly, now, it made her want to be sick. "Still not getting anything. Do you want me to try going outside?" She glanced back at him. "We're leaving anyway, so—"

"Okay, go—wait, wait. Look, there it is."

She looked back to the screen, which was a solid white haze now. Then something flickered, and an image came on the screen. "I thought it was coming in as code," she said at the same time he murmured, "What the hell?"

"You said she sent a digital image last time—"

"Encrypted into digital code, yes. It was just a string. I— holy shit, what does she think she's doing?"

And there, in her hands, in her own hands, CJ, her dead partner, flickered back to life. Living, breathing, full Technicolor life. It was hard to make out details on the tiny screen, but there was no mistaking the black-as-midnight hair, the tall frame, the expressive hand gestures as she spoke.

"Sorry," came a garbled voice.

"Oh," Tate gasped, clutching the unit more tightly. Hearing was even more daunting than seeing. Her heart squeezed so painfully inside her chest, she thought she might not be able to stand up to it.

"No time—code," CJ continued, though it was very, very hard to understand. There was no static, but there were gaps in the relay, lag in both the motion on the screen and therefore the verbal transmission.

"Couldn't tell you," she said, then there was a gap. "—had no choice."

"Tell me what?" Derek's breath was warm on the side of

her neck, but for once, she was barely even aware of his presence. "Come on, CJ."

"Not underco—" Then there was a gap. "—them. I'm work—" Another gap. "Us."

"What are you telling us, CJ?" This time it was Tate whispering.

"You—" Gap. "—in their sights. Get out. Don't—" More lag. "—Tate. Trust no—" Gap. "Life—death. Yours."

And then the transmission blinked out for good.

# Chapter 14

Derek shoved the walking stick at Tate and took the link from her, but nothing more came through. "Damn it to hell!" He trudged with frustrating slowness over to the chair beside the couch, his ribs protesting every step with the sling pressing against them, and no cane to balance his weight out.

"Here," Tate said, offering him the walking stick.

"Pain isn't such a bad thing at the moment," he said, levering himself down into the chair with a short string of rapid profanities.

Tate sat at the end of the couch, angled to face him. Her brain was a swirl, and the emotions rocking her even more tempestuous, but she struggled to rally them, corral them, stay focused on the matter at hand. "What's your take? I could barely make out what she was saying."

"Why in the hell did she risk an open transmission? I can scramble code, but I wasn't set up to scramble voice and video. She had to know that."

"Maybe she had no choice. She was clearly warning you, but of what?"

Derek looked at her. "She mentioned you, as well."

"I know. I heard. Is the information saved to the device? Can we view it again?"

"There is an auto-save to the memory card, but I don't have the tools here to play with it and see what else we can extract."

She got up and went into the kitchen and came back with a zippered laptop bag. "I know we were avoiding leaving any trail behind here, but I think we're well past that." She propped the bag on the coffee table and slid her notebook computer out. "Do you have an adapter for the card? If not, I have a multi-function—"

"In my gear bag."

She noted he'd already put what little stuff he had by the front door, so she went and got the black tote and handed it to him. "Not sure what we'll be able to do on my machine, but probably more than we can do on your link device."

"Let's move this to the kitchen table."

She pushed the walking stick at him. "I'll carry."

He didn't argue this time. He'd been pushing well past where he should be the past few days. Too much more and he'd be going backward instead of forward with getting healthy again.

She set the laptop and link on the table, then grabbed a few water bottles from the fridge while he lowered himself into the kitchen chair. He reached for the laptop the same time as she did.

"Wait," she said quickly, but he'd already popped the lid up.

A page full of text appeared. "What—"

She tugged the laptop around, but not before he'd had the chance to note that some of the text was partly formatted dialogue.

"What program do you think would work best?" she asked, making a few quick clicks on the keyboard. No doubt saving whatever file was on screen. "I have Internet access as well."

Derek knew he had no time for further distractions, but that didn't seem to stop him from asking, "What was that?"

"Like we said earlier, we don't really know each other outside of work."

"No, I guess we don't."

She turned the laptop back to him, but scooted her chair around next to him, angling the screen so they could both see.

"I'm willing to do the manual labor if it's easier, given I have two working hands. Just guide me on what to do."

He turned just enough to look directly at her, but she didn't meet his gaze. "Tate."

She glanced up then. "It's nothing to do with this, which is where we need to focus right now."

She was absolutely right, and still he didn't want to let it go. "For the record, the interest is sincere, not because it might have been work related."

"Appreciated. Now, let's look at the transmission again."

Derek sighed. Whatever CJ was trying to tell him wasn't good news. And he was suddenly exceedingly weary of always dealing with bad news. He wasted a precious extra second visualizing just chucking it all and moving to some remote island, where he'd soak up the sun, flirt with island girls, maybe run a little bar with old reruns playing on the television. He'd educate the locals on the scholarly merits of *Seinfeld* and *M\*A\*S\*H*. There would be full-fledged debates over which of *Charlie's Angels* was the hottest.

"Derek?"

He looked at her. "I always thought it was Jaclyn Smith, but I'm really starting to rethink the relative virtues of Kate Jackson. She was smart, beautiful, good at her job, and a wiseass. Never underestimate the wiseass."

"What in the hell are you talking about?"

"Nothing," he said, then turned back to the screen. He slipped the tiny disk out of the link device and slid it into a card converter. "Will your machine take this?"

She took the now marginally larger card from him, still smaller than an inch square and thinner than a wafer, and slid it into the corresponding slot on the side of her laptop. "I've only had this notebook for a few months, so it's relatively up-to-date. In a general, civilian way, anyway."

So many things he had a burning desire to know about her. Why did it seem such a shame to him now that, in order to do his job as effectively as possible, he'd thoroughly cut himself off in any meaningful way from those he'd spent the most time with? He hadn't been lying when he said he had no regrets about how he'd handled his job or the restrictions it imposed on his life. But, going forward . . . now he had questions.

He glanced at Tate.

About a lot of things.

He used his good hand to manipulate the touch pad and open the saved file. First he opened the photo CJ had sent during their initial communication.

He heard Tate's indrawn breath. "Definitely her. It's so surreal, Derek. I mean, I heard her voice, watched her move her hands when she talked, in that way only she did. And it's still almost impossible to believe, truly, that she's really alive."

"I know." He tapped the screen. "This is the building. Mean anything to you?"

She shook her head. "We didn't spend too much time in London, not together, anyway. I don't even recognize it."

"It's new construction. Still nothing on the name?"

"Harrison-Gambault you said, right? No. I looked it up—" She shot him a don't-even-say-it look. "Nothing, no connections I could find to anything we worked on, or with. It was my decision, Derek," she said by way of defending her actions. "I'm already harboring a fugitive agent. A little computer search-engine research was hardly going to compromise me further. Especially as it didn't bring anything to light."

He turned back to the computer screen and tapped open the other file. It brought up a small video play screen. A second later, CJ wavered once again to life, only this time complete with voice and video.

They listened to it several times, as originally transmitted, but there was little to take from it, other than she was clearly warning him, concerned he was in a deadly situation. And somehow she was involving Tate in her directives, but there wasn't enough there to figure out what she was exactly directing him to do about her.

"Help me, Obi-Wan Kenobi," Derek muttered.

"What?" Tate said, still distracted with the video.

"It's like when Leia sends the transmission via R2D2, only more frustrating."

"If you say so."

He turned to look at her, until she had to look up. "What?"

"Seriously? You've never seen *Star Wars*? Any of them? Ever?"

"Through osmosis, I know the basics, but no, not really my thing." When he just kept looking at her, incredulous, she added, "So I'm not into my entertainment centering around suspense or espionage, in any century. It seemed sort of a busman's holiday, you know?"

"But it was cinematic history, sort of like with *Jurassic Park* and dinosaurs." At her clearly flat expression, he simply shook his head. "You're so deprived. I never knew."

"Some people read books on planes," was all she said. "Now, about the—"

"What did you read, then? Let me guess, the classics."

"Dreary stories written by dead white guys? Hardly. Now really, this is no time to—"

"Then just answer the question. If you don't like the classics, and steer clear of suspense, espionage, spy books, science fiction, and, I'm guessing, by association, mystery, then what was Tate Winslow, super-agent's book genre of choice?"

"Seriously," she said, giving him the dead stare. "It's not like we don't have our own suspense-action-espionage moment going on right here, live and in color."

Then it hit him, and he smiled. Hunh, he thought, and leaned forward to tap on the touch pad. "You're right, we should—"

She slapped her hand over his. "What's with the oh-so-amused smile?" she wanted to know.

"What?" He was all innocence now. "I'm agreeing with you, we should focus." He lifted his fingers a little, rubbed them against hers. "I can't help it, you distract me sometimes. I find myself endlessly curious about you."

She snatched her hand away. "You're right, time to focus."

He chuckled and dragged the cursor back over the video screen gauges. "Focusing."

"Here, move," Tate said, suddenly all business as she manually backed up the video. "Right here, listen. Where she says 'trust no—' then breaks off?" She looked at Derek. "I assume she was saying to trust no one."

"Most likely." He moved the cursor back even further. "It's this part that I want to figure out." He replayed the segment where she said something about being undercover.

"Sounds like she's saying she's not undercover for someone, but the next word we hear is 'them.' Then the word 'working' then 'us.' We could take the linear translation, but—" Tate broke off, looked to Derek, confusion clouding her eyes. "Do you think she was trying to tell you that she's not working undercover for the group we infiltrated . . . but undercover for our side, on our side? How is that possible? Did she think you suspected she might have flipped to the other team and wanted you to understand she was still undercover for us?"

Derek didn't answer right away. Instead he turned up the sound and listened to that section again. And again. He smacked the table, making Tate jump. "I need my equipment. I could slow it down, clarify the words she does say, maybe pull something from the lag time, if there is even the tiniest bit of data being transmitted."

"It's got to be something else, something we didn't hear."

"You could have hit on it. If she thinks I think she's flipped, which would play given she contacted me outside of mandated channels, then she might be sitting there, worried about how I'm planning to extract her. So she risks coming back on, to make sure I know she's still on our side, not a double agent."

"Which plays," Tate continued, "except for that last part where she's clearly warning you. If she was just trying to save herself, or clarify her position, the one in danger is her, not you. Unless she's afraid her people know she's contacted you." She sat up straighter, started talking faster. "That part about having you in their sights. Maybe it's her side that's coming after you, and, by connection, me, if you'd contacted me. Maybe she was warning you not to contact me, now that she's been compromised, only she couldn't know it's too late for that. If she was needing you to extract her, then this all plays. Something had already gone wrong for her to contact you, she does, that gets found out, and she's trying to warn you." Then she gasped and looked directly at Derek. "The part, specifically, about being in their sights . . . maybe a reference to being hunted? Maybe they were the ones responsible for the attack after all."

Derek took in her rapid-fire rationale. It all made sense.

"Maybe home base isn't connected, which means, if you do some swift and serious damage control regarding your extended absence, maybe you could get back and have greater access to work on this. Now, with this transmission, you have enough to show someone on your team. I mean, it's enough they can't risk doing something stupid with it."

Derek just looked at her.

"You know what I mean. They can't bury it. You'd have to be leader on the mission, given your background and that you're who she's contacting. You could control how it's run."

"You trying to get rid of me?"

"I'm trying to figure this out. This is the most that any of this has made sense yet." She sat back in her seat. "Finally, a break."

When Derek didn't immediately agree, she turned to him. "What? What's holding you back? You have to admit this all fits. It's the best linear explanation we've got."

"I know, I know. But—"

"But what?"

"It's not it. I can't give you proof why, but I'm not feeling it's the right path, in my gut."

"So don't go back then, if you're still worried about what's going on at home. Go overseas, deal with CJ, find out for sure what's what. You come back with a dead agent, suddenly alive and well, and I'm sure amidst all the shock and awe, you can find some way to use that as your excuse for your continued radio silence with home base."

"I don't know. You're right, it plays . . . except it doesn't. I just don't think the guys who worked me over are CJ's. And I'm not entirely certain she was warning me that her team had found her out. It doesn't sound completely . . ." He rubbed a hand over his face. "I'm going to want to go over this before I decide, make sure we're on the right track with the warning she was delivering."

"What's the alternative? That my first conclusion was right? That your own people did it? Because, how could that be? That's crazy. I just misinterpreted. The other way makes more sense. If she was warning you that she was working undercover for us, spying on our own people, us . . . how is that possible? Especially without anyone figuring out who she is? Because, if she's undercover in her own branch—our branch—first off, she hasn't changed her appearance in any noticeable way. Her hair is longer, her face thinner, but no one who knew her, or had ever worked with her, would mistake that as being her."

"Except she's dead, so they wouldn't be looking."

"Which is fine, except if she's currently still operating, then anyone with intel on her, a photo, anything, would run it and figure out that somehow that isn't the case."

"I found absolutely nothing on her in the digging I did. If she's been in the game the past three years, she's either been so deep undercover, somewhere we don't have a presence, that no one knows she's back—which I presumed was the case after her first transmission—or she changed her appearance while under."

Tate sat silently for a moment. "Okay, I'm trying to stay open to all possibilities here. So, she apologizes, in the beginning. Says she couldn't tell you. About what? Then we get garbled stuff about not being undercover, only clearly she has been if she hasn't popped on any radar in three years. She didn't retire. So, stands to reason she's apologizing for not being undercover for whoever she initially said she was, or implied she was. Only . . ."

Derek turned away from the screen, looked at Tate. "Only . . . ?"

"I heard it, Derek. Then I saw her. Bullet hole, right here." She tapped her forehead. "I don't care how messed up I was at the time. I know what I saw. What they made sure I saw." She stared at the screen, at the frozen picture of CJ. "The other picture of her, could you did you blow it up? Look for any signs? Any scarring?" She waved her hand. "What am I saying? If that bullet hole was real, then she really was dead."

"I did look." He lifted a shoulder when she looked at him like he was the crazy one. "Cover all bases. I wasn't there. I don't know what you saw, but I know what you think you saw. So I looked."

"And?"

"Couldn't digitally enhance it enough to know for certain, but I didn't see any sign of a scar. Doesn't mean she didn't have it covered up, but I tend to go with your train of thought. If she had a hole there, she wouldn't be standing here three years later."

"Which leads me back to the beginning. When she died, but really didn't. If that was all really some kind of elaborate scam for my benefit, which obviously it had to be, since there she stands." Tate waved a hand toward the screen. "Then it can only follow that she somehow convinced them to keep her alive, and let me think she was dead." She abruptly sat up straighter. "Which is why I wasn't killed."

"Why?"

"To get the word out, to do exactly what I did, which was to resolutely confirm that I saw her dead with my own eyes. That I saw them drag her lifeless body out of the hovel we were in. You never found the body, so I'm the only witness. And I'm no good as a witness unless I'm alive to come back and tell everyone."

"If they'd killed you both, we might have never found either body and the end result would have been the same. Us thinking you're both dead."

"True, but that would have taken more time. To declare for certain. With no body, it could have taken years, even. And there was no absolute certainty I might not have died anyway, the way I was left, but the assumption could be made that I'd reveal what I knew before I died. This way, there is no active search for either of us, no open case file, nothing to slow down whatever plans they had for using her."

Derek nodded. "That follows. So then, a little alteration here or there, even temporary, and they have someone working their side with all the skills she possesses, not to mention the knowledge of our side, and we'd never go looking, because we have proof, via you, that she died."

"Exactly."

Derek rubbed at the still tender skin at his temple. His cuts and scrapes were healing, and they itched like a son of a bitch. "Which plays to your version of this."

"Except . . ."

Derek looked at her. Now what? "Except what?"

"Except she begins this transmission apologizing, stating she didn't tell you the truth, that she couldn't. Then it sounds like she's saying she's not undercover with them, which could be her way of saying she didn't flip, but she also could be saying she wasn't working with or for them at all, undercover or not."

"Which goes back to my scenario."

"Yes, but then . . . if we go that route, and she's not working overseas for the group that captured us . . . how in the hell did she get out of that village alive three years ago?"

"Maybe she started with them, then decamped. Or escaped. She said in her coded message that it was time to get out, time to come back, but she needed help and could trust no one."

"Get out, come back . . . both suggest she's elsewhere."

"Except in this transmission, she more or less says she wasn't telling the truth last time. But about which part?"

"Okay, we've already played out my scenario, let's play out

yours. If she's working for us, as some kind of internal affairs operative, then what 'back' is she coming in from the cold from? Do we assume that was the part she wasn't being truthful about? That she couldn't reveal? Because what if you'd gone off on a wild goose chase overseas looking for her? What the hell kind of game is she playing? I mean, you can't send someone an SOS, then go, oops, psych, I really meant x, y, and z. Besides, if she's been working with us the whole time, then why can't she suddenly trust her handlers if her handlers are us?"

"I assumed in her first message that she couldn't trust anyone in her immediate circle."

"Meaning a circle filled with the people who were holding us."

"Right. After this much time, if she was undercover, they trust her, or should. The fact that she was still there—supposedly—indicates she'd gotten herself way in. And, as a female—"

Tate waved a hand. "I really don't want to think about that, or—just go on."

"She didn't speak to that," he told Tate, "and I didn't get the sense that she'd been abused or harmed in that way. More that she'd painted herself into an intel corner she couldn't get herself out of, and needed extrication."

"So why come to you?"

"I was her team leader. She knows she can trust me, above anything else."

"But she didn't follow protocol. She came to you indirectly. Which, if we apply the new way of thinking, that she was working with us the whole time, then why? Why not use her own contacts? What couldn't she trust about them?"

"And, also," Derek added, "by coming to me, outside of regular channels, she outs herself, puts herself on the map of the living. So it wasn't a choice made lightly. Had to be life or death. Either hers or someone else's, that drove her to the surface. Or, that her dying would preclude her getting the word out about whatever the hell it was she'd discovered or gotten herself into that prevented her from using her own people to extract her."

"Hence the warning that you're not safe. Because her people are your people. Which would also explain why she contacted you in the first place. She says you're the only one she can trust, now she's warning you that you can't trust anyone either. So maybe it's both. She's stuck, and—"

"She's telling me I am, too."

"Maybe that's why she suddenly surfaced. Maybe you're the 'someone else' who was put in danger. When you came into it, she drew the line. It's a tougher scenario to make fit in some ways, but the timing is all there this way, too. Her contacting you, the attack right afterward, it plays, Derek. She said she couldn't tell you at first, and I wondered about the wild goose chase, but maybe she hoped you would hop a plane and go try and find her in the Middle East. That might have been her way of getting you out of the picture here, to buy her more time to figure out whatever had gone wrong. She might not have wanted your help in getting her out of anything, but just wanted you out of the way, somewhere safe. And the only way to do that, to make you believe it was her without question, and so as not to alert her superiors, was to contact you in a way only she could have. Untraceable to anyone else."

Tate was clearly on a roll, sliding all her puzzle pieces into place, making a case—his case, but perversely, even now, Derek wasn't so quick to follow suit. Maybe it was because he was trained to look at all sides, or maybe she'd made such a convincing case for her own scenario that now he was second guessing everything. Both scenarios fit, but choosing the wrong one could ultimately get any or all of them dead. His gut told him his scenario was it, which was why he wanted to be extra cautious, extra certain, that if he went in that direction, he was doing so for all the right reasons. Because she had made a good case for her take on the situation, and that made him want to play devil's advocate for his own.

But, ultimately, he had to be sure he was right, because it was one thing to imply that CJ had gotten herself saved by making a deal with her captors, only to once again find herself unable to extricate herself. But to imply she was working for someone inside his own organization, somehow against their own organization . . . he had to be damn sure.

"You're making waves," Tate went on, relentless now with his theory, which was sounding like it might be her theory now, too. "You're not happy with what is happening to the team, or with how the agency is handling our division. You say you think they're keeping an eye on you, and that you have a bad feeling that something is going down. Something you don't understand and are not a part of, but you're not sitting back silently. Which makes you a target."

"But of *what*? *For* what?"

"I don't know. You don't know." She nodded toward the screen. "But maybe CJ does. And she's risking everything to let you know. I don't think she'd do that just to save her own skin, but to save yours?" She nodded.

They both sat back and remained silent for a few minutes. Tate was the one to speak first. "But all this supposition still doesn't explain how she got out three years ago. Why our captors went through with the sham of making me think she was dead. I don't see them being in cahoots with some kind of private agency watchdog group for our side, no matter how nefarious in nature. What would they stand to gain?"

Derek had nothing for that, either.

"And that was a year and a half before the shake-up with the team, before you started to have concerns."

Derek nodded.

"How long after Northam signed on did your instincts begin to clamor?"

"Almost immediately. But that's still a significant gap between her supposedly being shot dead, and me starting to get bad vibes."

"Something like that would take a lot of planning. Maybe getting Mankowicz out just took that long. Maybe this has been in play much longer than you know, but couldn't have started to figure out until Northam stepped in. If you're right about something bad going down, maybe it's much, much bigger than you know, bigger than our team, our agency, which is why you can't find proof. You're not looking high enough up the chain, thinking big enough."

Derek thought about that, and though the very idea was appalling to contemplate, the sickening feeling of dread that started trickling in, even as she said it, made him already know what his instincts were going to tell him. "So, we have something big going on, bigger than our little agency, and somehow CJ gets signed up for a spot on the team, which includes extricating her from what is otherwise a certain death sentence. Which would tend to make a person agree to just about anything—"

"Except she wouldn't," Tate said. "I mean, she was going to die for her principles, for what she believed was right. She'd hardly sign on to something she couldn't morally sanction, even if it was for our own side."

"Why not?"

Tate just gaped at him.

"No, I don't mean that she'd compromise her integrity. I'm saying, she's facing certain death. Then along comes someone—from her own side—offering her some kind of deal. A deal which includes a get-out-of-jail-free card. I'd take it—" He held up his hand. "Let me finish. I'd take it, because a, it keeps me alive and gets me out, and b, I'd want to know what in the hell my own country was doing, to offer me something like that."

"So . . . she agrees, but she's more or less undercover, just . . . for herself. Staying alive, and hoping to find out what in the hell is going on. Working for us—without being actually affiliated with any of us—against us, or against whatever, and whoever, bought her with a get-out-of-dying card."

They both fell silent again. Then finally Tate said, "I don't know what I'd have done. What choice I'd have made."

"Don't you?"

"I'd have been mad as hell, thinking that the country I was risking my life for was going to use me to do something against our stated mission . . . whatever the hell that was. I might have been stubborn enough to let them just go ahead and kill me instead. I don't know."

"Which might be why CJ got the tap, and not you. I'm not saying anything against CJ, clearly she's played this, or tried to, to do the right thing. Or she's trying to now. We don't know what her role has been, or what she's done, or had to do, in order to stay alive. But maybe they knew you'd be too big a wild card to trust with the opportunity."

"They'd have been right."

Derek said nothing for a few long moments, thinking over everything, trying to find the hole in the logic, the time line, something, anything. He almost wished he believed Tate's scenario now. But . . . he knew, in his gut, he knew this was the track they should follow.

"I can't really believe it. Any of it. There are so many holes, but . . ."

She knew it, too. It was in her voice. She knew.

"I'm sorry."

"What are you apologizing for now?"

"If I'd known more of this, suspected anything on this scale—"

"How could you have? It was wild enough speculation just to wonder about your own agency being somehow corrupted. And you didn't drag me into this, remember, CJ did. She told you to come find me."

"That's the one part that still doesn't play in all this. If she's on the inside of our side, she knows you're retired. She knows you're well out of the loop. Why drag you in?"

"Because I'm the only one who could verify she was dead."

"How does that factor?"

"I don't know. I haven't figured that out yet. Maybe she needs a way to prove how she got out of the village. Maybe she needs to prove the scam happened."

"She's alive, so obviously some scam was perpetrated, given what you saw."

"What only I saw." She ducked her chin, rubbed at her temples. "I don't know. That part . . . I still don't know."

"Would she pull you in, risk you, to save herself? You said you didn't think she'd do that with me. Would she with you?"

"No. I don't think so. There's got to be something there—she does warn you in this transmission not to contact me. So she changed her mind, but I don't know why. Maybe she thinks I know more than I do, about what happened in the village. I can't know what she was thinking." She swore under her breath. "It's all so damn frustrating."

"Welcome to my world for the past eighteen months."

She nodded, perhaps understanding more clearly than ever before. He wished like hell that wasn't the case, that he'd never dragged her into it, that CJ had gotten to him with the truth, or more information, before he'd come out here and risked her life like he had.

"Most frustrating is, we still don't know what in the hell is going on. What team was CJ asked to play for? What is their mission? What is this covert operation about?"

"I don't know," Tate said. "Maybe they're a division going out there to do unsanctioned work. Meaning someone is playing renegade God and deciding what we do, to whom, and where, without a chain of command telling them to."

Derek thought about that, then shook his head. "I think our agency was pretty much taking care of what we could in that area. And I don't see an entire new secret team being assembled to be what, assassins or something?"

"Nothing is impossible. But you're right. This smacks of something internal."

"Meaning what, they're in place to police us? What's to police that can't be handled directly, or through already established protocol channels?"

Tate shrugged. "I have no idea, but this seems very internal to me, not another division out there working the opposition. If this plays out, it's got to be a team made up of our players, playing against our own team."

"But for what gain?"

"I don't know."

"Yeah. I'm sick to fucking death of not knowing."

She actually smiled a little at that, but it was a rueful one. "I've only been involved for forty-eight hours and I heartily concur." Her smile faded, and it looked like she was going to say something, then she stopped.

"What? And don't say nothing. At this point, nothing gets left off the table."

"It's not about that, it's just . . . if our supposition is right, about how she got out, then that means CJ took the deal, she knew she was getting out, and—"

"—and she was leaving you to die. You don't know if she bargained for you to be involved, too."

"If she thought I was going to be signed up, then why the hoax making me think she was dead?"

"Maybe that was the bargain she made."

"Meaning what?"

"Meaning what you said earlier, about them needing you as a witness to her death. If she agreed to save herself, then maybe she got them to see that logic, forced the sham, which—"

"Which meant leaving me alive so I could tell someone about it."

"It wasn't a guarantee, but it was more than either of you had before."

"They tortured me for another two days after she supposedly died. Then left me for dead."

"We have no idea how they got in to get to her in the first place, or what their limitations or boundaries were, in terms of what they had to work with. The fact that you were found so quickly after they left—"

"By some old villager—"

"In a completely destroyed town. He was the only one brave enough to venture in."

"He was old, and starving. Maybe he felt he didn't have that much to lose. We didn't worry about it at the time. It was surprising that anyone went there so soon after the occupation ended, but it wasn't impossible."

"Which is why we never really looked at it."

"So . . . that could have been a setup."

"All I'm saying is that CJ didn't necessarily abandon you to save herself."

"Yeah," Tate said, but it didn't sound like that made her feel a lot better about the situation. Which was certainly understandable, all things considered. She looked at him. "So, what is the game plan, now?"

Derek closed the computer. "We're getting out of here. Now."

"But—"

"Change of plans. You're sticking with me. But neither of us is sticking here." He pushed his chair back. "Grab your stuff."

She didn't question him, which both surprised and pleased him. She just stood and said, "Well, there's one good thing about this."

"Which is?"

"No flowery suitcase required."

"What?"

"Long story. I'll be ready in five minutes."

He noted that she didn't leave the laptop on the table, either. Well, he thought, as he stood up and moved his aching body, a road trip would give him a chance to solve two problems. The situation with CJ and his agency . . . and his growing fascination with all things Tate.

# Chapter 15

"Turn here."

She turned down the gravel road. "This doesn't connect to anything."

"It connects to my vehicle and the rest of my gear."

"Wow," she said, more to herself than to him. "I really have been away a long time."

"Why do you say that?"

"All this time, and I never once even thought about how you got into the valley in the first place. Do you think there is any chance the guys who followed you in have already had fun with your truck?"

"They didn't find my other gear. And I didn't exactly leave my truck on the side of the road."

"Right. So . . . are we swapping out, or just picking up your stuff?"

"Your vehicle can be tracked to you."

"And yours can't? If it's our people following you, they'll know from running the plates—"

"That's not going to be a problem."

She glanced at him, but kept her attention on the bumpy, narrow road as it wound its way up into the hills, through the trees. Normally on a job, they had all kinds of latitude with overcoming obstacles that might otherwise be a nuisance. Without the support of home base, however, anything he did to hurdle obstacles now was through his own channels, using his own ingenuity.

"Then what?" she asked, deciding she'd only ask questions she really wanted the answers to.

"I don't want to be too far out from home base, and I don't want to necessarily get back to civilization. Too many people means too much to keep track of, but I want to get away from this immediate area."

"If they come looking for me and I'm gone—"

"Will any of your neighbors think it's strange that you're not around?"

"I've never been gone for any real period of time since living there, but I'm not that close to any of them that they'd be alarmed. For all they know I'm away on vacation or visiting family."

"Family you don't have."

"They don't know that. As I said, I haven't grown that close." Not that she specifically wanted it that way, but she'd spent a good chunk of her first year just working to get as much of her health and range of mobility back as she possibly could. Along with beginning her . . . other endeavors, as she still thought of it. Which had turned out to be solitary in nature, and which she discovered she was perfectly fine with.

Being left entirely alone had felt good, and healing, and restorative to both her health and her spirit. She'd always figured when the time came where it felt reclusive and lonely, she'd do something about it. So far, that hadn't happened. But she had a burgeoning new career that was so shiny and new she still couldn't quite believe it was happening, and the long distance relationships that building her new career had created, had been stimulating enough, while having the double bonus of not being in her immediate day-to-day life. The perfect balance, really.

She glanced over at Derek. Until now, anyway. Now she was thinking about other things, things that weren't so solitary, and it was messing up everything she thought she'd long ago come to terms with.

She thought about her laptop, stowed behind her seat, and what Derek had inadvertently seen earlier. Apparently she'd kept him from getting more than a glimpse, and he'd mercifully let it drop. At least the timing of this whole . . . event, wouldn't screw her up too badly on that front. But it made her consider those other thoughts she was having, and . . . well, there were no answers there, so no point in wasting precious time and energy pondering. Very likely whatever happened in the days to come would figure it out for her. Life often had a way of doing that.

"Any ideas on where we should hunker down to plot and scheme?" she asked.

"We shouldn't stay in any one spot."

She glanced at him again. "Are you saying we should live out of your vehicle?"

He smiled a little. "It's a nice vehicle."

"You're just barely on the path to mending. Traveling all cramped up isn't—"

"Pull over right there," he said, motioning with his good hand to a spot up the road to the right, where the gravel track seemed to come to an end.

The road was deeply rutted and riddled with puddles and long stretches of red clay mud. "There have been other tracks back in here."

"It's used as an entry point to a county-owned wilderness area. They give out a number of hunting permits every year to maintain the herd of deer. It's popular with bow hunters. In the off-season hikers come back here."

"And you know this because?"

"Because I do my research. There isn't much activity here, but enough that any tracks we make, or vehicles left behind, won't look odd or unheard of."

"Where is your—" She broke off, gaping as she pulled to

the side of the road and stopped beneath a stand of towering pines. "Not on the side of the road, but not exactly out of sight." She swung her gaze to him. "Is that yours?"

"That's what the rental agreement says."

"I, uh . . . huh." What was there to say really? It was an RV. Not the long bus type, more like a mutant-sized pickup truck. "Very stealthy."

"I wasn't going for stealth. I told everyone I was going hiking, fishing, whatever, so this played the part."

"And because you do so much hiking and fishing, everyone believed you."

He shifted a little and looked at her. "Actually, I have."

"In all the time we worked together, I don't remember you ever taking personal leave, much less a vacation."

"You were always able to get in touch with me, I was your team leader, but you didn't know where I was half the time. Maybe more than that. You weren't exactly sitting around the office."

She didn't respond right away, but stared at him openly now. "So, you're saying that when I checked in with you, you could have been standing knee-deep in some frigid river, trout fishing?"

"More likely I was on a beach somewhere, but it could have happened, yes."

"Hunh." She leaned back, having no idea what to say to that.

"Just because you didn't take personal time didn't mean none of the rest of us did."

She eyed him. "Is that some kind of dig?"

"No, as your commander I loved your dedication to the job. I worried at times that you'd burn out, but you're one of those people who actually seemed to get energized by being in the field. You also struck me as the sort who'd ask for personal time if and when you wanted it, so in the absence of seeing any issues you might have been having, I left you to make that call."

"I appreciate that," she said, truly meaning it. "I'd have said the same about you, you know. That you were the energized type who loved being on the job. One of the things we all respected was that you were out in the trenches with us."

He nodded his appreciation. "And, by nature, I am like that. I loved my work."

She cocked a brow. "Past tense?"

"I don't know. I know it's not the same. I'm not the same."

"Do you want to leave?"

"I'm not sure where I would go, or what I would take on that gives me the same sense of satisfaction."

"So you've thought about it."

"Some. Out of frustration mostly, I think. I guess part of me thinks if I could just figure out what the hell is going on, and fix it, it would go back to the way it was. But realistically, and especially now, I don't see where that would be the case."

"The AWOL thing could be a problem," she said dryly.

"Yes, and no," he answered seriously. "I think I have proof now, with CJ's last transmission, that I'd at least have a valid cause for conversation if they tried to can me. But if our suspicions are true, then there's a whole lot more at stake here than just my job."

"Given the physical shape you're in at the moment, I'd agree with that." She continued to study him, even when he didn't immediately reply.

"What," he said at length.

"I don't know. I'm still trying to picture you kicking back on the beach. Sleeping in a tent I can envision, but only with your gear, and a full mission report laid out on the cot next to you. But then, in a million years, I'd have never expected that Austin Powers impression, either. You were the most gung ho, seriously serious one of all."

"I was that guy once. I used to live, eat, breathe my job. Things happen, make you reevaluate."

She didn't press. He would know from being her commander what her background was, that she'd lost her parents young, been raised by a relative who'd passed when she was in her first year in college. No other family. That she'd taken an interest in history, international politics, and criminal law, and had been recruited by the agency straight out of college. She didn't know much more about him than what was in his standard bio, available to anyone in the agency. She knew his childhood was somewhat similar in that they'd both been orphaned young, only he'd been recruited out of the military— Army—after his second tour, having signed up straight out of high school. She knew he'd been a Ranger, one of the younger commanders they'd ever had. He never spoke of it, any of it, but it certainly wouldn't have come as a surprise to anyone who'd worked with him.

The rest of him was a blank slate, and she'd never really thought about it, but she realized now that his still waters ran far, far deeper than she'd have ever suspected.

"I don't know if I regret not having sought more balance," she said. "I loved what I was doing. It was the adventure of a lifetime, and I was making a difference. My job was my life and I liked it fine that way. It wasn't like I had anywhere else to be."

"That must have made it even harder, it ending like it did. Understatement, I'm sure."

He didn't say that in an offhanded manner, so she answered seriously. "Actually, to be honest, the end . . . how it ended, was so, well, horrific, that I was, and still am, just thankful to be alive."

He shifted to look at her more directly. "You turned down the psych evals and post-mission therapy."

She nodded, realizing now that was maybe why he'd prodded her earlier about her mental state. "No regrets there. If I'd thought about going back, even entertained the idea of being back in the field again, I'd have gone in for all the counseling and testing they could put me through. If for no other reason than I'd have had to be one hundred percent certain I was ready and able to be back."

"You never once considered it? At any time, during or since?"

"In some ways, I'll be recuperating the rest of my life." She lifted a hand. "I don't mean to imply I'm having lasting problems, other than the physical limitations I'll always have. No PTSD, at least not as yet. But that's likely because I've found my peace, and made my peace, with myself, with what I thought was my future. I'm okay. And that's enough." She looked at him. "It's more than I thought I'd ever have when they pulled me out of there."

"Then we're not so different. Things happen, you reevaluated, too."

She knew he'd seen a lot, been through a lot, but to her knowledge, had never been captured or tortured. She wanted to ask, wanted to know, what it was that had caused such a pivotal shift for him, and the curiosity was more than idle in nature for her, which was stultifying enough to make her reconsider the idea. But that's not what stopped her. In the end, she didn't think she had the right to pry, despite the depths of what he knew about her, and the frank level of conversation they were having.

But neither one of them made a move to get out of her SUV.

"I've never talked about it," he said, as if he knew the direction of her thoughts.

"You don't have to now," she said. "But I'm willing to listen if you want to talk." Or need to, she thought. No matter how this panned out, he was facing a major crossroads in his life, and she knew better than most how much that played with your head. She hadn't had a sounding board. Her sounding board had been left behind in the desert, with a bullet hole in her head. Or so Tate had believed. So she'd coped, and thought, and thought some more, and finally decided, on her own. And she was okay with that, too. She'd had to be, and it was the least of her concerns at the time. It made her feel good, strong, whole to be able to resolve issues, whether small and insignificant, or huge and life-altering. And there were times when the former took on the same magnitude as the latter.

But she'd made it through.

Still, in all that time, and for all the good it truly had done her, had CJ walked back through the door at any point during the past three years, Tate knew, without equivocation, that she'd have flung herself in her best friend's arms and poured out every last thought and feeling and doubt she'd had, until she was bone dry and raw from the catharsis.

She remembered what he'd said, about having no one to "let his hair down" with. He'd done that, a little, with her. And she recalled how swiftly she'd shut him down, which now made her feel bad. She'd been protecting herself, which she didn't regret, but she didn't feel great about the cost to him.

"Did you ever wish you did?" she asked, when the silence continued. "Have someone you trusted to talk to about it?"

"I tried a counselor. I thought the impersonality of it would actually be the right fit for me. I could talk that way, but there was no danger of further emotional attachment, so I could just stay detached about it, too. Talk, listen to what they had to say, apply whatever principles made sense, and maybe just feel better for having put it out there. No personal risk."

"And?"

His gaze shifted out the front window. She wondered what he was seeing in his mind's eye, thinking maybe they shouldn't be talking about this at all right now.

"And, no pain, no glory. No risk, no reward."

"I'm sorry."

"I'm not. I mean, I tried. It wasn't right for me."

"So . . . what was?" She wondered how old he'd been. What time in his life had this happened? When he was in the military? Had he watched compatriots die? She had no idea what his service had involved, but it certainly wasn't outside the realm of possibility, even probability. Or had it happened while working for the agency? Which had been her initial impression when he'd first brought it up.

"Finding my own balance. I couldn't change things, and I

sure as hell couldn't fix them. But I could fix myself. So it would never happen again."

She shifted in her seat then, and looked directly at him, held that gaze until he finally turned his head and looked back at her. His eyes were dark, flat, but not emotionless. If anything, there was so much banked emotion to be found there, it was a surprise it didn't just come shooting out, like a blast of fire.

"And did you?" she asked.

"Did I what?"

"Fix yourself?"

He broke eye contact then, and she knew the conversation was over. "It never happened again, so I guess I did."

"Well, then that's good," she said, shooting for something helpful and understanding, and missing by a mile. It sounded like a lame platitude, even to herself. So, maybe she wasn't the best one to talk to, she thought. "Where am I going to park this thing? Should I move yours out first, then pull this in the same spot?"

He'd parked the truck, or RV, or whatever you called the hybrid between the two, on a hard-packed area of dirt and rocks with tall weeds growing in huge, bright green stalks. Which, after all the rain, followed by the very direct sun, would probably just get taller. Not tall enough to hide anything, but with the tracks in and out, it looked parked there for a purpose. Like an overgrown, unpaved parking lot. Such as it was.

"I think there's enough space on the other side, and you've got the ground clearance."

"Okay."

"But don't pull in yet. I want to check the truck and the surrounding area, and the less disturbance we make, the better. Just want to make sure no one has paid my truck a visit."

He opened his door and she popped hers open as well. When he gave her a questioning look, she said, "I'm not questioning your ability to handle the reconnaissance, but I'm better suited at the moment to do undercarriage checks, that sort of thing."

She smiled wryly. "I may be rusty, but I'm not completely useless."

"Never said you were." He carefully slid out, and she heard him grunt a little as he got his weight stabilized over the walking stick.

In some ways, it was hard to watch him be so physically restricted. He'd always been such a Superman on the job, to the point where none of the team would have been completely shocked if bullets had just bounced off his chest. Without benefit of Kevlar. He took on some of the most dangerous assignments, and was successful more often than not, getting in and out of places most of them would have thought impossible. And usually without so much as a scratch. They kidded about that—not to his face, of course. She hadn't been kidding when she said they'd all thought him the baddest of badasses. He was tough, really tough, and also fair, but he wasn't the kind or tender type. Which is why this whole couple of days with him was so completely surreal. How could she know so little about the man she'd fought in the trenches next to?

She also hadn't realized the degree to which his superhero abilities had instilled the trust and confidence she'd had in him, until now. She was seeing him as vulnerable, both physically, and through their conversations, emotionally as well. It was taking some effort to mentally adjust to that. Tate and the rest of her team had been good, often better than good, but ultimately they'd also been human. Not Derek Cole.

In other ways, it was hard to believe he was doing as much as he was already, given the shape he'd been in just a few days ago. She supposed it shouldn't surprise her that he'd be superhuman, even in this.

"You coming?"

"Yes," she said, scrambling down from the driver's seat. Her body wasn't as achy today, now that the damp was mostly gone from the air. Here in the woods it was more humid, but they wouldn't be here long. The ground was boggy, being in the trees, and hidden from the sun. The deluge they'd gotten hadn't spared the ground beneath even the densest of tree stands, which was why she'd parked beneath the pines. The needles would provide a stronger bed and barrier than pretty much anything else.

But that wasn't going to carry them all the way to where he'd parked his truck. "Be careful with the mud," she called out.

When he looked at her, as if questioning her mothering tendencies, she added, "The peg end of the walking stick is kind of pointy and it sometimes sinks down into the mud further than you think it will, especially if you're putting your weight on it. I learned the hard way by doing a face plant in a huge mud bog. I thought maybe I'd save you the trip."

He nodded, but said nothing. Apparently he was still operating on the aftereffects of the semi-revealing conversation they'd just had. Maybe he was concerned she'd pry. God knows she wanted to. He tossed out those tantalizing crumbs, she'd have to be numb not to be curious. But she hoped he knew her well enough to know that, outside of the job, she wouldn't poke, especially in an area that was so obviously sensitive.

"Hold back," he told her. "Let me do once around, then you can move in. The ground is pretty marshy over here, and we'll just track it up."

"Anything that might have been there would have been hard to date, with the rains beating down the imprints."

"If there's anything to be found around this truck, I'm not going to care when they were here, just that they found it."

She stood in silence by the front of her SUV and watched him slowly and methodically pick his way around the truck. Once he'd circled completely around, she said, "Find anything?"

"Hard to say. The ground is more water than dirt at this point."

"Even if you did, could be other hikers nosing about, checking out your rig. Or even looking to see if they could break in and get out of the rain, if they were caught out here in the storm."

He checked the body of the truck itself on his next go-around. Tate moved in closer and looked at the ground. He was right. It was more suitable for mud wrestling than walking. "I can't say as I'm all that excited about shimmying under this thing to check for bugs. Or worse."

He circled around behind her. "I don't think that'll be necessary. Even with all the wet ground, I'm not getting anything. Not even the slightest print. I think the storm, which was probably predicted ahead of time, kept the strays out. And I don't think we've had any other visitors."

"You're sure? I can always change clothes."

He smiled then, and it felt like it had been ages since he'd directed that suggestive grin her way. "And I'd be more than happy to help with that."

"So altruistic."

"A real Boy Scout."

"Uh huh."

"But even I'm not enough of a guy to make you crawl around in the mud for my own entertainment."

"A real manly man."

"You have no idea."

When he continued to grin, the air between them changed from dry banter to something with a lot more kick to it. And she'd been doing so well avoiding that particular brand of tension today. "I'm assuming we're going to stay mobile because this is our new temporary living quarters?"

"Until such time where it doesn't make sense, I think it's the best way to go. I don't know how much driving around out here you've done, but I'm sure it won't be that hard to get lost for a day or two."

Lost. In the woods. In a camper. With very tight living quarters. With Derek. And she thought the cabin had been a challenge. Not that she wanted him injured, but, at the moment, where self-preservation usurped all other concerns, it was probably the one barrier that was going to keep them focused on business and off of . . . well, the tightness of living space. Amongst other tight things.

"No, no it won't. Didn't that thing come with a GPS?"

"Yes, but if it's listed on the GPS, it's not lost enough for me."

"Understood." She started to walk back to her SUV. "I'll pull mine around and we'll move our stuff into the truck. Do you want to check the interior? Or would you rather I do that?" She paused, looked back. "You're a little more limited than before, given the sling, the ribs."

"I'll be fine. You'll need to drive."

"Not a problem." She could drive a tank if necessary. Which she knew firsthand. "And I did do a lot of driving around the county and adjoining areas, all over the valley, and most of the mountains. So I know it pretty well." When she got stuck on a particular passage in her writing, she'd discovered that driving helped to free up her mind so she could solve plot problems in a way that no amount of time spent sitting still and staring at her computer screen would ever do. Plus, just having the freedom to drive around through the lovely peace and serenity of the valley and all that surrounded it, without any bullets flying or fears of roadside bombs blowing her to smithereens, was such an absolute joy, she'd often taken off on drives just for the pure pleasure of it.

She often plotted routes for later work-related runs. She also was a champ at finding little hole-in-the-wall dead ends in the middle of nowhere, logging roads, roads that might have been intended to lead to new development but whose potential had never been fulfilled. It's why she'd traded in her nondescript little sedan and bought the SUV right after moving in.

She moved her vehicle while he did an interior sweep. He didn't find anything. She made quick work of moving their gear over, and less than ten minutes later, they were pulling out.

"Any ideas on where to take us?" he asked.

"I've got one or two." She wasn't sure how she'd explain to

him how she knew about them. It wasn't that her very newly begun career as a fiction novelist was something she wanted to hide from him, not in the way that he'd wanted to avoid talking about whatever life-changing event he'd been alluding to earlier, but it was very new, and, for her, very exciting, and she wasn't willing to share the specialness of that with anyone. At least not until she'd had a chance to wallow in all the lovely new layers of it a bit longer.

Eventually she'd probably become a stressed-out, jaded and cynical hack who'd talk about it to anyone who'd listen. But for now, it was a fantastical, still somewhat unbelievable, dream come true. An actual new chapter in a life already pretty fully lived. So much more than she could have ever dreamed for, and, on top of it all, it was perfect for her.

So, for now, it would stay all hers.

# Chapter 16

"Not bad," he told her, as she backed into a small patch of flat ground between two trees. They were deep in a wilderness area, off an old fire road which extended over the mountain and dumped out into West Virginia. If they had to make a move, there was more than one way out, but Derek didn't feel there was much danger they'd be tracked. It was heavily forested enough where they could move through without too much of a trail. And he planned for them to be gone again by daybreak.

"Unfortunately no hookups, no water," she said.

"I have a generator, so we'll have electric. And there's enough water in the reserves to get us through till morning."

"There is one thing we forgot."

He merely lifted his eyebrows.

"Food."

"We're covered."

She made a face.

"What?"

"Whatever you 'covered' us with has been sitting in this truck, rotting for the past few days. You'll have to pardon me if I'm not overly enthusiastic."

He shot her a wry grin. "You have gotten soft."

"What I've gotten is used to eating decent food. Every day.

Whenever I want. My days of not minding the occasional ant, roach, or maggot are well over."

"Wimp."

"Proudly."

He just laughed. They'd been on the road for a little over an hour. Not that they were that far away in miles from their initial spot, but the winding mountain roads were steep and narrow, with switchbacks that had taken some maneuvering in the big beast of a truck. Getting up the fire road and down the trail they were presently parked off of had been the easy part.

They hadn't really talked at all. He'd given her the time and space to get used to the demands of the vehicle and decide on where they should hunker down for the night. And, he thought, they both needed the time to mull over everything they'd talked about before leaving her cabin. He looked out the windshield at the glow of the setting sun, shafting through dense forestation. "Well, you found us a pretty good spot, so, wimp or no, at least you're still good for something."

"Careful, or I'll take my walking stick back."

He smiled, but didn't try to bluff that one. His entire body was one giant throbbing ache at the moment. Even an hour cramped in a seated position, after all he'd already done that day, had been about forty-five minutes longer than his body could handle. He really needed to lie flat for a bit and give his ribs and shoulder a chance to take a load off.

Which was when he considered the sleeping arrangements for the first time. There weren't too many options in the little RV. There was a short, double-wide bed in the loft space that extended up over the top of the cab of the truck. The little dinette kitchen table dropped down so the cushions from the bench seats on either side could slide in and form a second small sleeping platform. And that was it. Problem for him came from the fact that while the table-bed was the easier to access for someone in his current physical condition, there was no way he could contort his body to fit in that boxy space.

Tate wouldn't be stretching out there, either, and he had no idea what kind of effect that would have on her, but of the two of them, she was a better fit in both size and health. Which left him somehow maneuvering up to the loft bed.

Of course, the loft bed was big enough for both of them to lie flat, legs extended, fairly comfortably. And just the idea of being pressed full length against Tate in tight quarters brought another ache into play, which he quickly worked to quash. Now was not the time, and that cab bed was definitely not the place. He'd thought they'd have parted by now, working independently. The physical distraction of Tate would be a thing of the past. Or, at least a thing of less immediacy. He was beginning to wonder if he'd ever get her out of his mind. He'd spent the last hour thinking more about that than the mission. Not real reassuring in regards to him getting his head back in the game.

He just wasn't so sure about the game anymore. And he couldn't be blamed really, given how rapidly the rules seemed to be changing. But it went beyond that. He'd never really contemplated life after the job. Certainly not at this stage in his life or career. That was something to think about as the golden years approached, and he was several decades away from that. But he'd never planned on the job changing like it had, or him changing because of it.

And he certainly hadn't planned on Tate. Neither the contrast she was presenting to him at this particular point in his career, as someone who'd left the life and found contentment, or the distraction she was providing personally. And if he thought the distraction could be slaked by a few hours spent in the cab bed with her, then, injuries and all, he'd be tempted to see it through, just for the peace of mind of getting his attention span back. But Tate was proving to be a distraction on far more levels—dangerous levels—than mere physical ones.

"If you'll tell me what to do to secure the truck, you can go in the back, stretch out."

He blinked away images of Tate cooking in the kitchen, Tate helping him in and out of beds, chairs, Tate berating him, Tate being a smartass, Tate smiling . . . Tate laughing. "I'm fine."

To which he added the renewed image of Tate giving him "that look."

He had thought he'd been hiding his fatigue and pain management issues better than that. "Without water or electric hookup, there's not much that needs to be done."

"Okay. Well, maybe we should eat and then you can lie down for a bit. I'll go back over CJ's transmission, see if there's anything more I can get out of it." She paused, then glanced over her shoulder, then back at him. "Speaking of which, what kind of sleeping arrangement does that thing have? Because I can just bunk up here if—"

"There's room," he said, wondering if, by chance, her eagerness to sleep in the RV's backseat had anything to do with how she might be fighting the same kind of attraction-distraction he was.

He should be so lucky.

Except no, it was good if she wasn't fighting anything. And no one was getting any kind of lucky. That was what he should be hoping for.

Right.

"So, what's the setup?" she asked.

"There are two spots, one of them hardly better than up here, but at least back there you won't have seatbelts digging into your back."

"What is the arrangement?"

"Bigger bed is the loft, above here." He rapped his good hand on the roof of the truck cab. "Problem is getting me into it. Smaller platform bed would involve me curling up on my side."

"Right. Not happening. So we get you into the loft. Probably not going to feel all that good, but I can lever you up, or we can devise some kind of footstool to give you better leverage since you can't use your upper torso to pull yourself up and in." She smiled at him.

"What's amusing?"

"That you're more high maintenance than I am."

"Ha ha." He popped open his door, went to shift his legs out and enough of his body protested that the wince came out before he could cover for it.

"Perfectly fine. Right."

"I didn't say perfectly. There are levels of fine."

Tate laughed as she slid out of her side of the truck. "I'd say you're at about the lowest level of fine there is."

By the time she walked around the front of the truck, he was out and standing, if not exactly upright, at least under his own power. "Okay," he said when she just folded her arms and stared at him. "If it turns out we can get me up into that loft, then maybe it might not be a bad idea for me to stretch out for a bit. I'll show you how to run the generator so we can have light once the sun is gone. It's not that warm out, so I think we can just crank open the windows for ventilation. The screens will keep out the mosquitoes and flies."

"Sounds simply heavenly."

"So sincere."

"Well, it's one thing to rough it when you have to, for the job, for . . . whatever."

"This is quite a few levels up from roughing it. If we're still on the levels grading scale."

She smirked at him. "I just don't understand people electively doing any level of this for fun. Haven't they heard of hotels with room service and masseurs on staff?"

"They don't understand the kind of communing we've done with nature. We're a bit jaded on that score."

"You might have a point." She stepped around him and walked to the back of the truck and the door to the inside. "Come on, we should get started so we can get you resting and me working before the sun goes the rest of the way down."

She opened the door and stepped inside. Once he levered himself up the narrow aluminum steps, he moved in behind her.

"Cozy," she said, almost bumping into him just turning around.

"It is that."

She nodded at the tiny kitchen table. "You weren't kidding."

"There's enough room up top for two people to stretch out, if—"

"I'll be fine," she said quickly. Maybe a little too quickly.

He couldn't see her face, so he didn't know if she was worried about them keeping their hands off each other in closer confines . . . or if he was just projecting. And if she was worried . . . that wasn't supposed to be a good thing. Except it wasn't bothering him so much.

"Where is the generator switch?" she asked, sounding quite abruptly so-very-all-businesslike.

He fought a smile. So . . . not just him. Good to know. And bad to know. Now he just had to decide which was the bad part. "Here." He showed her how everything worked. Pointed out the tiny bathroom space, and the lever to lower the table for both table and bed conversion. She listened to what he had to say, nodded her head on occasion, then, when he was done, said, "Doesn't sound like rocket science. So let's get you in the bed, then I'll grab my laptop case and bring it back here to work on the CJ transmission."

She shifted back against the tiny kitchen sink to let him squeeze by, and he wasn't halfway past before he was forced to admit that he wasn't going to handle this—any of this—nearly as smoothly as he'd have liked to believe. Because his body was screaming at him, his head was pounding, but did he turn his back to her so they could shift positions? No. Did he stop when the two of them were pinned between sink and stove? Yes.

"Cozy," he said.

"Derek—"

"Tate."

She met his gaze, but said nothing.

"My body feels like somebody kicked the shit out of me," he said.

"Somebody did."

"So, why is it that it's more interested in paying attention to you, than it is getting some much needed rest?"

"So, now it's all your body's fault? You claim no responsibility for controlling your . . . urges?"

"Do you have urges, Tate?"

She didn't answer, which was telling in and of itself, but the way her pupils went wide and dark told him even more.

"Just because your mind wants to wander down a path, and your body thinks it might be fun to follow, does not mean—"

"Does your mind wander to me?" he asked, suddenly no longer teasing and flirting.

"Derek—" she started, then broke off and dipped her chin. "Bodies want what they want, that's just basic chemistry. And a mind—especially one that's been living alone in a cabin for quite some time—can convince you of all kinds of things."

He rested his weight, and the walking stick, on the range behind him, then tipped up her chin with the fingers of his good hand. "Is there something terribly wrong in that?"

She stared at him. "I have a hard time believing you're hard up for companionship when you want it. And, three years alone or not, I don't need a pity—"

He cut her off with a kiss. He cupped her cheek with his palm and slanted his mouth over hers, groaning when she softened and let him in. "Your mouth just begs to be taken," he murmured against her lips.

"So, now it's all my mouth's fault?"

He grinned and continued his assault. "Yeah, a guy can hardly think, looking at your mouth."

"Hunh. I've never found that to be a real problem before."

"Then you've been hanging out with the wrong men." He claimed her mouth again, only this time he didn't come up for air until he thought his heart might pound out of his chest. The adrenaline rush was instant and fierce. He wanted her, all of her, and he really needed to get a grip before he did something they'd both be sorry for.

And he realized right then that what he'd be most sorry for, what he couldn't tolerate, was that she just wanted the pheromone rush he was providing, after a long time without one. He wanted her to want him. Because she was right, if he was of the mind, finding companionship wasn't all that challenging. But this was far, far different from wanting a roll in the sack. He wanted—

"Shit." He lifted his head, and she wavered toward him before catching up and straightening away.

"What?" she asked, sounding a bit vague and looking like someone had just thoroughly kissed her. And someone had. The same someone who wanted to do that and a whole lot more, almost more than he wanted another breath.

"I want you, Tate."

She smiled and let out a half laugh. "Yeah, I'd sort of figured that part out."

"I mean, it's you. Not sex. Not just sex. That I want. Christ." He rubbed his hand over his face. "I'm usually better at putting thoughts into words, but—"

"But you're injured and your body, as well as your brain, is a little depleted. Hardly the time to be assessing needs and wants and—" She started to scoot away, but he reached out and blocked her with his good arm.

"Wait." He cupped her elbow, turned her back to face him. "I have been trying to be a good boy."

She looked up at him through her lashes, that wry quirk that was always hovering, played at the corners of her mouth. "Really."

"You have no idea. And it has nothing to do with being addled or beaten up—"

"Or facing a crisis at work, your entire career on the line . . . I could go on. But really, Derek, this isn't the time to be pursuing anything other than finding CJ and figuring out what in the hell is really going on."

"I'm incredibly well aware of that. And my discipline, in all things, has always been the foundation upon which I've built everything else. I know, above all else, in a world where trust is often an elusive, illusionary thing, that I can trust myself. To do what I need to do, what must be done, no matter what."

"What are you saying?"

"I'm saying that I don't seem to have a handle on that anymore. And I've been injured and messed with before. It usually makes the focus that much tighter."

"You're at a crossroads, Derek. In a place you've never been before. Nothing you've done or experienced in the past can guide you now. There is no obvious path forward now. Everything that was sharp and in focus, is kind of a blur now. Trust me, I know what I'm talking about."

"Tate—"

"Let me finish. Isn't it possible that you're transferring some of that confusion to me? I'm here, I'm convenient, and if you convince yourself that I'm really the source of all that is crazy in your world, and you can somehow work that out, in whatever way you need to, including sex, then that will allow you to get back to normality. Well, I'm here to tell you, if what we suspect—if even a fraction of that is true—nothing will ever be normal again."

Her words pummeled him, the truth behind them was inescapable. And still he wanted to reject that truth. Instinctively, he didn't want to think that she was just some representation of the frustration he was feeling, something he could "work it out" on.

"Did you?" he asked, before he even knew the question was there.

"Did I what?"

"Transfer your confusion. To someone."

"Not someone, no."

"Something, then?"

She nodded, reluctantly.

"And what happened?"

Now she looked away.

"Oh no," he said, turning her face back to his. "You don't go pounding me with your brutal truths, then shy away from the rest of the lecture."

"My word should be enough. You can trust that I understand where you are."

"What happened?" he asked. "You're telling me not to repeat your mistakes. What was your mistake? What price did you pay?"

He looked closely, expecting to see hurt, pain, anger, something. He saw none of those things, and this time, when she dipped her chin, he let her.

"What was it, Tate?" he asked again.

"I respected your privacy. I didn't pry."

He knew what she was referring to. "Did you want to? Did you want to know?" He leaned down, until he caught her eye, had her looking up without touching her. "Do you want to know me?"

She stared at him for what felt like eternity. "Yes," she finally said, so softly he almost didn't hear it. "But just because I'm curious, don't mistake that—"

"Is it simple curiosity?" He shifted his weight then, and his body made him pay, but he didn't really give a damn at the moment. He already knew there were entire realms of pain that had nothing to do with the physical. He was far more concerned with the emotional kind at the moment. He crowded her body, brushing against hers so she had to look up to see into his eyes. "Or a more complex kind?"

"If it was simple, I wouldn't be standing here."

"If it was simple, neither would I." He brushed a finger along her cheek. "You're right about the crossroads, and you're right about the future being a blur." He lowered his mouth. "But I'm not so sure you're right about the transfer part." He brushed her lips with his, his body tightening, both with pain and pleasure, when she moaned a little at the touch. "In fact, it seems the only thing I am clear-minded about, is not stepping back from this. From you. I tried. The timing is wrong, I'm the wrong guy, everything is wrong, and yet, when I do this . . ." He kissed her then, deeply, and with more emotion welling up than he'd allowed himself to feel in a very, very long time.

His heart was thudding in his chest when he lifted his mouth from hers, both from need, and from fear. But not from uncertainty. Fear always accompanied risk. And nothing worth having came without some of both. "When I kiss you, Tate, it doesn't matter. Because it feels incredibly right. And I know what right feels like."

"How?" she asked, her own voice rough, the question, and the look in her eyes, more sincere than he could recall seeing. "How do you know?"

"Because I had it right once before. And I blew it. To smithereens. And I swore, no matter what, I'd never go back there again. For my own sanity, and because I'd never risk hurting anyone again. Myself . . . anyone."

It was the closest he'd ever come to talking about it, and, for the first time, there was a part of him that wanted her to ask, to demand to know, to make him rip out of himself the dark place he'd carried for such a long time. Because he finally, mercifully, and somewhat terrifyingly, wanted it gone. Mercifully, because he didn't want to punish himself with it anymore . . . and terrifyingly, because it was what had forged him, and without it he had no idea what his boundaries would be.

But she had to know. If this was right, she had to know. She had to look at him, all of him, and still believe this was right.

"I don't know," she said.

"Do you want to find out?" he asked.

"I mean, I don't know what it feels like." She looked at him. "Whatever it was in your past that hurt you so badly . . . at least you knew how to feel that deeply, care on that level. I never had that. Lust, yes, but that's not what you're talking about. The closest I came was with my friendship to CJ. But this . . ." She lifted a hand from the sink where she'd braced herself and waved it between them. "I have no background, no gauge, no foundation." She looked at him then. "So, I don't know if it's so much about you being the wrong guy, but you may want to seriously rethink whether or not I'm someone you need to be taking a chance with."

His heart tripled in speed. She might not realize what she'd just said, so busy trying to warn him off . . . He leaned forward, trapping her fully against the sink now.

"Your arm—"

—Was screaming. He leaned in anyway . . . and she took the weight of him, shifted her own, until she fit there, just there . . . right there. Just right there.

He slid his hand beneath her hair, cupped the back of her neck, and drank his absolute fill of her. Her mouth, her slightly crooked nose, the way her chin was almost pointy, but not quite, which made her lips even that much more ridiculously earthy looking, tasting, and her eyes, he could stare into them for lifetimes. Seen so much, done so much, as had he. He'd get her, understand her, like no one else, and she'd understand him, too. "Earlier," he said, leaning down and dropping kisses so tender he hadn't known he possessed the skill, "you didn't answer because it turned out not to be a mistake at all, didn't it?"

"It could have been," she said, gasping and tilting her chin up, allowing him access to the soft side of her neck. "It should have been. I was crazy, fixated. It wasn't healthy."

He could feel her pulse pounding beneath his lips as he kissed her below her ear. "But . . . not a mistake."

She said nothing, but made no move to stop his very deliberate exploration. She gasped when he nipped her earlobe, shivered when he ran his tongue along the throbbing pulse point just below it, sighed when he turned her mouth to his and kissed her again. "In the end," he said against her mouth, slipping his tongue in, and back out, teasing hers, wanting her to tease him back. "Not a mistake."

He continued to tease her with his tongue, until she realized she wouldn't get more, wouldn't get him doing what she wanted, what he wanted, which was to invade her fully, feel her mouth tighten around his tongue and pull it in more deeply . . . until she answered him.

"No," she finally gasped. "In the end . . . no. It wasn't a mistake."

# Chapter 17

He was so . . . *relentless* was the only thing she could think, and she could barely do that. Relentlessly inquisitive, relentlessly searching, relentlessly interested, relentlessly demanding . . . and most disconcerting, relentlessly tender. She'd have never expected that from him, this gentleness of spirit inside such a dominant and aggressively alpha personality. He was the definition of go-getter, both mover and shaker, an inspiration to those around him. She'd never expected him to admit he had feelings, or that, if he did, that they mattered, much less take the time to examine them. And explain them. Along with examining hers as well.

There was darkness there, and pain, far deeper than the physical injuries he'd suffered. She understood that in the way that only the physically shattered could. She understood it wasn't the physical decimation that would ever have put that kind of darkness there. It hadn't in her, either. No, it was something much farther reaching than a shattered femur or a mangled hip socket. Something, or someone, had shattered something far more precious, and far harder to rebuild and regenerate. His heart.

She wondered about that, even as he was kissing the daylights out of her, this man who worked to save the many, but hadn't taken the time to save himself. And now that the foundation he'd worked from had shifted, and there was no security in even the things he had trusted, he had nowhere to land, because he hadn't ever defined himself outside his work.

No, she thought, as she pushed her tongue into his mouth, savored the taste of him, rubbed her palm over his whisker-shadowed cheek, sunk her fingers into the depths of his hair as she tugged him gently closer, took him deeper, pushed her way deeper into him. No, the person who hadn't taken the time for self-definition had been her. She thought she had now, since the accident, since her new life had begun . . . but she hadn't, not really. Not like he had. Her catastrophe, her altering event, had still, at the core, been all about her.

His hadn't been. She knew that, as well as she knew that no matter what he said, he was scrambling here.

And she had no idea how she felt about being the one he was scrambling onto. Except for one thing, one thought that wouldn't leave her, as her body came alive to his touch, his taste, and craved more in a way it never had, not ever. This transcended the need for sex, the need even for intimacy, to the need to feel full and primal and human and female. This . . . this presented risk.

She'd risked her life, which would seem to be the ultimate hazard a person could take. And she'd valued her life, had never wanted to die, had never spent a moment thinking that wouldn't be such a bad payoff. No, she wanted victory, and she wanted to keep on being victorious. It was what she did, who she was, what she was good at, and, so she'd told herself, what she'd been put here for.

For the past three years, she'd had to come up with new answers to the questions of who she was, what her purpose was. And she didn't have them all yet. She was exploring, and her new world as a writer was a brave, dangerous, and equally tantalizing one, even if the only people who could die in it were fictional. If they died, which they didn't. Because in a life spent, up until three years ago, mired in the tragedy and the relentless destruction of the human condition, and the horror of what one human being could do to another . . . had she taken up her pen and turned her imagination to that world? To mining, fictionally, what she knew best?

No. No. Quite outrageously, and against all odds, she'd done exactly the opposite. She'd mined the world of the heart. And she'd felt like such a total fraud. Except, in the absence of personal knowledge, it was the most exhilarating, self-indulgent journey she could take herself on, without risk of actually, you know, experiencing it. She hadn't had it in her to risk anything else, much less to relive her past by writing about it. She'd taken the ultimate risk, or so she'd thought, and survived it. She could be forgiven if she just wanted to take a pass on doing it again and wallow, for once, in the pleasures of the human condition.

It had been what she'd scrambled for, in a way that had made no sense and had even less likelihood of success, much less fulfillment, and yet she'd kept on, determined, fixated, pouring everything she had into a fictional story. It had been her therapy, her shoulder, her solace, her haven. And it had been so unrealistic to even consider that this, of all things, could be her future.

But she'd sent the manuscript off anyway, via a friend of an old work contact, who, she'd recalled, had connections in New York. Mostly, she'd told herself at the time, it was so someone would tell her, unequivocally, that she was crazy and to find another dream.

And then her first effort had sold. *Fools*, she'd thought, both giddily and guiltily. But, oh, the giddy part had been so good, so ridiculously good. If they only new how much of her fiction was truly fiction. She wrote about how she thought it should be, versus how she knew it could be. So then she'd finished her second book, certain they'd see the truth. But no. And so, here she was, a second contract for books three and four just signed, with book one due to arrive in stores in less than eight weeks. She still couldn't truly make herself believe it. She hadn't told a soul. But then, who would she tell?

Only now, here was Derek. And this could ruin everything.

He could ruin everything. He was making her feel things she hadn't felt, think about things she was far more comfortable just assuming than experiencing. What if he exposed her for the fraud she truly was? What if he made all her assumptions and beliefs seem silly and naïve?

Or worse . . . what if it was better than she could have ever hoped for or imagined? What if she let herself want, let herself need, let herself fall? Let herself take the greatest risk of all and let herself love . . . and fail? It could destroy everything she'd carefully constructed . . . and she knew, more than any shattered bone and mangled limb, it could destroy her. And she wasn't sure she could rise from those ashes.

In the end, that was what had her pulling away, pushing gently at his good shoulder, ducking her chin when he tried to get her to look at him.

"Tate . . ."

She liked hearing him say her name. No one had ever said her name just like that before. All rough with need, throaty from just kissing her senseless, and clearly not done yet.

She felt all those things, too, and wondered if he heard them in her voice. Wondered if even a fraction of the thoughts running through her mind were running through his. Only she knew they were, just coming from a different source. He was at a crucial turning point . . . she'd turned that corner and was heading down a bright and shiny new path that, while not perfect, was far more than she could have ever hoped for. She didn't know what lay in store for him. She didn't know what choices he'd have to make.

She did know that her new world was already being compromised far more than she'd ever anticipated it could be, by being dragged into what was, ultimately, his problem. The promise of reuniting with CJ was very powerful stuff . . . and absolutely nerve-wracking. She'd made peace with her dead friend, who had died while she had lived. It was hugely selfish, because a part of her ached to stand in the same room as CJ, hear her, watch her, hug her. Talk to her. Laugh with her. Whereas an even bigger part wanted to keep things just as they were. Because if CJ's dying wasn't real, then Tate wasn't sure she was prepared to handle whatever other secrets her former best friend and partner had withheld from her. Better to think her partner a hero who had died fighting a just cause, than a human who might have . . .

She shut her eyes. "There's so much," she whispered. "So much about this to think about, to handle." She made herself open her eyes, look at him. "I don't know if I can handle it, and think about you, too. I know it's not fair, or even logical, but I'm not sure I want to take the same risks you're willing to take."

"If I could extract you from this situation, I would. And there still isn't any absolute proof that I won't be able to, once I connect with CJ. I'd think you'd want some of those answers, too. Whether you were in this or not."

"I do. And I don't. It's hard to explain."

"I think I understand better than you imagine."

She stared into his eyes, and thought maybe he was right. "Maybe you're the only one who could. But I already feel like I'm standing on a cliff, about to have it crumble beneath my feet again, and I'm stuck there, forced to fall and just take the impact and absorb whatever it does to me."

"I know this might not seem like much, but you can talk to me. I won't leave you alone in this. If that's what you want, if it would help, then we'll stick together, no matter what. I'll be here throughout, if you want me there."

"We'll do what we always do, and that is whatever it takes to get the job done." She reached out, touched his arm, then let her hand drop. "But the gesture, the offer, means a lot. I don't know you, Derek Cole. I really don't. And I do want to. In another time, or another place. I wish I could say I'm the woman who can handle anything, anytime, and maybe I once could have. Or maybe I could have never handled anything like this. I don't know. I do know I can't—or won't try—to handle it now."

"The way things are now isn't the way they'll be forever."

"No," she said. "No, they won't."

"Then this isn't no, forever. Just not right now."

"Derek—"

"If the CJ situation was resolved, along with my situation with the agency, and if I came to you, unfettered by those things, would you try?"

"That's a lot of ifs, and more than you can offer right now. Maybe more than you should offer, at this juncture. You don't know me, either, Derek."

"I know enough."

"How—"

He placed a finger across her lips, and damn if it didn't make her tremble.

"Because I do. Sometimes, you just do." He smiled then, and it was both dark and mysterious, sexy, and a little sad. "You just have to trust me on that."

He let his finger drop away, but he didn't move away. He was clearly waiting for a response to his question.

Only she didn't have one. Her knee-jerk response was to run, hide, say no, never, can't happen, don't wanna try. Only her gut knotted up a little at the thought of never seeing him again, never finding out the things she was suddenly so curious to know. Never knowing what it would be like to laugh hard with him, fight with him, make up with him . . . feel the weight of him on top of her . . . inside of her. So many things . . . And worse and completely out of place was the thought that she most definitely didn't want him doing any of those things with anyone else.

She wasn't the jealous type, or the possessive type. Her career, her life, wouldn't tolerate such things. So it was a bit shocking to realize that she felt a little of both right now. And for a man she had worked for, for years, but didn't even really know.

*Sometimes, you just do.*

His words echoed in her head . . . and in her heart. Where she thought, maybe, just maybe . . . he might be right.

"We have a long couple of days, at least, in front of us," he said. "And I should probably get horizontal as quickly as possible, if I want to have any hope of being of any use to you during that time."

He was giving her an out. Sort of. Or at least letting it drop. She nodded, started to shift back so he could move in front of her, toward the cab bed. She'd fall in behind him, do whatever was necessary to help him up there, even if it included shoving him up there entirely under her own power.

But then he was pausing, and turning, and once again she was inside his personal space, and unable to move, or even breathe, because he was lowering his head, bringing his lips toward hers, and she knew what they tasted like now, and had to fight against her body's desire to close the distance faster by moving herself.

It wasn't a soul kiss, like before. Or even a fierce, claiming one. In fact, it was barely a brushing of the lips, which turned out to be far more insidious to her defenses.

"It's not no, forever," he murmured, then turned and moved slowly toward the bed.

She took a moment to find her balance, grab hold of her equilibrium, realized there was a fat chance of doing either, and finally decided she'd have to just take the same attitude with him that she'd taken when her agent had called to tell her they'd gotten a two-book offer on her first manuscript and she realized they hadn't figured out she was a fraud. Fake it.

"Here," she said, "let me give you a boost up on your good side. Your ribs won't like it much, but I don't think there's a real way around that. Unless you want the table bed."

"I'll live and I can get up here." He stared up into the loft, then down, as if looking for something to use to hoist himself up there. "There was supposed to be a ladder, but hell if I know where it is."

"I'm stronger than I look," she told him. "I'm plucky."

That got a half-laugh out of him and he looked back at her. "What?"

"One of the nurses in the hospital, after I'd started recovering, she said I had pluck. I kind of liked the image of that."

"Okay, Plucky. Since I don't see any other way up there, short of tearing up my shoulder further, or banging more ribs, I guess I'll have to take your word for it."

"Trust the pluck."

He just grinned and shook his head. "Right."

She moved in closer and crouched down so he could put one foot into her laced fingers. "Use the walking stick to lever yourself up, and maybe you'll save your ribs a bit of agony, too."

He looked at her, braced and ready, and shook his head, a half-smile still on his face. "I'm more solid than I look."

I know, she could have told him. I just felt the weight of you, pressing me into the sink. She didn't need to think about that right at the moment. It was bad enough that her crouched position put her in line to stare at parts of him she had no business staring at, if her plan was to keep things all business. "I got you, semi-conscious and half out of your mind, from my living room floor to my bed. I can manage this. Come on," she told him, sounding more impatient than she meant to, but she really needed a few minutes alone to gather herself.

He angled himself around, then put his weight on the walking stick as he stepped into her waiting hands, and a second and a grunt later, he was up.

"You okay?" she asked, as he lay on his side, still.

"Yeah," he said, his voice tight. "I'm plucky."

She couldn't help it, she grinned. "Can I help you with anything else?"

He shifted then, onto his back, and pulled his legs up behind him, until he lay flat. Then he turned his head to look at her. "Do you really want an answer to that question?"

"I'll go get my computer. Get to work. You get some rest."

"Right," he said, but the amused smile was back.

And as she let herself out of the back of the camper, she heard him make clucking noises. *Let him think I'm chicken*, she thought, smiling despite herself. It wasn't far from the truth really.

She'd never been one to shrink away from . . . well, anything. Fear, risk, possibility of failure were all accepted parts of her job.

Only this wasn't a job she was signing on for. This was a lot more complicated. A lot more demanding. And a hell of a lot scarier. Which, considering how she'd spent her years in service to her country, said a lot.

She climbed into the cab and retrieved her laptop bag. She thought about just sitting up here and working, only that seemed too cowardly. Besides, he'd likely be asleep already. She knew he was pushing it far harder than he should. Which was another reason for her to keep her figurative distance from him. If only she could keep her physical distance from him, too, it would make life a lot simpler.

"But God forbid things be simple," she muttered as she made her way back around to the camper door. The sun was low enough now that she'd need to get the generator running so she'd have light to work by. She opened the door and stepped inside as quietly as she could. The curtain that closed off the upper bunk was still open, but he seemed to be resting comfortably. His eyes were closed, and his chest rose and fell evenly, so she did her best to be quiet. Rather than put the table up, she sat on one of the banquettes, stretching her legs out the length of it, and propped her computer on her lap to work. The light from the screen was enough, at least for now, so she didn't risk waking him by having the generator suddenly cut on.

In fact, it was kind of nice, the twilight of the evening, the sounds of the forest creatures rustling about, the frogs and crickets . . . it was almost as good as being at home. Her gaze drifted up to the loft bed. Almost, but not quite. If she'd thought him a distraction before . . .

Her mind returned to her work and she spent a moment or two considering opening up her newest work in process, which she'd just begun . . . but she couldn't seem to stop looking up to where he slept, and eventually decided now was not the time to be writing about . . . what she wrote about. Like she wasn't worked up enough at the moment.

And yet, even as she opened the transmission file, she caught herself wondering if this time, even though brief, that they were spending together, would alter the way she approached her writing, if what she had to say would change given the things he'd made her feel.

"All the more reason to avoid feeling anything else," she murmured. She didn't know why her manuscripts were selling, and she still didn't know how well they'd sell to the public, but she'd passed the starting line and entered the race under her own power, and it was far too early to go changing her routine. For whatever reason, her way was working. Even if she didn't understand why it was working, why risk messing it up with a new reality?

So she resolutely opened the file and booted up the video transmission. Having to watch her dead partner talk would surely pull her head out of this place he'd put it in.

"You hungry?"

She hadn't even begun the video. With an inward sigh, she tried to ignore the truth that was niggling at her. Which was, that as long as they were working together and, more to the point, living together, she didn't stand a prayer of not getting more involved with him. She looked up to find him rolled partly to one side, watching her. She was hungry all right, and it had nothing to do with whatever he had stashed in the cupboards. "Doesn't lying like that hurt your ribs?"

"Everything hurts my ribs. So, are you hungry?"

"I thought you were napping and I was working."

"No. Mostly I'm lying here trying not to think about what we could be doing up here on this nice, wide mattress and hoping you're down there wondering the same thing." He smiled. "But there would probably be napping after."

She rolled her eyes. It was that or lick her lips.

"So, instead of giving in to my more basic nature, I'm proving I can be a gentleman despite my carnal interests and keep things on a professional level."

"Is that what you're doing? Talking about mattresses and ways to spend time on one?"

"Am I wearing you down?"

He had no idea. And she didn't plan on changing that fact. "Not in the way you want to be, no."

His grin changed to a frown. Well, it was more of a pout. She never would have imagined Derek Cole even capable of a decent pout. Turns out she was wrong. He had a pretty damn adorable one.

He rolled to his back. "You know, I have been pushing it pretty hard. Maybe you should come up here and play mean nurse and yell at me for being a bad patient."

She had to work really hard not to laugh. Who knew he could be this cute? "Is that a particular fantasy of yours? Because, I have to tell you, I've had way too many doctors and nurses in my life for it to ever play into anything sexual for me. Probably ever."

He sighed, ever so pathetically. She bit her bottom lip to keep from smiling.

"So, does this mean I'm on my own for food, too?"

"So, it is true, then."

He rolled his head just enough so he could see her. "What's true?"

"Sex and food. Provide both and a man will never want for anything more."

He looked back to the roof of the camper. "Not true."

"Really? Because you're playing right into that stereotype."

"Beer."

"What?"

"An occasional well brewed, really cold beer. Food, and sex. There could be some variations on that theme, but that's pretty much the triple play."

"I'll keep that in mind."

He sighed again. "Well, I guess that's a start."

"Stop," she told him.

"Stop what?" he asked, entirely too innocently.

"You know what. If I'd had any idea you had the ability to pour on the charm like this, I'd have left you on my porch. In the rain."

"You think I'm charming?"

"I think you likely possess all kinds of talents I don't know about and am wishing I never did. Although I'm beginning to see why your mission ratings were so high. Here I thought it was because you were a methodical, calculating machine who never, ever let anything distract him from his goal. When I thought about your probable skill set—not that I did—it never included things like teasing and flirting and quoting Austin Powers. But I begin to see where developing those angles only made you the more well-rounded agent."

.    "Is that what you think this is?" He rolled back to his side, his tone absolutely serious, besides the wince of pain. "Do you think I'm working you as a mission? Doing whatever is neces sary to succeed?"

So she responded in kind. "I don't know what to think. This is uncharted territory for me. You're definitely uncharted territory, and proving to be quite tricky terrain, to boot. And given I never saw any of this in the man I worked for, it's hard to say, for absolutely certain, if I'm being played."

"Why?" he asked flatly, and if she wasn't mistaken, a bit heatedly.

"Why what?"

"Why would I 'play' you, as you call it? What would be in it for me?"

"Besides the obvious benefit, you mean?"

"You said sex wasn't a hard thing for me to get, and you'd have been right about that."

"I have no doubt. And saying that to me, in that way, could be calculated to get me to lower my defenses."

"Again, why?"

"Because I'm here, and available. Do you need more than that?"

"In the past, on occasion? No. From you? Most assuredly yes."

She didn't have a sharp retort for that one. Because she'd mostly begun this line of conversation as a dodge. She'd been up close and very personal when he was saying those things to her earlier. And unless he was an Oscar-worthy actor, he hadn't been faking any of that. But now that she'd started it, it did get the mind to wondering. "You sound angry."

"You're questioning my integrity."

"You mean to say that you've never used the various facets of your personality, or other abilities, to get the job done? Been less than one-hundred-percent truthful, or true, in how you've conducted yourself?"

There was a pause, then he said, "I don't think of you as a mission I have to accomplish."

"You could still think that I'm in cahoots somehow with CJ."

"I don't think you knew anything about CJ until I told you."

He wasn't teasing and she'd run out of diversionary steam. This was completely backfiring, as it was only furthering her attraction to him, not distancing herself from it.

"We might be working together on this, but my behavior with you . . ." He trailed off and shifted his gaze to the ceiling again.

She had no idea what he was thinking, but she felt bad now for badgering him. "Derek—"

"Yes," he said, "I've certainly been less than truthful when working to get a job done. I've done whatever was necessary, much, I suspect, as you have."

He sounded completely like her old boss now, and nothing like the Derek she had just started to get to know. "I'm sorry, I shouldn't have—"

"Oh, but you should. In fact, I encourage it. If you have

questions, doubts, concerns, bring them on. I want the opportunity to respond. It's better than letting the idea of what
might be, or the unknown, fester in your mind."

"You're so very different. The real you, I mean. From the
man I worked for."

"I'm absolutely exactly like the man you worked for. Nothing about my work persona is false or created as a professional
screen. I merely filter out the parts that I don't deem appropriate for a team leader and commander, especially given the level
of commitment I require from my agents. I imagine you did
much the same. All of who you are wasn't on display while
you were on the job."

"No, that's true, but I don't think the parts of me that
weren't . . ." Now she trailed off, then half-laughed at herself.
"Actually, I was completely myself on the job. I didn't hide
anything, or filter anything. Some of my thoughts and reactions maybe, so I wouldn't get fired if I didn't agree with something, but—and maybe this is pathetically revealing—I was my
job. That was all there was to me."

"I think most of us have that in common."

"But there is so much more to you."

"There is to you, too."

"There is now," she agreed. "But that's because my world,
my life, has expanded. Which sounds funny given that the
scope of my job included such a big part of the world. But my
personal world is very different now. And I'm a different person in it."

"Which I think is why I'm so attracted to you. I always respected you, but this . . ." He rolled to his side again and she
winced for him. "You're right, there is more to you now, whether
it's merely a reflection of your new life, or a new life that has
allowed the parts of you that were always there to surface,
who's to say? But I think it's your very grounded, very realistic
approach to things that allows me to be more of myself with
you."

She remembered what he said about her having CJ to "let

her hair down" with, and in that regard, he was right. They mostly let their hair down about work and more work, but it was an outlet. She couldn't imagine having worked as well as she had without that vent. She didn't have it now, except where it was related to her newfound profession, but she wasn't close to her agent or her editor in that way that invited those kinds of discussions or intimate revelations. Most especially not those kinds, given her personal feelings about her real abilities to do her job well. The last thing she wanted to do was alarm either of them in any way that she was less than a hundred percent ready to tackle this new mission in her life.

"How did you handle it? The job, I mean, without having someone to, well, if not talk to, at least unwind with?"

"It's just the way it was. But I made sure I did. Unwind, as you call it."

She didn't push too hard there, as the little seedling of jealousy reared its very shocking head, again. She didn't want to think about how he unwound, or who with. Although she tried to picture him in pick-up basketball games with a bunch of buddies, the picture that formed in her mind might have involved getting hot and sweaty, but there was no basketball court in sight.

She thought about the last time they'd had this conversation, and his quasi-revelation that he'd suffered some kind of tragic—she assumed—event that had altered the way he approached balancing career and self. Now she was more curious to know the whole story than before, but felt she couldn't press for several reasons. One, it wasn't any of her business. Not if she was going to make a go of trying to keep this professional, it wasn't. And two, by just asking, she was making a statement to him about her level of interest in him.

And, thirdly . . . whatever it was, she had a feeling it would only put her that much deeper into his personal space, his intimately personal space, which she was already fighting very hard to stay out of. It was one thing when he teased her, cajoled her about wanting her. When she provoked him, he seemed quite willing to get very serious, and very direct.

Something she might want to consider as she continued figuring out the boundaries of their new living situation.

"Okay," she said, setting her laptop on the floor and swinging her legs around. "I'll rustle us up something to eat."

"Nice dodge," he said, half chuckling.

She hadn't realized how much she could enjoy the teasing, flirting, the making him laugh, even at her expense. Especially when he was just as willing to laugh at himself. He was entirely too endearing and she had no idea what to do about that. "You have no idea," she said, and started digging through the cupboards.

# Chapter 18

Derek tried to get comfortable on the banquette, but there wasn't much room to squeeze in around the table, and having his arm strapped in front of him didn't help matters any. "Thanks for putting this together," he said, picking up the sandwich.

"It's tuna and some chips. Not exactly five-star fare."

He washed down the sandwich with bottled water. "Tastes like it to me, at the moment." He nodded toward the open laptop. "Were you able to come up with anything?"

She looked at him like he'd sprouted two heads.

He paused with the sandwich halfway to his mouth. "What?"

"I'd barely parked my butt on the bench seat when you started badgering me."

"Badgering? I asked if you were hungry."

"Which led to me making a meal. At what point do you think I got work done?"

He smiled over his sandwich. She'd said he was charming. Somehow at the moment, he didn't think he was pulling that off. "Well, look at it this way, now I can help." He laughed. "From the look on your face, I don't think I want to know your opinion on that."

"Good thing," she said, but he could see her fight a smile as she bit off another chunk of bread. "I don't know if it was wise for you to climb back down here. You could have eaten up there and then crashed for the night."

"I'm tired, but not sleepy. I'll feel better if we get somewhere with this transmission."

"Me, too," she said, and turned her focus to the computer screen as she continued with her meal.

Just the mention of work seemed to settle her some, which made him feel marginally bad for pushing the personal element of their developing relationship earlier. She was dealing with a lot at the moment, and he wasn't helping matters any. But he also knew the very fact that she was struggling to deal with him, meant he was getting to her. And this was too big, too much, too . . . everything, for him to just let it drop. He'd spent a few minutes before getting her to help him down from the bed, asking himself if it wouldn't be better to stick with the business at hand, get the situation figured out, then pursue whatever this was that was happening between them. Except once this was over, he'd have no reason to be around her. He could find some way to stay in the area, but there was no guarantee she'd have anything to do with him once she could hole up in her cabin again. She was far too good at putting up walls and erecting boundaries.

And if he thought, for one minute, that she truly wanted to be left alone, he'd honor that. But he'd seen the look in her eyes, felt the hunger in her kisses, tasted the passion that was simmering inside her. And he'd be damned if he was just going to walk away from that.

He'd finally—finally—opened himself up to the possibility of feeling like this again. The timing sucked, the place sucked, pretty much none of it was well conceived. But then, wasn't that how life worked? It was a miracle to him that he was even tempted to let his guard down, but with Tate, it wasn't like he even had a choice. He felt what he felt. And it was powerful, tantalizing stuff. It had to be, for him to be putting himself, and her, through this.

So, here he sat, mixing business with pleasure, because with Tate there was no separating the two.

"I think what I want to do is try and figure out what she might be saying during the gaps in the transmiss—what?" She looked up and caught him staring, with God knew what kind of dopey expression on his face.

"Nothing. I'm listening."

"You're staring."

"I'm eating and looking at you. You're nice to look at."

"It's—" She just shook her head and looked back to the screen, but he could tell from the set of her shoulders that she was self-conscious about it.

"Tate."

"Hmm," she murmured, very studiously eating her sandwich and playing the transmission back.

"I'm not going to leap over the table and attack you or anything. I can barely even fit on the damn seat. And I'm hardly in any condition for feats of athletic prowess."

She looked up at him, her expression both wary and resigned. It should have been off-putting, or at least stultifying, but it didn't set him back in the least.

"I'm not concerned with you jumping me."

"Good to know."

Now she sighed. There might have been an eye roll. "Given what we were doing earlier, I also know that short of having all your limbs completely severed, you'll find a way to get your hands on me if that's where you want them. That's not what I'm having a problem with." Seemingly realizing where that line of conversation was leading her, she abruptly shut up and looked back to the screen, though he'd have bet money she wasn't seeing a thing on it.

"Really," he said, trying not to sound amused and failing spectacularly.

"Yes, really," she said. "Don't be smug. It's not becoming."

"So, I'm not getting to you, then. At all. Take me or leave me."

"Of course you are. I'd have to be dead without a pulse not to be affected by you. Now stop fishing and let me work."

He was about to say he wasn't fishing, but maybe he was. Not intentionally, and not because he needed some kind of validation. Maybe it was because he couldn't seem to leave it alone, so he didn't want her to have that luxury, either.

"So," she went on, her tone brooking no argument, "I think we should try and work our way through the transmission and see if we can figure out what she's saying during the audio breaks. Especially in the beginning, where she talks about who she's working for."

The conversation they were having was so much more interesting to him than anything having to do with work, which was a new and different experience for him, but he let the matter drop. For now.

"Maybe if I listen and don't look, don't let seeing her distract any of my thought processes." Tate closed her eyes and hit PLAY. Derek watched her without interruption as she replayed the voice transmission a half dozen times.

"What are you looking for, listening for?" he asked, finally. He was listening, too, without watching, but it wasn't adding up to anything he hadn't already heard.

"I'm focusing on tone, the cadence, as best I can, even the gaps, and the words, both whole and fragmented." She listened several more times, never once watching, just listening. "I'm trying to get the rhythm and timing of CJ's speech patterns. I know what she sounded like—sounds like—and I'm trying to mentally superimpose her cadence over the fragmented audio. My hope is to try and gauge how much is missing, how many words, how much more could be being said. And possibly piece it together."

Derek nodded, but Tate wasn't watching him, or even looking at him. Other than replaying the transmission, she was sitting with her eyes shut, focusing. He tried to focus on the transmission, too, but found himself mostly watching Tate.

"Are you getting anything from it? Any ideas what is missing?"

She opened her eyes, looked at him. "Do you read lips very well?"

His eyes dropped to her mouth, he couldn't help it. But she was asking seriously, so he answered in kind. "I'm fair with it."

"Same with me." She sighed, looked back at the screen. "With the rhythm in my head, of her speech, of how much is missing, I think if I look at her mouth more closely, I might be able to put together at least a close approximation of what she's saying, or at least how many words we're missing. But we need to enlarge the image for that. It's too tiny, and I can't make out her mouth well enough to read anything."

"Sounds like a huge puzzle with a lot of possible right or wrong answers."

"Unless you have audio equipment we can use to enhance the transmission, it's more than we have right now," Tate responded. "And if it gets us any closer to understanding what she was apologizing for, and what she was specifically warning you about, then I say we have to at least try. I understand it will just be one potential scenario, or theory, but we've got nothing but supposition at the moment." She shoved the computer back toward him. "Get me in for a tighter look at her mouth without too much pixelation, if you can."

He didn't look at the computer. "Were you always this bossy?"

"I prefer to think of it as determined. It's part of my charm."

"True, actually. It is." And while she chewed on that, he slid his arm out of the sling and rested it on the table. Even with his fingers taped, two hands would be faster than one. He stuck in his universal Internet card, then tapped his way online, resisting the surprisingly strong temptation to run a quick search on her desktop for that document she'd hurried to shut down earlier that day. There'd be time for that later. Maybe they'd both play show-and-tell.

"With the timing thrown off by the transmission delay, her

mouth moving doesn't match the audio track anyway," Tate said. "Maybe what we need to do is enlarge the video and turn off the audio all together, just read her mouth and see where we can fill in any of the gaps. We might get the whole thing that way."

He slid the computer back further so he could rest his fore-arm on the table, but he was still pleased to feel more muscle-related pain in his hand and shoulder from all the physical therapy he'd been doing, than actual injury-related pain. Now he just had to not be stupid or impatient, and push too hard, too fast. Or any harder and faster than he already was. On the down side, his ribs still hurt like someone was shoving hot shards of glass between them, but he'd take what progress he could and focus on that.

Pain he could manage, and shove aside when duty called, but the distraction of Tate's personal life and how much more he wanted to know about it, was something that was proving yet another struggle he had to find a way to deal with.

He shoved the global DSL card in the slot, then quickly got online. While he got busy hacking a program download for a digital photography program, Tate had snagged a legal-size notepad out of her computer bag. A handful of pages had been dog-eared and flipped over the back. A quick glance revealed every line was crammed full with what looked like a never-ending stream of handwriting.

He turned his attention back to the download. If the pro-gram came through okay, he should be able to do moderate edits and enlargements of at least the video part of the trans-mission. Enhancing the voice would be a lot trickier and de-mand a much more involved program he doubted he'd be able to hack with the limited entry points he had on her system. He'd have to hack his way through several levels of secure sites before he could get to where he needed to be, and not only would that be too time consuming, but possibly too danger-ous.

"Oh. My god." Tate looked up from the page where it looked

like she'd been sketching out the transmission dialogue in script format. Her eyes were wide, her jaw a bit slack.

"What?" Derek demanded. "What did you figure out?"

"Let me see that." She tugged the computer around.

"Wait, I was downloading—"

"I just need to see where—" She stopped abruptly as she pulled up the video transmission screen.

"What?" he asked, when she simply stared.

She finally looked at him. "I know where she is." She looked back to the screen. "Or where she was, when she recorded this."

Derek swung the screen around. CJ was standing in front of what looked like a low, stacked-stone wall. Behind that was a thick stand of trees that blocked out the view of anything else. The image was tiny, still the size it had been on his satlink screen, but from what he could see, there were no buildings in sight, no signs, nothing else, not even the sky.

"She's here. In the States."

Derek glanced up. "Do you know this place?" She'd been diagramming the audio when she'd realized it, so he wasn't sure what had triggered the realization.

"No, not personally, but I think I know where it is." She tapped her pen on the pad. "I was writing out what she'd said, leaving spaces for where the gaps are, and I don't know why, but my mind just wandered and I was picturing her as I was writing, thinking about how it still doesn't seem real to me, even though I'm watching her, hearing her, that she's alive. And then it hit me."

Derek didn't interrupt, he just let her work through it.

She looked at him, but he was betting she was seeing something else entirely. "I was never one to make close friends easily, mostly because, for most of my life, growing up anyway, I found the people around me annoying and irritating." She smiled briefly. "I'm sure they'd have said the same about me. And they would have been right. Anyway, one of the reasons

CJ and I bonded like we did, was because we had that in common, the lack of strong childhood bonds."

"Where did you grow up?" He half expected her to say foster care. He had her bio and full dossier from when she came to work for his team, but all he recalled at the moment was that she'd grown up somewhere in New England, raised by a relative after her parents passed away.

"Boarding school," she said, which had him raising his eyebrows. "My parents both died when I was very young—"

"I know, you were raised in New England, by a family relative, right?"

"I was only six when they died, and the only one left in my family was an elderly great uncle. He had no idea what to do with me, so he shipped me off to boarding school. CJ's story was almost identical, except it was her grandmother who did the shipping. She was in a fancy boarding school out west, Washington state, and I was in New Hampshire. Anyway, we never felt like we belonged there, mostly because we didn't, and the exposure I got to the hierarchy of the rich get richer and the poor get bullied was, in large part, why I went the direction I did in college and afterward, into working for the government, and, eventually, for you." She sighed and put her pen down. "None of which is important, except CJ and I used to have long talks about the BS Years, as we called them. At my school, I stayed year round. My great uncle sent cards, money, and I stayed and ate holiday dinners with the staff and their children, which were actually my most favorite times of the year as they were the only times I felt I could relax and just be myself.

"CJ went home on holidays to stay with her grandmother, who was richer than Croesus but crazy as a loon. She lived on a mountain that she mostly owned, in this rambling old stone house that had been in the family since the dawn of time. Anyway, her grandmother apparently left CJ the place along with a giant wad of money to maintain it—nothing for CJ directly, mind you, but a half a million to some charity organized to find the cure for some kind of blighted plant lichen or something. She was truly an eccentric individual. CJ didn't mind that she didn't get anything, but she didn't want to be saddled with the estate, and all the property.

"But her grandmother had set it up so it was tied up in mountains of legal crap, so CJ couldn't sell it, so she leased it out, set up a trustee to manage the fund and oversee the tenants, and never looked back really."

"And you think that's where she is?"

"She described the place more than once, and mostly she went on about how Norman Bates would have felt right at home there, that it was dark and kind of creepy, but I remembered her talking about the grounds and how she spent most of her time there playing outside." She held Derek's gaze now. "In the wintertime, the snow was deep, and I remember her saying how it wasn't until she was there in the summertime that she even knew there was an old, stacked-stone wall around the whole place."

Derek looked back at the screen, and the stone wall that CJ stood in front of.

"And you think that's the stone wall."

"I don't know what her situation is, but if she wanted to go somewhere no one would think to look for her—"

"Wouldn't there be a paper trail of her owning it? I'd think the least bit of digging—"

"That's just it. She hasn't been there since she was in college. It never figured into her adult life, at all. I don't know what connection would come up in regards to the trust that oversees it, but I'm not even sure it makes any real dent anywhere in her history except as a sidenote in her background sheet. But that's not what I think is most important, what is most important is that she's dead. In the eyes of the law, anyway, and she didn't leave any blood relations behind, or a spouse, so I don't know where the estate ended up, or who it ended up with. It's probably not even hers anymore."

"Except if anyone is looking for her, they might piece it together like you have."

"If she hadn't mentioned it to me, I'd have never known. Did you know? Do you remember that from her background file?"

"No, but that doesn't mean it's not easily discovered."

"No, it doesn't. But regardless, I think that's where she went. It's familiar to her, but not to anyone else. I don't know what the setup is there now, or who even lives there. Or if she's even still there."

"So, do we head west, then?"

"It's the best place to start, I think. The only place we have that fits the scenario we think is right. And if she was in London the first time, and is here now, then her original code message that she needed an extrication wasn't about getting home from overseas. Clearly she managed that on her own. So, it looks even more now like you were right, it's all tied together, and it all starts and ends here." She held his gaze. "I'm sorry."

"Me, too. We can fly out in the morning."

"Do you think we can board a plane without being tracked? Even a private plane, if we're being watched in any way . . ."

"The drive would take us several days, but there's nothing to say we can't drive partway, and fly from there. I'm reasonably sure we haven't been tracked here from your place, agreed?"

"I don't think I was followed, and you did a scan for bugs, so I don't think we're being electronically tracked. If we were being watched, it might take them a day or two to find my car, then figure out we're in your rental, that is if they tracked that already."

"We can be several states away by then, and on a plane west."

"You're right," she said. "Okay then, we'll leave before dawn."

# Chapter 19

Tate shifted position for the hundredth time, and for the hundredth time debated on leaving right then. She could get them all the way to Indiana or Missouri by lunchtime. She realized they were heading out on what could only be deemed a wild goose chase, but it was the only trail they had at the moment. She had sat up with Derek after her revelation and they'd discussed other options, including him going back to home base as if he was just returning from his vacation and seeing what he could figure out from the inside while she headed west. But his injuries were still debilitating enough to restrict the kind of latitude he might require. Not to mention having to explain how he'd sustained them in the first place, possibly to the very people who had been responsible for torturing him.

They'd decided it was best to stick together and work from the outside. At least for now. She'd lain awake thinking about Derek's position, what his superiors were doing or thinking about his prolonged absence, the fact that no one was trying to make contact with him, as well as CJ's possible role in all of it and why she'd sent Derek after her, of all people, then warned him away. They'd tried to enlarge the video, but it had pixelated so badly, she couldn't read CJ's lips at all. They needed more sophisticated equipment, which is what had led to the talk about him possibly going back, working from the inside.

They'd even talked about her going back, under the original plan of pretending she wanted her job back, while he headed out to find CJ, but she wouldn't have access to the necessary equipment, at least not without running serious risk, with few options for explaining herself if she got caught.

She'd tried to come to terms with the fact that there was something nefarious going on, possibly inside her own agency, and definitely reaching far beyond it. She'd devoted her life to what she considered a patriotic cause, fighting to right injustices, and she'd never had any qualms about the fact that her team was developed outside the normal chain of command, and that very few in national security even knew of its existence. But the very fact that they did exist, and had for some time now, operating at a very complex, in-depth level inside the most dangerous elements of the international security community proved that her government was certainly capable of creating other, highly secret agencies as well.

It was the idea of exactly what the other agency may have been assembled to do that made her blood run cold. It wouldn't be beyond consideration that they were in place to police, in some manner, the operations of her team, given their extreme latitude in how they operated. Those checks and balances were already in place with their chain of command, who had to answer to someone in the NSA, at least in part, but if there was feared corruption at a higher level, then perhaps some policing was necessary. None of which explained why they'd hunted down, drugged, and beaten Derek in the hopes of extracting some kind of information from him. What would he know that made him that kind of target? A target who might not have survived the ambush?

She turned over again, and grunted a little in frustration at the small confines of the converted bed table. She knew it was imperative that she get as much rest as possible, as she'd be doing the driving. She needed to be alert to any possibility they'd been tracked. She rolled to her back and glanced up at the loft, where Derek, damn him, seemed to be sleeping quite peacefully. "Of course. He's all stretched out nice and flat," she muttered beneath her breath.

She'd helped him back up there not too long after they'd eaten and discussed their plans for the trip west, and he'd been out shortly afterward. At least one of them would be getting some good, restorative sleep.

She stared through the night gloom and allowed herself the luxury of watching him, though he wasn't much more than a darker outline on the mattress. Her thoughts strayed back to what had happened earlier, when they'd first gotten into the camper together. Which, if she was being completely honest with herself, had far more to do with her current sleepless state than the size of her sleeping quarters or concerns about the next stage of their mission. She should be thinking about the possibility that she'd be reunited with CJ soon, and the myriad of confusing thoughts and feelings that that eventuality roused. And she'd done her share of that, too, but even that monumental, possibly life-changing event, hadn't interrupted the chain of thoughts she couldn't seem to stop having about her former boss and current partner.

A man she'd always had great respect for and whose professionalism she'd admired and tried to mirror . . . and who she now couldn't stop thinking about stripping naked and devouring whole.

She blamed that entirely on him. She'd have never acted on the surprising reaction she had to him when she'd first brought him into her home. She'd have thought about it, maybe even fantasized about it, especially in light of her current work in progress, which she'd have probably blamed it on. She might have compared, contrasted, and—who was she kidding? If he hadn't kissed her in the kitchen that first day, she'd have likely jumped him at some point. Especially given the way he teased her, and joked around, and behaved in ways that weren't remotely like her reserved, oh-so-professional-at-all-times boss and team leader.

She rolled to her side and punched at the flimsy piece of fabric-covered foam that some idiot who'd designed this thing thought could pass for a pillow. She'd spent more nights than she could count sleeping on a lot less, with nothing under her head, but for three years she'd slept in a lovely, feather-topped, specially ordered and designed bed, on incredibly soft, high thread-count sheets, with a pillow under her head that was like a cloud. The redesign of the bathroom had been a necessity, but the bed . . . that had been her one serious self-indulgence. And she missed it, dammit.

She hated that she was back in this kind of grind, this kind of constant, nausea-inducing adrenaline rush, never knowing anything for certain, operating purely on instinct, staying so finely tuned at all times, all her nerve endings and receptors were all but quivering. Which probably explained her heightened awareness of Derek, too.

She hated all of it. If she'd ever wanted confirmation that she was okay with the turn her life had taken, and the exit from the career that had defined who she was, this was certainly providing all the proof she'd ever need.

She flopped to her back again, her gaze going to Derek. Again.

"For the love of God, will you just come up here and stretch out and get some rest?"

The unexpected sound of his gravelly voice, all deep and slurry from sleep, had her freezing in place. "Sorry," she whispered. "I'm fine. Go back to sleep."

She heard a patting noise against his mattress.

"Up here. Seriously. You're not fine, and neither of us is getting any sleep."

She begged to differ. He'd been conked out for almost three straight hours before she'd even made her bed. But she didn't think it was wise to get into a debate with him at the moment.

"If you're worried I'm going to jump you, don't be. Not that I don't want to, mind you. I don't know what the hell I did yesterday but I'm in no shape to be doing anything but lying flat on my back at the moment. You'd be doing the injured invalid a great service by climbing up here next to him and getting some sleep, so he doesn't have to listen to you toss and turn and huff and sigh."

"I do not huff," she said, at length.

Which earned a sleepy chuckle that was far too sexy and libidinally motivating to make getting anywhere near him a good idea. She didn't care how injured and sleepless he was. Because the sad, sorry truth of it was, while he might be able to control himself and not jump her, she wasn't suffering from any such physical limitations—quite the opposite—and wasn't at all certain she'd be able to maintain as high a level of control as he apparently could. And no way was she making the first move.

She blinked into the darkness, as she realized what she'd just admitted to herself. Had she been waiting for him to make another move? Because, why? If he did, then she could keep excusing herself from any culpability in what might happen next? Like, she didn't want this as badly as he did?

That wasn't a very flattering self portrait . . . and she wished like hell she could refute it. But her body was already damp and clamoring, just hearing his gravelly voice . . . and he wasn't even coming on to her!

"I'll be quieter. Go back to sleep."

"The way you're banging around, that bed is going to leave you more crippled than I am. So, two choices. You come up, or I come get you."

The idea of him coming after her had all kinds of connotations, and not a single one of them bothered her like it should. Quite the opposite. "Big words for a guy in a sling, using a cane to stay upright." Hopefully he was too sleepy to hear the need and frustration even she could hear in her voice.

"There are a few really inappropriate responses I could make to that, but I'll refrain in hopes that it'll encourage you to stop being so damn stubborn and come here where you can get some sleep."

"Easy for you to say," she muttered under her breath.

He slid one leg over the side of the bed. "Okay, time's up."

"Derek! For God's sake, don't do something stupid, just because—" She broke off and clambered around on the bed until she was standing beside the loft mattress. She pushed her bedhead hair from her face. "You're really insufferable, you know that?"

"Takes one," he responded. He pulled his leg back onto the bed and moved away from the edge. "Climb up, then we'll switch sides so you don't bang my bad shoulder."

He had it all planned, and it all sounded so innocent. She didn't know just how tired and grumpy he was, but her thoughts were anything but innocent at the moment. "Brace yourself," she told him, thinking there were all kinds of levels to the meaning of that.

"Ready," he told her.

She used the bench cushions to help heave herself up and over the side. She banged into him and he felt big and solid and was taking up a whole lot of room in what suddenly felt like a very small bed. "Sorry," she said, quickly trying to pull her legs up so she could stretch out beside him.

"No worries," he said, sounding sleepy, and sexy, and way up too close and personal.

"How do you want to switch places?"

"You go over, I'll slide under."

She could hear the amusement in his voice, damn the man. "No funny business," she said.

"Who me?"

Oh, yeah, so innocent. "Ready?"

"Always."

"Derek."

"Tate," he mimicked. "I'll be a Boy Scout, I promise. I told you, I'm in no condition to—"

She couldn't stand it. She made her move only she didn't swing her leg far enough and ended up all but dragging her body over his. "Sorry, sorry."

He grunted, but as she moved, she felt, very distinctly, that he was a whole lot more affected by her than he was letting on. "Hey—"

"Keep moving," he said tightly.

She managed to lever herself off of him and landed on the far side, banging into the wall of the front of the cab top. "Sorry."

"So you said."

"Yeah, well, Mr. Boy Scout—"

"I can't help if some parts of my body think they're ready."

"Well . . . okay." She slid down and lay flat on her back.

He moved around a bit, got settled, and then was still.

She just lay there, supremely aware of him, all big, warm, solid . . . and hard.

"Relax, Tate," he murmured, sounding almost asleep.

*Right,* she thought. *No problem.* But apparently it wasn't much of one for him, as he seemed to drop off almost immediately. His chest rose and fell and she could hear his even breathing. *Oh sure,* she thought rather unkindly, *just go right on off to sleep like it doesn't matter that I'm lying here, an inch away, ridiculously turned on and needy, with zero chance of ever getting any sleep.* She wiggled a little bit, trying to get comfortable without actually moving or breathing. Fat chance.

"The hell with it," Derek muttered. "Come here." He snagged her arm with his good hand and, with surprising strength, tugged her so she rolled right up next to him.

"I thought you were asleep."

"Right," he snorted, as if the possibility were so remote as to be ridiculous. Which made her perversely happy, just knowing she wasn't the only one affected.

"Curl up," he told her, urging her to snuggle up next to him.

"Your ribs," she said, stupidly, because it wasn't like she was actually going to do as he suggested. That was crazy.

"Can't hurt any more than they do right now." He slid his arm under her and rolled her in tight.

"Derek," she said, her face smothered against his T-shirt-clad chest.

"Shh," he said, stroking his hand down her arm. "Sleep. Big day tomorrow."

"Right." The mission. She was half draped across him, and he was thinking about work. Which, she should be if she had half a brain in her head. But her head and the brain inside it had apparently gone on vacation, because the mission was absolutely the last thing on her mind at the moment.

How he smelled, fresh, like her soap and fabric softener, and how absolutely rock solid he felt, that was what she was thinking about. And she knew exactly how good his rock solidness felt pressed into her body from when he'd trapped her against the sink earlier—no, don't think about that for God's sake. He was warm, and steady, and—

"Sigh like that one more time and even an Eagle Scout wouldn't be held responsible for his actions."

She went still. And yet all she could think about was that his lips were pressed against her hair, which meant all she had to do was tilt her head back a little bit and—

A heartbeat later her mouth was crushed under the force of his, and he was devouring her like she was his last meal. It took a second for her to realize that she wasn't just fantasizing this, that it was really happening, and then she caught right up.

Any concern for his shoulder, his ribs, blanked from her mind. He'd have to be responsible for that, because it was all she could do to keep up with the giddy way her body was responding to his onslaught.

And then, as quickly as it had started, it was over, and he was yanking his mouth from hers. "No," he said, his breath coming more heavily, "not like this. Christ, Tate."

"*I* didn't do anything!"

"You sure as hell—" He broke off and let his head drop back on the mattress. "I'm sorry," he said, at length. "You're right. You didn't ask for that."

"I didn't exactly shove you away," she said, grudgingly, needing to be honest.

"No, but . . ." He swore under his breath.

She put her hand gently on his chest. It was warm, and his heart was pounding. It matched her own. "Derek. Half the reason I couldn't sleep was thinking about you up here. Not the cramped sleeping quarters, or CJ, or any of it. This is just as much a thing for me as it is for you, so you can stop apologizing." Wow, she so hadn't intended for that to just come blurting out, but there was nothing she could do for it now.

He turned his head and she could see the glimmer of his eyes in the dark. "Is it? A thing for you?"

"You knew that from before."

"The timing sucks."

"I'm not sure there was ever going to be a right time for this. You and I—" She broke off, then finally said the rest. "Maybe this is the only time we'll ever have. Sucky or not."

"Earlier, you said—"

"I'm very aware of what I said, just like I'm very aware that I can say—and mean—a lot of things, but apparently that doesn't mean I'm going to be able to back them up, just that I want to. Or, more to the point, I know I *should* want to. My wants are definitely at odds with what's best for me at the moment."

He nudged her chin up with his bandaged fingers. "And what's best for you is being isolated and alone?"

"Alone doesn't equal lonely. And the isolation has been as big a part of my healing process as all the hundreds of excruciating hours I spent in physical therapy. More so, maybe."

"And the isolation has to be complete for you to feel whole? Is the idea of sharing your life so at odds with anything you can envision that might be healthy and happy for you?"

"You're talking about sharing my bed, not my life."

"You have no idea what I'm talking about."

That caught her up short. "You are probably more right than wrong with that statement, but not for the reasons you think."

"Then tell me why." He slid his hand up her arm and curled her more tightly against him.

"Your ribs—"

"What ribs? Stay here. It's the best medicine in the world, trust me." He rubbed his hand down her back, kept her close. "So, is it the risk? I understand about that."

She settled carefully against him, not in any real hurry to leave the surprising comfort of his arm around her, now that she'd felt it there. "That's just it. I've risked pretty much everything. Risk is a concept I'm thoroughly familiar with."

"And it's understandable that you don't want to invite that back into your world."

"It's not that, or not only that." She sighed a little, and he immediately rubbed her arm with the wide palm of his hand. It soothed her, and she couldn't recall a single time in her life where anyone had ever soothed her, for anything. It felt so damn good. Intoxicatingly good, even. She knew how soft she'd become when she was forced to admit that it would take very little for her to get used to this kind of give-and-take. And soft suddenly didn't seem like such a bad thing to be.

"What is it then?" he asked, and his voice, all deep and languorous in the dark, was seductive in ways that went far beyond the physical. It invoked trust, which would be all too easy to give.

"I understood the risk I was taking with my job. I understood what failure might mean, every level of failure, including how things ended for me. Death wasn't the only risk, and possibly not even the worst thing. But I knew, going in, what I was taking on, what the consequences could be. So it was an educated choice and I willingly accepted the ramifications."

He slid his hand up into her hair, as he half pulled her on top of him, sliding his other arm to the side, out of the way.

"Derek—"

"I think I understand," he said, pulling her so close that even in the dark she could see his face, his eyes. "You said before this was uncharted territory for you. By 'this' you didn't mean just the attraction, or even the beginning of affection, you meant putting your heart into play. That's the risk you don't want to take. Because it's not an educated choice. Because you don't know what you're risking. Not to scare you further, but sometimes—most times—it isn't even a choice. You just feel what you feel, no matter what you tell yourself."

He'd gotten it. Exactly. "How do you know that?" she asked.

"Because I have been there. I remember how terrifying it was. To want that badly, to take that kind of chance, hand someone that kind of power over you. It went against everything I believed in, that I'd trained for. But I had no choice, the feelings were there anyway. She already had the power without even asking for it."

Tate lay there, feeling his heartbeat beneath her, staring into eyes that knew, that understood . . . She also realized he was revealing something about himself, giving her a part of himself she didn't think he easily shared. And she knew, without knowing how, that the "she" in question here was responsible for whatever life-altering event he'd gone through that had so thoroughly changed him.

Which then brought about a fully humbling realization, when it sunk in, that in order to make sure that never happened again, he'd kept himself unencumbered from personal relationships . . . and yet here he was, pursuing one with her. She didn't know whether to feel flattered, terrified, or both.

"Tate . . ."

"Will you tell me?" she whispered. "What happened? I know it's part of what you started to tell me before, so if you can't—"

He pushed his fingers through her hair, cupped the back of her head, nudged her face closer to his. "Was I right? About the risk?"

"Yes," she said, knowing she couldn't give him anything less than the truth now, not with what she was asking of him. And a part of her already knew, as he'd said, that it wouldn't matter what she did now. She felt what she felt. The risk had already been taken.

She felt his breath ease out, his chest relax.

"Were you really worried it wasn't?"

"I was really worried you wouldn't acknowledge it, or let yourself believe it. It's damn inconvenient, and scary as hell, I know, but—"

She shut him up with a kiss for a change. And the instant her mouth brushed his, his hold on her was so tight, she thought she might not be able to breathe. Except it felt so good, so strong and solid and right. She wouldn't have cared if she'd passed out. She'd have gone with a smile on her face. And in her heart.

Christ. She'd really gone and done it.

"That," he said, when she finally lifted her mouth, "was the single best kiss I've ever received."

She laughed a little at that. "You have really low standards."

"On the contrary, I have standards so high, I didn't think a kiss like that was even possible."

"Meaning?"

"It was a gift. For me. To me. Me, Tate."

She knew what he was saying, and it made her eyes burn a little. "Yes, that's true. It's definitely, specifically you."

His hold tightened again, and she thought he'd kiss her again, maybe push for more, and, regardless of his physical condition, she didn't think she'd have stopped him this time. Or possibly ever. She had no idea where this would lead, or what in the hell she was really getting herself into, but she was already into it, so fighting it any longer seemed a useless waste of time. Time that could be spent right here. Doing this.

Because time was the one commodity she had no guarantee for.

He didn't kiss her though. Instead, he tucked her head back down on his chest, and kept his arm snug around her. "Do you still want to know?"

She knew what he was referring to. "Only if you want to tell me."

"I've never told a single living soul, not all of it. My part in it."

"Derek—"

"But I have to tell you. I need to tell you. If you're going to kiss me—me—then I need you to know all of who you are making promises to."

"Promises—"

"That kiss, Tate, was a promise, whether you know it or not."

She thought about it, and realized he was right. She'd claimed him with that kiss. He was hers . . . for now. For how long, or for what kind of ride, she had no idea. But her heart was in play. And she believed his was, too. Which was both scary as all hell . . . and the most exhilarating feeling in the world.

"I . . . I know it," she told him, then smiled against his chest at his murmured, "Hot damn."

"I'm going to ask you for something, then, too," he added.

She propped her chin up. "What? What do you need to know?"

"I want to know who I'm kissing, too. Who I'm claiming."

"You do know. What you see is what you get. I don't have a lot of levels."

"You'd be wrong about that, but that's not what I mean."

She thought about it, then realized what he might be getting at. And further realized it was the one thing she had that was exclusively hers, that she hadn't shared with a soul. In her case, it was an exciting thing, a life-altering thing, too, but not a tragic thing, as she feared his was. But it was still a fair trade, swapping pieces of themselves, trusting the other to hold on to it with reverence and respect. And understanding.

"You want to know about what you saw on my computer."

"Because it's something that's yours, that you clearly don't share, for whatever reason, and that intrigues me to no end. I don't even care what it is, it's the idea of its existence that gets after me."

"So, you want an exchange then. An exchange of trust, so to speak."

"No, I already trust you. I've always trusted you with my life. Now I trust you with far more fragile parts of me, possibly the only vulnerable part I have."

"Derek—"

"You'll do with that what you will, Tate. And I won't hold it against you either way. You didn't ask for it, it doesn't work like that. It's just yours." He smiled then, she could feel it. "Which could be the best gift ever, or the worst. You'll have to be the judge. But just because it's given freely, doesn't mean it will be accepted. That's the risk part. I can't control that. I can only hope for the best."

"I know," she said, feeling every word he said resonate deep inside of her because she identified with each one. How terrifying was that? But, as he said, there was no choice for it. Risk already taken.

"Good," he said, and there was such warmth in his voice, such . . . happiness. And it was such a wondrous thing, knowing she'd been the one who'd caused it. She was amazed that she had the power. Then immediately, the full importance of the risk sunk in. She had the power to please, which meant she had the power to hurt.

And so did he.

"About the other," he went on, "I'm not blackmailing it out of you. I want you to want to tell me. And I can wait for that. I don't care when, and it certainly doesn't have to be now. I'm going to tell you my part, because I need to, because I can't go further without telling you. I'll wait for yours until you feel the same. And hope that, at some point, you will."

"Patience hasn't exactly been a virtue. For either of us."

"I can stick this one out."

"You won't have to," she said, already knowing it was true. Suddenly it seemed silly, the secret life she'd been harboring. What he thought of it mattered to her in that she wanted his respect, but beyond that, she trusted that he'd listen, then handle the information in whatever way she asked him to. "What you saw on the screen—"

"Wait," he said.

"I trust you, Derek."

"Do you want me to know? Because you're bursting at the seams to share?"

She thought about that, and realized that while it might sound like he was splitting hairs, he really wasn't. She could give him what he'd asked for, merely as a show of trust, knowing he'd handle it, a secret safely shared. But that wasn't what he was asking for at all. It wasn't a test she had to pass. She'd already passed whatever test there was in the choosing of a partner, just based on who she was to him. No, he was asking for something far more elemental, and it wasn't something she could fabricate. She either had to feel it, or not. She could choose to share the feeling or not, but she couldn't choose feeling it.

"I get it," she said, as much to herself as to him. "I truly get it."

"And?"

"And, I don't know."

There was only the briefest of pauses. "Okay."

She laughed a little. "It's so not okay, but you don't have a choice, I know that, and I'm sorry. But honesty is imperative to me, and I'd think it would be mandatory for someone like you."

"Yes, someone like me would like to think that someone like you would never be anything but honest."

"Was that part of the thing? From your past? Honesty, loyalty?"

"No," he said.

"Okay." She felt better about that.

"I would expect it regardless, from anyone. If I didn't have that from you, I wouldn't be here, talking to you like this. So, I may not like it, but never shy away from speaking it."

"I won't. And . . . with my thing . . . it's—I could tell you right now, but it would be more an act of bravery, and I'm very good at being brave. Proving to myself and you that I can. Because I do trust you, and I know now that telling you will be fine. But that's not what you're asking of me, and I get that. So, to do it now . . . it seems more about proving something than sharing something I'm excited and giddy about and want to run and tell you about because I can't wait to share."

"You have it exactly right."

"Then you'll have to wait." She reached up and cupped his face. "Not because I can't, or don't want to, but the moment has to be mine. And this moment . . . this one is yours. Does that make sense?"

He tugged her up, so his lips were brushing hers. "Yes," he said quietly, almost reverently. "Thank you."

"For?"

"Getting it. Getting me. And waiting so you can have your moment. You deserve that."

"We both do."

"Yeah," he said, then sighed. "Mine isn't going to be—"

"Shh," she said, brushing a kiss against his lips. "I know. But you need to. And I need to know. It'll be okay. I'll be okay."

What was surprising her most, was that she was traversing the path into this new, uncharted territory, and while it was both scary and exciting, it was also not so daunting or mystifying. She hadn't known how she'd act, or if she'd feel awkward or lost. But she didn't feel lost at all. Which was kind of wild, because she'd always felt perfectly fine, just with herself, by herself, for herself. But, lying here in his arms, feeling his heartbeat, the warmth of his body, his deep voice . . . she'd never felt less lost in her life. And never more at home.

"We can save all of this for later," she said, knowing she'd sleep now. Knowing they both would. "It's been a really long day, and maybe just knowing we will talk about it is enough for now."

"Now is better," he said, surprising her a little. She'd thought he'd take the out, for now, enjoy their newfound bond. But he sounded almost . . . anxious.

"Okay."

"Is it?"

"Yes," she said, knowing it was the truth. He needed her now. Now is when she'd be there for him.

He slid his fingers into her hair, tucked her head so it was snuggled in the crook of his neck and shoulder. His fingers lightly massaged her scalp, then toyed with her hair, but she'd bet the actions were more to soothe him, than her. Which was another thing that made her feel good, that he instinctively reached for her to be soothed.

"I was married once," he said, "and we had a son."

She went completely still, and her heart squeezed tightly, knowing what was coming, even before he said it. She'd been expecting . . . something. Something bad, something tragic, so why this stopped her heart, why this caught her so badly off guard, she didn't know.

Tears were already burning, and had he been anyone else, had she been at all capable, she would have scrambled down off the bed and raced out of the RV and into the woods. Because a second ago it had been all about trust, and soothing, and excitement, and arousal . . . now it was going to be about pain, and loss. And she'd known it had to be something like that, and was prepared to soothe him in whatever way she could—even if she was awkward with it, she'd try her damndest to be there for him.

What she hadn't counted on, is that the one who'd need soothing, who'd hurt just listening to it, would be her.

"He died. He got sick, and he died, and I wasn't there. I wasn't there to help him, to help her, to hold either one of them. I thought what I was doing was so important, saving the world, and that she was exaggerating, because of course I knew everything, I knew best. So I left her there. Alone. With a sick child, who got very much sicker, very fast. Too fast, too fast for me to do anything, to get back. So, I left her there, alone, to do the hardest thing any human being could ever have to do, to hold her own son—our son . . . my son—and watch him die. Without me. The only other person she had.

The one who would never let her down. I let them both down, I let me down. I—I let my son down."

She instinctively clutched him to her, and pressed her lips against his neck. They were wet, and she realized the tears were her own. She never cried. Never, not once. Not during her entire time in captivity, not during her entire time in rehabilitation. But he clutched her right back, and held on tight, and she felt his chest quake, felt his trembling lips press against her hair, and she cried. Hot streaks burned down her cheeks, and they wouldn't stop coming.

And that's when she realized the true meaning of having the power to hurt. Because she was just hurting for him, and it was almost unbearable. She couldn't imagine the pain and anguish of him hurting her directly, even if he didn't mean to, if he couldn't help it, if he had no choice.

And she held on to him, more terrified than she'd ever been in her life. Held on to him . . . and she shook, and she cried. For him, for his dead son, for the loss of his family, and for herself. Because he was both the only thing that could soothe that pain, that stark terror . . . and the only one who could cause it.

What in the hell had she done?

# Chapter 20

What had he done?

He'd made her cry. And not just little tears of sympathy . . . she was brokenhearted with them. And she was breaking his heart with them, too. What in the hell had he done?

"Tate—"

"Don't," she whispered raggedly. "Just . . . let me hold on. You . . . hold on."

So he did. And, with her wrapped tightly around him, crying for him, his own tears came. Finally. He'd raged, at the world, at himself. He'd been numb, he'd drowned in the pain. He'd been everything, done everything . . . except this. It had been a long, long time ago . . . but it was forever yesterday in his heart. He'd made sure he was the best at what he did, best in the field, best leader, best strategist, best trainer. He risked his life, and those of the men and women he commanded, but he made damn sure they were as prepared to deal with what the mission handed them as they could be.

What he didn't do, what he never did again, was let himself care. About the mission, about his people, their safety, yes . . . but not with his heart, not with the part of him he couldn't control. If he never loved like that, he couldn't hurt like that, destroy like that. Like he'd destroyed his family. He was so busy saving the world, he couldn't save his own family.

It was too late. For all of it. When he got back. It was too late.

But he'd learned. Learned he wasn't going to take a risk like that again. And he would find balance, find time to put the job in perspective, if it killed him. He'd take time away, so he understood the balance necessary. For himself, for his job, for his team. Everyone would benefit if he understood balance.

But he never saw himself falling in love again. Even with that understanding, he never saw himself taking the risk. He'd pour himself into the thing he knew he did well, and he'd take his harshly, so harshly learned lessons, and apply them there. And to himself. But he wouldn't risk another person, not intimately. And he sure as hell wouldn't risk a child. He knew himself. He was a crusader, he wanted to save the world. And if it meant finding balance within, he'd do that in order to do what he did to the best of his ability.

Then that world changed. And he didn't know what he was crusading for. He supposed it came with getting older, a new perspective, and he wondered what his role was, what he should be doing, and if, perhaps, in his single-mindedness, he'd overlooked the importance of broadening his scope.

And then there was Tate. And it didn't really matter what had come before, or what might come after. She was there. And his heart was in play. He knew it, knew the signs, the feelings, even before she'd dragged him into her home, and as he'd stayed, and as he'd fallen, he'd wondered how in the hell he'd ever thought he could live the rest of his life without this.

Maybe things happened for a reason when they did. He'd never be able to reconcile the loss of his son. He'd been the cause of losing his wife. And now, here he was, in a place that should be so petrifying . . . and yet it was the opposite of that. It was grounding, and renewing, and validating. Proof that what he was fighting for was worth it. Worth this. Freedom . . . to live, to love.

Maybe he was falling now because he was ready to fall. Tate thought it was because he was at a crossroads and clinging to something, but that was not it. In fact, that was the last thing he'd do in uncertain times. Drag someone else in and cling to them to regain his own sense of balance. And yet, it was uncertain times, but the person at his side understood that, had lived it. Like he did. So it didn't matter. They balanced each other, because they'd both learned to stand alone. It made it exactly the right time. The right person. Maybe the only person.

Her tears slowed, then stopped. He kept stroking her hair, leaving the dried tears on his cheeks, feeling the tight skin there from the tracks, as he continued to soothe himself by soothing her.

"I'm sorry," she said, but didn't elaborate. She didn't have to. That was the thing about this. Why he knew that of course she was the one he'd love. Of course she was.

"It should scare me," he said. "This."

"Does it?" she said, her voice rough from the tears.

He pressed a kiss to the top of her head. "No. It's too right for that." He tipped her face up, kissed the corners of her eyes, and down the salty tracks left from her tears, until he ended at her mouth. "You're too right for it to be anything other than glorious. It's too good to waste any of it worrying. I've learned. I've learned what will happen, will happen. I don't want anything bad to happen. But I know what to do. What not to do. I found balance, Tate. I know my place in the world, and what's important, and I know my place in this. I wouldn't make the same choices, the same mistakes. And the rest . . ." He kissed her again. "It doesn't do any good to worry. I'd rather spend the time I have doing this."

Her mouth was soft, warm, damp with tears, and pliant beneath his. She was still sad, still mourning for him, and he let her work through that as he continued his soft kisses. It eased him, too, helped him mourn all that was, that could never be. Even as he slowly brought them back to what was going to be, with the promise of all those kisses.

"Derek—"

"Shh," he murmured.

She shook her head, broke the kiss long enough to lift her head and look at him. "No, I need to say this. Thank you."

"For breaking your heart?"

"For sharing that part of yourself. With me. For letting your heart break again. For trusting me to hold all the shattered little pieces."

"But I shattered you, too."

"I know." She smiled a little then, and it was so beautiful, like the sun after the rain, the promise of new life to come. "It was because you could that I knew what to do. I knew what I needed, so I knew what to give. I'm not making any sense."

"You're making perfect sense."

She laid her head back down. "We should sleep."

"We should." He nudged her chin back up, and kissed her again, only this time it wasn't about easing, but about the promise of new life. And, once he'd started to unleash it, the hunger for it, to start it, it almost swamped him. He knew it was the boomerang of being so wrenched just before, but he didn't care. It was the right bookend to it, the right launching pad for what came next.

And Tate was right there with him, kissing him back with the same hunger, the same fervor, the same voracious need, like she could consume him and it still wouldn't be enough to sate her.

He knew the feeling.

He pushed her to her back and rolled to his side. Her hand came up to brace him. "You said, before . . . you said, 'not like this.' You shouldn't be—we shouldn't—"

He let his ribs scream. His shoulder echoed the sentiment. But he leaned down over her anyway. "Now we should. I wanted it to be between two people who knew, who'd accepted, who are ready to look forward. It had to be all that, with you. Nothing less would be right."

She smiled then, broadly, white teeth flashing in the dark, and it was truly the sun at the end of a long, very long storm. "It feels perfectly right . . . but—"

"I know I'm not a hundred percent, I'm a little busted up at the moment, but what I feel for you is a hundred percent."

"Then that's all that matters. We can wait, until it's pleasure and not pain for you. It shouldn't hurt. I don't want it to hurt."

"I'm pretty sure I won't feel the least bit of pain." Then he leaned in to kiss her and his rib gave him such a vicious pinch, he sucked in a gasp before he could control it.

"See?" She gently eased him off of her. "Lie down." She kept pushing. "Lie all the way back down."

Flat on his back again, the fire in his side immediately ceded, but the one in his heart . . . "This is so not how I wanted our tempestuous union to begin."

She smiled and leaned over him. "I hate to be the one to break it to you, but it's already started." She kissed him, then kissed him again.

He groaned as his body raged to life, feeling only pure, unadulterated pleasure at her taste, her touch, that she was the one kissing him, pleasing him . . . nothing had ever felt this good. His hand came up to brace her, then to pull her down. "Seriously, about the injuries—"

"Shh," she told him now. "Let me the rest of the way in."

"You're in," he told her, groaning deep in his throat when she brushed her hands across his face, traced his tender cheekbone, ran her fingers across his lips, then began working her way along his jaw with a string of kisses that were sweeter than he thought existed.

"Then let me have you," she murmured, pressing a hot, sweet kiss to the tender spot beneath his ear. "Let me learn you." She lifted her head, looked into his eyes. "Trust me with this," she said, pressing the tips of her fingers over his heart. "Trust me with you. You'll have your turn, your time . . . but this time, is my time."

She slid down, kissed the spot where her fingers pressed. Then she leaned over and kissed the tips of his bandaged fingers, and every single one of his ribs, so feather soft, her lips so warm and sweet.

His eyes burned again, only it had nothing to do with mourning a loss. How . . . what had he done to deserve the gift of her?

"You gave me the same gift," she said, sliding further down, continuing her journey of healing, of loving.

He hadn't known he'd even spoken out loud. Then the burning behind his eyes, and the squeezing of his heart instantly eased as his body twitched and pulsed to life. "Tate, you don't—"

"Oh," she said, with the most delectable, devilish amusement in her voice, "but I do." She slid her hand down his belly, and over the rock hard bulge below, circling him, holding him . . . stroking him.

He lifted his head and watched her, watched the pleasure it gave her, the grin on her face, like she was unwrapping a present Christmas morning. And he found himself grinning, then chuckling, because it felt like Christmas for him, too. "I promise I was a very, very good boy."

She giggled then, and he didn't think he'd ever heard that sound from her. "Nice to know," she said. "You'll have to tell me if I am a very good girl."

And then she pushed up his shirt . . . and pulled down his boxers, freeing him to her touch, her taste, her—"Dear, heavenly God," he groaned, letting his head drop back on the mattress as she took him into her mouth. "Santa is going to be very, *very* good to you later," he promised, then he was pretty sure his eyes rolled back in his head because there were no more words, only the most intense, insane pleasure he'd ever experienced.

She teased, she tormented, she explored, she enjoyed. And she pleasured. Oh, sweet Lord, did she pleasure. But as he felt himself begin to gather, and knew there would be no stopping the rush to release this time, no easing back to prolong the delirium that was Tate's mouth on him, he knew that this was not how he wanted their first joining to be.

"Tate." He sunk his hand in her hair, then covered her hand, wrapped around him, with his own. "Tate, come here. I want . . . I want inside you."

She stopped, but kept her hand around him. "Derek, it's okay, I want—"

"Me, inside of you." His hips were still moving, her hand still around him. "Straddle. My hips."

"Your ribs—"

"Trust me, I am feeling absolutely no pain right now. Wait, shit, in my wallet—protection. I really didn't plan—"

"We're safe. After what happened to me, I can't—we're safe."

His heart squeezed, and he wanted to pull her back up to him, kiss her, hold her, for the losses she'd suffered, too. But her hand was still on him, and—"Please."

She smiled as she moved onto her knees, sliding out of her pajama bottoms as she did, and carefully moving over him. "Well, if you're going to say please . . ."

He gripped her hip with his good hand, his other hand slid up her thigh, and they both groaned in unison as she slid down over him. She arched back, taking him deeper, and his hips bucked off the bed at the sensation of all of her, gripping all of him, in the most intimate of embraces. And then she was leaning forward, bracing her hands on the bed . . . and moving.

They found their rhythm easily. He wasn't sure who was driving and who was riding. He was panting, she was groaning, then he felt her begin to tighten, begin to move faster, and the force that gathered inside him was so strong, he thought he might truly explode.

"Tate—"

"Yes," she said, then said it again. She was driving him, moving almost mindlessly now, the whimpers and groans of her own pleasure mingling with his until he thought he might lose consciousness the intensity was so insane.

"Derek. Derek!"

He opened his eyes, just as she leaned forward and claimed his mouth, cried against his lips, into him, as she came, convulsing around him. And that was all it took. He shook hard with the force of his release, and she continued to rock on him, saying his name, claiming him, mind, body, and soul as she kissed him, first fiercely, then more softly, and finally, tenderly, as their bodies slowed, and the air was filled only with the sound of their deeply drawn breaths.

He wanted to pull her down on top of him, but she was already sliding off of him, carefully lying next to him. He tugged her close, held on tight, so far beyond feeling pain at the moment that there was nothing that could spoil it. "That—" he began.

"—was exactly perfect," she sighed.

"—was just the beginning," he finished, and they both laughed.

He nudged her chin up and leaned down enough so he could kiss her. It was a promise of more, sealing what they just experienced.

"So," she said as she settled into the crook of his arm, careful, always careful, not to press against any of his injuries, "what in the hell was I waiting for, anyway?"

He chuckled. "To think we had that big ol' bed of yours, but noooo."

She air-swatted him. "You were in no shape for this."

"I believe I just managed quite well."

"Several days later, yes."

"And several days more, look out," he said, tugging her up hard against him so he could kiss her fast and deep.

"I'm not sure I'll survive it," she said, on a gasp.

"We might need to get another one of those walking sticks of yours."

"His and hers," she said with a snicker.

He grinned into the dark as he rubbed his hand up her back, and kept her close. He couldn't remember a time when he felt this good. Even before, when he'd loved, it hadn't been like this. This was deeper, with far greater understanding, and, if possible, more profound joy.

Now, all he had to do was figure out the rest of his life. And how to keep her in it.

# Chapter 21

Tate settled herself behind the wheel of the truck and waited for Derek to finish securing the back door. It was hard to believe she'd just parked this thing less than twelve hours ago. An entire lifetime had taken place inside that camper since then.

She closed her eyes for a moment and thought about last night, about that moment when he'd said her name, with all that want, all that need. And when she'd moved over him, and he'd moved inside her . . . She pressed her thighs together now in memory of how much better it was than anything she'd ever experienced. Certainly than anything she'd ever written.

She smiled, and laughed a little. "Boy, I was even more a giant fraud than I thought."

"What?" Derek was opening the passenger door and climbing in.

"Nothing," she said, still smiling. "Are we all set?"

"We are."

She smiled at him, and he smiled back, making her feel like a ridiculously giddy teenager, which she'd never once been even when she'd been a teenager. So, fair was fair, she was getting the chance now. And she didn't care who knew it.

His hair was still damp from the shower and her body responded to him just being close to her. They'd hooked up the generator so they could each take what amounted to a quick, hot rinse in a cubicle made for stick figures. He'd tried to snag her under the spray with him, but the small space made that impossible. She was surprised he'd managed to shower at all without injuring more body parts.

"Sunrise is pretty," she said, as she carefully pulled out from between the trees.

"Possibly the nicest one I've ever seen."

She laughed and looked over at him. "Are you sure you didn't take any happy pills this morning?"

"Just you," he said. "That's all the happy I need."

She tried to roll her eyes, but she was too busy grinning like a loon to pull it off. "Yeah. I know the feeling."

She slid the piece of paper over with the crude map she'd drawn earlier in the morning. "I think that's our best trail out of the area," she said. She'd keep them to back roads until they were most of the way through West Virginia, then hit the highway west in a straight shot all the way to Kentucky. She looked up. "How do we reserve tickets without creating a paper trail?"

"We don't. We pull cash out of the nearest bank branch, so they can't track us any further than the Virginia state line. If we're lucky, anyone keeping an eye on our whereabouts will assume we're staying in the area, close to home base. They might monitor the local airports and train stations, but I doubt they'll figure out our target destination."

"Unless they know where CJ is, too. I thought about this while you were showering this morning, but we don't know if CJ is alone, being watched, or what is going on with her."

"See, while I was in the shower, I was thinking about slippery wet skin and all the things I could do with that, and how I should have reserved an RV with a shower stall bigger than a phone booth."

"Work first, then play."

"Oh, no. If you wait to play after work is done, play never happens, because there's always more work."

She looked over at him. "If we get this particular work done, we'll have nothing to do but play."

"If you want to risk it, sure, go ahead. But I'm telling you, taking play breaks is highly underrated."

"Really." She looked back to the road, a grin slowly curving her lips as she imagined what a play break with Derek Cole would be like. An injured Derek Cole could already make her forget her name when he made her the focus of his attention. A healthy Derek Cole . . . a healthy, playful, Derek Cole . . . She couldn't help it, she squirmed in her seat a little. "I'll take your suggestion under advisement."

"Oh, please do," he said, resurrecting Austin Powers again.

"Somewhere, Mike Myers just cringed."

"Mike Myers would kill to be me right now."

She laughed at that, and forced her attention to the road, and away from the crazy, sexy man seated beside her. Her former boss. Now her lover. A man she'd trusted with her life . . . suddenly, somehow had ended up as the caretaker of her heart. It was really unbelievable, in so many ways. If she let herself think about it, about what she'd done in the past twelve hours, the past several days really, it was downright mind blowing, considering all that had come before, and where she felt so solidly planted now. The distraction potential was off the charts. And she needed to be focused, clear-headed, sharp, if they were going to handle the situation with CJ and, at the same time, resolve the mystery of what was really going on behind the scenes at home.

And, at the same time, she felt perfectly within her rights to soak up all the pleasure, all the joy, all the Derek she could. He was right about not postponing the good stuff. She knew exactly how fragile life could be.

She had no idea what the next few days would bring, much less all the ones that came after it. And she didn't want to dwell on what she didn't know. She wanted to wallow, to revel, in what she did. For as long as she could.

"You know . . ."

"What do I know," he said, glancing up from her map and directions.

"I was thinking about your work/play ethic, and it has me wondering."

"Yes?"

"Are airplane bathrooms any bigger than RV bathrooms?"

"Hmm," he said, pretending to take it under very serious consideration. "Considering we're going private and not commercial, I'll have to see what I can work out."

"Just a suggestion," she said.

"I'll take it under advisement," he said, making her laugh.

They came down off the mountain and eventually into a small town with both bank and gas station. They planned to go as far as a single tank would get them, then get to the nearest airport, hire a pilot and head west. After the bank, she pumped gas and Derek went inside to stock up with what he termed "road trip necessities."

He came out with a bulging bag, which had her shaking her head as she finished up and closed the gas cap. She climbed back in the cab and buckled in. "What in the world did you get? One of everything?" The station store had been only slighter bigger than the RV shower.

"A granola bar breakfast just wasn't going to do it for me." He propped the bag on his lap so he could dig inside of it.

She smiled. "Well, a guy with a work/play mantra does need to keep his stamina up."

That had him slanting a look her way. "Up with stamina is going to be my new motto."

She laughed at his near reverent tone. "You know, it's just as well you filtered this part of your personality out when we worked together."

"I get no respect."

"Wow, your Rodney is even worse than your Austin. Hard to believe, really."

"Rodney would also kill to be me right now. Do you know, when I was younger I thought Dangerfield was such a cool name. Total action hero."

She smiled over at him. "You are an action hero."

He started to shoot back a retort, but he lifted his gaze to hers just then, and must have seen something in her expression, because he ducked his chin, but not before she thought she saw an actual blush rise to his cheeks. She looked back to the road, and wondered if her cheeks would freeze like this from grinning all the time. "For the baddest of badasses, you are ridiculously cute sometimes."

She thought he might have choked a little. "Seriously, don't ever say that in front of the team."

"Don't worry." She turned her full attention back to the road. "They'd never believe me anyway."

They stopped for coffee, then wound their way into the mountains of West Virginia and got down to some serious driving. Derek worked his way through at least half the bag of food, while she munched on a blueberry muffin and mulled over exactly what course of action they should take once they got out to Washington.

"I know the estate was in a little town called Spruce Lake, or just outside it anyway. I looked it up on the computer this morning when I was putting the map together and it's a good three hours from any major airport, but only forty-five minutes from the county airstrip. Do you think it's worth the risk to land there and narrow our window of opportunity?"

"Depending on how small a town it is, landing a small private jet would probably get jaws to wagging. We might lose any element of surprise."

"They wouldn't know it's us."

"They'd know it was somebody, and that's more of an edge than we can stand to lose."

"I hate to lose the time, though. I don't know . . . when I woke up this morning, I just had this feeling of urgency."

"That was just me. You spoon really well, by the way."

She gave him the eye. "You know, if it wasn't for the fact that it's your bad arm closest to me, you'd have gotten thwacked just now."

He covered the sling with his good hand. "So violent. Although, when it comes to the way you climax, violent is kind of good. Great actually."

She . . . didn't know what to say to that.

"What?" he asked, apparently noticing the stunned expression she knew she had on her face.

"Nothing. I guess I'm just not used to—I'll have to get used to you just saying things. Like that. You just came right out and—"

He started chuckling.

"You know," she said, evenly, "that might not be the best way to optimize your chances of a play break in the plane bathroom later. Just saying."

"I can't help it, I find it's kind of cute that you have literally seen the dregs of humanity and been in situations that were as real and down and dirty as it gets, but talking about sex makes you blush."

"Yeah, well . . ." She had nothing for that. "That's different. This is personal."

"It's our personal, so we get to talk about it. You and I. And celebrate it, revel in it. I could go on, in fact, in great detail, about what your body feels like, wrapped around me. It was an almost spiritual experience, feeling you come. The way I came. In fact, I might even be poetic."

If the way the muscles between her thighs were tightening up, along with her nipples, was any indication, her body just loved hearing him talk like that. She just smiled over at him, shook her head, and kept driving, letting the idea of true intimacy, and all the various levels and layers that it evidently carried with it, sink in for a bit.

He was making notes on her map and polishing off another bottle of water when she said, "So . . . violent is good then? Because you're a bit . . . volcanic yourself when you come. I liked that."

It was very gratifying to see him half choke, and half spray the swig of water he'd just taken. "Mmmf," he managed, around a mouthful of pretzel. Which was followed by either "Good," or "God," she wasn't sure which, but decided it didn't matter.

She just grinned and relaxed back in the seat a little. She'd get the hang of this. This whole relationship thing. "Remember, I was always a fast learner."

He swallowed, took another swig of water, then dug in the bag. "More protein bars. And vitamins. We're going to need those."

She laughed, and he chuckled, and it was easy, right then, to forget their eventual destination . . . and the great unknown that yawned, wide and vast beyond it.

She wanted him. She wanted everything she could have with him. She also wanted her life in the valley. The solitude to write, to think, to simply be. She slid a glance at Derek and wondered how he'd fit in to all that. And wondered if she was prepared to make that sacrifice if he couldn't.

He dozed for awhile, reminding her that even superheroes needed time to heal. She hoped their . . . activities from the night before wouldn't prove too big a setback for him. But he seemed clearer, stronger, and sharper this morning, so she didn't think it had. But nonetheless, she was glad for the drive, and the flight, if for no other reason than it would give him time to rest.

It was early afternoon when she rolled into the rest stop just inside the Kentucky state line. "Derek?"

"Mmm," he responded, not opening his eyes.

"We're in Kentucky. Do you need a break, get out to stretch, or do you want to push on to the airport?"

His eyes blinked open. "Kentucky? How the hell—what time is it?"

"A little after two. I didn't think you'd sleep this long, but figured it might not be a bad idea to just let you get as much rest as you can."

He looked . . . grumpy. And she wondered if he was a morning person. She couldn't really judge by the few mornings he'd woken at her cabin, given the state he'd been in. And this morning . . . she closed her eyes briefly and recalled how amazing it had been to come awake and realize it was his solid arm holding her tight against the length of his wonderfully warm body . . . and that had all felt perfectly natural. For a woman who'd slept alone her entire life. Perfectly natural, like she'd been doing it forever. It had felt pretty spectacular, actually.

"Tate?"

"Huh?" She blinked her eyes open, looked at him. "What?"

"Maybe you need a break. I can get us to the airport."

"No, no I'm fine. I was just thinking about . . ."

He lifted his eyebrows when she didn't finish.

"I need to stretch my legs."

"Yeah, okay," he said, his amused tone telling her he wasn't fooled for a minute.

What kind of look had she had on her face anyway? Blissful was a possibility. She smiled, and wondered why she'd dodged him. So she turned back to him as she slid out of the truck. "I was thinking about waking up next to you, and how it felt so normal."

"That was pretty good, wasn't it," he said, his smile warm now, happy, and perhaps a little suggestive. She liked that combination on him. She liked even more that she was responsible for it.

She closed the door and walked up to the little brick building, and decided she'd have to do that more often. Just tell him what was on her mind. Especially when what was on her mind was him. It was so odd to think that she could make someone else happy like that, so simply. That she could do that for him. Whenever she wanted. And the payback was twofold, because making him happy had the same effect on her.

Seriously. Why had she waited so long to figure this out?

The two books she'd written were powerful and dynamic, lots of passion and emotion, but these little things, all the various tangents, were things she hadn't really thought about. And yet, they were what added the color, the depth, the richness to the whole thing. The passion and the power were great, but the nuances . . . the real dynamic was in all the details.

She was so lost in thought, marveling over her little revelations, and how they were going to alter how she viewed her
work—had to, really—not to mention her whole entire life,
she wandered back out of the ladies' room . . . and smack into
Derek, who was waiting for her by the door.

"Sorry," she said, moving back quickly as he took hold of
her arm to steady them both.

"Come here." He tugged her around the corner, to the side
of the building that was in the shade, off the pathway, and out
of direct view of the other commuters using the rest stop.

She tensed, adrenaline kicking in immediately, as her senses
went on full alert. "Why? What's happened? Is someone here?"

"No. I just needed a moment to do this." He pushed her up
against the smooth red brick and moved in so his body was
molded against hers, or as much as it could be with the sling
between them. He cupped the back of her neck so her mouth
was lifted to his, so he could take it. Deeply, slowly, and quite
thoroughly.

Talk about passion and power.

She was almost light-headed when he lifted his mouth from
hers.

"I thought I was dreaming about that." He smiled, dropped
another kiss on her tender lips. "Good to know I was just
dreaming about you." He ran his hand up her side, snuck it
under her shirt, and moved it between them, out of anyone's line
of vision, not that anyone was around, and cupped her breast.

"Oh," she gasped, bucking her hips against him at the surprise jolt of pleasure that went shooting through her.

He rubbed his thumb slowly back and forth over her now-
hard nipple, making her moan a little, which he captured with
his mouth. "I had a very long dream," he murmured against
her lips. "So many things I was doing with you . . . to you . . .
for you . . ."

Her legs went a little weak at that.

He slowly pushed his hips more deeply into hers, and she
felt every inch of what he wanted to do to her.

"See what happens when you let me sleep. I get all . . . reju-venated."

"I—yeah." It was all she could manage. He was completely undoing her with his hands, his oh-so-clever fingers, and that mouth.

He abruptly broke the kiss and slid his hand from her shirt.

"What's wrong?" she said, fighting her way out of the haze of desire she was presently in.

"Nothing a little change in location can't fix." He slid his hand in hers and tugged her around the corner, back toward the RV.

It was the fastest she'd seen him move—and without the walking stick, even—since he'd arrived in a heap on her porch. He circled the back of the RV and opened the door. He was boosting her up inside before she could stop him. "Derek—"

But he was already inside, right behind her, the door shut and locked before she could do more than turn around. A heartbeat later her back was pressed up against the closed bathroom door. He slipped his arm out of his sling so he could move both hands up her stomach and close them over her breasts.

"Derek—"

"Consider it physical therapy. Come here," he said, and nudged at her cheek with his nose, until she turned her face to his, and he captured her mouth in a kiss that was as fierce and claiming and demanding as any kiss they'd ever shared. Some-how, while she was swimming along on the pleasure cruise of his kisses and fingertips, he had her shirt unbuttoned and halfway down her arms. Her bra quickly followed. "I want to taste you."

He didn't wait for her reply, but shifted back, bracing her hips with his hands now, so he could feast on the tightly bud-ded tips of her breasts. She grappled for something to hold on to, and settled for weaving her fingers through his hair, and holding on tight, which had the added benefit of keeping his mouth right where she wanted it. Then his hands were moving again, and her pants were unbuttoned, unzipped, and—

"Oh," she said, on a very long sigh as he slid his hand inside the elastic band of her panties.

"Mmm," he said, "I'm not the only rejuvenated one." He lowered himself to his knees and shoved her pants down, and his tongue found her before she could gasp another breath.

The pleasure was so intense, so sudden, it yanked her equilibrium out from under her, and all she could do was ride the wave of pleasure as she tried to remain upright. It rushed up to a powerful crescendo so swiftly, she was clutching at his hair just to keep from sinking to the floor.

"Derek," she said, as her thighs trembled hard and she felt herself roll up to that first peak.

"Present and accounted for," he said, then flicked his tongue over her as he slid one hand up and rolled her nipple between his fingers, shooting her past the edge and thundering down the other side in a cascading waterfall of pleasure so intense, she swore she saw stars.

He stayed with her, as she peaked, and peaked again, then he was bracing his hands on the door behind her, levering himself upright, and turning her around, pulling her back against him.

She felt him pushing between the backs of her thighs. She moved her hips into him, and he slid his hands around her waist. His bandaged fingers had no problem finding her other nipple, while his good hand slid downward and over her as he pushed into her. They both groaned long, and deep, as he slid all the way in, even as his fingers teased her along, up the path again, toward another climax. She wasn't sure she'd survive another, with him filling her the way he was, but she reached for it just the same.

He kept her clamped to his hips, pushing, driving, as she pressed her palms flat against the door and pushed back, making him growl. They both worked themselves into a rhythm of thrusts that had him almost shouting when he finally came, and her trembling so badly she was hardly able to stand.

When he slid out of her, he turned her around and pulled her against him. It was the first time she'd been fully against him, without the sling between them, and it felt so incredibly damn good to be in his arms like this. She didn't even bother chastising him about his ribs, or his shoulder, or any of it. She just floated along on the bliss of the moment, and let her body find its center again.

She pressed her palm against his heart and tipped her head back to look at him. He was watching her, and there was . . . so much there in his eyes. So much, she felt her own eyes burn.

"Shh," he said, kissing the corners when tears leaked out. "What's this? Did I hurt you?"

"No. Never. I—" She wanted to tell him everything that was in her heart, but there weren't words for it. It was so encompassing. And she didn't want him to think she was ever confusing sex—mind blowing as it was—with why her heart was completely his. "I want you, Derek Cole," she said, then reached up to cup his face. "It's exactly, totally, and completely you."

It was as close as she could come to finding the right words. The rest would come, too. She knew that. And it was exhilarating to contemplate even saying them, much less all the meaning there would be behind them.

Just looking into his eyes right at that moment, was enough for her. If he never spoke another word, what she saw in his eyes right then would forever be enough. And so much more than she ever thought she'd have.

"So," he said, at great length, so much emotion still there, even as his lips curved into one of his sexiest grins. "That whole play/work thing. What's your educated opinion on that?"

She rested her head on his good shoulder. "Oh, it's totally getting written into my mission statement. There might be T-shirts. Bumper stickers. A banner or two. Perhaps a tasteful blimp."

He laughed and turned his head to capture her mouth. "You are so tough, and so soft and sweet, and so incredibly easy to love."

Her heart tripped a little just then, and squeezed so tightly that she shifted her head back so he could see clearly into her eyes when she spoke. "I could say the exact same thing about you."

His grin was so swift, so brilliant, that she had to laugh.

He pulled her into such a tight embrace, it had to hurt him, but he was nothing but smiles when he finally let her go. "Come on," he said, helping her to find her clothes and straighten his own. "Let's go hunt down your former partner and catch a few bad guys. Because I'm going to need a whole hell of a lot more play time with you."

# Chapter 22

The puddle jumper they'd hired to get from Spokane to the county air park near Spruce Lake landed with a hard bounce on the cracked asphalt runway.

Derek clamped his teeth together as the jarring landing set his ribs to singing, but was happy enough to have cut out the three-hour drive time in favor of the quick thirty-minute flight to keep any piloting complaints to himself.

"It's raining," Tate said.

"Welcome to Washington," Derek said.

"Have you spent any time out here?"

"Not in Washington, no. You?"

She shook her head.

Her cheek was still creased from where she'd slept with her head on his good shoulder from Kentucky all the way to Spokane. He'd slept, too.

"The rental agent back at the airport said we could get a car in Redland, which is one town over from Spruce Lake. They weren't sure about getting from here to Redland, though."

The pilot looked over his shoulder and said, "Hardy will probably be happy to give you a quick lift. He's the mechanic here and all around handyman. Unless he's in the middle of something, he usually doesn't mind."

"Thank you," Tate said, and the pilot nodded.

There were no hangars. The pilot actually taxied them all

the way around to the front of the small airpark building. "Here you go," he said. "Pleasure doing business with you."

"Appreciate you getting us out here so quickly," Derek said.

"Where are you folks from?" The question was asked innocently enough and the pilot looked like he was just making friendly conversation, but Derek opted to err on the side of caution.

"Back east. We're here visiting an old friend." He gathered his gear and shifted toward the door. "Thanks again."

The pilot didn't seem put off by his lack of geniality, and sketched a brief salute as they debarked. They'd opted to leave most of their gear back in Kentucky in the RV, and travel as light as possible. To that end, they had his small black gear bag, one small shoulder tote for Tate, and her notebook.

As it turned out, Hardy was a short, grizzled man, somewhere between the age of seventy and a hundred, who was more than happy to get them to Redland in his equally old pickup truck.

Tate shot a dubious look to Derek, who just shrugged. "We don't have many options, and I'd like to get out to the estate before it gets too much later. With the rain, we're already at a disadvantage on light."

"Good thing you folks got in when you did. Probably have to shut the park down early," Hardy said. "Supposed to storm something good, later on."

"Perfect," Tate muttered.

Derek offered to pay Hardy, or at least fill his gas tank, but the old man just waved them off. "Had to come into town anyway. You all enjoy yourselves."

Derek felt like his entire frame had been rattled to death. Every part of his body protested when he slid out of the cab of Hardy's truck, but he did his best to duck and run toward the little rental building, Tate in tow, which was in the corner of a tiny strip shopping center. It was raining harder now, so Tate scooted in front of him and opened the door for them both. "I guess we should pick up some rain gear," she said, as they brushed the water off their skin after stepping into the tiny front office. "You doing okay without the walking stick? We should have brought it with us."

"I'm good," he said, knowing he was anything but, but he also knew that when the time came, the aches and pains of his body weren't going to stop him from doing whatever needed to be done. He could rest up and heal later.

Thirty minutes later they were in a small SUV, a bag of carry-out food between them, and two army-green rain slickers in a bag on the backseat. "I hate to think what the storm is going to be like if this is just the prelude."

There was no thunder or lightning, but the wind was whipping something fierce, making the rain seem even heavier than it actually was, and reducing visibility even further.

Tate took the hamburger Derek offered her and took a huge bite. "I'm starved," she said, making short work of it, then moving on to the bag of fries.

Other than the packet of cheese and crackers they'd had on the flight west, they hadn't eaten since his road-trip food that morning. "It's actually not bad," Derek said.

"Cardboard would taste like steak right now, I'm so hungry."

Derek grinned around his French fry. "Keep that thought. The hungry part."

She didn't say anything, but she stopped eating, and put the car in reverse. "I guess we should get on out there."

"You okay?"

"Fine, why?"

"Tate."

She sighed a little. "Usually I like it when you say my name."

"I'm not questioning you being ready for whatever we have to do out there, mission-wise. I'm asking if you're okay—"

"With possibly seeing CJ again?" She swung the car around and exited the parking lot, heading toward Spruce Lake. "I don't know what I am with regards to that. I'm trying not to think about it."

"You need to be ready for . . . any possibility."

"I know," she said, quietly. And he knew that she, of all people, did.

There had been no further transmissions from CJ and they hadn't been able to get anything more from the garbled one they did have. They'd come out here literally on a wing and a prayer, hoping to find her and get to the bottom of it all, once and for all. He hated being so unprepared, but there wasn't much they could do that they hadn't done already to prepare themselves.

They drove the rest of the way out to Spruce Lake in silence. Derek polished off the rest of the fries, and they both finished their drinks. They didn't stop in the small town center, but kept on going to the outskirts on the other side. Tate had used her computer to map out a circuitous route around the small town, hoping they'd find the place that way. It was a rather unwieldy loop, but the country roads were few and far between. It might take them some time because of that, but there weren't enough roads total to make the hunt an impossible one. "I'm pretty sure she said it was west of town, so we'll start here."

"I wish we had time to dig into the county records, find out who owns it now." He'd tried to do some digging during their trip west, but the county here was small, they had no online presence and nothing, apparently, had been digitized.

"We'd have a hard time doing that and not standing out like a huge, waving red flag."

"Turn there," Derek said, studying the map in the steadily graying light, "then take a left, and we're out on the first leg."

The rain had picked up, forcing her to turn the windshield wipers on high. "I can hardly see a foot in front of the truck, much less anything on the sides of the road."

"I'll look, you drive."

It took them another full hour of trekking up and around mountain roads, before the low stone wall finally came into view. It was on Derek's side. "Drive past the entrance, keep going. Let's see what we can see from the road."

It was early evening, Pacific time, and though it usually stayed light until close to nine at this time of year, the storm made it much closer to full dark. "I can't see anything," Tate said. She kept going though, and eventually a road branched off to the right, and she followed that around, too. The stone wall rolled along beside them.

"You weren't kidding about this being a big piece of property."

"I seem to remember that she owned pretty much the whole top of the mountain. Look," she said, pointing. "There, up to the right, a small sign—"

"'Service entrance,'" Derek read. He turned to Tate. "We either go in now, or as soon as the sun comes up."

"I'm not sure the sun comes up in Washington."

"It's pretty bad out there."

She let the engine rumble, foot on the break. "What's the call?"

He sighed, swore under his breath. But there was only one way to play it. "We're at too big a disadvantage. I say we risk the few more hours, pray the storm is keeping everyone inside."

"And off the phone. All we need is for word to spread about the two strangers who flew into County Park and rented a car in Redmond."

"We could pick an entrance and park for the night, keep watch for comings or goings."

"There is no side to the road. One car or truck comes around the bend, and we're toast. Besides, with two entrances, how do we choose without knowing who is up there? Maybe we should go back and get a second car in the morning."

"I don't want to waste the time. Tomorrow we can get out

on foot." He didn't really want to think about how he was going to fare over rocky, marshy, muddy ground with is half-gimpy body, but he'd figure something out. He wouldn't let Tate down.

"Then we'd best find a place out here to park this thing and get some rest. We can put the seats down in the back so you can stretch out. I don't think staying in town is a good idea, and I don't want to be all the way out in Redland."

"Agreed," Derek said, "but you can take the back. I'm good up here."

"Right. That's not going to happen, so don't argue."

He grinned, his teeth a slash of white in the growing gray gloom. "So bossy."

"You'd roll right over me if I wasn't."

"Not that that doesn't have some mighty fine connotations to it, but yeah, you're probably right."

She moved on down the road. "Check the map, see what you can find road-wise."

It was full dark, with the storm in full fury by the time they found a place they felt secure enough to tuck the truck away and hide in.

Tate climbed over the seats all the way to the back, then flipped the seat backs forward, creating as much flat space as she could. "Where's the crappy foam pillows when you need them," she muttered.

"We can get a room," he offered. "We'll—"

"Leave too big a trail that way," she finished. "I don't mind. I'm more worried about you."

"Don't be," he said, but he was touched that she was. He was still getting used to that, and he couldn't deny it felt kind of good. "Okay, I'm going out my door and in the back side door." No way was he going to be able to get himself over the seat without risking a healthy setback to ribs or shoulder. He popped open the door, had his breath sucked out of him by the blast of wind and rain, then ducked out and slammed the door behind him. Tate popped the side door open and he climbed in as fast as his body would let him. "Damn, that's some nasty shit weather."

"It seems to follow you around," she teased.

"Be nice, or I'll hug you right now and make you damp in ways you don't want to be damp. However, in the ways that you do, I'm also available."

She had nothing for that, and he smiled to himself in the dark. She was such an odd mix. It was such a turn-on to him, all the little discoveries he was making.

"I'll climb up front," she said, scooting around him.

"There's enough room back here."

"One of us should be ready to pull out and drive if necessary, so I should sleep up there."

"Who said anything about sleeping?"

"Derek."

"Tate."

She sighed. He chuckled. "Just come here for a little while, then you can climb up front. I'm not in any condition—"

"Don't even try that. You haven't been in any condition since you came barging back into my life and it hasn't slowed you down a bit. I'm almost afraid to think how I'm going to keep up with you once you're in condition."

He liked it when she talked about the future together like it was a foregone conclusion. He didn't know the hows and whys of it yet, but he did know it was exactly what he wanted. As long as it was what she wanted, too, then they'd find a way.

He slipped his sling off, then took off his damp flannel shirt, leaving his T-shirt, which was mostly dry. He reached for her. "Come here. Just for a little while."

"You're wet."

"Barely damp," he said. "You, on the other hand . . ."

She snorted, but she was already scooting over and shifting around to lie next to him.

He rolled up his flannel shirt as a pillow, then snugged her up against his good side. "Better than crappy foam?" he asked, when she tucked her head on his shoulder.

"Maybe," she said, clearly not wanting to give him an inch.

He had a bunch of inches he wanted to give her, but he promised himself he'd behave. They both needed to be sharp, and while play breaks with her were invigorating, he was pretty sure he was all invigorated out at the moment. "Well, as long as we have that settled then."

They lay there in the dark, holding each other, not talking, just listening to the rain beat a hard tattoo on the roof of the truck.

He wasn't sure how much time had passed when she finally spoke.

"I should be more excited," she said, keeping her voice hushed and soft. "About seeing CJ. I'm not. I'm nervous. And even a little pissed off."

"All normal reactions. You've mourned her, missed her, and she's been alive the whole time. It makes sense to be all of those things."

"I need some answers from her, before I know how to feel."

"We both need some answers from her."

She fell silent again. "Tomorrow," she said, a few minutes later. "Everything happens tomorrow."

"Tomorrow," he said, then kissed the top of her head.

He must have drifted off to sleep then, because the next thing he knew was Tate kissing him, and him thinking that it was finally quiet. No more rain.

When he was on a mission, he rarely slept soundly, and yet he'd done it often during his time with her. Even injured, he usually stayed more subconsciously alert. It must be a sign how much he did, in fact, trust her, but it also made him wary. He didn't want to leave her fending for herself. Ever.

Not because she couldn't handle it. Because he couldn't.

"It's tomorrow," she said.

"Yeah." He blinked his eyes open. She was sprawled, half

sitting up, half stretched out, next to him. Her hair was a tangle, and her eyes looked a bit hollow. It made him worry, even though he knew she'd never tolerate him saying so. "You ready?"

"No," she said, quite bluntly. "But I'm going to go anyway."

"Let me get out, stretch my legs. Then we'll head out."

She just nodded, then went to scramble back up front.

He reached out and put his hand on her leg. "How are you feeling? Your leg okay? Your hip?" He didn't care if it pissed her off, his caring. She did the same with him, and though he didn't need her to worry, he'd found he didn't mind so much that she did. Maybe she'd feel the same.

"Better than yours," she said, "which probably isn't saying much."

"What a team, huh?"

Her lips curved the tiniest bit then. "We're not so bad." Then she moved up and over the seat and got herself settled behind the wheel.

He liked that she was competent and just got on with things. But it didn't want to make him coddle her any less. Tate Winslow needed some coddling. And he'd make sure she got some. Whether she thought she needed it or not.

It took him slightly longer than he'd hoped to dress, take care of business, and get himself situated up front. His stomach was growling, but even before she turned her head, he said, "I think we should just get on with this, before it gets much past dawn." He pulled his gear bag up and fished out a bottle of water and two granola bars.

"Mmm," she said, humorlessly. "Breakfast of superspies." But she took one, then pulled out. "Service or main?" she asked, as they wound their way down the mountain toward the estate.

"Let's find out what we can see from the road this morning." The sun wasn't really up yet, so it was still dusky, and there was mist clinging in the trees and across some of the low-lying clearances, but it was a hundred percent better than the night before. "I want to see if there are any vehicles, how many, and what kind of security the place has."

"We don't even know who lives there," she said. "I don't think I've ever gone into a mission so unprepared."

He reached across, squeezed her hand.

"Hey," she said, surprised at the contact and looking over at him. "No sling?"

"I don't want any hindrances. I can tuck my hand in my shirt if I need to rest the shoulder, but it's doing pretty good. It's just stiff."

"Ribs?" When he didn't answer, she glanced at him.

"Water bottle?" he offered.

She looked back to the road. "That's what I thought."

"I've worked with worse, Tate, I'll be fine."

"And I'll worry about you anyway. Deal with it."

"Ditto."

She scowled at that, which made him smile. What a team, indeed.

They rolled past the service entrance and she slowed without turning in. "No security service signs, no hot wire. And the wall is low enough a small child could scramble over it."

"Maybe out here security isn't really an issue."

"Maybe," she said. "Driveway is too long to see anything. You can't even see the house from here."

"Go on around the front."

They did, and Derek let out a slow whistle. "The Addams Family would think they'd died and gone to heaven."

"Wow," Tate breathed. "CJ wasn't kidding. It's like some kind of nightmare out of a gothic novel."

"I see now why she played outside."

She gave an exaggerated shudder. "So, what's the game plan?"

"We need to get up there. See what's what. There are plenty of trees for cover, and no security at all from what I can tell. Drop me here, then double back to the service entrance. You take the back side, I'll take the front, and we'll meet somewhere on the far side of the house."

She swung into the driveway just enough to get off the road, the nose of the SUV even with the stone wall on either side. "The heaviest forestation looks to be on that side," she said. "It's probably where she filmed the message. Go that way first."

He grinned. "Yes, ma'am." But he was out of the car and working his way along the tree line inside the wall before he could hear her retort.

# Chapter 23

Tate rolled to a stop at the end of the service entrance. It curved and ran around to the top of the hill. The house would be just past the bend, behind the trees. She wished there was somewhere to stash the car on this side of the wall, but that was a wish that wasn't going to be granted. So she pulled in, turned around, then pulled off to the side of the driveway in the only flat space she could find, so the front of the SUV faced the exit.

She got out and made her way slowly to the house, using the copious shrubbery and stands of trees for cover. She sure as hell hoped that security wasn't an issue up here, because they'd left this place all kinds of wide open to possible entry. She was formulating plans in her head, deciding if she wanted to approach, if there were cars, maybe spin a story to whoever answered the door, work her way inside. But with CJ working for their own side, it would be just her luck that if it was an agent who opened the door, he—or she—would recognize Tate. And she was quick with her feet and her wit, but she doubted she could run fast enough or talk her way out of that one.

Once she got the house in plain sight, she spied the garage attached via a walkway, off the northwest corner of the house. Dammit. She'd have to get right up on it to determine what was inside. And while the wall hadn't been wired, there was nothing to say the buildings weren't. She was doing a slow visual scan with each step, but there were no cameras, nothing in the trees, nothing mounted on the house, no wire in any window or on the roof of the garage. So she went with the assumption that it was wide open for trespassing, but maintained her level of alert all the same as she got close enough to peek inside the window on the far side from the house.

No cars in the garage. That was interesting. In fact it was swept clean. Even more interesting. She crept around and looked for a good line of cover to get up close to the house itself. The back side of the closed walkway from the garage to the house provided that cover. She inched along, and worked her way over to the first low window. Her heart was pounding far out of sync with the level of danger she felt at the moment. She knew it was anxiety. The idea that CJ could be standing on the other side of that window, or pop up anywhere, at any time, was more than a little unnerving. Her feelings on confronting her former partner hadn't gotten any clearer overnight.

She edged closer and peeked inside. Empty, too. Her heart sank. The place looked empty. Maybe with CJ's death, it had fallen into some kind of legal bind. "Or maybe no one wants to live in the house that Frankenstein built," she murmured.

She went past two more windows, maintaining as much stealth as possible. Just because the estate appeared unoccupied, didn't mean it was entirely empty. CJ had been here. The stone wall was definitely one and the same. That transmission had been sent, live, two days ago.

She stopped short as that thought replayed itself through her mind. She crouched down, her back against the stone wall of the house, as she thought through what had caught her up short. What if CJ hadn't been transmitting live? What if she'd filmed that at some other time, then sent it? She thought back over the other transmissions. The time frame between the London communiqué and the garbled message they'd gotten while at her cabin had been approximately nine days. More than enough time to travel from the UK to the States. But just because CJ had sent a still picture while holding a live-time text conversation didn't mean she'd been in London at the time.

"Dammit." Tate continued to swear under her breath as she realized that they could have both been royally played. But for what purpose? If CJ was truly trying to warn them, then why any subterfuge? Which led her to believe that the Spruce Lake video was, if not live, certainly close to it. But the London photo . . . that one still stuck. Why had she been in London if she was working with a US agency against US operatives? Unless they were working on a global scale, tracking their own agents overseas.

Her mind was spinning in too many different directions, and she knew she had to shake that loose for now and focus on the place and task at hand. But she couldn't stop thinking they'd been set up. But why? "Either to get us out of the way, or—"

"Lure you into a trap."

Tate went stock still. She knew that voice. Knew it as well as her own. Slowly, she straightened from her crouched position, too numb to even tremble. There was no amount of regrouping that was going to prepare her for what came next, so she just turned around.

And looked right into the very live eyes of her formerly dead partner.

"CJ."

She was thinner, without the curves she once had that drew the eyes of men in every culture, and had been the bane of her existence on more than one assignment. Her dark hair was longer, but still full and wavy, which made the contrast with her face that much more severe. Her features were drawn, her cheeks were more prominent, her lips, always full and curved into a natural smile, were flat and humorless. Her eyes . . . Right at the moment, Tate couldn't look there. There was too much to see, and too little. And it didn't matter, because all she saw in her mind's eye was the way they'd been the last time she'd seen them.

Open . . . and lifeless.

If felt like a million separate thoughts and emotions were rioting through her, all at the same time, but that didn't come close to the number of questions begging to be asked. She supposed, in the end, it all boiled down to one. "Why?"

"I wanted to tell you. If you don't believe anything else, believe that."

The numbness ended abruptly, replaced by a pain so swift and severe it felt like the lifeblood was being squeezed from her heart. She wanted to press her fist against it to keep it from shattering apart. But when CJ brought her hands up from her sides, the sleek black Glock with a silencer on the end kept Tate immobile. "No," was all Tate said. All she could say.

"I did save you. They spared you."

A cold descended over Tate now. Because she realized, in that moment, that her former partner, the person she'd lived beside, trained beside, laughed beside, and almost died beside, had died that day in the desert. Whoever this was, standing before her, trying to tell her she should be thankful, while pointing a gun at her head . . . she didn't know who the hell that was.

"Well, gosh," Tate said, finding her voice along with the fury, "I'd hate to see what they do to someone when they aren't spared then. Oh, wait, that's right, they shoot them in the heart. And in the head." She ran her gaze over her former partner's face and body. "You heal miraculously well. Did you have some work done? Because I can hardly see any scarring."

"I don't blame you. For hating me. For being angry."

"That's good. Because I was going to lose sleep over that."

CJ took a step closer, but nothing came to life on her face, it was still flat, emotionless, despite the words she was speaking. "I know it sounds trite, but I can explain. I've wanted to. Every day. I knew you made it out. I knew you'd left the team. Started a new life. And so I thought—convinced myself—that maybe it was for the best this way."

"What, letting me think you died a hero in service to the

people of your country, when all this time you've been working against them?"

"No. Tate—" She stepped closer, and Tate stayed completely still, but tensed every muscle in her body. She had no idea what CJ was capable of, or what her priorities were at the moment, so she tried to ready herself for fight or flight. When they'd stopped for food in Redland yesterday before heading to Spruce Lake, Derek had gotten a couple of hunting knives and a pair of binoculars when he'd bought the slickers. She had one strapped to her ankle and the other tucked in her waistband. That and her wits were all she had.

And none of those were going to stop a single one of the bullets in CJ's gun if she chose to use it.

"I told him not to bring you," CJ said. "I warned him. You came anyway."

It was the first time she'd mentioned Derek, and it made Tate's heart freeze in stark terror as she wondered if CJ had already used the gun once. It was shocking how swiftly terror turned to fury, and it took every scrap of willpower she possessed to not let it show on her face. Even harder was the will it took not to launch herself at her former partner and rip her limb from limb if she so much as hurt a hair on his head. She had no idea she was capable of such a violent streak. Maybe Derek was right.

No, she couldn't think about him, especially the teasing him, and must keep a clear head.

"Yeah, that memo got to us a little too late," she said.

She was close enough now for Tate to see how pale her skin was, and the tension in the line of her jaw. It was at odds with the complete lack of emotion on her face. But the entire moment felt so surreal to Tate, she was having a hard time processing it all.

"I will explain," she said.

"I hope you have some time set aside, then. I have a few questions."

"I know. I'm sorry, Tate, but I'm being watched right now,

and if I have any hope of keeping us both alive, I have to make this look real."

She was thinking that CJ's eyes looked almost more lifeless alive than they had dead, so her words took a split second longer to register, and Tate missed the one brief moment where she could have reacted. By the time Tate assessed her intention, CJ had already chopped the hand holding the Glock in a swift move to the right, connecting with Tate's temple.

There was swift, blinding pain. And then there was nothing.

# Chapter 24

"**A**nd me without a single, fucking bullet." Derek watched CJ drop Tate with a single blow, and knew if he'd had a gun, he would have gone against every training protocol there was and dropped CJ with one shot. And it wouldn't have been to the back of the shoulder.

As it was, he was pinned behind an overgrown bush at the far end of the house, too far away to see their faces, much less hear what was being said. It hadn't appeared either one of them was upset . . . but there was a distinct lack of a reunion going on with both of them keeping their distance. Then CJ had raised her hand with a gun in it, and Derek thought his heart had permanently stopped.

One thing he knew right then was that he was completely and totally compromised. Because no way was he putting mission over partner. No way was he putting anything before his partner, including his own life. And if CJ understood even a fraction of that vulnerability, she'd own him. He'd been the one to train her to exploit exactly that kind of weakness.

The pain in his body didn't touch the pain in his heart. He had the small binoculars he'd gotten along with the hunting knives. They'd only had one set small enough to be functional for their mission, and he'd taken them at Tate's insistence that they might provide a slight edge given his physical limitations. He'd pulled them up the moment he'd seen CJ standing a few feet away from Tate, but the angle of their bodies gave him a view of CJ's back, and nothing at all of Tate, as CJ stood exactly between the two of them. Which is what prevented him from zooming in on Tate when she'd dropped to the ground, so he could see if there was any indication at all of her level of consciousness. He refused to even consider that she might be out permanently.

CJ didn't so much as crouch down and check her pulse. Instead, she looked up at the house, as if checking something. Derek did a swift scan with the binoculars of the windows lining the upper floors above where CJ stood. Nothing. He moved them immediately back down to CJ, who had finally bent down next to Tate.

Derek palmed his knife, the only thing he had, and if CJ so much as twitched a finger on her gun—

But instead she checked Tate's pulse, then slid the gun in the back of her waistband, and scooped Tate into her arms. He'd thought CJ looked thinner and weaker than before, but she handled the smaller, shorter Tate with no obvious struggle.

She started around the far side of the house, and Derek struggled not to immediately race after her. CJ had been looking at something on the second floor, and he couldn't risk being seen by anyone else . . . if he hadn't been marked already. Maybe they thought he'd come in after Tate . . . which might not have been too far off, given how he felt at the moment. Or, if he was lucky, they had no idea where he was. He'd stayed much further back from the house than Tate had.

He swung the binoculars up again to do one last scan of the upper level, then caught sight of something on the roof. He had to back up a little, still keeping the bush between him and the house, but eventually he realized that what he'd seen was the tip of a helicopter prop. He tried to back up enough to get any markings on the small, black chopper, but the gabled roof front and multiple chimneys blocked the rest from view. It was parked deep in the center of the roof of the sprawling mansion, which is why they hadn't seen it straight off when they'd pulled around the front of the house.

At least that answered the question of whether CJ was alone. Unless she'd trained in the past three years, she didn't have a pilot's license of any kind.

He went back the way he'd come, toward the front of the house. It took a little longer, but if he was picked out . . . or off, he'd be of no help to Tate whatsoever. He hadn't seen any vehicles along the drive or in front of the house, and he didn't hear anything like the garage door opening, so when he finally had the front of the house in view, and CJ and Tate were nowhere to be seen, he could only surmise that she'd taken Tate inside.

"Great, just fucking great."

He wasn't mad at Tate for getting captured. He hadn't seen how CJ had gotten the drop on her, or even if she had. By the time he'd come around the back of the house, the two were already squared off across from each other. No, he didn't blame Tate.

The only thing running through him at the moment was fear. Fear that she wasn't okay. Fear that she'd regain consciousness, only to find herself in a captive situation again. Fear that anyone else would lay so much as a finger on her. Ever again. She'd taken herself out of the game. She shouldn't have to bear that. Of all things . . . not that.

Now it was a matter of choosing the best way in. He wished he could see more of the helicopter, determine if it was one of theirs. He hated having no idea who he was dealing with. And he had no idea what the situation was with CJ, but he had to treat her as hostile until proven otherwise. Then he had a thought and backtracked to the side of the house. He remembered a trellis, almost buried in ivy, that climbed all three stories up to a chimney at the end of the roofline. There were only small windows on the side, so if he could get up to the house itself without being seen, he could take the trellis to the roof, and start with the chopper—and whoever might be guarding it—and work his way in from there. Beyond a possible sentinel, he doubted they'd be looking for a threat from that direction.

Now all he had to worry about was whether the trellis would hold him . . . and whether his shoulder would hold up to the climb. After a thorough scan of the windows, he went in low and fast, covering the open ground as quickly as his body would allow. The extra adrenaline punch was a definite benefit.

He checked the trellis up as high as he could see, and, other than being so clogged and overgrown with ivy that it would make finding purchase even more challenging, it appeared it would hold him. Hell, he thought, it was holding a couple hundred pounds of plant, what was a few hundred more?

He used the knife to slit the tape on his bandaged fingers, freeing them for full use, then clamped the knife between his teeth. He pulled himself up with his right hand, using the left to hack at the ivy, creating foot- and handholds that would minimize the use of his left arm and shoulder as best he could. It definitely left his ribs worse for wear, but he moved up fairly swiftly and still had a functioning arm and shoulder by the time he rolled to the roof.

Surprisingly, no one was posted by the helicopter, which meant whoever had flown in wasn't particularly worried about visitors. Derek was perfectly happy with that scenario as it gave him the element of surprise . . . and kept him from having to take out a posted agent who could possibly be playing for the same side. He still had no idea what was going on, but one thing was now certain: CJ was real, alive and breathing. And she was still in trouble. She was on American soil, and . . . He trotted in low to the chopper and checked its markings, and the inside for gear. Nothing except call numbers . . . but that was all he needed. He knew that special code added to the end. The bird was government issued, NSA.

Which brought up another possible scenario. CJ was working for the US, but for the wrong side, and the right side had caught her. That could be who was inside, too. Dammit, he hated the lack of intel, and the lack of backup. He had nothing but his own wits and a damn hunting knife.

*You are a superhero.*

Tate's words popped into his mind and he felt humbled all over again, because she hadn't been teasing when she'd said it. "Well, I don't know about the superhero part," he murmured under his breath as he crossed the roof in a low, crouched trot, "but I'm coming in, and either we both leave, or no one leaves."

He went in through a narrow door to the stairwell. No one posted on the inside. He moved the knife to the center back of his belt. He moved down the stairs without making a sound despite his screaming ribcage. He hadn't told Tate, but given the continued high level of pain, he was fairly certain he was dealing with a fracture or two. Or three. He'd wanted to believe they were just badly bruised, or that his extracurricular activities with Tate were prolonging the healing process. But now that he was back in the swing of things, using his body as it had been trained to be used, he was getting a much clearer picture of what his injuries actually were.

At least his shoulder was holding up.

The house turned out to be a freaking nightmare of construction. Nothing was laid out in any sort of structured sense. It was all winding halls and little alcoves, and places where walls had been erected or torn down to create different sized spaces, some that required going a completely different direction to get around, and some that could be walked through to a door on the opposite side.

As he moved through the top floor, he tried to be as methodical and thorough as he could, but he quickly realized it was like being in a maze, as he'd pass the same door again, swearing that should be on the opposite side of the floor by now. He listened outside every door, paused to listen whenever moving into a new section, but heard absolutely nothing. The rooms were completely empty. Hardwood floors, and blinds or curtains in the windows, and that was it.

He finally came to a side staircase situated at the west end of the top floor and decided to descend. Chances were, even with the escape vehicle situated on the roof, whoever was running the operation was likely doing so from the main floor.

A similar experience on the second floor upheld that supposition. He'd found the main staircase down, but it emptied right into a broad foyer with no cover. There were huge arched, open doors into the front rooms of the foyer, on either side, and from his position, just as it had been on the upper two levels, both looked like they were also entirely empty of any furniture. Which gave him nowhere to go. So he opted to continue on to the east end of the second floor and look for side stairs. Which he found minutes later.

He moved even more slowly now, as the air in this stairwell was warmer and more humid. Trying to mentally superimpose the layout of the house on the framework of what he'd already discovered, he'd bet this staircase led down to the kitchen.

There was no smell of cooking food, but the heat emanating from below didn't have any other likely source. A fireplace, perhaps, but one at the end of the back of the house, where he was, was also probably in the kitchen area. And, from his experience, it was oftentimes the gathering place for operations.

As he neared the door at the bottom of the stairwell, he slowed, tried to get both his heartbeat and breathing as even as possible, so he could hear even the tiniest of sounds.

One sound came through loud and clear a second later—the whistle of a tea pot.

*Bingo.*

Without floorplans, he had no idea how the stairwell door factored into the layout of the room beyond it or how visible his entry would be. So he crouched, despite the very loud protest from his midsection, and positioned himself as strategically as possible, in case anyone opened the door before he was ready to open it. The adrenaline rush was quickly shifting from the first punch of energy to the prolonged saturation levels that worked the opposite of the initial boost. He was weary, bone weary. His body wasn't ready for even a fraction of the activity he'd just put it through. Not that that would stop him, but he had to gauge his actions accordingly, and use what energy and strength he did have left as wisely as possible.

He listened closely, but heard no voices, no clattering of dishes, no sounds of utensils being scraped across plates. Just that damn whistling kettle.

But the fact that it was whistling meant that someone would come tend to it. And Derek decided he was done with not being informed. One of the only ways to change that was to get his hands on someone who was informed, or at least more informed than he was. Even if he ended up taking a household employee, they'd have valuable information. And if he got a member of the team . . . even better. They might be better trained to handle capture and interrogation, but Derek was quite . . . motivated at the moment and thought his rather aggressive approach might get him the results he needed. In fact, when the whistle suddenly cut off and he went through the door, he was almost hoping it wasn't a maid or a cook.

A little aggression therapy might do him a world of good right now.

But, what waited for him on the other side of the door was neither agent nor cook.

He'd come in low, knife at the ready, but faltered badly when he saw who was standing at the stove.

The older man turned, and, to his credit, looked mildly surprised, perhaps even a little impressed, before he blanked his face into an expressionless mask. "Why, there you are, Agent Cole."

Derek straightened and tightened his grip on the handle of the knife. "Mankowicz. What in the hell are you doing here?"

# Chapter 25

When Tate came to, she discovered she was bound to a chair, ankles to the chair legs, hands cross-tied to the slat back. She was groggy, and her head hurt like hellfire, but fortunately no one was in her immediate line of sight when she woke up. Which was her only edge at the moment, that who-ever had her didn't know she was awake.

Without moving her head, she scanned as much of the room as she could. She had to squeeze her eyes shut several times, trying to get the blurred vision under control, then finally closed them altogether, resting them while she worked through the events that had led to her current predicament.

*CJ.*

Her heart squeezed, but her temper kicked in right along with it, along with a healthy dose of hurt. And not the kind presently playing the bongos against her brain. She knew she'd taken a pretty good hit if she'd been out long enough for CJ to get her in the house and trussed up like this, so she tried to work slowly and methodically, as best she could, without pan-icking or getting frustrated.

Good luck with that.

It wasn't lack of recent training this time, or that she'd gone soft. She was just really pissed off. It was personal this time, dammit, and so far, she wasn't all that thrilled with the way the reunion was going.

She went over the entire confrontation, trying her best to recall everything that had been said, looking for clues as to why she'd gotten her head half bashed in and been taken captive. She knew CJ was in trouble, and that she'd reached out to Derek, and, temporarily, to her.

So . . . had that all been set as a trap? Because it was hard to find another way to explain why you'd strike down the very people you'd called to come help you.

Then something CJ had said, right at the end, tickled at the corners of her memory. Tate had been distracted for a moment, thinking how lifeless CJ's eyes were now, which was even more chilling than how she'd seen them last. And a second later had come the crack to the skull. But CJ had been saying something right before then. What was it? *Dammit.*

Tate could feel her pulse accelerate, which caused the throbbing in her head to intensify, so she worked to calm herself in hope of clear thinking.

*I have to make this look real.*

That's what CJ had said, as she swung her hand. Tate tried to think through that moment, then adjust her thinking, extracting the personal element, for a moment at least, and put herself in CJ's place, try to figure out what kind of situation she could have gotten herself into. If Tate had heard her correctly, then she was in a position of having to prove herself to someone. And considering that when she'd contacted Derek she'd been in trouble and asking for help, led Tate to conclude that the trouble had caught up to CJ, and now she was having to wiggle her way out, whatever way she could.

It could explain the total lack of emotion or expression on CJ's face, which were at odds with the words coming out of her mouth. If someone had been watching her, unless they could read lips or had her wired for sound, from appearances only their confrontation had looked like a meeting between two people who had no love lost for each other. And Tate had unwittingly played right into it.

She had no idea, even with hindsight, if that had been the

best way to handle it, but she hadn't exactly been thinking clearly at that first moment. CJ had never had to grieve, process, deal with, and move on . . . she'd always known the real story. Whereas, up until that moment when Tate had turned and laid eyes on her partner, person to person, Tate was having to rethink, reprocess, and deal with a whole new reality that brought with it an avalanche of confusing and very conflicting emotions.

She wanted answers. She needed to understand. Which meant she had to find a way out of this damn chair and these godforsaken ropes. She had no idea where Derek was, but she had to believe he was still at large and figuring out a way to breach and infiltrate the estate. If anyone could do it, even with a bad arm and busted ribs, it was Derek Cole. She had every faith in him, but she couldn't let that be her plan. She couldn't simply wait to be saved and willingly remain helpless and trapped. Besides, if Derek had met with the same fate she had, then he might be the one who needed saving.

She heard footsteps and let her neck go lax, chin resting on her chest, eyes closed, as if still unconscious. Hopefully whoever was coming would talk freely, assuming she was still out. Any information was more than she had now.

Only one set of footsteps entered the room, which was disappointing as there was less likelihood of conversation. But just as those footsteps drew closer and Tate willed herself not to tense any part of her body, another set, a heavier set of footsteps sounded in the background.

"Still out?" asked a man's voice.

Someone paused next to her and it took incredible skill and determination not to flinch or react in any way when someone prodded her eyelid open, then let it go. The action had only afforded a dark blur before her eyelid closed again.

"Yes."

CJ.

"We'll want to question her when she comes to. I'll be in the kitchen." The heavier footsteps drew away, then paused. "Good thing you didn't kill her."

"She was the best at the game. She doesn't go down easily," came CJ's voice, flat and emotionless. "I had to make certain she'd stay down. I'll keep an eye on her, let you know."

There was a pause, then, "You do that, Agent Rampling." The tone had been slightly condescending, with an edge of warning. The footsteps continued and a moment later were out of hearing range.

The last time Tate had been this acutely alert she'd also been tied up. She could do without feeling like this ever again. She listened as CJ sighed, heard her pace quietly away from where she sat. She debated risking opening her eyes even a slit, but—

"Finally," CJ said, then swore under her breath. "Davis is like part hawk, part snake. Okay, no one is watching us. This might be our only time to talk. But keep your head angled exactly as it is, eyes shut. If you understand what I'm saying, twitch your right pinky finger."

Tate's heart skipped, then raced forward. CJ was talking to her, and sounding exactly like her old self. She knew Tate was conscious. So much for her being the best in the game. She could choose not to respond, make CJ wonder if her assessment had been correct, which would draw her close again, but Tate was bound too well to be able to use the element of surprise to move or attack in any way.

Which left working with her old partner. Or letting her think she was willing to work.

She twitched her pinky finger.

"Good. I don't know how much time we have before he comes back, so I'll try and give you the condensed version."

CJ didn't come closer, or untie her, which Tate could take a number of different ways. She hoped it meant that she had CJ as an ally, but that she just couldn't spring her. Yet. First, however, she'd listen to what her former partner had to say. Her head hurt like hell and she wasn't in a real forgiving mood at the moment.

Speaking in hurried, hushed tones, CJ went on. "I'm sorry I had to hit you, you have no idea. I'm sure I sounded like a freaking zombie out there, but they were watching, so I had to make it look good. There's too much to tell you now, but one thing I meant was that I did do everything I could to save us both. I didn't know if it would work, but the alternative was pretty much a foregone conclusion."

"They shot you," Tate said quietly, evenly, while maintaining her droop-necked, eyes-closed position.

"Shh. Davis could pop around the corner any second and I can't risk him seeing you move, speak, anything. The longer you can go without them questioning you, the longer I have to plan on how to get us out of this. I'll explain, and you still won't believe it. I've been in it for three years and I still don't believe it."

*In what?* Tate wanted to shout, but maintained her assumed posture.

"I was pulled into a secret task force, set up by Jack Garrison, who is the head of the entire—"

Tate twitched her pinky finger, signaling she knew who he was and to go on. Garrison was Howell's contact and the de-facto leader of their little secret division. He was the direct contact to the Oval, and the NSA. If Garrison was the one who'd set this thing in motion, then it was as big and broad-reaching as Derek had feared it could be. Garrison had gar-nered enormous respect from a heavily decorated career in the military, and on beyond that in advisory positions very high up in the White House. Because of that, he'd been given a great deal of leeway in coming up with solutions to . . . problems. The agency Tate worked for had been his brainchild.

And if Garrison had been given free rein to create a secret counterterrorist agency, then God only knows what else he had been able to create.

"He's the one who promoted Paul Mankowicz to the UN ambassador's position, but that was a front. He still works for Garrison. Northam was pulled in because he was easily con-trolled."

Tate's focus sharpened and she stopped thinking about what

might be what and listened intently. Paul Mankowicz? Her former chief, involved in something like this? He'd been the most patriotic flag-waver she'd ever met, which was really saying something with the folks she worked with and for. Frankly, she'd always been surprised he'd agreed to run their under-the-radar agency. She figured it was the chance to make a significant difference, protecting the country he loved so much and whose dominance he so often touted, that had ultimately lured him in. That, and that Jack Garrison had clout and prestige. Working under him was never a bad thing.

Or so she'd thought.

"Garrison created another agency, only this one was set up to police our own security operatives, or that's what I was told initially. Seems Garrison had an entire network of teams out there, not all of them sanctioned or even known by his own chain of command. They'd given him way too much autonomy, but he had such a high level of respect and trust at every level, no one questioned it.

"Apparently, Garrison had serious issues with the direction our government was going in terms of dealing with global security threats and so he decided to do something about it. Only it wasn't the global factions he was taking issue with. He felt we were corrupted within our ranks and government, and that was what was preventing us from making the difference overseas, that he needed to 'attack the cancer within.'

"He's gotten a little crazy, almost evangelical, with the power he's assumed, and has taken it upon himself to decide how things are going to go. Our agency, our team, put on a good show and diverted attention away from his other activities at first, but lately he hasn't even cared about that, which was supposedly his initial reason for this whole thing. He lets Northam take the heat there, while he plays little Caesar. The power has completely seduced him and he's so caught up in playing Emperor Terminator, I'm honestly not sure he's still entirely sane."

Tate took it all in, but was also busy scrambling to figure a way out. If this was as far-reaching as CJ said, with CJ somehow smack in the core of it . . . there weren't going to be too many places to hide.

"Our original team was good, very good," she went on hurriedly. "Which basically kept him in power. So, while we were racing around the world trying to save it, he was setting up teams of what amounted to paid assassins to take out, alter, or otherwise deal with whoever he thought was getting in the way of us getting our job done the way he believes it should be done."

Tate sat and listened in stunned silence as CJ ran down a list of both agent terminations and public figures who had met with various issues, up to and including death by a variety of means, none of them done in such a way that anyone would think they had been targeted assassinations. *Holy shit.*

"It's big, Tate, and very well planned, and exceedingly well financed by a few people in this country with very—very—deep pockets, who privately approve of Garrison's methods. I was recruited, as were a number of other agents who were extracted from situations much like ours, where the opportunity to further serve our country or be left to die, made the choice pretty simple."

Tate could hear her pacing now, but still maintained her limp pose.

"I was basically being recruited to work for our very own terrorist faction. And the target wasn't other designated terrorists, it was ourselves! You know I'd never get involved in that kind of bullshit." More pacing, as her voice grew more agitated, but she still kept it low. "But what choice did I have? So, the gunshots, the bullets . . . two of the men who'd been beating the ever-loving shit out of me for seventeen days were actually ours. *Ours*, Tate. They were supposedly deeper undercover than we were, also working for Garrison, or so I was told, and had to go through with the interrogation of us so as not to blow their cover.

"I was offered an out, but with very serious stipulations. When they proposed the plan to get me out, then did it, I realized they'd been telling the truth about Garrison's new endeavor, but not in the way I'd originally been told. I took the offer, because alive is always better than dead, but I quickly realized his new policing team was more like a hit squad. I knew right from the start I'd either be looking for a way out, or a way to take them all down. I talked them into making you a witness to my death, so I could be resurrected in Garrison's little underground army . . . and the rest you know."

"Three years," Tate hissed before she could stop herself. "*Years*, CJ."

"I was trying to get further in, figure out how I could get the proof I needed to blow the lid off of it and bring Garrison down. But it's big, too big, and I was only one person. So I . . . got closer in the only way I could."

Tate's heart stopped for a moment. CJ . . . with Garrison? He was like, seventy-something. And married for fifty or so of them. It was a huge part of his profile. His public profile anyway. But then, apparently he was quite good at hiding a lot of things. And why any of it surprised her, she didn't know. Things like that happened all the time, especially, it seemed, with men drunk on power. Still . . . *Garrison?*

"I got close to Paul Mankowicz," CJ went on. "To the world, he's a UN ambassador, but, in truth, he's Garrison's right hand. I thought . . . I thought it was the only way I might be able to get my hands directly on any kind of proof or documentation to support my charges."

Mankowicz. That made much more sense. And they had a history together. Paul was a staunch flag-waver, but even though he was almost two decades CJ's senior, he'd never made a secret of the fact that he thought his best agent in the field might also make for a great partner in the sack. It had been of a joking nature, and, though inappropriate from a superior, CJ heard stuff like that all the time, and had fielded it as such. To Tate's knowledge, nothing had ever come of it, but it would be the perfect angle to exploit . . . if you were willing to do that.

CJ had, apparently, been willing.

"Mank was the one who set up my whole new life, my new role, so I worked it. Worked him. He was more than a little intoxicated with his new power and I took full advantage. I knew exactly what I was doing, and I have no regrets. If I could take down his self-serving, patriot-on-the-surface, condescending lounge-lizard asshole in private self, I'd have done ten times more." She stopped pacing and risked crouching down next to Tate. She made a show of checking her pulse.

Tate opened her eyes, and looked directly into CJ's.

"I knew you survived, that you got out for good," CJ whispered. "I envied you. You have no idea. I've wanted out so badly. But the more I saw, the more I knew I had to try. I never contacted you. Much less Derek. It was bad enough I was in it. I wasn't going to compromise you."

"Then why?" Tate whispered.

CJ stood and paced away again, and Tate closed her eyes, surprised to feel the burning there. She squeezed them more tightly shut, willing back the sensation. Now was the very last time she was going to let her emotions get the best of her. Later, later she would deal with this, with what it meant, with what it made her think, and feel, and she'd decide. Right now, she was still tied to a chair, with Derek out who the hell knew where. Right now, she had to focus on getting out. And while she appreciated that she knew now what had happened, if it came down to saving herself, or saving CJ . . . well, she didn't want to have to make that choice, but given the fact that CJ had dragged her unwillingly and without benefit of any intel into this mess, she could be responsible for getting herself out. She apparently excelled at that.

"Mank started to get suspicious. Little things. I was getting anxious as they were ramping up and I might have overplayed it. I wasn't as eager to go on assignment, which, in truth, I loathed, but I tried to make him think it was because I wanted to be with him. I tried . . . all kinds of things," she said, the last part ending on a weary note. "But, unbeknownst to me, instead of gaining his trust back, I had only made him more wary, and he eventually put an agent on me. On me, as in, on assignment. Me, Tate. The woman he was sleeping with. And I know, I know, you lie down with snakes . . ." The pacing stopped. "I never saw it coming. It was only on a fluke I missed getting hit. We were in London, supposedly having some personal time alone, away from the prying eyes of . . . everyone. I should have known the prying eyes were his. He set me up, on foreign soil. But he picked the wrong agent to do the hit. It was someone I'd worked with once, a long time ago, and I made him. I ran. I had no base, no help, no one I could trust. Anywhere in the world. Except . . ."

"Derek."

"I panicked, I didn't know what to do, but if I was going to die, then dammit, it wasn't going to be without someone knowing what the hell was going on. I didn't put in three years wallowing with the slime and doing things I'll surely go to hell for, for nothing. I figured if anyone would take up the mantle, or believe me, it was our former boss. So yes, I did. And then I found out he was already being targeted. Apparently Northam was complaining about him getting out of hand and making waves. And I tried to warn him—Derek—but—"

"Why send him to me?" Tate whispered heatedly.

"Because you were the only other one with the balls to fight this and you were on the outside, so they wouldn't track you, or be suspicious. I didn't know then that he was being tracked already, I didn't know I was leading all that to you. I couldn't let it all go for nothing, to die, for nothing. I sent him to you. You were the only one there, you saw me shot and dead. If you knew I was really alive, if he showed you that much proof . . . I thought—"

"Shit," Tate swore beneath her breath. She hated it. All of it. She hated that she'd been dragged out of her safe life, and back into this. She hated that CJ hadn't kept her out of it. Hadn't kept Derek out of it. But most of all she hated knowing that if the situation had been reversed . . . she would have done the exact same thing. *Dammit.*

"How'd you get back in with Mankowicz?" Tate whispered. "After the botched hit?"

"I decided the best way to survive was from the inside. I went back to him, told him I realized he'd try to have me hit. I was angry, furious, insulted, you name it. I put on a hell of a show. I made him air his concerns about me, and told him if he was that damn afraid of me, that I'd do whatever I had to do to prove otherwise. He hated that I'd implied he was afraid of anything. I did what I had to do. It was that, or die, Tate. And Derek . . . I didn't know what he'd do. I didn't know then, that day, that he was on the list."

"Mank wanted you to get Derek," Tate whispered, as the whole thing fell into place. Hand over your former boss and ye shall be redeemed. And she'd already contacted him once without Mankowicz knowing it. She knew he'd try and get to Tate. Which explained the ambush.

"The first chance I had to warn him, I did. I swear. I told him to leave you out, that he was in danger himself. But . . . things were already in motion. I—there was nothing I could do to stop it. It was going to happen anyway . . . but I tried to stop it, tried to stop you. Then you showed up here—"

And, Tate realized, CJ had had to continue with the game.

"And, I hope you understand, but I'm taking credit for this, for getting to you. I'm doing Mank a favor—"

"*What?*"

"I don't mean I'd kill you for him—"

"Good to know."

"But I have to play the role, keep him pacified. Right now, he's all high on Garrison handing him the keys to the regime. He's setting up here to run operations on this side of the country. I happened to know about the perfect piece of real estate, this place, and directed him to it, so between that and his distraction with his new role, and now you both coming here, I'm pretty sure he's more or less convinced that he has nothing to worry about with me. How I handle you, and Derek, will make or break that."

Tate pondered that . . . and wondered how far CJ would, in fact, go, if it was her or Tate. And Tate was afraid she knew the answer to that one already. "So, what's the plan?" Tate whispered.

"I don't know. If we run, we have nowhere to hide. Neither Mank or Garrison would leave me on the loose, and I think that would unfortunately extend to you and Derek now as well. We have to figure this out from the inside. We have to figure out how to end this, once and for all."

"But—"

Just then two sets of heavy footsteps echoed in the hallway. "Well, well, CJ, look who has decided to join our cozy little party." *Mankowicz.*

Tate's heart froze. There could only be one person joining—

"Agent Cole," CJ said, her voice once again completely flat. "What a surprise."

# Chapter 26

"And here I thought you'd been expecting me," Derek said, trying to keep his gaze from straying to Tate even for so much as a blink. "I must say you're looking rather well. For a dead woman."

"Yes, well, you're the one who trained me to have nine lives. I hadn't used them all up yet, as it happened."

Mank's monkey, who Derek didn't know, but had heard him referred to as Davis, pushed Derek deeper into the small room. There were boxes piled up in one corner, and a desk in another. "Homey," he said, looking around. "Funny though, I never took you two for the Morticia and Gomez type."

Mankowicz strode across the room, pompous as all hell. Derek was still piecing things together. His former boss had told him nothing so far, but it was clear that whatever his reasons for being here, it wasn't to ride in and save the day. Quite the opposite, Derek was afraid.

"Be careful now," Mank said. "You're looking at the future West Coast headquarters." He went over and stood next to CJ, and even though he made no overt physical contact, or even acknowledged her, really, it didn't take a rocket scientist to figure out that their relationship had gone far beyond its original incarnation.

"Headquarters to what?" he asked. "I thought you were with the UN."

Mankowicz's smile reminded Derek of some of the fanatics he'd tracked down in his day. Specifically the ones whose belief systems had gone a bit around the bend, taking their hosts with it. Mank had always been a bit of a zealot where his patriotism was concerned, and that gleam in his eye spoke directly to that, but now it was even more intensified.

"'Were' is the key word there," he said, and Derek realized what the difference was. Paul Mankowicz had preached and expounded often about the strength and dignity and enduring presence of his beloved country, but the thing that had kept it from being fanatical was the earnestness behind his strong beliefs. Now . . . now there was a level of smugness, almost condescension, that had replaced the somewhat blind faith that had been there before. It would have been disconcerting, even disturbing, to anyone who noted it, but it was downright chilling to someone who'd been trained to understand exactly what it meant.

"Garrison needs help with the expansion of the agency," CJ said, linking her arm through Mankowicz's and putting to rest any doubts Derek might have had about his assumption. "He's tapped Mank to run the West Coast." She looked at her former boss and now . . . lover? Partner? Derek couldn't be sure, but there was only glowing admiration to be found on CJ's face. He prayed to God that was an act of self-preservation on her part.

Because he'd hate to have to be the one to make sure that this time, dead was really dead.

Derek raised his eyebrows. "Garrison is expanding, is he? That's . . . interesting. Because it seems like lately our agency has been taking on fewer missions, not more. Are we expanding our Asian operations then?"

"You could say we're expanding operations, yes," Mankowicz said, patting CJ's hand, then removing it from his arm and walking to the other end of the room, keeping himself between Derek and Tate. If CJ was insulted by the overt brush off, she didn't show it. "Fortunately, CJ had this property, which has been plagued with legal issues since her unfortunate demise, so we pulled some strings, and bought it outright. Worked out well for all concerned, didn't it?" He addressed that last part to CJ, who merely nodded.

Derek was trying to piece together the information being revealed, well aware they wouldn't be talking so freely if they had any plans to let either him or Tate leave here alive. Which meant Mank was wasting valuable time essentially gloating. And it was that newly unbridled, self-congratulatory attitude that would eventually bring him down.

Davis chose that moment to walk over to Tate and, without warning, slapped her cheek. Hard. "Time to wake up, Ms. Winslow. Have some questions for you."

The sudden action almost had Derek leaping—almost. "Careful there," was all he said. "She's no longer on our payroll. She's got nothing for you. Except, perhaps, a nice fat civil suit if you all continue abusing her."

Mankowicz laughed and Davis kissed ass by chuckling with him. CJ merely smiled and shook her head, as if it was nothing more than a "boys will be boys" moment and amusing to her.

Derek understood she was in a tight spot, doing whatever she could to maintain, but given a few minutes of alone time, he'd take great pleasure in setting his former operative straight.

Mankowicz was still smiling, openly arrogant and patronizing now. "I've got a dead agent standing here, whose previous curriculum vitae included working for a privately sanctioned security agency who took care of business in ways that were anything but civil." His smile didn't waver, but as he walked over to CJ, Derek saw Mank's eyes were hard as glass. "And who I'm now fucking whenever I want, because I can."

Derek glanced at CJ in time to see understanding dawn in her eyes, before she carefully blanked them. So, she hadn't been playing the middle as well as she'd hoped, apparently.

Mank jerked CJ against him, shoved his hand between her legs, and squeezed. "Isn't that right, sweetheart? I own this, and I own you." Then he simply dropped his hands and moved away, as if she didn't even warrant the energy required to shove her aside. He turned back to Derek. Any vestige of a smile or good-will, fake or otherwise, was gone now. His features looked like they were carved from stone, and his gaze was hell-frozen-over cold.

"I hope you got a piece of that before you got here," he informed Derek, nodding to Tate, who hadn't been roused by Davis's slap. "Because you sure as hell won't be getting any more of it." He turned his gaze to Davis. "Wake her up, we don't have all goddamn day." He glared at CJ. "You better be praying right now that you didn't damage the goods too badly in your misguided hopes of impressing me with your loyalty."

He strode toward Tate, and Derek fought to stem the ensuing wave of fury, knowing he couldn't afford to make one wrong move right now, or Tate was going to suffer far worse than a hard slap. "Let me," Derek said, walking between Davis and Tate, getting there before Mankowicz.

He crouched down, working not to show the fiery stabs of pain shooting through his ribs, and tipped up Tate's chin. Her eyes opened the merest of slivers that only he could see. He had no idea how long she'd been alert, but she was purposely playing unconscious. Unfortunately, Davis chose that moment to lean down behind him, so Tate had no chance to signal him in any way. Did CJ know she was alert? He couldn't risk looking toward her to find out. "Wake up, Tate," he said flatly, unable and totally unwilling to watch her get smacked around again, no matter what plan she thought she had worked out.

She blinked open her eyes and did a pretty damn good impression of someone just coming to after a severe blow to the head. What he hated is that she had personal experience in knowing exactly how to make that look real. "Derek? Where are—" She went to move, then jerked as she realized her bonds. She went still, then slowly turned her head, her expression carefully blank. "Oh," was all she said.

"'Oh' is right," Mankowicz said.

She straightened in her seat and lifted her head to look at

her former boss. It was Derek's first opportunity to see the gash and swelling on her temple. He shot a look at CJ, but she had turned her attention toward the window, apparently lost in her own thoughts at the moment. Not surprising after Mankowicz's crude, dehumanizing little display.

The tide was turning and turning swiftly, and Derek was pretty certain CJ wasn't going to survive the impending crash against the shore either, if Mank had anything to say about it. And Derek understood why. He'd gotten what he needed out of her. The property was his now. And she'd snagged him an agent—the agency's team leader no less

And then the rest fell into place. The tranq dart, the interrogation. Mank had sent them—his own—after him. They hadn't known about Tate, or possibly even CJ's contact with him, at that point anyway. But they had been suspicious when he'd taken off—and given what was being revealed here, with good reason. They'd wanted to know what he knew, why he'd really taken off. At that time, he'd only had vague suspicions and the very recent knowledge of CJ's return from the dead, which he apparently hadn't given up even while drugged, or he wouldn't have been left alive then.

He wasn't going to be given the same grace this time. Mank had CJ, the house, and now Derek. Tate was either a bonus or a nuisance, but she'd be dealt with either way. What was another body disposal to deal with? Hell, Mank could stick them all in the basement of his mausoleum to rot and no one would find them until they were long dead and gone.

Derek didn't ask permission, he simply began untying Tate. By his estimation, it was now three against two. Mank's first mistake had been overtly cutting CJ out before he'd taken care of Derek and Tate. But then his ego was already so swollen, he apparently felt certain that it would take more than a few agents to bring him down.

Derek still didn't know what Garrison's role in all this was, but he doubted Mank was setting up Asian operations headquarters here, which meant Garrison was involved in setting up something other than counterterrorist teams. And if Garrison was running this, then there was no telling how deep this went. Mank's supreme confidence led Derek to believe that whatever power he thought he had was both unmonitored and far-reaching. Which, given he had a sick feeling this new agency was internally or domestically focused and not internationally geared, had him realizing that this wasn't simply going to be a matter of getting away from Mank and his monkey, Davis. If Garrison was at the top of this food chain, there was literally no place to hide.

Derek tugged at the knots at Tate's ankles as they were the closest in reach. His fingers brushed against the strap that, to his shock, still held the knife he'd gotten her. Which meant CJ had been the one to truss her up . . . and the one to leave her armed. So, perhaps she'd been on their side all along, and not just as a result of Mank's public rejection.

Mank had two of Derek's knives and the binoculars, but hadn't been foolish enough to step in, alone, and pat him down. So Derek was still armed as well. And if CJ still had her gun . . . well, he started to feel immeasurably better about their chances. Unfortunately, his bum fingers slowed him down a little on the untying, giving Davis a chance to block him before he'd gotten her released.

Derek barely reined in the automatic reflex action that would have dropped Davis like a stone. An unconscious one. Dropping Davis was the least of his problems right now and would only provoke Mank, who was unpredictable at the moment. With Tate still tied up and Derek not seeing how either of them had any leverage at all in prolonging their usefulness, he had to pick his targets and timing carefully.

"Are you telling me you need to keep her bound in order to ask a few questions?" Derek asked, poking a little, seeing where the tender spots were. "She's been out of the field for three years, and—"

"And probably in your pants for at least the past three days,"

Mankowicz said. "So, yes, for now, let's just leave the lady tied up. Move back."

Davis stepped in and there was no opportunity to communicate anything to Tate. However, when he straightened and was stepping back, CJ moved so she was behind both Davis and Mankowicz for a brief moment. She motioned to Davis and Mank, then slid a finger across her neck. She pointed to herself and nodded at him and Tate, and held up three fingers, then squeezed them in a tight hold with her other hand, indicating they were a team now. He wished he had more faith in that. Her loyalty seemed tied to whoever would keep her alive. He supposed he'd just have to make sure she believed the only person capable of doing that at this point, was him.

Mank turned just then, but she'd already dropped her hands to her side and was, once again, looking toward the window.

Derek thought he understood the general dynamics of the situation, but he also didn't take his conclusion as the only possible one. Given his former boss's crude references regarding CJ, her signal that she was aligning with Tate and himself, and wanted Davis and Mank neutralized, made sense. However, the truth was also that CJ was standing there, living proof of the lengths to which Garrison and Mank were willing to go to set somebody up to believe something that wasn't true. So he didn't buy into it automatically. That gash on Tate's temple, delivered by CJ, was no fake.

However, time was tight, so he went with the higher percentage scenario. For now. Which was to keep as many potential players for his team standing as possible. First step was to buy more time. As long as Mank still thought CJ was his bitch, so to speak, he might leave them alone at some point, which was when they'd put a plan into motion. All he needed now . . . was a plan. And to formulate a plan, he needed information. And he didn't have time to waste. So he went straight to it.

"So," he asked, keeping an open, direct path between him and Tate, as much as he could, "why the tranq, why the attack?"

Mank didn't even blink. "We had to know what you knew."

Well, that was a step in the right direction. Mank was behind the attack, or knew of it. Which meant scenario number one was, unfortunately, looking pretty good right now. At least Mank was so confident in the outcome here, he was willing to talk. Derek was very willing to listen. "A shame you wasted your time and manpower like that," he replied.

"Not entirely a waste," Mank replied, with a sly smile. "I'm certain you're less than enthusiastic at the moment to tackle any sort of physical altercation."

So, he'd given them nothing. Thank God. That information alone gave him an even stronger mental edge now. "I generally hold my own."

Mankowicz looked to Tate. "Well, you certainly went to the right person for that." He walked toward Tate and Derek had to fight to stand his ground. "I don't know that I've ever seen any agent, man or woman, stand up to the interrogation like she did." He glanced at CJ. "I was worried perhaps we went with the wrong recruit." Then he lifted a shoulder. "Then you gave up, and I realized we'd done the best we could with that situation."

Derek carefully blanked the emotion from his face. "That situation? How involved were you, in that 'situation'?"

Mankowicz didn't answer, but he didn't have to. Derek glanced to Tate then, who had dipped her chin and was staring at the ground, but was likely seeing something entirely different in her mind's eye. He had no idea how it would feel, to find out that all you'd suffered, all you'd willingly put yourself through in the name of protecting your country . . . had been perpetrated *by* your country. Or at least a few members of it, anyway.

Derek curled his busted fingers into a fist and fixed on that pain, trying to find some center that would allow him to keep his shit together until he found a way out of this. But he decided right then and there, he wasn't leaving until he'd had the opportunity to repay Mank's . . . patriotism.

"You should have stayed retired, Winslow," Mank said in lieu of a reply. He moved closer to Tate. "In the end, perhaps you were the smart one. Cowardly, but smart. Get out, stay out. A shame you didn't stick to that."

"I heard you'd gotten out, as well," she said, speaking for the first time. Her voice was flat, emotionless. "Promoted out. An ambassador, wasn't it?"

"You should be reading about my retirement from that position any day. Or, would have, at any rate. Had you stayed home."

Derek had no idea how she was holding it together, but then, she'd been through worse. And though, supposedly, Mankowicz was on the same side, a terrorist was a terrorist, regardless of origin. And Tate, above all else, was trained to deal with exactly that.

"I'm guessing your future plans to work out here for Garrison won't be mentioned in the same article," Derek said, his dry tone drawing Mankowicz's attention away from Tate, as he'd intended. "Perhaps you should take your own advice and stay retired."

"You might believe your team leadership qualifies you to speak on the matter, but you would be wrong," Mankowicz said, his tone both lofty and denigrating. "Dead wrong, as it happens. You were low level management, at best."

"The agents I've kept alive and the missions we've successfully completed might speak otherwise."

"In that particular battle, you and Ms. Winslow here were merely foot soldiers. Quite skilled and adept foot soldiers, I'll grant you, but your boundaries, while broad, weren't limitless, and ultimately you were followers, doing as you're ordered to do. There is no shame in that. Without foot soldiers, leaders would have no one to direct to do their bidding."

"And yet, you answer to Garrison, don't you?" This from Tate. Who was clearly drawing the fire back to her.

Derek wanted to tell her to let him handle it. But he supposed he had about as much chance of that happening as she would of getting him to back down. So, he figured as long as they didn't work at cross purposes, two heads might just, in fact, be better than one.

"The difference, my dear," Mank said, condescension fairly oozing now, "is that I trained under the master with every intention of becoming the master."

"And now you are?" Derek asked, forcing Mank to play a little head Ping-Pong, with his attention split between him and Tate. Clearly Mank was confident. Derek also noted he was in total command here, given Derek wasn't tied up next to Tate. Davis wasn't entirely sure where to keep his focus when he moved about. Mank seemed unconcerned. That would be his second mistake. "Does Garrison know this?"

"I'm here, aren't I?"

"Still seems like second-in-command to me," Tate said, lifting a shoulder.

"You cannot bait me, Ms. Winslow," he said with a cold laugh. "My position here, and the power that comes with it, renders titles and rank completely unimportant."

Derek took a step to the left, drawing Mank's attention a scant bit further away from Tate. And from Davis. "So, what, exactly, is your new role? What are you and Garrison doing?"

Mank looked to CJ for the first time since dismissing her. His gaze was flat and completely empty. He looked back to Derek. "Why don't you tell me? You've been chatting with your former operative almost regularly of late. Surely she's shared."

"If she had, surely your operatives would have discovered that while drugging me and interrogating me."

Derek kept moving to his left and, from the corner of his eye, he noted that CJ had casually begun easing farther to the opposite end of the room, between Tate and Davis. Good, she'd figured out Derek was trying to separate Davis from Mankowicz. The only problem here was he didn't know how well armed Mank was. Davis wouldn't be an issue, as he'd be the first to be dropped. Leaving them Mank to deal with. And Mank to deal with them. Would he simply shoot first and ask

332 Donna Kauffman

questions later . . . or did he like to have others do his dirty work?

"Unless you're admitting that perhaps your foot soldiers aren't all that well trained," Derek continued. He walked a little closer. "Why don't you tell me what the plan is?" he suggested. "Perhaps I can be of some use to you. After all, I assembled a pretty damn good team for Garrison."

Mankowicz merely chuckled. "Somehow, Mr. Cole, I don't think your temperament is what we're looking for."

Now Derek grinned. "You have apparently assembled a team thus far by snatching agents from the jaws of death and offering them a way to rise from the ashes. I'm assuming you're not planning on just letting us stroll out of here. I might be inclined to undergo a . . . temperament adjustment." He lifted his good shoulder in a casual shrug. "Look at it this way, you tell me what you've got cooking out here and I can agree to sign on and help keep you in power, much as I did before. And if I say no, well, we can go back to your original plan. Either way, no harm, no foul to you."

Mankowicz's smile vanished, and Derek wasn't entirely sure what he was thinking. He only hoped that if Mank went for his gun, that CJ would go for Davis. At least level the playing field a little bit. The only thing really holding him back at the moment was the fact that Tate was still tied up and, therefore, quite vulnerable.

But Mankowicz didn't go for a weapon. Instead, it appeared as if he was giving Derek's offer some serious consideration. Which was all the leverage Derek needed.

So he pressed. "If it's not Asian operations, which, admittedly, wasn't my specialty, then what is it? Are we going into South America? Pick up the war on drugs? The Washington home base would be a brilliant plan then, as everyone would assume southern California or New Mexico. After all, we operate from the US for European ventures." He walked to the far end of the room. "Although, I have to admit, while tackling South and even Central America is a pretty big task, I don't know that it puts you anywhere near on par with Garrison's work in Asia and the Middle East. I mean—"

"I'm not heading international affairs," Mankowicz snapped.

"I'm surprised Garrison isn't using your contacts made through your post within the United Nations. Seems a waste not to mine the potential there for networking and intel."

"We have our systems well in place for that," he said. "I'll be leaving there to head up a . . . domestic division of the agency."

"What," Derek asked, "like internal affairs for the international teams? We have our own policing for that, built right into the system. It's why you—and now Northam—and Howell, have been put into place by Garrison. Unless you think Northam isn't up to the job, and frankly, if you want to know why I was rattling so many cages, it was because I was afraid that Northam and Howell were more interested in playing golf than fighting the war on terror. Your stand on patriotism and the fight for our country is what led us into battle. Northam hasn't been exactly a visionary replacement, much less a motivational one."

Mankowicz waved his hand. "We've work to do here before I can concern myself with that. It is precisely the current domestic policy that is preventing us from having broader success overseas, so we must focus here, at home, first. These are much bigger issues."

"Bigger? Bigger than the war against terrorism? I'm not sure I follow. How could anything domestically related—"

"We cannot win the war on terror overseas, until we clean out the terror here on our own soil." Mank's eyes took on that edge of fanaticism again, only this time instead of a wild gleam, there was that icy, soulless quality that was far more disturbing.

"You mean foreign operatives working here? We've long since established teams whose sole function—"

"No!" he shouted, showing real emotion for the first time. "I've come to realize, as has Garrison, that it's hopeless to ever rise above, to eradicate the disease and human toxins plaguing this world of ours, until we get ourselves into position here to move forward as we wish, as we need to. Too much divisiveness, too much corruption, too much politicizing, too much greed and narrow-mindedness. When did we lose sight of the big picture? It's amazing we get anything accomplished given we're rotting from the core out."

"And you—and Garrison—are sanctioned to tackle this massive clean-up job?"

"We have the power," Mank thundered, "because we've taken the mantle of it into our own hands. We're the only ones with the vision to see the bigger truth, to see a future where internal strife and corruption topples us from power, leaving us to be the unwitting victim of the earth's infidels. We—*we*—are the ones with the vision, the power, the will, to risk everything to bring this country to its full potential and glory!" He strode toward Derek, clearly far past the grasp of rational thought—and clapped him on the shoulder. "And if you have any love for this country, for what it stands for, for what we can do to right this world and rid it of evil, then you should join us. Help us conquer, help us rule, help us be the ultimate global power we have fought so hard to become."

Derek couldn't keep from dipping slightly when Mankowicz clapped his hand on his bad shoulder. But then Mank gripped and held on, driving Derek down slightly as he found pressure points in the still damaged tissue, and sunk his fingers in.

"Perhaps I can interest you in a position," Mank said, his demonic grin the very definition of the toxic human waste he purported to want to eradicate. He drove his fingers in deeper, and Derek continued to sink lower, ribs screaming as he crumpled, but taking the torture without reaction, both because he knew Mank was testing him, and because it kept Mank's focus tightly on Derek. "But I will need proof that you are wholeheartedly committed to our vision."

"Anything," Derek said with a grunt, allowing Mank to believe he had him right where he wanted him. It made him wonder if his former boss had any real idea of what his agents had to handle out in the field. Because, in the realm of torture, this didn't feel so great, but it was child's play compared to the sorts of torture they'd been trained to endure.

"Good," Mankowicz said, and abruptly released him, causing Derek to stagger back a few steps. He motioned behind Derek to where he knew Tate was seated. "Our first mandate is to neutralize or otherwise rid ourselves of those who we deem to be an obstruction to our pursuit of eventual global peace."

Derek didn't bother to point out the irony that he was using the exact corrupt, heinous type of action that he was supposedly trying to rid the world of in the first place. "Understandable," was all he said.

"So," Mank said, that unholy grin once again sliding across his face, "your first target is seated over there in the chair."

Derek's heart stopped, but the only outward sign of his twin reactions of fear and fury was a jaw so tight he was surprised bone didn't snap. "I thought you just got done chastising Agent Rampling for being too rough with her. Now you want her dead?"

"I didn't say anything about killing her. I want to know what she knows. I want to know if she's been operating for the agency, from outside the agency, much in the way I set CJ up to do the same."

"Why don't you simply ask her then?"

"I think we have ample evidence that it takes far more than simple questioning to elicit a response from her. In fact, I'd like you to demonstrate your interrogation skills. Consider it a job interview of sorts. An audition."

"I'm not certain why you'd require one," Derek said, trying to think fast. Hurting Tate was the very last thing he could ever do, even if the bigger purpose was the hope of saving them. Which, he was certain, was the exact reason Mank had chosen her. "I would think my past work and my win record would be all you'd ever need to see in regards to my capabilities."

"Yes, but that was operating against foreign threats. My agency will require a much more . . . dedicated mindset. Your targets won't be foreign. And they might very well be someone you have previously worked for, perhaps even admired. I have to know, without doubt, that you'll trust my decisions, follow my orders, and do whatever I deem necessary to bring us to the next level."

*Sure,* Derek thought, *you fucking insane despot.* How in the hell had he gone so far around the bend and not attracted any attention? For that matter, how had Garrison done the same?

Mank motioned to Derek, then Tate. "Go on. No time like the present."

Derek nodded. "Not a problem." He thought he heard an audible gasp, but considering the direction it had come from, he had to assume it was from CJ. He turned and looked directly into Tate's eyes. She held his evenly, without a speck of emotion. He prayed she trusted him, prayed her training would never completely leave her. Because the two of them were about to give the performance of their lives.

He strode over to her and immediately began to untie her hands. Davis moved in. "Call him off, Mank," Derek ordered, his tone cold and all business now.

"I would, if I understood why on earth you were releasing your target."

Davis took another step and Derek stopped what he was doing. "If he comes a step closer, I will be happy to give a demonstration on how to take out multiple targets simultaneously. And I won't be held responsible for whatever methods I deem best to use. So ask yourself . . . is your man here expendable to you?"

Mank actually laughed. "You know, I think I might have misjudged you, Cole." He waved his hand. "Back away Davis. Unless, of course, you'd like to prove yourself."

Davis said nothing, but stepped back. Mank laughed again. "So noted, Davis. Keep an eye on your back."

Derek could feel the hate emanating from Davis, which was good, it would keep him from paying attention to anything else. Hopefully CJ would realize that he was her target. He finished untying Tate's hands and she quickly brought them around and moved her wrists and rubbed the life back into her arms.

"Again, Agent Cole, why are you releasing her?"

"Anyone can dominate and interrogate a captive. You know Ms. Winslow was one of our most formidable agents. I thought perhaps you would like to see me neutralize someone operating at full ability."

"As you said, she's been out of the field—"

"He trained me," Tate said. "It will take a lot more than a couple of years to dull that out of me."

"Not to mention we all know I'm not at full ability right now," Derek added.

A quick glance showed Mank nodding, further impressed. "Go on then."

Tate quickly finished untying her ankles and Derek blocked the view so she could check the ankle strap, make sure the knife was accessible.

"Stand," he instructed Tate as he backed away. He looked to CJ. "Move. I won't need your assistance." He gave a head gesture, motioning her to stand off to the side. Right next to Davis. Who still had a death stare locked onto Derek.

Perfect.

The sound of a cocked gun had Derek glancing to his left. Mank held a small Walther PPK in his right hand. "Continue," he said.

Okay, not as perfect. But it was a hell of a lot better situation than they'd been in five minutes ago.

He moved so his back was to Mank. And the barrel of his gun. "*Hit me*," he mouthed to Tate, then moved in as if to strike.

She instinctively moved to slash at his bad shoulder, only when he feinted, she hit his ribs instead. She'd hit low and to the inside, to minimize the blow to where she knew he wasn't as injured, but it definitely made him see a few stars. She definitely hadn't forgotten her training.

Her body was in ready stance. Her eyes, however, were filled with remorse, which Mank could clearly see from his position behind Derek.

Proof of that came with his next statement. "Ms. Winslow," Mank said, "you might want to think of this as an audition as well. You win this little battle, and we'll discuss an offer to prolong your stay on this earth."

She nodded tightly and her gaze went steely. *Good,* Derek thought, make Mank pay more attention to the show and less attention to what we're truly trained to do . . .

He moved in, she feinted right. They moved around one another, coming in on attack, the other always narrowly escaping, in a complex dance so demanding that it could have only been accomplished to look that real with pre-planned choreography. And yet they performed it seamlessly, as if somehow psychically connected.

Derek was intentionally working her around so they drew closer and closer to Mank, who still held the gun, but seemed to have forgotten it in the riveting display.

"I'm impressed with the evasive skills," he informed them, as they continued their maneuvers. "But if neither one of you can determine how to get command over the other . . . then I'm afraid I have no use for either of you."

Derek swung in right then, Tate feinted left as he'd known she would, so he feinted as well, and grabbed her arm, spinning her and wrapping her against his chest, right in front of Mank. Her surprised gasp at the sudden shift in power wasn't faked, which kept Mank riveted, and Derek used the moment to simultaneously bind her wrists in one hand behind her back and put his mouth next to her ear. "Kick now," he whispered.

By anchoring her wrists and her weight against him, he gave her the leverage to kick up and out, sending Mank's gun flying.

"Now, CJ!" Derek commanded as he and Tate moved in low and took Mank down.

He had no time to see if CJ followed, but they were dead either way if she didn't, so he had to trust she was on their side. The ensuing scuffle on the far side of the room told him that something had started anyway. He prayed her element of surprise had given her the edge.

Mank howled and grabbed his shattered wrist where Tate had connected with the toe of her boot when she'd kicked, and Derek dropped him by taking him at his knees. Derek paid the price with his ribs and throbbing shoulder, but anything was better than dying.

He rolled with Mank, whose preservation instincts finally took over and he began to fight for his life. He got his good hand on Derek's face, his thumb dangerously close to Derek's eye socket, before he froze when Tate swung in behind him and put the point of her knife at the corner of Mank's eye.

"Move your hand away," she said, and even Derek didn't think he'd ever heard her sound so cold and deadly. "Or lose an eye. And I won't do it cleanly."

Mank moved a shaky hand from Derek's face.

"Roll away," Tate commanded, talking to Derek now.

Derek carefully shifted, but was in no position to help Tate until he could get to his knees or feet.

As it turned out, she didn't need his help.

"Get up," she told Mank as she moved back. She used the toe of her boot to forcefully dig into his now gimpy knee. "Up," she commanded.

Mank grunted when she prodded his knee again, but slowly stood, wobbling dangerously with both knees clearly no longer fully functioning.

Tate moved back, her knife still at the ready. Derek scooped up Mank's gun. "He has my knives on him somewhere," he told Tate.

"He won't ever get the chance to use them," Tate said.

Derek slid a sideways glance and was a little alarmed at the deadly cold expression still on her face.

"We're good," CJ called out, and he risked a fast look across the room, to where CJ stood over the inert body of Davis. He didn't know if Davis was out, or dead, and, at the moment, found he didn't much care.

She walked over and joined them. "Need my assistance?" she asked, clearly more than willing to help further subdue her former boss and lover.

"No," Tate said softly. "I can handle this all by myself." She smiled then. "Consider this my job interview," she told Mankowicz, who visibly swallowed. "Let's see how you hold up under a little questioning. After all, I can't work for a man who can't take what he dishes out. We already know what I'm capable of handling. Let's see how you do when I use those very same interrogating techniques on you." She reached out her hand. "CJ, will you get me that drill I saw lying over there on the desk?" She smiled back at Mank. "Not to worry. I'm sure you won't even show it when I drill holes in both of your kneecaps."

"Tate—" Derek began.

"He was responsible for having me tortured." She never once took her eyes off Mankowicz. "By our own operatives, Derek."

"I know, but—"

"The drill!" she commanded, and CJ walked over to get it. Tate looked back at Mank and shook her head. "Gee, I don't think you're going to do very well at this." She glanced down to where the floor had grown suspiciously wet. Then she darted a quick glance at Derek and winked before turning a stone cold visage back to Mank. She took the drill from CJ and pressed the power button a few times. "Now," she said, "why don't you tell me exactly where Garrison is, and what he has planned."

CJ moved around behind Mank and put her fingertips on two precise pressure points by the base of his neck. "If you so much as twitch a finger, I will drop you, and let Tate have fun with power tools while you're powerless to do anything about it."

Tate crouched and put the drill bit dead center on Mank's kneecap. "You have two seconds to start talking."

"I c-can't. Garrison will never allow me—"

"One . . . two . . ." She pressed the power button just enough so the spin of the bit caught the fabric of Mank's pants and twisted them tight.

His eyes rolled back in his head and he hit the floor a second later.

Tate rose and looked at CJ and Derek, a smile on her face. "Somehow I don't think we're going to have any problems getting all the information we need."

CJ put her hand out. "Give me the drill."

"I'm not really going to—"

"You get a turn." CJ looked at Mank's inert body. "Then I get a turn."

"Seems only fair," Derek offered.

Both women looked at him.

He grinned. "Remind me never to piss either one of you off."

# Chapter 27

Tate sat in the D.C. hotel room reserved for her by the United States government. She was numb, thoroughly and utterly numb. Five straight days of testifying, having to go over, in excruciating detail, what happened to her three weeks ago . . . and three years ago. Garrison's fall from grace, and the attendant fallout from the revelation that he was running such a massive underground operation, was the biggest scandal to rock the country since Watergate. Maybe even bigger. It reached so far and touched a country already angry and weary and scared of the war, both at home and on foreign soil, that the furious backlash had been swift and colossal.

For her part, she just wanted to crawl back into her cave, go home to her little cabin in the valley, go back to writing stories about love, and triumph, and redemption, and far, far away from corruption, evil, and greed. She'd given at the office. She wanted to be excused now, please.

She had been kept sequestered for the past several weeks as federal agents, investigators, lawyers, doctors, you name it, questioned her and prepared her for what was to come. She hadn't been allowed to talk, much less see Derek, or CJ.

Both Mankowicz and Garrison were in prison, charged with crimes against humanity. And she, Derek, and CJ—the agent risen from the dead—were the rock stars of the hour. She hated it. All of it.

To make matters worse, her book agent and editor had been in almost constant contact, pressuring her—hard—to use her current global notoriety as a means to give a huge push to her first book release, slated to happen the following month. They'd been honestly surprised that she hadn't been willing to milk that, and had thrown all kinds of incentives her way to get her to agree. She'd forced them to keep silent about her new job, threatening all kinds of legal hell if they "accidentally" leaked so much as a squeak. She'd already decided long before this happened to publish under a different name—not Tara Wingate, but something one step further removed from that—and that decision was going to stand as well. Which she was very thankful for now, because with everything that had happened, her brief stint as Tara Wingate wasn't a secret any longer, either.

If she had any hope whatsoever to continue on in any kind of peace and solitude, no way was she inviting this insanity into her future world. She would make it or break it on her own merits, without any reliance on her former job or any glory it might bring her.

Her agent and publisher were seriously unhappy with her at the moment and she knew the pressure wasn't over yet. But they had no idea who they were dealing with. Did they honestly think that she'd cave in to whatever demands could be made by a book publisher? Had they not been paying attention to exactly why she was in the news at the moment?

She got up and paced, then went back and lay on the bed. Her back, hip, and leg were killing her. She hadn't been taking proper care of herself. The long days, the constant attention and demands of her time and energy had wreaked havoc on the routine she used to keep her body functioning. She glanced at the walking stick propped in the corner, then looked away. It reminded her of Derek. Of before.

She couldn't afford to think too much about that, about him. About how he was holding up. She wasn't even allowed to watch television or read so much as a magazine until this was over. Her lawyers kept her informed about the level of hysteria this trial was reaching. Just making it in and out of the courtroom every day through the frenzied throngs gave her an indication of the level of global attention this was garnering. The number of satellite trucks alone, clogging the streets for blocks around the courthouse, was staggering.

But now, after today, and possibly by morning . . . her part in it would all be over. She couldn't put herself through much more, and she'd told her lawyer as much. She'd told the prosecuters, repeatedly and in far more detail than was warranted, every single thing she knew. The interest now seemed almost prurient to her, rather than productive, and finally her lawyer had stepped in and demanded that they show proof of what further use they thought she could be to their case, or cut her loose. She wasn't the criminal here. And now she'd been told that her release from her agreement to further testify could come as soon as tomorrow morning.

Part of her couldn't wait to get home. Back to her old life. Only she suspected, given what she saw outside the courthouse, that the fixation with her wouldn't stop when she stopped giving testimony. Her book agent, who she'd retained as her temporary publicity manager, just to manage the insanity—not because she intended to take advantage of it in any way—was already fielding offers from everyone from *60 Minutes* to *Oprah*. She'd instructed her agent to refuse them all. That hadn't won her points with her publisher either.

She just wanted to disappear.

But first, she wanted—needed—to see Derek. She had no idea what he was going through, or what kinds of choices he might be making about his future. She couldn't imagine he'd enjoy any of this time in the spotlight, and she knew he'd been at a delicate point in his career when this happened, but he might want to take advantage of this very public housecleaning and step in to see what could be done, where he could help, with a war that would continue overseas despite what was happening at home. She had no idea what his feelings were on that at this point. They'd never had the chance to discuss it.

After they'd interrogated Mankowicz, who'd babbled almost incessantly without much more provocation than the power drill lying on Tate's lap, they'd had to figure out who they could call who would be most willing to tackle a case of this magnitude. Garrison had friends in very high places, so high that the sudden disappearance of a UN ambassador and a few trained agents—current and former—would be nothing to take care of. Especially given the line of work Garrison was in these days.

So, they'd gone the only route they could. They'd gone to the media, to the news agencies, while simultaneously going to the United States attorney general, and made it very clear what their plans were. Which led to a global release of footage, filmed in CJ's Washington estate, of Paul Mankowicz willingly exposing Garrison and everything he knew, while simultaneously, federal agents had raided Garrison's private Hamptons club and arrested him, along with several other high ranking officials named in Mankowicz's confession.

From there, the free-for-all had begun. And she and Derek hadn't been alone since.

A knock on the door brought her out of her reverie. "Room service," came a quiet voice on the other side of the door.

She hadn't ordered anything, but maybe her attorney had, for her. She'd been so exhausted when they'd left the courthouse a few hours ago, she'd asked to just come back to her room to rest.

She got up and limped over to the door, checking the peephole first. While her profile was high enough, and the court case vast enough, that she didn't fear her imminent demise, it wouldn't be completely unheard of for something to happen. She had a guard stationed on her floor, but—

Her mind blanked as she looked at the face staring back at her. She had to blink, twice, to make sure it wasn't wishful thinking.

Then she burst into action. She yanked the chain free and flipped the lock and tugged the door open so fast it almost clipped her in the shoulder. "Derek?"

"Shh," he cautioned, then wiggled his fake eyebrows, which made the silly bell-captain hat jostle on the wig on his head.

She moved back and he rolled the cart into the room and she quickly locked the door behind him. "What if someone finds out, what if—"

That was all she got out before he swept her up against him in a tight hug. "Oh my God, you feel even better than I thought you would," he said, his face buried in her hair.

The cap and hairpiece had fallen off and as he leaned back to look at her, he let her go with one arm, just long enough to pull off the fake eyebrows and mustache.

"Derek, how—"

"I couldn't stand it another second. I went AWOL."

Her heart was pounding, but the grin on her face was so huge she thought her face might freeze like that. It was really him. He was really here. "You know, you seem to be making a habit of going renegade and ending up on my doorstep."

He spread one arm wide. "But alert, alive, and no longer busted up. So I'm improving on the routine."

"Everything is okay?"

"A little tender in spots, but . . ." He took her hands and put them on his shoulders, then moved them down his chest, over his ribs, then tucked them around his waist. "All in one piece." He tugged her back into his arms. "Thanks to Super-woman, here."

"It was a team effort."

"You know, I have an entirely different sort of team effort in mind."

"Do you?" She couldn't help it, she ran her hands over his face, through his hair. "Sorry," she said, still grinning, "I just . . . I've missed you so incredibly badly, and I had no idea what you were doing, thinking, and I—I've never felt the absence of anyone in my life before, except maybe CJ, but never like this. I can't believe I got so used to having you there when I needed you . . . and now—"

"I know, we've both been through the ringer, and I hated that we had to be apart, but it was worth it if it means the opposition can't find any loopholes to discredit our testimony in any way."

"I know, I know, but then you risked it by coming here, and—"

"I'm done. As of yesterday. Finished. Free."

"Then, why the disguise?"

"To protect you. I know I should have waited until you were done, but I walked out of that hotel—well, the back service entrance of that hotel because of the mob out front—a free man with my entire life in front of me, and there was only one place I absolutely knew I wanted to be." He ran his fingers along her cheek, then tenderly kissed the bruised spot where CJ had hit her. "Right here. With you. That's all the future I need to know. That is if you'll have me in it. I know you're used to your solitude, but—"

She cut him off with a kiss. And it was no buss on the lips. It was everything she'd been feeling these past few weeks. The terror, the pain, the anger, the fury, the fear, the uncertainty . . . all of it. But most of all, it was the passion she knew she had for this man. "I missed you, Derek. Missed *you*." She looked at him. "I don't want to miss you anymore."

"Then you'll never have to."

"I—" She looked to the window, then back to him. "I don't know what I'm going to do. They told me I should be out of here by tomorrow. My attorney is arguing on my behalf right now. And . . . I want to go home, but I don't know if they'll let me." She motioned to the window. "I mean, all of them. I couldn't stand to have my home invaded." She smiled a little. "Once was enough for me."

He kissed her, and he didn't end it past the initial burst of want. He continued to kiss her, until the frenzy of reunion shifted to the hunger of need. "I won't be going back," he said. "I'm done."

"What will you do?"

"Well . . . I have an idea," he said, still running kisses along her jaw, then to the sensitive spot on the side of her neck.

She laughed, and it felt so damn good. Joy. She wanted that back. And she'd be damned if she'd let herself get robbed of it now. "While I like where this is going, I'm not sure a person can live off of that alone."

"I have ideas for that, too. But first . . ." He scooped her up into his arms, eliciting a surprised gasp from Tate.

"Your ribs—"

"I'm fine. And you feel even better than fine." He carried her into the bedroom, then let her feet drop to the floor so they stood next to the bed. "And I want to make very fine love to you. On a real bed. I wish it was our bed, but I'm afraid I'm not patient enough to wait that long."

"Good thing," she said, then grabbed the lapels of his hotel service jacket and spun him around and onto the bed.

"Hey," he said, on a surprised laugh.

"You said you were fine," she said, climbing on top of him, straddling him.

"I think maybe your little display in Washington has reenergized your training skills."

She had begun unbuttoning the jacket, and followed with the shirt. She leaned over her busy hands and smiled. "Don't worry, I never use my skills for evil."

"Well," he said, as she yanked his shirt free, leaving his chest bare, as she went to work on the trouser button. "Never let it be said I didn't encourage my agents to keep their skills sharply honed at all times. You never know when you might need them."

She slid down, taking his pants with her. "True. So very, very true."

And then, just as suddenly, he sat up, slid his hands under

her arms, and a second later she found herself flat on her back, undergoing a similar disrobing ritual. "I also think that it's important you know, at all times, that your team leader hasn't let his own skills go lax in the face of his agents' impressive show of dedication." He slid down and kissed the skin below her navel, then shifted even lower, until her hips bucked off the bed.

"Yes," she said. "Dedication is really, really a good thing." She gasped as his tongue found her. "Downright motivational."

She sunk her hands in his hair and let herself rush up and over, marveling at the very idea that after all that had been her past . . . that this could be her future. Their future.

He moved up her body, having shrugged out of the rest of his clothes, and pulled her legs around his hips as he moved between her thighs. "I'm very motivated," he said, then slid into her. And the talking ended as they began.

He moved inside of her and she lifted to take him deeper, reveling in the feel of him, filling her, the weight of him, so stabilizing and grounding. She'd never thought she'd need anyone but herself for that, and she knew, without doubt, that she could rely on herself now, just as she had before. But it felt so much better to share, to give, to take, to be the grounding force for someone else, and know there was someone who wanted to be that for her.

So she reached up, and she took it. And she gave it back.

And she found the peace she'd been fighting for.

Afterward, Derek pulled her close. She nestled against him, more content than she could ever remember being, than she thought she could ever be.

He tilted up her chin then, looked into her eyes, and she found even more there. "I love you, Tate. I can't not tell you that. You don't have to—"

"I love you, too." She beamed then. "Wow, that felt really good."

"Good," he said, wrapping her in his arms. "Because I could definitely get used to hearing it."

She cupped his face, turned it to her. "I want you to know that I understand, with what happened in the past—"

"Is past, now, Tate. Truly. It was like a beacon, my own North Star, reminding me of what I had to do . . . but it was also a weight, dragging me down. I will always mourn the loss, and there will always be guilt—" He pushed her hand down when she pressed a finger to his lips. "You can't suffer the loss I did and not feel that. But it's okay. Now, it's okay. Because now I know that I should use what I learned not to hide from it, or run from it, but to do it again, and do it right. If I'm ever going to honor him, honor what I lost . . . then I can't be afraid to do it again. To get it right."

She kissed him then. "I'm so glad I get to be the one you do it right with."

He laughed. "Well, I haven't pulled it off quite yet."

"Yeah," she said, smiling, and rolling him to his back. "But that's the fun part. Getting there." She moved on top of him. "First we might want to figure out where we go from here. Literally."

He grinned. "Actually, I have an idea about that. In fact, I did a little research this morning before going AWOL, and I have a lead on a new life."

Her eyes went wide. "New life? Doing . . . ?"

"A whole lot of what we're doing now, if we're lucky."

"Love is great, but it doesn't put food on the table."

"Ah, that's where you're wrong."

She looked confused. He laughed.

"You love your newfound profession, right?" He frowned for a second. "The insanity—" He gestured to the windows. "That hasn't changed things for you in any way, has it?"

She hadn't told him yet, about her new profession, but he must have guessed at least some of it from what he saw on her computer. "No. It hasn't made things easy, but I'm still on track there."

"And, can I assume that you don't have to be in a specific

place to continue with this job of your heart? This job you love?"

"No. All I need is a computer, an e-mail account, and possibly, on occasion, a plane ticket to New York."

"That can certainly be done." He didn't ask any further questions, and if there were any lingering doubts, they vanished. She'd follow him anywhere. Even better was the knowledge that she was pretty sure he'd do the same for her.

She propped her chin on his chest. "So . . . are we living off of my love then, or . . ."

He grinned. "Oh no, I have a new love interest of my own." He pulled her up and kissed her soundly. "Never to be outshone by you, of course."

"Of course," she said dryly. "What is it?"

"I've never told anyone about this. It's always been more the dream for when I couldn't stand my job any longer, or when I retired. I never really thought I'd actually do it. But now it seems like the perfect thing."

"What?"

He whispered in her ear and she leaned up. "Seriously?"

"Seriously."

"Where? Do you have a place picked out for it?"

"Maybe." He rolled them to their sides. "Would you really consider it?"

"Of course I would."

He kissed her. "It really is a brave new world. And I hit the jackpot."

"Well," she said, grinning and pulling him on top of her this time. "You always did have good aim."

"Now that you mention it . . ."

# Epilogue

"Tate, honey, come here. I need you to settle an epic question for us. Yours will be the deciding opinion."

Tate looked up from her computer and sighed a little. It was a good thing she loved him so dearly, because the man did not understand about deadlines. But then, he didn't have to worry about things like that.

She marveled at how perfectly at home he looked behind the bar. His skin was golden brown from the sun, his hair was long and shaggy, and his eyes twinkled with fun and more than a little mischievousness. The baddest of badasses superhero agent had been left behind in D.C. . . . and what was left was the real Derek Cole, the warmhearted man who could quote Jim Carrey and make love to her until all hours, then make her laugh until dawn, only to make love to her again. The man who'd found paradise half a world away, where there were no cameras, no newspapers to speak of, and the only thing on television were the sports and old television reruns he had beamed in via satellite hookup.

He'd set up his bar, bait, and tackle shop on Aitutaki, in the Cook Islands. She had the sun, the water, and the endless smiles of the locals, who had adopted them as if they were their own. The fact that the love had increased exponentially when they'd been introduced to the cinematic blondeness that was Cameron Diaz, thanks to Derek's extensive DVD collection, hadn't been lost on her.

"Hold on," she told him, from her shaded spot on the side porch of the bar. "Let me—"

Just then CJ burst into the open-walled thatched building, making the "Derek's Angels" sign swing on its perch above the bar. "The plane, the plane," she said.

"Wow, you're actually worse than he is," Tate said, shaking her head at her best friend's lame Tattoo impression.

"Besides, everyone knows it's 'da plane,'" said Tupa, a local who was sitting at the bar, his gap-toothed grin wide and adorable.

"Yeah," Derek deadpanned. "Everybody knows that."

"No, really." She stopped in front of Tate, blocking her view of Derek and Tupa. "*The* plane. With the mail?"

"Ooh!" Tate jumped up. "I'll be right back."

"But, the debate—"

"Can wait." She and CJ raced down to the docks where the seaplane sat as Fernando unloaded supplies and the mail.

"Is there a box for me, is there, is there?" She all but jumped up and down, waiting, almost breathless.

CJ was beside her, equally excited.

It never ceased to amaze Tate how she thought she could have been happy and fulfilled, holed up and cut off from the world. Of course, it could be argued that she was cut off from a substantial part of the world, living in the South Pacific. But that world had gotten all they were going to get of Tate. At least in person. About every seven months they could buy a piece of her at their local bookstore.

Here, in this world, she had her blessed and much needed peace. She'd earned that and didn't feel a shred of remorse for taking it. But she also got to have Derek, who was everything she could have ever wanted in a hero. Fiction couldn't live up to the man. And she had CJ, best friend, confidant, and the only other person in the world who knew exactly what she'd been through, and what she'd become.

She'd worried at first that CJ might have cut herself off from finding the same fulfillment that she'd found with Derek . . .

only why she'd been concerned, she hadn't had a clue. CJ had never once lacked for companionship, and being a world away hadn't changed that any. In fact, she just now noticed that CJ was looking at the very studly—and very young—Fernando in a way that . . . Hunh. So that's why she was always hanging out, waiting for the supply plane to come in.

"Here it is, Miss Tate!" he said, thrusting the box into her hands. "I will be bringing a copy for you to sign with me next time."

"I'll be happy to sign another one for your mother, Fernando—"

His blush was apparent even with his dark skin. "No, Miss Tate. I . . . the first one you so kindly signed for her? I read it, I confess. And . . . this next one . . . it will be for me."

Tate beamed at him. "Great! I'll be happy to sign it."

Fernando looked to CJ, then back to Tate. "You write of love. I am finding I like reading about it." He darted a look back to CJ. "A lot."

Tate smiled at the two of them, then clutched her package to her chest. She looked to CJ. "I'm going to go back, show Derek."

"I want to be there, but—" CJ looked to Fernando, who would be leaving shortly after his supplies were unloaded.

"No, that's fine. I kind of want to do this in private anyway."

CJ smiled and waved her off. "Go, hurry then."

Tate did. She raced back to the bar.

"Trapper John, or Hawkeye," Tupa demanded when she came busting in.

She looked at Derek. "This is your epic debate?"

"The balance of world power, not to mention my profit for this week, could rest on your answer."

"Ah. Well, then, it depends. Do I want a friend or lover?"

"You want both, of course," Derek said.

"Hawkeye."

"But—"

Tupa slapped his hand on the bar. "Free round!"

"Tate—"

"Give the man his beer and come with me."

He'd barely had time to slide Tupa his suds when she pulled him out from behind the bar. "I need to show you something."

"I'm working."

"Didn't stop you from interrupting mine just a few minutes ago. Consider us even."

He just grinned and shrugged and let her pull him away, "I got nothing for that. Busted." He stopped when they were on the back deck, which was deserted at this time of the morning. He tugged her into his arms, even with the package trapped between them. "I can't help it. I love having you with me all the time. You don't have to write here, you know. We built you that whole office—"

"I know, and it's okay. Now, it's my turn."

"What?"

She pulled away and put the box on the deck railing and tore at the tape.

"What is this?" he said, taking a penknife from his pocket and slicing the tape open for her.

"This," she said proudly, "is my moment."

"What?"

"Remember, back in Virginia, when you first told me about your past, because you couldn't go another minute without telling me? That was your moment. I could have told you about my writing then, but—"

"But it's not exactly a secret now."

"No, but you didn't find out about it from me. You found out during the trial." Her publisher had found a way to get the word out, and it had launched her career into the stratosphere, but it had also been the deciding factor on moving to the South Seas.

"I wished it had been otherwise, I didn't want to rob you of telling me yourself, but—"

"It's okay. Really. Right now is my moment. Right now is

when I can't wait to share something with you. Right this very second is when I have to tell you something, or I might burst—"

Derek's eyes went wide. "You're not—I mean, I know we talked about trying, but—"

It took her a second, then she realized. "No, I'm not pregnant. That would be an even bigger moment than this. This is just my moment, with you, just the two of us."

"Okay," he said, smiling very adorably and twinkly at her. "I like moments with just the two of us. What is it?"

She pulled the advance copy of her upcoming release out of the packaging. "Here."

He looked at the cover. "It's wonderful," he said, but it was obvious he wasn't sure what the moment was exactly, as he'd seen her first two books already when they'd been released and he'd already seen the advance cover of this one.

It was touching that he didn't want to hurt her feelings. She was still beaming. "The first two I'd written before you came back into my life. Before . . ." She surprised herself by getting a little teary. "Before you became my life."

"Tate, honey—"

"Open it," she said, sniffling. "Read."

He opened the book and read, then looked up, his own eyes a little glassy. "This is a pretty damn good moment." He looked down, read it again. "You dedicated it to me."

"You."

"You never dedicated a book before. You said there was no one—"

"There is now. Only one."

He put the book down and pulled her into his arms. "Thank you," he said a bit hoarsely. "You give really great moments, you know that?"

She tugged his face down for a kiss. "I hope it's just one of many."

He kissed her back, then scooped her up into his arms. "Well, there is that other special moment we were just discussing . . ."

"Do you mean it? Are you sure?"

He nodded, kissed her, and scooped her up in his arms. "I've never been more sure of anything in my life."

"Then let's go make ourselves a little moment."

"Yeah," he said, grinning. "Let's go do that."

If you liked this book, pick up
KEPT,
the seond book in
Jami Alden's Gemini Men series,
available now from Brava. . . .

"What's up with you going where you're not supposed to?"

The deep gruff voice slid around her, grabbed her, and wouldn't let go. Alyssa couldn't have held back her smile if she'd wanted to.

His eyes were hidden in shadow, but his mouth curved into a half smile, and a dimple creased the left corner of his mouth. His lips were firm and full, and she knew they'd be hot against her skin.

"Do I even want to know why you're hanging out at the servants' entrance looking like you're about to stick your thumb out?"

"I didn't want to have to deal with the crowd on my way out. And now my driver got into an accident, so it looks like I'm stranded for a while."

Derek was silent for several moments, and though his eyes were shadowed, she could feel him studying her.

*Ask me.*

"Can I give you a ride home?" He almost looked shocked that he'd asked.

She didn't let that stop her. "Sure," she said without hesitation.

A slight frown creased his forehead, but he gave her a curt nod and left without another word to get his car.

As she waited she shifted on her sky-high heels, restless, alive with anticipation. After so many months on her best behavior, a reckless urge was pulsing through her. Uncontrollable, unstoppable. She needed to forget the consequences and do something outrageous.

But this time it wouldn't be for attention, publicity, or her father's censure. This time it would be all for herself. She'd been so good, watching her every move for so long. Surely she deserved a little treat?

A silver Audi rumbled up to the driveway, and Alyssa wasted no time sliding into the passenger seat. The leather was cool against her bare thighs, and the interior of the car was full of his cedar and soap scent.

He backed out of the driveway and turned the corner, passing the snarl of limos and guests crowding the circular driveway of the Bancrofts' estate.

"Where to?"

Nerves warring with desire, Alyssa rummaged in her bag and dug out her lip gloss, slicking on a coat to give herself something to do.

Derek stopped at a stop sign. "Where are we going?"

She swallowed hard, her throat suddenly bone dry. What she was about to do was crazy. Stupid.

Necessary.

"You know, it's so early," she said, and turned to face him. She kept her eyes locked with his and placed her hand deliberately on his thigh. "And I'm not quite ready to go home."

He stared at her hard for what felt like an eternity. His thick, dark brows drew together in a harsh scowl.

Her stomach bottomed out as she realized he was about to turn her down.

"You want to get a drink somewhere?"

The moment of truth. She slid her hand farther up his thigh, delighting in the swells and ripples of rock-hard muscle hidden beneath wool gabardine. "I'm not much for crowds. Why don't you just take me back to your place?"

And don't miss
THE EDUCATION OF MADELINE,
Beth Williamson's Brava debut,
in stores now. . . .

She made excuses to herself to visit him during the day when she was home. The hours at the bank gave her time to cool herself off, but then there were the times she was home and temptation was within reach. Each time, no matter if he wore his shirt or not, her heart and her body reacted as one. Reaching for him, wanting him. Needing to know what it felt like to touch him. What it felt like for him to touch her. Her experience was limited to simple kissing and hugging, but she could imagine quite a bit more. Especially with the help of the medical texts she'd read. Although none of them quite explained the exact details of fornication, she was fairly certain she had figured it out.

Now she couldn't wait to try it. If only she hadn't agreed to give Teague a week to decide. A week was too long. Far too long. She should have given him one day. No more. She had to find some way to distract herself from *thinking* about bedding him. An idea struck her.

"Do you play any games, Teague?" Maddie asked as they left the dining room after supper.

He didn't answer, so she turned to look at him. A mischievous grin played around those beautiful lips, and one eyebrow arched over humor-filled eyes. "What kind of games?"

Madeline felt a bit flustered, and she hoped it didn't reflect in her cheeks. She didn't want him to know her self-control was melting like an icicle in July.

"Checkers, chess, backgammon. Those kinds of games."

When his grin turned into a full-blown smile, Madeline gripped the doorjamb to stay upright. She thought she was prepared. She was so very wrong. That smile was devastating. It lit up his whole face, made his eyes crinkle at the corners, and turned her into a puddle of unrequited passion.

"No, but I play a mean game of poker. Do you play?"

Madeline shook her head, disappointed. That canceled her distraction idea.

"Would you like to learn?"

She felt an urge to blurt, "No!" but grabbed it before it could be let loose. The proper lady wasn't going to make the decisions this time. Proper ladies may not play poker, but Maddie Brewster was going to learn.

After searching for thirty minutes, they found a deck of cards in her father's old desk. Teague suggested they play in the kitchen since it was in the back of the house and relatively private.

When they settled at the table, the lamplight threw a cozy glow over the room. Madeline watched Teague's hands, fascinated by how quickly he shuffled the cards. His fingers were lithe and strong at the same time. She wondered how those fingers would feel on her skin, making her temperature rise degree by degree.

Teague explained a game called five-card stud. The rules were a bit complex, but Madeline understood most of them. He let her play a couple of practice hands, and then they started to play in earnest.

Madeline lost five hands in a row before she started to really enjoy playing the game. She won the next hand. Teague actually looked surprised. "Very good, Maddie. You're getting the hang of it."

Madeline smiled. "I think I understand why gamblers like to play this so much. Can we gamble, too?"

Teague threw back his head and laughed. It was the first

time she'd heard him laugh, and the rough, raspy sound of it did something strange to her equilibrium.

"Don't you think gambling is the root of all evil?"

"No, I don't. I've seen the root of evil, and it's definitely not poker."

He looked like he wanted to respond, but he didn't. He shrugged. "I don't have money to play for."

Madeline watched his hands as he shuffled the cards again.

"How about we play for truths?" he said without looking up.

"Truths?"

"Yes, each time one of us wins a hand, we get to ask the other a question, and the loser must tell the truth."

His hands shuffled faster. By the time the cards started flying off the deck, his fingers were a blur of motion. In a few seconds, five cards lay in front of her.

"I'll play for truths. There isn't much I've got to hide, anyway."

Madeline lost the first truth hand.

"Are you ready for the first question?" he asked with a small grin.

"Yes, I'm ready."

"Why did you paint your house blue?"

It was her turn to laugh. "I thought you were going to ask me what color my bloomers were."

His eyebrows rose. "Now you've spoiled it. That was my next question."

"I painted it blue because it was my favorite color, and I wasn't allowed to wear anything that bright. After my father died, I indulged myself."

He nodded. "That answers why it's so damn bright."

She laughed and waved her hands at the cards. "Deal again, Teague. I'm itching to ask you a truth question."

This time, Madeline won. She pondered her question for several minutes, earning a sigh and rolling eyes from the sore loser.

"Why didn't you say no to my proposition to bed me?"

He clearly hadn't been expecting a personal question like that. The cards he'd been shuffling fell out of his hand like an explosion, raining down all over the table and floor.

"I had to stop myself from saying yes too quickly."

Heat pooled low and insistent in her belly, and a throbbing began between her legs.

"Does this mean you're saying yes to my . . . proposal?" she asked. Her mouth felt as dry as cotton. "I mean, it sounds as though you're going to say yes."

He stood abruptly, and she could see the outline of his penis clearly in his pants. My, oh, my! That certainly was a large-looking organ. Much larger than ones in the drawings in the book.

Teague let the rest of the cards fall from his hands and came around the side of the table. The primal way he walked was enough to make her nipples pucker. He clearly wanted her. *Her*. Madeline Brewster!

When he reached her side, he knelt down on the floor next to her and cupped her face in his big hands. "Why me?"

She shrugged, somehow. "I need a big man. I'm not . . . petite or feminine like most women. I didn't want my teacher to feel embarrassed by the size difference if I was bigger. You . . . You're bigger than me. And . . ."

"And?"

"Just looking at you makes my body hum."

His pupils widened, and he licked his lips.

*He's going to kiss me!*

Madeline closed her eyes. She expected his lips on hers. What she didn't expect was feather-light kisses along her brow, down her nose, across her cheekbones, to her chin. Small, jittery kisses that made her ache that much more. "Hurry up and kiss me," she demanded.

He chuckled against the corner of her mouth. "If you want me to be your teacher, you're going to have to be the student. Can you hand over the reins, Maddie girl?"

Madeline thought long and hard about that question. It wasn't a matter of being under his thumb like her father. It was trusting that he would teach her what she wanted to know without doubting or interfering in his methods. "Yes," she breathed.

She felt him smile. "Good. Now just close your eyes and feel. This is lesson number one."

"Wait! Does this mean yes?"

Here's a peek at
IMMORTAL DANGER,
by Cynthia Eden, coming next month!

His back teeth clenched as he glanced around the room. Doors led off in every direction. He already knew where all those doors would take him. To hell.

But he needed to find Maya, so he'd have to go—

"Don't screw with me, Armand!" A woman's voice, hard, ice cold. Maya.

He turned, found her leaning over the bar, her hand wrapped around the bartender's throat.

"I want to know who went after Sean, and I want to know now." He saw her fingernails stretch into claws, and he watched as those claws sank into the man's neck.

"I-I d-don't k-know—" The guy looked like he might faint at any moment. Definitely human. Vamps were always so pale, it looked like they might faint. But this guy, he'd looked pretty normal until Maya had clawed him.

"Find out!" She threw him against a wall of drinks.

Adam stalked toward her, reached her side just as she spun around, claws up.

He stilled.

She glared at him. "What the hell do you want?" she snarled, and he could see the faint edge of her fangs gleaming behind her plump lips.

It was his first time to get a good look at her face. He'd seen her from a distance before, judged her to be pretty, hadn't bothered to think much beyond that.

He blinked as he stared at her. Damn, the woman looked like some kind of angel.

Her straight hair framed her perfect, heart-shaped face. Her cheeks were high, glass sharp. Her nose was small, straight. Her eyes wide and currently the black of a vampire in hunting mode. And her lips, well, she might have the face of an angel, but she had lips made for sin.

Adam felt his cock stir, for a vampire.

He shuddered in revulsion.

Oh, hell, no. The woman was so not his type.

Her scent surrounded him. Not the rancid, rotting stench of death he'd smelled around others of her kind. But a light, fragrant scent, almost like flowers.

What in the hell? How could she—

Maya growled and shoved him away from her, muttering something under her breath about idiots with death wishes.

Then she walked away from him.

For a moment, he just studied her. Maya wasn't exactly his idea of an uber-vamp. She was small, too damn small for his taste. The woman was barely five feet four. Her body was slender, with almost boyish hips. Her legs were encased in an old, faded pair of jeans, and the black T-shirt she wore clung gently to her small breasts.

He liked a woman with more meat on her bones. Liked a woman with curves. A woman with round, lush hips that he could hold while he thrust deep into her.

But, well, he wasn't interested in screwing Maya, anyway. Not with her too thin body. Her too pale skin. No, he didn't want to screw her.

He just planned to use her.

Adam took two quick strides forward, grabbed her arm, and swung her back toward him.

The eyes that had relaxed to a bright blue shade instantly

flashed black. Vamps' eyes always changed to black when they fought or when they fucked.

Sometimes folks made the mistake of confusing vamps with demons, because a demon's eyes, well, they could go black, too. Actually, Adam knew that a demon's eyes were *always* black. And for the demons, every damn part of their eyes went black. Cornea. Iris. Lens. With the vamps, just the iris changed.

Usually demons were smart enough to hide the true nature of their eyes. But the vamps, they didn't seem to give a flying shit who saw the change. 'Course, if a human happened to see the eye shift, it was generally too late for the poor bastard because, by then, he was prey.

Gazing into Maya's relentless black eyes, Adam had a true inkling of just how those poor bastards must have felt.

A growl rumbled in her throat, then she snarled, "Slick, you're screwing with the wrong woman tonight."

No, she was the right woman. Whether he liked the fact or not.

So he clenched his teeth, swallowed his pride and, in the midst of hell, admitted, "I need your help."